Praise for *Welcome to the Pine Away Motel and Cabins*

"Katarina Bivald talks about her characters like you talk about your best friends. She gives her story absolutely everything she has. You'll care when you read because she really, really cared when she wrote."

—Fredrik Backman, #1 *New York Times* bestselling author of *A Man Called Ove*

"Hopeful, heartening, and humane, this is the novel I needed to read right now."

—J. Ryan Stradal, author of *The Lager Queen of Minnesota* and *Kitchens of the Great Midwest*

"Bivald delves into what's important in life in this bittersweet tale about life after death. In a story about the lives a single person can touch, the highlight is fittingly Bivald's memorable characterizations, as she makes each person and their needs distinct and complex. This is a winning novel about the lasting impact of love."

—*Publishers Weekly*

"A celebration of life in which friendship, community, and a room for the night are gentle antidotes to prejudice."

—*Kirkus Reviews*

"Remarkable...unquestionably a page-turner and full of wisdom. A brave, unusual book, which powerfully portrays friendship and love."

—Felicity Hayes-McCoy, author of *The Library at the Edge of the World*

"A novel of irresistible characters who make you believe in the power of hard-won wisdom and second chances, *Welcome to the Pine Away Motel and Cabins* is a delight!"

—Linda Francis Lee, author of *The Glass Kitchen*

"...harming, heartwarming, and thought-provoking novel will ...age is turned."

—*Booklist*

Praise for *The Readers of Broken Wheel Recommend*

#1 Indie Next Pick
#2 LibraryReads Pick
Amazon Best Book of the Month

"A manifesto for booksellers, booklovers, and friendship. We should all celebrate these little bookstores, where our souls find home... *The Readers of Broken Wheel Recommend* is one of those books you want to live in for a while."

—Nina George, *New York Times* bestselling author of *The Little Paris Bookshop*

"*The Readers of Broken Wheel Recommend* is one of the more surprisingly improbable and delightful books I've read in years. What begins as an unlikely international friendship based on a mutual love of books becomes a sweet and soulful discovery of America. Quirky, unpredictable, funny, and fresh—a wonderful book."

—Nickolas Butler, international bestselling author of the novel *Shotgun Lovesongs* and the short-story collection *Beneath the Bonfire: Stories*

"This classic fish-out-of-water story will steal your heart. It's smart, sweet, absorbing, and endearing, just like the town of Broken Wheel. It's a story for everyone who believes in the magic of books to enlighten, heal, and restore. A treat for readers everywhere!"

—Susan Wiggs, #1 *New York Times* bestselling author of *Starlight on Willow Lake*

"Heartwarming and utterly charming... Will captivate fans of Nina George's *The Little Paris Bookshop* and Gabrielle Zevin's *The Storied Life of A. J. Fikry.*"

—*Library Journal* Starred Review

ALSO BY KATARINA BIVALD

The Readers of Broken Wheel Recommend

Welcome to the Pine Away Motel and Cabins

KATARINA BIVALD

Translated from Swedish by Alice Menzies

sourcebooks
landmark

Published by Sourcebooks Landmark, an imprint of Sourcebooks
P.O. Box 4410, Naperville, Illinois 60567-4410
(630) 961-3900
sourcebooks.com

Originally published as *En dag ska jag lämna allt det här* in 2018 in Sweden by Bokförlaget Forum.

Library of Congress Cataloging-in-Publication Data

Names: Bivald, Katarina, author. | Menzies, Alice, translator.
Title: Check in at the Pine Away Motel : a novel / Katarina Bivald ;
   translated from Swedish by Alice Menzies.
Other titles: Dag ska jag lämna allt det här. English
Description: Naperville, IL : Sourcebooks Landmark, [2019]
Identifiers: LCCN 2019009897 | (trade pbk. : alk. paper)
Classification: LCC PT9877.12 .I93 D3413 2019 | DDC 839.7/38--dc23
LC record available at https://lccn.loc.gov/2019009897

Printed and bound in Canada.
MBP 10 9 8 7 6 5 4 3 2 1

Alis volat propriis. (She flies with her own wings.)
—Oregon state motto

"You can check out any time you like,
but you can never leave."
—The Eagles, "Hotel California," 1977

"Here Is Henny's Sand"

MY FUNERAL BEGINS IN AN HOUR.

I'm pretty sure I'm going to miss it. Right now I'm sitting on the motel rooftop, looking down on an almost-empty parking lot.

I imagine myself floating through the air, higher and higher, as if I've finally gotten the hang of flying. So high that everyone is nothing but tiny black dots, making their way to the Pine Creek United Methodist Church. Dad is probably already there, waiting patiently inside, an especially black dot on my own internal map. Cheryl will be with him, no doubt, like the supportive Christian neighbor that she is. I try to be angry with the two of them, but I don't seem to have the energy anymore.

Before long, they'll be joined by friends and former classmates, vague acquaintances, teachers I once had, Dad's neighbors.

A confident guess at who will attend a funeral in Pine Creek: everyone.

They'll try to sing along to old-fashioned hymns, and they'll listen to the pastor's empty eulogy. Dad will be sitting at the front, brave and desperately proper.

And then I'll be cremated. A rather bold and surprising choice from Dad. I approve, but I'm apprehensive as well. On the one hand, I'd rather burst into flames than be shoved underground. I've always been a little bit afraid of the dark. But on the other hand, I worry that this—what's left of me, my soul or consciousness or whatever you want to call it—will disappear when my body does.

I don't think you can go on being a ghost forever. No matter how much you want to. There'd be more of us around if you could, that's for sure. Maybe most people never even get the chance to stick around and see how their loved ones are doing. Maybe I should be grateful for the opportunity.

I'm talking about smoke and picturing myself engulfed in a wall of flames, but that's not how it works. The body—my body—will be heated through calcination. Everything organic, roughly 97 percent of me, will first turn to liquid and then become hot gas. They'll add oxygen so that the body can burn entirely without flames.

All that will be left of me is ash. Surely no soul can survive it?

Ash is actually a pretty misleading word. It's not like a fine ash automatically appears afterward, ready to be stored in an urn or buried under a headstone or sprinkled somewhere, whatever Dad plans to do with it. You need a special processor to grind the remains into a kind of fine-grained sand.

But I don't think that has quite the same ring to it. For the relatives, I mean. "Here is Henny's sand."

The whole process takes around two hours. I wish I knew exactly when everything was going to happen, so that I could prepare myself. It would be awful to disappear midthought. Or be thinking something completely meaningless when it happened—*I wonder what time it is*—and then nothing.

No, I want my very last thought to be grand and beautiful and important. A final message, even if I'm the only one who hears it.

Below me, the motel is closed for the first time since a snowstorm left us without power for three days in 2003. The reception area is dark, the computers switched off. The restaurant is eerily empty, all the chairs upside down on the tables. The rooms are locked. Only two cars are there: Camila's and MacKenzie's.

On the other side of the parking lot, the *Pine Creek Motel* sign glows faintly in the daylight.

Vacanci s. The *e* has stopped working.

Beneath that is a patchwork of strange little signs made from cheap metal, in all imaginable sizes, colors, and styles:

Vacant rooms!

Cabins!

Forest views!

Microwaves in every room!

Air-conditioning!

Now with color TV!
Restaurant!
Bar!
Pool!
Open
Vote No on Measure 9!
Oregon—Proud home of anti-gay ballot measures since 1992!
MacKenzie added the last two.

CHAPTER 1

Caucasian Female, 33 Years Old

MY VERY LAST THOUGHT ALIVE: *MICHAEL'S BODY*.

I was thinking *Michael's body, Michael's body, Michael's body*, as if repeating a miracle I still didn't quite believe in.

Every detail on the road was familiar to me, and yet they all felt magically new, as though I was seeing them for the first time. The asphalt, which looked even more worn-out in the afternoon sunshine, the gravel at the sides of the road, the sweet scent of pines. I was smiling. I know that. I had been smiling the entire weekend.

The next thing I remember is standing there on the road, feeling slightly bewildered, looking at a strange heap some twenty feet away.

At first, all I feel is a vague sense of curiosity. I don't realize it's a body, and the idea that it could be human doesn't even cross my mind.

It's only as I get closer that I can make out a right leg, unmistakably human, bent at an unnatural angle. While that initial shock is still sinking in, I recognize my good jeans and what's left of my favorite blouse.

The bright-red polka dots are clear enough, but I'll never be able to get the rest of it white again.

I don't recognize my hair. The pale-brown strands are mixed with gravel and engine oil and what I guess must be blood. My left arm is sticking straight out from the body, and my right arm is...missing.

Instinctively, I look down at my own right side, but my arm is still there.

Up ahead, a truck is straddling both lanes of the road. A man in his forties is leaning against the right-hand side of the hood. His eyes are fixed on the ground, and it looks like his knees are about to give way beneath him.

He takes two unsteady steps toward the edge of the road, where he bends down over the ferns. I look away when he starts throwing up.

Somehow he manages to make it back to the truck without falling apart. He's slim, his shirt a little too big for him, and his hands are shaking as he pulls out his phone and calls the police. *Accident. Pine Creek. Near the motel. Just after the exit. One…injured.*

We're alone here among the pines. He rocks back and forth as he mumbles to himself, and I can't think of a single thing I can do to help. I try patting him on the shoulder, awkwardly and apologetically, but it doesn't make much difference.

Then I hear what he is saying.

It's like some kind of mantra. Over and over again.

"Don't be dead, don't be dead, don't be dead."

Just fifteen minutes ago, I was head-over-heels happy.

I'm thinking about that as though happiness should be some kind of shield against being mowed down by a truck. And I'm thinking about how quiet everything is around us, as if nothing bad could ever happen on this old road.

This is a nightmare; that's all it is. Any minute now, I'll wake up in the Redwood Cabin and be fascinated by how such a familiar room can look so different when you're lying on your back in it.

Before I open my eyes, I'll reach out to check if Michael's body is still there beside me. Then I'll smile when it is.

Providing everything with Michael even happened, of course. If all this is just a dream, then maybe Michael was, too.

Maybe I'll wake up in my own bed, alone again, and get back to cleaning motel rooms as usual.

The truck driver stops mumbling to himself, but that just makes things worse. He stops rocking, too. Instead, he starts shaking.

When Sheriff Ed Carmichael arrives, I run toward him, relieved. I want to grab hold of his arm, harder than I've ever grabbed anything before, and force him to walk faster, do something.

Sheriff Ed will know what needs to be done, I think.

He's the third generation of Carmichaels to be sheriff here. When he started at the sheriff's office, both his grandpa and father were still alive. He'd dealt with that the way he dealt with everything else in his line of work: stoically, with valiant patience and calm competence.

I didn't think anything could shock him, but I was wrong.

"Jesus," he says. "That's Henny Broek."

He calls for an ambulance first, then the state troopers, who promise to send "a couple of cars" as soon as they can.

Sheriff Ed turns to the truck driver. He asks some routine questions about the man's name, driver's license, and registration, and then moves on to what happened.

"I...I didn't see her. She just stepped out into the road, and I tried to brake, but..."

The truck driver starts rocking again, and shaking. The sheriff fetches a blanket from the trunk of his patrol car, wraps it around the man's shoulders, and guides him over to the back seat.

"The state troopers will be here soon," he says. "They're going to take you down to the station. They'll need to take some samples. Breath, urine, blood. Do you understand? They have to do all that."

Sheriff Ed studies the truck driver as he talks. Maybe he's looking for signs of intoxication. Maybe his work as a sheriff has made him suspicious.

But I'm pretty sure it happened just like the driver said. I was thinking about Michael. I was happy, my body high on adrenaline and exhausted from too little sleep, and suddenly I was lying in the middle of the road.

"Henny Broek," the sheriff says with a shake of his head. "She was always such a good girl."

The ambulance is the first to arrive. At the sheriff's request, paramedics give the truck driver a quick, uninterested once-over, and then they move on to me. Not that there seems to be much they can do. They cover my body and lift it into the ambulance. The state troopers arrive just as they are leaving.

Their sirens sound muted even when they're right next to us, and I blink at the revolving, psychedelic blue lights. Fragments of conversation: "What a waste." "Do you think he was drunk?" The state troopers are strong and tough, and they all look incredibly young.

The commanding officer walks over to Sheriff Ed while the two others set up a detour with a flashing sign reading *Lane Closed*. A car passes, slowing down so the driver can take in as much as possible, and I feel embarrassed by all the fuss. *I never meant to cause this much trouble*, I think.

"Sir," says the commanding officer. As their sirens fall silent, I can hear the sound of the yellow-and-black plastic tape flapping in the wind.

"Did you know the deceased, sir?"

The deceased.

"Henny Broek," the sheriff replies automatically. "Caucasian female, thirty-three years old. Works at Pine Creek Motel and Cabins." He nods down the road toward the motel.

"Worked, sir."

"Huh? Yeah, right. She *was* in charge of the motel, along with MacKenzie Jones. They both live there. The motel has three cabins nearby, so I'm guessing she was on her way to or from one of them. From, I'd say, given the direction the truck was traveling. The driver's name is Paul Jackson. Resident of Pine Creek. Says she ran into the road without looking. He tried to brake, didn't make it."

The deceased, the deceased, the deceased. I fight the urge to laugh.

"MacKenzie and Henny manage the motel, but they don't own it. The owner doesn't live in town anymore. For a cheap motel, it's a pretty good place. Not much trouble. They have to kick out difficult guests from time to time, but that's all. Nothing unusual."

The state trooper doesn't come out and say he doesn't care about the motel, but I can tell he's thinking it.

"And next of kin, sir?"

"Just her father. Lives at 17 Water Street. Her mom's been dead a long time."

"Maybe just as well," the trooper says, and Sheriff Ed pulls a face.

So this is what it's like to be dead, I think. Shouldn't there be...I don't know, *more* to it? Should I really be able to stand here on the road

WELCOME TO THE PINE AWAY MOTEL AND CABINS

beneath the trees, smelling the same old, dusty asphalt, pine needles, and ferns?

Not that the trees care about what happened to me. They were here long before I came along, and they'll be here a long time after me. What I did during my short life doesn't matter to them. Not how it ended, either.

"You want me to inform her father?" Sheriff Ed asks.

"That might be best, sir," the trooper replies, sounding relieved. "Better if it comes from someone he knows."

"Sometimes I really hate my job," Sheriff Ed says, sighing wearily.

CHAPTER 2

"She Didn't Feel Any Pain"

JESUS IS WATCHING OVER US IN DAD'S LIVING ROOM.

I rode over here with the sheriff. When he started walking toward his car, I just climbed in and sat behind him in the back seat. It was only once I was sitting there that I realized I'd walked straight through the locked door.

Dad and Cheryl are side by side on the couch. Cheryl is Dad's closest neighbor, and she came over the minute she saw the police car. The sheriff is sitting in the best armchair, the one Dad normally uses for reading in the evening. There's a floor lamp right next to it, to save Dad's eyes, and the armchair is angled toward Jesus, to fill Dad's soul with godliness.

On a shelf behind the couch, there is a small plastic figurine of the baby Jesus. It's a cheap Christmas decoration, but Dad has had it out year-round for as long as I can remember. Next to the shelf is a portrait of Jesus wearing a crown of thorns, his face meek and downturned. The local artist who painted it has more religious zeal than talent, and it looks like Jesus is wearing a bird's nest on his head.

The sheriff turns resolutely toward Dad. Dad's hands are clasped in his lap, and he seems defensive and confused before the sheriff even opens his mouth to speak. All his life, Dad has been obsessed with doing and saying the right thing, but nothing could have prepared him for a visit from the sheriff on an ordinary Sunday evening. He's probably wondering what the neighbors will think.

"Sir," Sheriff Ed begins. "There's no easy way for me to say this. I'm very sorry, but your daughter, Henny, died earlier this afternoon, in a traffic accident just outside the motel."

"The motel," says Dad.

Cheryl raises her hand to her mouth and says, "Oh, Lord."

"Yes," says Dad as though that should have been his reaction.

"If there's anything I can do..." the sheriff continues.

I pace back and forth across the living room floor. I shouldn't be here. I should be back in the Redwood Cabin, with Michael.

Strictly speaking, I should be at the reception desk to relieve MacKenzie from her shift. It's several years since Dad's old wall clock stopped, but I'm pretty sure I must be really late. MacKenzie has already worked all weekend because of me.

"Henny was always such a good girl," Dad says suddenly. "She always did as she was told. There wasn't a child on the street as polite and well behaved as my Henny. It's true. I'm not the only one who says so. You can ask anyone."

The sheriff's eyes are drawn back to the baby Jesus. "Like I said, if there's anything I can do, anything at all..."

Dad looks helplessly from the sheriff to Cheryl and then back again. "I'm... You'll have to forgive me, but I seem to have forgotten what to do."

"Sir?"

"I've buried my parents and my wife and *her* mother. But I don't seem to be able to remember what I do next."

"The funeral parlor will be able to help you with all that," the sheriff reassures him. "I'm sure the state police will release the body shortly."

MacKenzie! I think. *She'll* be able to fix this. I need to find her and explain what happened.

"What...what does it look like? The body. Henny, I mean."

"She didn't feel any pain," says the sheriff.

"She was always a nice kid," says Dad. "Never caused any trouble."

She didn't feel any pain.

Of all the idiotic things to say, I think as I walk quickly toward the motel. It's definitely not true.

I might not have felt anything as the truck slammed into me, but it definitely hurts now.

MacKenzie isn't at the reception desk. She isn't in the restaurant. She isn't in her room. I walk through the entire motel without registering anything else. Afterward, I can't even remember who *was* in the reception area. All I could think was *Nope, not here.*

We argued the last time we spoke, but now I have an intense longing for her. I want her to pat me on the shoulder in that encouraging and slightly dismissive way of hers. Dismissive of my problems, not my feelings. I'll sort it out. It'll be fine. It's not so bad. *Come on, Henny, are you going to let a minor detail like this stop you?*

MacKenzie has a joke for every occasion, so maybe she'll be able to joke about this, too.

Henny, have you been playing chicken with a truck?

At least you can stop cleaning rooms at the motel now, Henny. Because you've gone to that big motel in the sky.

You've gone to the place where Netflix can't follow you.

Once, when I had a hundred-and-four-degree fever and could barely even smile at her jokes, she pushed my hair back from my face. Gently, with her fingertips, a calming almost-movement. It sounds motherly, but MacKenzie really isn't the motherly type. The fact she pushed back my hair was a gift. It was something unexpected, not something she does all the time.

"How're you doing, my friend?" she asked me. Cool fingertips against my forehead.

I miss that now.

That's not what she said the last time we spoke, of course. On Saturday. *Yesterday.* It was the second time that weekend that I'd asked her to cover my shift at the reception desk, and now she knew why. I assume she had gone through the reservation system. She tried to make me see sense, but I refused.

"It's been fifteen years," she said. "You're not the same people you were. You don't even know why he's back, or how long he's planning to stay. Last time he left without even saying goodbye."

"But you like Michael."

"That's not the point. I don't know him anymore. And neither do you."

"I don't know why you're so determined to stop me from being happy. What difference does it make if it eventually ends? He's here now, MacKenzie. He came back."

"And what exactly do you think is going to happen? That he'll spend one weekend here and then move back to a town he's always hated? Or were you thinking that you could just have a nice weekend together and then stand here and watch him leave without having your heart broken again, like always? Do you really think you're strong enough to handle a one-weekend stand?"

"Can you cover my shift or not?" I asked.

MacKenzie folded her arms.

"Fine," I said. "I'll stay here at the desk. If that's what you want."

"Henny..."

And so I sat there, desperately unhappy and with nothing to do, while Michael, my Michael, was only five hundred yards away. But MacKenzie came back after half an hour and made a weary gesture with one hand. I snuck off immediately, before she had time to change her mind, pulling on my favorite jeans and my favorite blouse, the one with the red polka dots, and running over to the cabin as I tried to make my heart beat like normal.

That was the last time I saw her.

I eventually find her car parked outside Timber Bar, the local dive where we always hang out. Darkness has fallen, and the streetlights are illuminating the deserted parking lot.

I walk straight through the door without thinking about what I'm doing, then pause and blink in the gloom. The dark wooden tables are empty, and the room smells faintly of sweat and stale beer.

Buddy and two of the other regulars are in their usual spots by the bar. All three look acutely uncomfortable and are staring straight down at their beers.

Word of my death has already reached them. Catastrophe spreads fast in a small town.

It's about respect, too. Grief is raw and naked and revealing, so they show consideration by looking away. It's like when our kindergarten teacher's mother went crazy and started walking around town in her underwear. No one laughed. You looked away. You tried desperately not to see her shuffling down Main Street in her rabbit slippers and lace underwear—*lace*—while our teacher hurried after her with a jacket that she kept throwing off.

MacKenzie is alone by the dartboard at the very back of the bar. She has a beer next to her, but she isn't drinking. She is wearing one of those huge men's shirts that she loves, a flannel one that has become silky smooth through years of wear. Even rolled up, the sleeves are too long for her. She keeps having to shake her arms to free her hands, an unconscious gesture so natural and familiar that, for a moment, it feels like everything is right again, everything is normal. I just need to buy a beer, and I can keep her company.

But then I notice how tense she is. Like an animal frozen midflight: every muscle, every synapse, is utterly under control. When she eventually throws the dart, it comes as a relief.

It hits the board too hard and bounces back to the floor.

MacKenzie doesn't care. I'm not sure she even notices.

She throws another dart.

"I bought her a backpack when she was nine," MacKenzie says.

I don't know who she's talking to, but Buddy and the other regulars all jump.

"Did you know that? It was the most pathetic backpack you could imagine. Ugly purple canvas. No Disney print, nothing. A real low-budget backpack."

I smile for the first time all evening. I remember it.

"And backpacks were important back then. All the others got a new one at the start of the school year. Henny had gotten one, too, but I didn't know that when I bought it."

The room is silent. It feels like everyone is trying to merge with the walls or become one with the bar's dark counter. Not even Bruce Springsteen is singing. Buddy's constant companion, an old CD player, is silent next to him.

"I just wanted to give her a gift. Dumb, huh? But right as I was about to give it to her, I realized her dad had already bought her a new backpack. A big, fantastic one, with some kind of print on it, whatever was cool that year. I don't remember exactly, *Beauty and the Beast* or *The Little Mermaid* or something. Anyway, there it was in the hallway, all shiny and new, and it made the backpack I'd bought look ridiculous. I'd already wrapped it up, so I couldn't exactly pretend it was for myself."

She throws another dart. This one misses the board completely and burrows into the wall.

I lean against the table, the one I usually sit at while she's playing darts, right by the wall and out of her line of fire.

"But do you know what the stupid woman did?" she says quietly, sounding almost confused. "She wore my pathetic backpack to school every day for years."

MacKenzie falls silent, as though she suddenly realizes that she's standing there, talking, and doesn't know why. When she picks up her beer, her hand is shaking.

"MacKenzie..." I say, but she doesn't react. No one does. They can't hear me anymore.

I walk over to her and place my hands on her shoulders. I want to shake her, *force* her to see me, to laugh again, to be the old, tough MacKenzie that I know so well.

"I'll fix this," I say. "I swear. Somehow. It'll be okay."

Then I turn away. I suddenly can't bear to see her blank face.

"I can't be dead," I say. "I've barely even started living."

Buddy gives us a ride back to the motel. He's six foot five and weighs at least 330 pounds, but he was still shaking a little when he refused to let MacKenzie drive herself home. "Friends don't let friends drive drunk," he mumbled as he stared down at his shoes.

Buddy is a handyman in town and at the motel. Anything we can't fix ourselves, we leave to him. He always knows a guy who can lend him the right tools. But he can't fix MacKenzie. I can tell from his eyes that he is longing to put things right with a forklift truck or a steel saw, but there's nothing he can do. MacKenzie doesn't say a word the whole way home, and by the time Buddy drives away from the motel, he has broken out in a cold sweat.

MacKenzie goes straight up to her room and slumps onto the bed, but she doesn't fall asleep. I keep her company as she twists and turns.

I'm sitting on the windowsill in a room that quickly becomes claustrophobic with anxiety. I abandoned her over the weekend; I can't leave her now.

I want to reach out and run my fingertips over her forehead. *How're you doing, my friend?* Swap roles completely. As incomprehensible as me speaking and her not listening.

My head feels like I've been battling with some kind of impossible puzzle for hours: *If a train leaves...* My brain feels swollen and overheated, as though it's pressing against my skull. All I want is to switch it off and take a break. *If a body is loaded into an ambulance going in one direction, and a soul grabs a ride in a police car going another...*

Eventually, I leave her there. My feet find their way in the darkness without any input from me. Suddenly, I'm just walking toward the Redwood Cabin. That's where Michael is, and it's where, only twelve hours earlier, I felt so unbelievably, intensely alive.

I try to be brave, I really do, but it's hard when you don't even know what is going on. Everything seems worse in the mockingly familiar area around the motel. I can *hear* the wind rustling the silver birches, but I can't feel it. I'm walking around in the middle of the night, wearing nothing but a thin blouse and jeans, and don't feel the slightest bit cold.

A silvery moon flashes on the dark surface of the creek. Beyond that is the complete darkness of what I know are the mountains.

Michael is asleep; his breathing is deep and calm. The faint glow of the moon seeps in through the open curtains, across the bed. He is on his side, and all I can see are his left cheekbone, his eye, and his nostril. Half of his mouth, slightly open. He's snoring, but he stops when I curl up against his back.

I bury my face in the nape of his neck and feel absurdly grateful that I can still make out his scent.

"You know, Michael," I say. "The strangest thing happened to me today..."

CHAPTER 3

Once Upon a Time, Boise Was a Coastal Town

IN THE BEGINNING, WE DIDN'T EXIST.

Michael used to tell me about how everything began. Four and a half billion years ago, the earth was just a fiery ball of lava and smoke and darkness. Nothing could live here, he said, but he didn't sound sad about that. In his world, rocks had always been most important.

We were seventeen. Michael hadn't gone off to college yet, and he hadn't begun his nomadic existence as a field geologist. But he already knew everything there was to know about Oregon's geology. Rocks were his first true love.

And where were we? I asked.

We?

Oregon.

There was no Oregon. In the beginning, we didn't exist. Hundreds of millions of years ago, when all the land on earth was gathered together in one big supercontinent that stretched from pole to pole—Pangaea—there was only ocean where Oregon is today. One big ocean, Panthalassa, as big as all of our current oceans put together. Its waves rolled onto Idaho's beaches. Boise would have been a coastal town.

He only said *Idaho* and *Boise* to amuse me. He loved how stubbornly I tried to force our own insignificant geography onto the earth's impressive history.

Our enormous mountain ranges, from the Cascades to the West, to the Klamaths in southwestern Oregon, and the Blue Mountains over here by us in the northeast, were still just isolated volcanoes. Some of the land around here was still at the bottom of the ocean. If you walk around

Pine Creek now, you can see traces of the volcanic islands we once were, surrounded by shallow bays and rivers and coral reefs.

Were there trees? I asked, and Michael laughed. He might have loved rocks, but I wanted something living, something that changed over time.

Rocks change, too, Henny.

I loved listening to Michael talk about geology. I loved the double approach to time and space that he had; the way he could stand on the barren banks of Pine Creek, with the high mountains and tall pines behind us, and see coral reefs.

I always wanted to hurry past the Permian-Triassic extinction event, past the dinosaurs and *their* extinction, to quickly skip over billions of years of history and get to our mountains and trees.

Our?

Pine Creek's.

I wanted to get to the mountains that had been worn down into sand to become the concrete that built the motel, the trees that had grown and been felled to become the cabins we built that summer.

CHAPTER 4

Flight HI1284 to Heaven: Delayed

I'VE NEVER BEEN GOOD IN A CRISIS, AND THIS WHOLE DYING thing is clearly no exception.

I spend all night lying beside Michael, thinking about everything I should have done differently. I make a list, just as Michael would.

Mistake number one: I shouldn't have let my body be taken away without me. That was a rookie error. How am I supposed to hover above it in a hospital room, suddenly returning to it and opening my eyes?

Although they might just have taken me straight to the morgue, and I really wouldn't want to go there. I'm pretty sure I'm supposed to be in a hospital bed.

At least, that's what I remember from all those "other side" films. People in comas in hospital beds suddenly finding some way back to their rooms, and voilà! Everyone is happy and relieved. Some beautiful song starts playing, and then the credits roll. Like they did in *Just Like Heaven*.

At the very least, I've never heard of anyone having a near-death experience and then coming back and talking about having been to the local bar.

Speaking of near-death experiences. *Mistake number two*: I definitely should have started looking for the light immediately.

Isn't that what everyone who has been through something similar says? They die, they see the light, they come back and find themselves looking up at their nearest and dearests' relieved faces. They *don't* come back and say that they saw a weathered old motel sign where the *e* was missing from *Vacancies*.

I'm not exactly longing for that light, but what if it's a two-way system where you need to find the light in order to pull away from it and return to life?

I'm looking for it now, beside Michael in bed, but I can't escape the feeling that it might already be too late. Shouldn't the light have been bright enough for me to notice it right away, even if I was in shock and distracted by all the police cars and sirens and the poor truck driver?

I wrap my arms around myself and try to focus on the sound of Michael breathing.

He doesn't even know that I'm dead, I realize. He isn't in touch with anyone in town, so unless MacKenzie called him as soon as she found out, I can't see how he would know. And I don't think she did. I don't think she would have been able to say it out loud.

This brings us to the biggest mistake of all: I shouldn't have run out in front of a truck. If only I'd left Michael's cabin fifteen minutes later! Let's say an hour, so I could have slept with him one last time. And maybe I could have taken the trail back to the motel, rather than the big road, just to be on the safe side.

Surely not even I could have managed to get hit by a truck *there*!

I don't know enough about philosophy or theology for this kind of thinking. Maybe our time on earth is predetermined. Maybe someone up there has measured my life and said, *This is how much Henny gets. No refills. I'm afraid we can't serve you anymore. You can have one last weekend with Michael as consolation, but that's it, okay?* Or maybe they threw in that weekend with Michael as a particularly cruel joke. I don't know.

Maybe I would have tripped on a root and hit my head if I'd taken the other way home.

There's no meaning behind it, Henny, Michael would have said.

And MacKenzie: *Sometimes bad things just happen. It is what it is.*

Fatalism isn't any consolation, I discover, but at least it's not as provocative as thinking of my death as the will of some kind of God.

If God exists, he hasn't even realized that I'm dead yet, or I would be up there by the pearly gates checking if Saint Peter has a reservation for me. But maybe it's just as well. Heaven would be too big and scary for me. I'd get tongue-tied among all the new people. And I'm really not cool enough for hell.

MacKenzie would have been much better at this...whatever this is. *She* would have seen the darn light, or maybe she would have created it herself. Made her way straight to heaven, fascinated by the new experience.

If she hadn't ended up in hell, that is. That would really have annoyed her. "Cheryl Stone and the rest of Sacred Faith Evangelical Church will be unbearable when they find out they were right about me," she'd say, but she would at least have found some comfort in the fact that they would definitely end up there, too, sooner or later.

Maybe I'm just stuck in some kind of waiting room at an existential airport?

Flight HE0847 to hell: delayed

Flight HI1284 to heaven: delayed

But that can't be how it works. People would have complained.

The restaurant is full of people. We serve the best breakfasts in Pine Creek, and today the food also comes with an irresistible side serving of fresh disaster. Eggs and bacon aren't the only things cooking; the air itself seems to be sizzling with rumors.

The restaurant is a long, narrow room with booths along the windows, smaller tables in the middle, and high stools along the bar. From there, the guests can enjoy the spectacle of Dolores's cooking. Or, on days like today, her dramatic tears. The place is so full that people are actually standing in the narrow walkway between the tables and the booths. Others are crammed in behind the people sitting at the counter, ordering over their shoulders. MacKenzie leaves the reception desk to help with serving.

I nervously follow her movements. I don't know whether she should be working today.

She's an unreliable waitress at the best of times, more likely to be making chitchat with her favorites than remembering strangers' orders, and today is worse than usual.

I walk alongside her, patting her awkwardly on the arm as if I'm trying to calm an anxious horse, but it has zero impact. She is clutching the coffeepot in front of her like a shield, refilling cups at random without even pretending to take down people's orders.

"I was drinking tea!" an old man protests, but another shakes his head and sits down next to him to explain the scale of the catastrophe that has struck us.

"Not much over thirty... Worked here all her life... They were... friends."

"Yes," the old man says irritably, "but what am I supposed to do with my tea now?"

If MacKenzie can hear them, she doesn't show it. Her face is so blank that people instinctively move out of her way.

Before long, Dolores's son, Alejandro, develops a system of simply following her around the room. We become a kind of team: me by her side, constantly patting her on the arm, and him one step behind, swapping coffee cups and amending orders as necessary. MacKenzie doesn't notice a thing.

People keep flashing her concerned glances when they think she isn't looking. Her dogged expression makes them far more uncomfortable than Dolores's hysterical sobs, which can be heard from the kitchen every now and then. All the regulars are used to Dolores. Her emotions make the breakfasts taste better; she's never as masterful as when she's in the grip of a mood swing. A few tears in the scrambled eggs or pancake batter are just right in a situation like this. It's MacKenzie's expressionless chill that unnerves people.

Clarence, who has been living at the motel for a few years, takes out his hip flask and spikes his breakfast coffee. As a rule, he normally waits until after nine.

Cheers, Clarence, I think.

As the morning wears on, the majority of breakfast guests slowly drift away. The only person left is a man who happens to be passing through town. He has no idea what all the fuss is about, and he grabs MacKenzie's arm as she walks by.

"Excuse me, miss," he says. He has an incredibly whiny voice. "I ordered pancakes."

MacKenzie looks down at his hand on her arm. He quickly lets go of her.

"And you got a breakfast burrito," she says.

He gives her an expectant look, assuming she is about to apologize and correct her mistake. But MacKenzie just smiles at him—more of a wolf's grin than a smile, really—and the man leans back as far as his seat will allow him.

"Enjoy!" she chirps before Alejandro gently takes the coffeepot from her hand and places it on an empty table.

"But my pancakes!" the man says.

"Eat your blasted burrito," MacKenzie says, and Alejandro takes hold of her shoulders and pushes her out through the door.

Pine Creek Motel and Cabins was built during a time when the open road was the great miracle, when cars were exciting and nature boring. Every single window at the motel looks out onto the parking lot.

It's a motel built for dreaming, I'm sure of that. There are dreams in the walls here. Dreams, and hard work and family and friendship. You just have to know how to see beyond the drab colors and the hand-sewn curtains that have started to fray at the seams.

I know many people think that motels are impersonal, or boring, or sometimes even slightly, well, shabby, but that's only because they don't know them like I do. Our kind of motels are run by families. They're temporary homes created for others by moms and pops and sons and daughters working together.

Sure, it's the kind of motel that has never had enough money or staff, but that's part of the charm. That's what makes working here so interesting. The last owner sewed the curtains by hand because new custom-made ones were too expensive. Michael, Camila, MacKenzie, and I painted the walls, back when everything was still a game and it didn't really matter whether we were paid or not.

So now, every time I look at anything here, I see me and MacKenzie and Michael and Camila, the most glorious friendship that has ever existed; and Juan Esteban, Camila's uncle, who made it all possible with his dreams and visions and occasional madness. *That's* what a motel is.

The design of the motel is like a kind of sideways L, where the long side is a two-story building containing just under thirty rooms. Even numbers downstairs, odd ones upstairs. We have coffee makers in every room and microwaves in roughly half, and on a good day both the fans and the air-conditioning work.

The familiar, homey environment cheers me up. I can't do anything about the mistakes I've made so far. The real question is what I'm going to do *now*.

Not that I have an answer to that, of course. But I run after MacKenzie as she cuts across the parking lot on her way toward reception. A lone car is parked outside. On the other side, the neon sign glows even more faintly in the sunlight.

The first thing she does as she steps inside is to kick the couch.

It's old, battered, and uncomfortable, but it hasn't exactly done her any harm. The floor lamp next to it is also largely innocent, but she gives that a kick, too. The rip in the dusky-pink shade has been there for some time. The brochures full of tips about local tourist attractions are tired and dog-eared, but it's from age rather than any guests flicking through them. They cascade sadly to the floor as MacKenzie gives the stand a shove.

"Crap," she says. "Crap crap crap crap crap."

The wall is next on her list of targets.

She slumps down behind the desk. For several minutes, she just stares straight ahead as though she can't remember what she is doing there. Then she leans forward and starts hitting her head against the desk. Slowly and methodically. Each one makes me wince.

She straightens up and calls Alejandro to ask if he will take over from her at the desk.

"Sure," he quickly says. "Anything. No problem. You just have to ask."

MacKenzie rests her forehead on the desk. Closes her eyes. She is still clutching the phone to her ear after Alejandro hangs up.

"I'm going to have to tell Michael," she says.

She finds him around the back of the cabin. Michael is looking out at the creek, toward the mountains, and he seems... He looks *happy*. Rested and tanned and utterly carefree.

I was right. He doesn't know. The level of interest at breakfast showed that news of my death has spread across town, but Michael isn't in touch with anyone here. His face is calm and relaxed, his gaze lively and amused, his body strong and full of energy. To him, it's just another sunny morning.

I turn sharply toward MacKenzie and hold out my arms to stop her from getting any closer. "Don't tell him!" I beg her. "He'll just be upset. Me and Michael can have one more happy day together, can't we? Tomorrow. You can tell him tomorrow. If you really have to."

MacKenzie looks about as reluctant as I am to go over to him. She just stands there, dithering, until Michael spots her.

"MacKenzie," he says, sounding surprised. He's smiling. To him, this is just an unexpected but welcome encounter with an old friend.

MacKenzie doesn't return his smile.

He seems confused by her stony face. They haven't seen each other in fifteen years. "Is this about Henny?" he asks.

MacKenzie seems relieved. "How did you know?" she asks. "Did someone...?"

"You're worried I'm going to hurt her, right? Did you come over here to tell me to leave her alone?"

"Jesus, Michael."

"Or to ask what the hell I'm playing at, coming back like this, without giving you any warning? I hope that's not what this is, because I can't give you any answers. I was just driving through Oregon and couldn't help myself."

He gives her a convincing smile, as though he is trying to make her laugh both with and at him. "Come on, MacKenzie," he says. "Is it really so bad? We're still friends, aren't we?"

"Could you just shut up a second?"

"Okay. Not friends, then."

I glance back and forth between them, paralyzed by the acute need to do something, say something, anything at all to protect him and keep him easygoing and happy for just a few more hours.

"If you don't shut up, I'll never be able to say this," MacKenzie says. "I can't... There's no easy way to tell you this."

"MacKenzie, what is it? Did something happen?"

"She's dead. Henny's dead, all right?"

All around us, everything is just like it was a few seconds ago. The sun is shining. The clear, icy stream is glittering in the sunlight. The mountains are in the background. The scent of rosemary is in the air. But Michael can't see any of that now. His face is worryingly pale.

His jaws are so tightly clenched that it hurts even to look at him. Cramped, tensed muscles in his arms, his thighs. It looks as though he wants to launch himself at something and just punch and punch and punch.

It takes real effort for him to relax enough to say even a single word. "How?"

"There was an accident. A truck. That's all I know. Sheriff Ed called the motel."

"When?"

"Yesterday. It happened sometime in the afternoon."

"Where?"

MacKenzie hesitates. "On the road between the cabin and the motel."

Michael instinctively turns his head toward the cabin. "She was leaving here."

"I guess so."

"She was in a hurry. She'd stayed too long. She had to get back to work."

"It doesn't matter now."

"She said..." He struggles to swallow and doesn't manage to say anything else.

"Michael..." I don't know whether it's me or MacKenzie who says that.

"I should've... If I hadn't..."

"It's not your fault," MacKenzie says. "She could just as easily have been walking over there anyway. Besides, it's as much my fault. She was heading back to take over from me in reception."

But Michael is already striding away from us. His body explodes into motion. When he reaches the cabin, he jumps into his car and tears away, tires screeching. The car skids on the gravel. He's gone before I even have time to react.

I stand there like an idiot, watching him leave.

"Are you sure you should be working?" Alejandro asks, but he immediately gets up from behind the desk so that MacKenzie can slump onto the chair. Maybe he's scared she will collapse if she remains on her feet. The brochures are back in their stand, and the lamp is in its usual spot.

"Why not?" she says.

"Shouldn't you—uh, I don't know—get some rest or something? You look a little weird."

"I'm fine. What would I do otherwise? I can't spend the whole damn day in bed. I'd really go crazy then."

Alejandro nods. Then he leaves her alone.

I assume that MacKenzie is going through the reservations, but when I peer over her shoulder, I realize that she is on Facebook.

She is working her way through the list of people called Camila Alvarez.

Camila. Being hit by a truck clarifies a lot of things in a person's mind, and I suddenly know without a shadow of a doubt that we shouldn't have let her leave all those years ago. Technically, this motel still belongs to her, but more importantly, *she* belongs here. If I could still drive a car, I would jump right into it, take off to California, and get her back here.

But I guess a Facebook message is a start.

We haven't seen her in fifteen years, but several people can be dismissed right away: One is too white. One is too old. One too young. Every time MacKenzie spots someone who could fit the bill, she sends them a message: Henny is dead.

I guess she thinks it'll mean something to one of them.

Henny is dead. Henny is dead. Henny is dead.

CHAPTER 5

The Redwood Cabin

THERE USED TO BE FOUR OF US. ME, MACKENZIE, MICHAEL, AND Camila. And then there were only two, right up until Friday, when Michael showed up at the motel.

He just walked right in like he had never left.

We were surprised to see each other, but I was the only one who had the right to be. He must have known he would run into me sooner or later, given that he was checking into my motel. Still, he tensed up. Kept clutching his two backpacks, didn't put either of them down.

When he first left me, I used to daydream about him coming back just like that. I would be standing in reception on a perfectly ordinary day, except that I'd look unusually pretty. Wearing my best jeans and having a good hair day. He would say: *Henny. I've missed you. I've changed my mind. I can't live without you.*

"Henny," he said.

I wasn't wearing my best jeans.

He was standing too close to the automatic doors and they kept trying to close on him, so he had to take a half step forward. He put down his bags and glanced around.

"I... Sorry, I should've..."

His eyes swept over the stand of tourist brochures about Pine Creek County and Oregon, then focused on the painting above the desk, by a local artist from Baker City. For some reason, he found the oil painting of Hells Canyon at sunset fascinating. He stood there for a long time, just staring at *it*.

The depressing thought that I matched reception crossed my mind. Drab, gray, and nondescript, like I always had been, but older and wearier than when he saw me last. I tried to smooth my hair and wished I had organized the brochure stand. And vacuumed. And put on some makeup.

He smiled, half-embarrassed and half-apologetic. "I should have come up with something to say in advance, right?" he said.

I can still hear how my heart started racing in my chest. *Dunk-dunk. Dunk-dunk. Dunk-dunk.* It feels weirdly calming to remember that now, but at the time, all I could think was that not even fifteen years of absence had taught my body to stop reacting to his.

"And I shouldn't be feeling this shocked. I wanted to see you. I just thought... I didn't think."

"Clearly," I said, noting with satisfaction that it was precisely what MacKenzie would have said.

"I'd like a room, please. Obviously. Otherwise I wouldn't be standing here with my bags."

"You could have just wanted to say hi on the way to your parents' place."

"Christ, no. Definitely not."

"No, then you wouldn't be quite so surprised to see me here."

"Not surprised, just..."

"Shocked."

He smiled again. "I didn't book a room."

"I know."

Did he think he could have booked a room without me noticing?

We had vacant rooms, of course. Nothing changed while he was gone. Both reception and I had been gathering dust ever since he left.

I gave Michael the Redwood Cabin, but if he was thinking about the night we had spent there fifteen years ago, he didn't show it. I followed him there, using the back trail while he took his car. We got there at the same time. After I opened the door, he took the key and looked around with an entirely unreasonable neutral expression.

Seeing him as a grown man was like being given the answer to the question you ask when you're young: *What will we be like when we're older?*

He was a stranger I still thought I knew. There were a few strands of gray around his temples and deep laughter lines around his eyes, but those things just made him even more handsome. His eyelashes were still absurdly long and dark, and his eyes seemed brilliantly blue against his tanned skin. I remembered them being cooler, grayer, though maybe the amusing awkwardness of the situation made them glitter like that.

The portrait inside the dust jacket of his book didn't do him justice. That was how I had kept track of him over the years. I already knew that he had become the geologist he always wanted to be, and that he had traveled to all of the exciting places he had dreamed of as a boy. Then he had taken his nerdy love for rocks and written a popular science book: *Fantastic Rocks and Where to Find Them*. For a few weeks, he had been everywhere. On the *New York Times* bestseller list, in *People* magazine, even on a TV couch or two.

And now he was here. In my cabin. Neither of us had moved from the little hallway by the door. It smelled of wood and old rugs.

"I read your book," I said.

He looked happy, but also a little embarrassed.

"It was like hearing you speak again, after all these years," I continued. "I could hear your voice in the anecdotes about rocks. It was almost like being there with you, despite everything."

"Henny..."

I moved deeper inside the cabin. Confusion made me sound briskly efficient. "Kitchen," I said. "Stovetop, refrigerator, silverware in this drawer, pots and frying pan in this cupboard. There's some tea and coffee. Bedroom in here." I quickly skipped over that. "Bathroom."

He ran a hand through his hair. It seemed darker than I remembered, though maybe that was just due to the contrast with his new silvery strands. It was messily overgrown, too. I instinctively reached out to smooth it, but I realized I no longer had the right to touch him.

I cleared my throat in embarrassment. "Hand towels," I said. "Just let us know if you need any more."

"I wondered whether you'd still be here," he said.

I looked up at him in surprise. "Where else would I be?"

"It's a big world, Henny."

"Not for me."

As I moved past him, he instinctively reached for my arm. I gasped. My entire body was intensely focused on that patch of skin beneath his fingers.

"Did you ever think about leaving?" he asked.

"No."

A lie.

"Did you ever think about coming back?" I asked.

"Yes."

I couldn't tell whether he was telling the truth.

"I have to get back to the reception desk," I said.

He dropped my arm. Without thinking, I touched the place his hand had been resting. My skin felt hot, like a burn mark of longing.

When I reached the front door, I paused. Turned around. He was still standing in the same place.

"Do you ever feel like life went...wrong?" he asked.

"Yeah."

The truth this time.

CHAPTER 6

Tree Terror on Elm Street

"HIS CAR IS STILL GONE, BUT SURELY HE'LL HAVE TO COME BACK. His stuff is still here. I could see his bags through the window. And the rocks. He'd never leave without *those*," I say.

I'm sitting in the passenger seat beside MacKenzie. Michael has been gone for over three hours now, and I've spent the whole time wandering back and forth between the cabin and reception. When I saw MacKenzie going out to her car, I followed her. I desperately wanted a distraction, anything to avoid having to think about the look on Michael's face.

It doesn't work. As we drive toward town, I can still see that look clearly. It seems much more real than the sunshine and the trees around us.

"He has to stay," I say. "He can't just leave. I'm going to fix this mess. I can, can't I?" And then: "MacKenzie...has your shirt been *ironed*?"

Yes, it has. It's also white. I didn't even know she owned a white shirt. Her fingers anxiously drum the wheel.

She parks outside the grocery store in Pine Creek and grabs a bunch of flowers at random from the bucket outside. It's a pathetic little bouquet, drowning in cellophane, but she doesn't seem to have noticed.

Her face is still expressionless, her eyes blank, and she barely seems to recognize the pastor from Dad's church, even when she almost walks straight into him.

I think the pastor means well when he pays his condolences and says that I'm in God's hands now, but it makes me want to lie down on the ground and kick and scream like a three-year-old. *In God's hands? In God's hands? I'm right here, damn it! In Pine Creek! I'm not in anyone's hands, I'll have you know!*

Then I feel bad. He means well. I like the pastor. He's always been on our side. But I don't think he should have said those things to MacKenzie. He knows what she's been through when it comes to God.

"It's easy to doubt God's existence in moments like this," the pastor says in his warm, kind voice, "but these are precisely the moments when we need Him..."

"Oh, I've been sure that God exists for years now," MacKenzie interrupts.

Something about her tone of voice makes the pastor's eyes dart nervously.

"This whole thing with Henny has just reinforced that."

"Oh, well—"

"It's just that I'm also pretty sure he's a jerk."

"Don't you think—"

"The same way I've never liked Santa. If he exists, he gives more presents to the rich kids."

"I don't really think it's quite the same—" the pastor begins.

"Of course it's not the same. No one abuses or harasses anyone in Santa's name. That's one thing we can't accuse him of."

And on that parting shot, MacKenzie storms off toward her car.

"She didn't mean it!" I shout over my shoulder, hurrying after her. "I think. Maybe. And I really do hope God exists, because I could do with a miracle right now."

MacKenzie pauses, holding the flowers over a trash can, but eventually she opens the car door and tosses them onto the passenger seat. I squeeze in between the bouquet and the door.

I think MacKenzie could do with a miracle, too, because by the time she turns off onto Water Street, where Dad lives, she has started talking to herself.

"I'm sorry about..." she says. "Mr. Broek, I'm so sorry..." She even tries out a hesitant: "Robert...?"

She pulls up outside Dad's house, slams the car door a little too hard, and winces guiltily. Then she leans in through the open window and grabs the flowers. She keeps them half-hidden behind her back, as though she already regrets both the bouquet and her own presence.

But she's come this far. She knocks on the door.

Nothing happens.

She knocks again. Louder this time. No one answers, but both MacKenzie and I see the kitchen curtains stir.

"Mr. Broek?" she says loudly. "Robert?"

This time, the only effect is that the neighbors' curtains start twitching, too. When one of them sticks their head out the window, MacKenzie quickly returns to her car. I barely have time to jump in after her before she tears away in relief.

I instinctively grab her arm, even though I know she won't feel it. "The pastor," I say. "The funeral. Dad. My body. *That's* what I should have been focusing on. I won't be able to fix anything until I find my body."

The only problem is that I have no idea where they keep dead bodies around here, and it's not like I can just Google it. Still, Dad will have to plan my funeral at some point, and my body will have to be transferred to the funeral parlor. If he would just arrange to view the body, I could follow him over there and then...well, then I have no idea what I would do. But it's a start. It's *something*. And who knows, maybe I'll have some kind of realization or revelation when I see it. Me. When I see myself.

MacKenzie pulls up outside Hank's Restaurant, but only long enough to wind down the window and hold out the flowers to one of the old men sitting outside.

He takes the bouquet out of sheer surprise, but also feels obliged to point out that he's married.

"So give them to your wife," MacKenzie tells him.

"The shock would kill her," the old man replies.

MacKenzie pulls away, but I don't go with her. I'm still outside Hank's, frozen to the spot and staring at a four-wheel-drive Hyundai parked a couple of blocks down Main Street.

Michael's car.

He is standing with his back to me, looking down the street.

It doesn't matter that he can't hear me. I have to say something, explain that I'm still here and that nothing has changed and that I'm going to sort all this out. I'll tell him how much the weekend meant to me, how I don't want it to end, how he has to *stay*...

"We've got elms now!" I blurt out.

Great, Henny, I think.

But it *is* true. Nowadays, the elms flank the street from the crossing by Hank's Restaurant all the way to the pretty, traditional sign on the edge of town: *Welcome to Pine Creek.* The leaves have just started to turn red and yellow, and proud American flags flutter between each of them, reaching right up to the treetops.

That is: shoulder height.

"They never really got any higher," I say. "No matter what the town tried to do. I guess they just never really...took. But by that time, they'd already changed the name of the street."

The elms make everything else look disproportionately big—the neighboring buildings towering toward the sky and the mountains grazing the clouds in the distance. The bike leaning against one of the trees must belong to a giant.

"The *Pine Creek Gazette* called it 'Tree Terror on Elm Street,'" I say. "But I think they're cute. Like some kind of hybrid tree-bush."

I've finally managed to find him, and I'm blabbering about *trees*?

"A lot has changed since you left. Bittersweet Café closed. The hardware store on Oak Street is an attorney's office. They specialize in bankruptcy. There are two new secondhand stores on Woodland Street."

And then I say: "Michael..." I don't sound anywhere near as cool and indifferent as I had hoped, but he finally turns around.

His face is as grief-stricken and gray as MacKenzie's. His skin seems thinner, almost transparent, as though life has managed to wear him down in just a few hours. His eyes are completely empty. It's the first time he has ever looked at me without a smile in his eyes.

"*Michael,*" I say.

He walks straight past me into Hank's and slumps exhaustedly onto a chair by the bar. The old man with MacKenzie's bouquet is sitting a few seats away. Next to him is a cold cup of coffee.

Long before our time, Hank's Restaurant was a café. His wife had thought that was more fitting than anything else, and though it's a long time since she left both Hank and town, her influence remains: there are worn lace curtains in the windows, and the wooden tables in front of them are small and dainty, made for delicate coffee cups and tiny saucers rather than enormous hamburger plates. Above the counter, there are a couple of signed Ducks T-shirts. A serving hatch connects the main room with the kitchen—there are definitely no plans to let any squeamish guests see how the food is made here. Michael is smart enough to stick to coffee, though even that has its risks.

"Michael, it's not as bad as it seems," I say desperately. "I mean, Hank's coffee is. *That* hasn't changed."

My attempt at a joke isn't particularly successful.

"But I'm not really gone. I'll be back. I'm going to fix all this. Somehow."

I try placing a hand on his shoulder. It feels surprisingly intimate to be sitting so close to him, touching him so openly.

His body has changed over the years. I told him that during our weekend together, and he said, "Be nice, Henny. I am fifteen years older."

But I hadn't meant it like that, and he wasn't really upset. He was still slim and nicely muscular.

What I meant was that his body was *more human* now.

In the past, he was a tense ball of restless, repressed energy. Whether consciously or unconsciously, he always seemed to think that his muscles and soul and brain were meant for *more*. More speed, more challenges, more movement. His body was never relaxed. Even when he slept, his arms and legs and hands would twitch.

But not now. Now, he can sit perfectly still, not even drinking from the coffee cup in front of him, not paying the slightest bit of notice to the old man going on and on about the insults he has had to endure as a result of the bouquet.

Michael lets the man's words wash over him. When Hank and the old man aren't looking, he closes his eyes as though he needs to summon all his energy just to sit quietly.

"You can't think I would leave you now that you're finally back," I say. I swallow.

"I know we never decided anything about, you know, the future. What we were going to do, or anything like that. But what we had last weekend was magical and real. It was *right*. It should've happened a long time ago, and you know that, too."

I look down at my hands. Wring them in front of me. Just twenty-four hours ago, I could touch him, but now I can't.

I only have three of my senses left: I can see, I can hear, and I can smell. So, I breathe in the scent of him, his deodorant, familiar after three days together. There's the cold leather of his jacket, too, and when I put my hand on his shoulder, I can almost pretend that it's an ordinary afternoon, that we're just grabbing a cup of coffee in town, chatting with a depressed old man at Hank's.

For a brief moment, I swear I can feel the warmth of his body. It fills me with a new sense of hope. My heart, my skin, the blood that used to flow through my veins—all that is probably in a morgue somewhere, but if I can still feel this... Surely it can't be too late?

Unless it's a phantom attraction, that is. Like phantom pains in an amputated leg. Maybe I just haven't realized that my heart has stopped beating.

No. "I'm still *here*," I say.

"Is it too much to ask to be able to enjoy a cup of coffee and shoot the breeze with a few friends?" the old man asks. "What the hell am I going to do with these flowers? The wife'll think I've been cheating on her."

"I'm going to find my body," I say. "You just need to give me a little time. I need to search for the light and find my body and, well, fix all this. But I can't do that if I'm constantly worrying about where you are or if you're going to leave while I'm gone."

I study his face intensely, searching for some kind of sign. Something that lets me know he has understood, that shows some part of him can hear me, or that tells me what he is planning to do. But his face doesn't reveal a thing.

"A couple of days," I say in desperation. I try to tell myself that he has heard me. That we're on the same page. He can't leave until then.

"Hold on a second," says Hank. "Aren't you Michael Callahan? Derek's little brother?"

He fills Michael's coffee, even though he has only taken a couple of sips.

The old man pulls a sympathetic face. "Take it easy with the coffee, Hank," he says. "We don't know how much the boy can handle."

"What brings you back to these parts?" Hank asks.

Michael shrugs. "I was just passing through."

"You staying out at the motel? I guess the place is okay for a few days, if you just need a place to crash." He leans forward. "Did you know the place is run by two dy—"

"I knew Henny," Michael interrupts.

"Right, right. Sad business. But still."

The old man studies Michael. "Condolences," he says. "Don't suppose you'd want a bunch of flowers as comfort?"

CHAPTER 7

A Tiny Piece of Oregon

AFTER MICHAEL CHECKED IN, I SPENT THE WHOLE AFTERNOON pacing restlessly around the reception desk.

It was impossible to think about anything else.

Michael, *my* Michael, was only a few hundred yards away.

Don't be stupid, I said to myself. *He left you. Fifteen years ago, he vanished without even saying goodbye! He probably hasn't missed you or anything else in Pine Creek.*

But I couldn't stay still, and I couldn't be sensible. Being holed up in the reception area only made things worse. I was standing behind the check-in counter. Behind me was our small, always chaotic office, and ahead of me were the same things I looked at every day: carpeted floor—reasonably clean, reassuring guests that the sheets may be, too—and an old sofa by one of the walls—seldom used, put there for appearance's sake, to create the illusion that we might sometimes actually get a line of customers checking in at the same time, and that some of them might want to sit down while waiting. The entire room was familiar and safe and suddenly so very *boring*.

Was this really my life? Michael had gone away and experienced things, but my entire existence was right here. The weekend stretched out ahead of me like it always did, with nothing to look forward to but work and hanging out with MacKenzie.

I should have been happy with that—it was *my life*—but suddenly all I could see was a kind of unbearable grayness: work that never ended, the utter meaninglessness of cleaning a room one day only to have to do it all over again the next.

Eventually, I gave up and called MacKenzie, asking her to cover my shift. She didn't ask why, and I didn't tell her.

I leaned over the sink and studied my reflection in the mirror, trying to see myself through his eyes. Had I changed? Were the lines around my eyes pretty or depressing? My hair was the same as ever, a boring shade of brown, neither long nor short. Practical and unassuming, like everything else about me. I thought about the women he must have met over the years, how dull I must seem in comparison. I knew nothing about him, but he already knew everything there was to know about me. *She's still here. She hasn't done anything with her life.*

I applied a few quick strokes of mascara. Sprayed perfume onto my wrists and behind my ears. The scent caught in my nose.

Lipstick! MacKenzie had given me one as a gift, but I had never used it. It was far too deep a shade of red, far too exotic for me, but suddenly I wanted to seem mysterious and exciting. I rummaged through my makeup bag, finding most of it old and dried up from lack of use. But the lipstick was still there. Practically new. I followed the contours of my pale, colorless lips and smacked them together, now blood red. I could taste lipstick and expectation. My cheeks flushed, and my eyes glittered with nerves. *Wild and exciting.*

I even tried applying a little wax to my hair. Messed it up slightly, gave it more volume. My fingers turned sticky.

Then I saw the new version of myself in the mirror. With strange hair and ridiculous red lips. The lipstick distorted the rest of me, like a mocking reflection in a fun-house mirror. A strand of hair clung to my forehead.

Ridiculous, ridiculous, ridiculous. You're an idiot. He probably has a girlfriend.

What was I thinking? That we'd had a grand love affair fifteen years ago, and he had finally come back to me? This was Pine Creek, for God's sake. Grand love stories didn't happen here. Unplanned pregnancies happened here. Marriages that drove people crazy or to the bottle happened here. We were just two kids who broke up after high school, and now we were ordinary thirtysomethings who didn't know each other. Suddenly, I could taste lipstick and shame.

I furiously rubbed off the makeup. Splashed my face with cold water. Tried to get rid of the redness on my cheeks and smoothed out my hair. The old Henny stared back at me. What was the point in pretending to be someone else?

I jogged over to the cabin and knocked on the door before I had time to change my mind.

"Henny." Michael sounded surprised.

I hoped the darkness would hide my burning cheeks. "I thought I would come over and...chat."

Even his cheeks looked a little red then. "Chat. Sure. Sounds nice."

He was still standing in the doorway. When he realized he was in the way, his cheeks flushed even darker, and he stepped to one side to let me in.

"Wine!" he said, relieved. "I mean, would you like a glass? Did you eat already? I bought a nice organic wine in Eugene when I passed through. Perfect with salmon, apparently."

The kitchens in the cabins are small, designed for making simple dishes that could be eaten at the table in the living room. But he managed to pour two glasses of wine without bumping into me too often.

"Did you eat already?"

"No, I..."

"I don't have any salmon, unfortunately. I meant to do some shopping here, but I got delayed on the way and there wasn't much choice at the convenience store. Still, I'm sure this wine goes just as well with, uh, hot dogs."

I laughed. The sound was unfamiliar. Tonight I was someone who didn't clean rooms or try to pass the time behind a reception desk.

"Dolores will kill you if she finds out you ate hot dogs instead of going to the restaurant," I said.

"Would you... Would you rather we ate there?"

I quickly shook my head. Took a sip of wine. Tried to make my heart stop beating so fiercely in my chest.

Half an hour later, we were eating hot dog omelettes and drinking his excellent organic wine at the table in the living room. We washed the dishes together afterward. The whole thing was over far too quickly. A saucepan, two forks, two plates. Suddenly, I no longer had any reason to hang around. I drank the last of my wine and washed that glass, too. Carefully dried it and put it neatly in the right place.

Michael followed me back into the living room. While I had been struggling to focus on my job in reception, he had unpacked. There were now four backpacks along the wall, and there was already a pile of rocks in one corner.

"Are those things you need for work?" I asked. I was trying to drag out our time together. I didn't want to go back to my real life.

"Kind of. I try to see as much as I can of the places where I work. It feels stupid to be staying in these incredible places if I just spend all my time down in a pit. So I've got equipment for warm and cold climates. Most of it works for both: lightweight tent, warm sleeping bag, camping stove."

I nodded to some tools spread out on top of a laminated map on the TV cabinet. "And these?"

"My tools. A rock hammer, for taking rock samples." He handed me a small, round plastic object, barely bigger than a ring. "Magnifying glass," he said.

"And a compass?"

"It's a Brunton compass. It shows you the direction, but also the angle and depth. It makes it easier to follow and document a rock formation."

I picked up one of the rocks. Honestly, it looked incredibly plain. Just an ordinary stone he had scrawled a few digits onto in marker pen. I looked at Michael, a question on my face. *Why this one?*

"No reason. It's just a rock. I'm a geologist. We get depressed if we go a long time without taking a rock sample."

He could see my skepticism and laughed. "Maybe you'll like this one better," he said, holding out a pretty purple-and-violet rock. "An amethyst," he explained. "From Australia."

"Did you collect these yourself?"

He nodded.

I smiled happily. "It's like a photo album of rocks."

I reached out for another rock. "And this one?" I asked.

He seemed embarrassed and took it from me. "That's just an ordinary rock." He picked up two others from beside it and put them back into the bag.

"But where are they from?"

"They're from here. This is a piece of basalt. It's everywhere here."

I was standing so close to him that I could feel the warmth of his body as he held up a beautiful, shimmering green stone. "Serpentinite."

He hesitated, but eventually handed me a rock that was a deep shade of grayish-blue. "Blueschist," he said. "Whenever I want to remember Oregon, this is what I think of."

I weighed the rock in my hand. All of my senses felt heightened, as though I was experiencing everything through a microscope. The rock felt warm and rough against my skin, the colors exploding right before my eyes, swirls of blue and thin streaks of something gray and glittering.

"God, I'm really blabbering," Michael said. "I always talk about rocks when I get nervous. You must think I'm an idiot."

But I was amused. I pictured him somewhere far from home, in some exotic place I could barely even imagine, with a tiny piece of Oregon close to him.

"I'd actually prepared what I was going to say to you if you came by after that debacle at check-in."

I smiled. "You wrote a list?"

That was what he always used to do.

"Three, actually. Suggested topics of conversation in case we had nothing to talk about. What I wanted to say to you. What I shouldn't say."

"That last one sounds the most interesting. But maybe I don't want to know?"

"I know that nothing has changed," he said. "I'll be leaving, and you can't be happy anywhere else. And it's probably been too long. We're so different. We were too different even when we were young, and things are much worse now. You've got your own life. Of course."

"Michael," I interrupted, but he continued, seemingly unable to stop.

"I just don't want you to think I expect anything of you. I'm not going to show up out of the blue and think that everything is fine between us and that we can try again just like that. Nothing has changed. I don't even know why I came back."

"You think too much," I said, and then I finally kissed him. I held my hand on his cheek, leaned forward on tiptoe, and gently pressed my lips to his.

It made him stop talking, at the very least.

He would move on and leave me again. I knew that, but to my confused heart, that was just another reason why I should kiss him. While I had the chance.

And then I stopped thinking about anything at all. Michael kissed me back as though he was trying to express fifteen years of longing, or maybe that was just how it felt. He pulled my blouse up and over my head, and I struggled feverishly with his shirt buttons, and then finally felt his warm skin beneath my hands.

His body was just how I remembered it, and completely different at the same time.

CHAPTER 8

A Lot of Food and Flowers

THE HISTORY OF PINE CREEK STARTS AND ENDS WITH THE forestry industry, and MacKenzie always says that the end came many years ago. We've just been in denial ever since.

Before that, the forest was the basis of our existence. The boys who graduated from Pine Creek High School during the seventies never had to worry about getting a college education or taking out student loans. No one moved away. They knew they could get a job that paid twelve dollars and eighty cents an hour, with fantastic benefits.

That isn't to say that the outside world wasn't already making a mark. By that time, feminists, hippies, Californians, and Christians had all started moving to Oregon to start collectives and pursue alternative lifestyles. Still, they could be swatted away like flies, swarming at the edge of Pine Creek's existence—irritating but ultimately harmless.

It was later that things started to go downhill. Across all of Oregon, not just in Pine Creek. A third of the people employed by the forestry industry lost their jobs. A few years after that, another thirty thousand positions went up in smoke. Thousands of others were forced to accept reduced hours, lower wages, or cuts in benefits—or all three. As always, the federal government was very supportive and introduced measures to protect the spotted owl. The spotted owl!

I have to admit, I've always loved those owls. I just make sure not to tell anyone. They're still a sore topic around here. The protection of the spotted owl's habitat saved millions of acres of trees from being cut down, but it was about more than that, too. We built this country. Literally. But when times got hard and we were struggling, those politicians in DC didn't give us a helping hand. They slapped us with environmental protections instead. I'm sure it wasn't the owls' fault, but people were right about one thing at least: there had been three sawmills in the region during the late seventies. Just twenty years later, they had all closed down.

And yet here we are. MacKenzie says it's because we're too stupid to leave, but she's just kidding.

There are tall pines all around me as I walk into town, and I realize that, in a sense, the forest is still saving us, because a lot of people now make a living from the tourists who come here to hike, hunt, or fish. Some of the men call themselves guides. Fishing guide. Hunting guide. Hiking guide. All you need is a decent jacket, a good pair of boots, and marginally more intelligence than the tourists. Which, as MacKenzie says, isn't particularly hard.

Things might have changed around here, but we're still a traditional town at heart. We take many things seriously here. God, for example. And death. There are three funeral homes in Pine Creek, and I've decided to visit them all.

So here I am the next day, walking into town. Driving a car is only one of many things I can't do anymore.

There must be a quicker way to move around as a ghost, but I haven't discovered it yet. Maybe I'm still bound by the laws of nature.

Maybe I just don't have enough imagination to picture myself hovering above the ground.

Hover, I think, but absolutely nothing happens.

Maybe I could teleport.

I close my eyes and think *Elm Street*, but I don't move an inch from the side of the road. Walking it is.

Unfortunately, funeral homes seem to have been designed specifically so that the recently bereaved won't stumble onto their unfortunate newly departed. They're more focused on finding the right coffin than the right body.

By lunchtime I've seen more tastefully arranged caskets than I really want to. One of the funeral homes has an entire showroom dedicated to them; the other two let people choose from expensive-looking bound catalogs.

There are white coffins, coffins in polished oak, coffins lined with silk. One section demonstrates how you can personalize your coffin with American flags or photos from the poor dead person's life. Another section showcases environmentally friendly burials using recycled materials or cardboard. It seems more fitting for Portland than Pine Creek, but perhaps times really are changing.

How can they expect people to *choose?* I feel suddenly very sorry for Dad. He'll be overwhelmed by the desperate need to make the right choice. He'll try to find the most traditional and correct coffin there is, and I'm guessing it will be expensive. MacKenzie would have an easier job with it. Her choice would inevitably be fun and personal and completely irreverent.

I'm beginning to think that is the only reasonable approach to death.

I lurk around a bit in the back of all the funeral homes, walking right through random doors—still a disconcerting experience—and mostly just getting lost. At the third one, I walk through a door only to find myself standing in front of a young couple, both looking stunned and uncomprehending. Worse than crying. It's like they're still too shocked to even be shattered by their loss. I back away quickly, automatically mumbling apologies no one can hear.

I retire to the safety of the street.

Any further search will have to wait. I can't take any more death today.

I pass Dad on my way home. I get there at the same time that he returns from his shopping, carrying two grocery bags. Cheryl is with him, doing her neighborly duty as always.

There's a strange pile of things outside his door. Dad moves closer to inspect it, and I lean in beside him.

There are a couple of Tupperware containers, neatly marked with the date and their contents. Flowers. Several cards, some simple and handmade, others store-bought. White with sober black edges, crosses, and the words *Our Deepest Sympathy*.

Dad puts down his shopping bag and glances at the pile as he fumbles for his keys.

They start coming before he even has time to open the door, one by one, a procession of human compassion. Some are embarrassed, some eloquent, others quiet. They hand over dishes of food, an orchid, a bag of canned food, more flowers, a bowl of homemade potato salad. "It's all we had at home," the woman who brought it whispers in embarrassment.

Dad's arms are overflowing as he tries to balance everything. He blinks in confusion.

A woman who lives a few houses down comes over with an apple pie. She puts it down on top of one of the other ovenproof dishes.

"I know it's not much," she says quickly. "But when my mom died, I could barely bring myself to eat, so I thought a pie might tempt you." She leans in and whispers: "Not that you have to eat if you don't feel like it. Just throw the food in the trash and give the dishes back. That's what I did."

Cheryl looks down at all of the food and flowers and cards, and her eyes fill with tears. "Oh, Robert," she says.

"I wish people would just leave me alone," Dad mumbles.

CHAPTER 9

You're One with Your Body

I THINK THERE ARE CERTAIN THINGS YOU'RE NOT SUPPOSED TO do alone, and visiting funeral homes is one of them. I could try again on my own, but I decide to wait for Dad. I'm not sure if it's for his comfort or mine.

I only needed to do a bit of eavesdropping to find out the time for his meeting there. So here I am.

Cheryl is here, too. I like her better for it. I know it's easy to imagine her having some sort of ulterior motive for keeping Dad company all the time. He is, after all, a reasonably good-looking and somewhat normal widower. These things happen, I'm sure. But Cheryl is very happily married to a very patient husband, and I know her only reason for being here is to be a good Christian to a friend in need. They're not members of the same congregation—he's Methodist, she's Evangelical—but she's never let a small detail like that get in her way. She found Jesus late in life, and she seems determined to make up for lost time.

Her T-shirt today reads *All I need today is a little coffee and a whole lot of Jesus*.

"I wish you were wearing different shoes," Dad tells Cheryl as they stand before the funeral home.

She's wearing a pair of turquoise sneakers.

Dad, on the other hand, is wearing a suit jacket. He has a manila folder tucked beneath his arm. The word *Funeral* is written on the front in his neat handwriting.

Cheryl is Dad's polar opposite. Dad has always radiated a kind of gloomy resignation, while Cheryl is always surrounded by an air of happy determination. Dad endures life; Cheryl tries to transform it into

God's likeness. But right now, she looks touchingly uncertain. I catch her glancing at the folder under Dad's arm several times.

The funeral home Dad is using is in one of the handsome turn-of-the-century buildings a few blocks from Sally's Café. Huge oak trees shade the whole street, on which a number of old family doctors and prominent lawyers are also based. The wrought-iron sign above the door reads *Annie Smith's Funeral Home*.

Annie Smith herself comes out to meet them in the reception area. "Mr. Broek," she says. Her steel-gray hair is slicked back, and she is wearing a dark suit and a pretty, cream-colored blouse, buttoned right up to her prominent chin. When she speaks, her voice is deep, with just the right amount of professional compassion.

"I am so sorry for your loss," she says, showing Dad and Cheryl into her office.

I linger in the doorway, peering down the corridor, but since I can't figure out where they keep the bodies, I decide to follow Dad and Cheryl inside.

Annie Smith closes the door behind us. All other sounds grow faint. It's as if the thick walls and soft carpets are shielding us from the world outside.

The sudden silence makes Dad nervous. He pats the pocket containing his keys and seems slightly reassured to feel their shape through the thin fabric. His other hand is clutching the folder to his chest.

"Please, take a seat," Annie Smith tells them.

The armchairs are soft and creamy white. The receptionist, a motherly woman with unruly gray hair, brings coffee, and Dad tries in confusion to juggle his folder, the cup, and the thin china saucer.

The office we are in is as timeless as the china. Pale-striped wallpaper and beautiful woodwork, with soft curtains over the high windows, preventing both nosy glances and too much sunlight from entering the room.

The walls are covered in black-and-white photographs from the era when the parlor was known as *Smith and Sons*. Several seem to be of Annie Smith's father; they have the same dignified, broad forehead and deep-set eyes, and identical charcoal-gray suits.

"I brought my folder," Dad tells her.

Annie gives him a warm glance.

"I've prepared everything. Coffin and flower arrangements and psalms."

Jesus Christ, I think.

"For myself, that is. For my death. So that everything would be ready for Henny. But now, well, I obviously have no idea. She wasn't supposed to die first. But I thought it could be...helpful..." His voice trails off.

He eagerly tries to hold out the folder, like a child with a piece of homework, but he has it upside down, and everything spills out onto the floor.

Neatly written psalms, newspaper cuttings about coffins—all at least fifteen years old—a completed form marked *Testament*, a whole stack of paper about flowers, and three different drafts of an obituary scatter around their feet.

Dad doesn't move. He sits still with his full cup of coffee and his empty folder as Cheryl and Annie bend down and try to gather everything together.

Annie takes the folder from him and carefully, almost tenderly, puts the papers back inside. Dad's cup rattles, and both Cheryl and Annie turn to look at it.

"Oh, Dad," I say.

"You don't need to make any decisions today," Annie explains. "We can just have a little chat. There's plenty of time before we need to decide on anything."

Dad sits upright. Straightens his spine, raises his chin. His cup is still trembling slightly, but this time he resolutely places it on the floor beside him.

"I've buried my parents," he says. "I've buried my wife. I've even buried my mother-in-law, though God knows I often doubted *that* day would ever come. I'm perfectly capable of both discussing and making any necessary decisions here today."

He steels himself. Takes a deep breath. "I want her to be cremated."

"But...*cremated*?" Cheryl says. From the tone, it's clear that she thinks cremation is for hippies and hipsters. The kind of people who want to scatter their ashes in the ocean or at a microbrewery. In her mind, normal people are buried. In a proper coffin, with a proper headstone.

"Yes." Dad is firm. "Cremated."

"But where will people leave flowers or candles?"

Dad hesitates. "Maybe a headstone, too. But I want her to be cremated."

I swallow. Cremation. I don't exactly want to be trapped in a dark, stuffy coffin, but...fire? Heat? It sounds so violent. I try to picture it, what little I know about it, probably from one film or another. A coffin slowly rolling into an oven. Or is it lowered into it? I don't know.

"I...I just can't bear the thought of her lying there in the darkness. Shut away in a coffin. It would have been fine for me, but not her. She... I don't know what she would have wanted, but not that. Not in the darkness."

Maybe he's right. I don't want to imagine a group of dignified, black-clad people standing around a coffin, either. A hole in the ground. Earth being thrown down onto it, maybe a rose or two. *Ashes to ashes, dust to dust*, and then being stuck six feet under for all eternity.

I force myself to remember the most important thing here: none of this is going to be necessary. I'm going to find my way back.

"And I think I'd like to see her body."

I nod eagerly. "You're on the right track now!"

"Are you sure you..." Cheryl begins.

"Of course we can arrange a viewing," says Annie. "But perhaps not today? Henny died in an accident. She's a little...the worse for wear. Naturally we'll make her look fantastic for the funeral; there's nothing we can't fix. But right now...she doesn't look the way she did when you last saw her. Death changes all of us, in both big and small ways."

You don't say, I think.

"What do you mean, fix?" Dad asks.

"That's what we do here. We make sure that relatives can have a dignified goodbye, regardless of the circumstances. We once had a man who had been beheaded. Industrial accident. But he had an open casket funeral."

Cheryl looks sick, Dad alarmed.

"No need to go into detail," Annie says. She decides to change the subject. "Have you given any thought about an open or closed casket for the funeral? That affects the time frame. If you want an open casket, the funeral will need to be held within the next day or two. For...practical reasons. Any out-of-town relatives that need time to get here?"

Cheryl answers for him. "No," she says.

"I don't care about the casket," Dad says, and then he looks embarrassed by the outburst.

"Let's just go for the closed option, then, shall we?" says Annie. "Gives you plenty of time to prepare things. Talk to your pastor. Perhaps just a private viewing before that?"

"I want to see her now. The way she really looks. Before you...change her."

Annie studies Dad. He stares stubbornly back.

"As you wish," Annie eventually tells him. "But I want to reiterate that this isn't standard procedure."

She gets up and walks over to her desk and makes a brief phone call. Five minutes later, she leads us down a winding passage to a more modern addition to the building, pausing to unlock a door before leading us through.

Everything in here is stainless steel: practical and functional for dealing with bodies on a daily basis. Along one wall, there is a cabinet with the kind of hatches you see in mortuaries on TV, only smaller. Nine doors, space for nine bodies. One of them is open.

Along another wall: a workstation, also stainless steel. I refuse to look at the tools set out on top. Or the bottles of chemicals on the shelf beyond. And yet I still manage to catch the word *formaldehyde* on the bottle closest to me.

In the middle of the room, on a stretcher-like table on wheels—stainless steel, again—is a body covered by a sheet. There's no mistaking the shape.

My body.

The room makes me feel uneasy, but I know I have to do this. I just have to be strong for a tiny, tiny bit longer, and then I'll be able to come back to them. *Do it for Michael*, I tell myself. *And MacKenzie.* You'll be able to see her *smile* again. That grayish tinge will disappear from their faces.

Dad walks straight over to the table. Determined, without hesitating. Cheryl has to force herself to follow him. Annie stands at a carefully considered distance, ready to provide comfort but also offering space. All I can hear is the hum of the refrigerators and the faint, stifled sound that Cheryl makes as she looks down at the table. The bright lights gleam on all of the steel.

I walk around the table and fight to keep my eyes on their faces for as long as I can. Dad's, impassive; Cheryl's, shocked; Annie's, calmly participating. There is so much at stake here that I don't know where to begin.

Annie slowly and respectfully folds back the sheet covering the body. I look down.

That's not me lying there.

It's a stranger. I don't recognize her. My stomach turns with compassion and sorrow for the dead woman in front of me. Her poor face is flat and sunken, not at all like mine. She's around my age. Did she have someone she loved, too? Family and friends who miss her?

And then I feel a selfish flash of hope, sudden and unreasonable. There's been an awful mistake. Maybe it wasn't me who was run over, maybe I'm still alive somewhere, I don't know where, *but that isn't me on the table.* Someone else has died, and God help me, all I feel is relief.

"She looks so...strange," Cheryl says.

"Her jaw was broken," Annie explains. "That changes a person's appearance."

I turn around and run.

The last thing I hear is Annie saying: "And Henny's...partner? She couldn't come today?"

I head straight back to the motel.

I check reception, the restaurant. It's the middle of the lunch rush, but how can anyone think about food right now? I check the corridor outside the rooms, in case MacKenzie is cleaning. Eventually, I find her in the laundry room, where endless loops of white material spin around inside the machines.

"You have to do something!" I say. "My body is just lying there.

How am I supposed to come back with my body looking so weird and nothing at all like me?"

Then I freeze. "Or worse! Who knows what chemicals they're going to pump into me. Formaldehyde doesn't exactly sound healthy. We need to do something. Before it's too late."

Yes, it would be nice if they managed to reunite me with my right arm before I came back, but I have a strong suspicion that I'd be a bit like Frankenstein's monster. Patched up or sewn together in a way you can hide under clothes. Who knows? Maybe they would just glue it on.

I shake my head to get rid of the thought. "Everything's going to be fine once I get back. It'll be like nothing even happened. We can fix my jaw later. But someone has to do something. I don't really know what. CPR? Electric shocks to get my heart going again?"

MacKenzie doesn't reply. She is busy throwing a white wash into one of the tumble driers. Her face is so waxlike that I find myself getting annoyed. Who's the dead one here, me or her?

"MacKenzie," I say firmly. "Concentrate."

But nothing happens.

Okay, I think. *I'll have to do this on my own.*

Society is built on rules, Henny.

It's not up to us to decide which of the rules we like or not.

Our country wouldn't exist if people broke the rules whenever they felt like it.

Committing a break-in is pretty easy when you're a ghost. The difficult part is ignoring a lifetime of good manners.

The old house is even more beautiful at night. A streetlight casts a faint glow onto the ornate letters on the sign above the locked door.

So, Henny, I think. *Let's do this.*

Thankfully it isn't pitch-black inside the funeral home. The light from the street outside seeps in, and the lamp above the empty reception desk is dimmed rather than switched off completely. I glance around to make sure I'm alone. Stick my head around the door into

Annie's office. Empty. The desk is neat and tidy, all of the papers in perfect order. Ready for another working day.

The next room is bigger, with rows of plastic chairs and a kind of altar up front. You can choose to have the ceremony here rather than at the church, something that's probably wasted on a religious town like Pine Creek. Maybe it looks different when it's full of flowers and people, but right now the room just seems sad and tired. More like an empty conference room than a place to say your goodbyes.

And there it is. The door we went through earlier. I straighten up and quickly rush through it.

I stare at the refrigerator. *Which door was open?* I re-create the image from earlier that day. Second row. Far right.

I haven't really thought any further than this, but I'm assuming that I just need to get into the compartment somehow, and then lie down on top of my body. Float into it the way you see people do after a near-death experience on TV. A white light lowering toward the body in the hospital bed.

This would have been much easier if my body was in a hospital bed, but I'll just have to do my best. I close my eyes again. Swallow. Psych myself up and practically dive through the door.

It's *definitely* dark in here.

Jesus Christ, it's dark. And cramped. I wonder if there's an echo?

"Helloooooo?"

No echo.

Okay, Henny, pull yourself together. You can do this. You know what you have to do.

"You are one with your body," I say.

I squeeze my eyes shut and repeat it, with more emphasis this time, like a mantra. Pressing the tip of my middle finger to my thumb. I say: "You are one with your body. You're a white light lowering over your body. You're going to open your eyes and be alive. Trapped in here, Christ alive, but don't think about that right now. One thing at a time."

I press my fingertips more firmly against one another.

"One with my body, one with my body, *one with my body*, Jesus Christ, it's dark in here."

What a fiasco.

I don't even last twenty minutes before scrambling out of the dark and running back to the safety of Michael's cabin.

I have no idea what I'm going to do now, but I know one thing. I'm *not* going back to the funeral home. I'll have to find another way to get myself back.

I'm still shaken as I climb in bed beside Michael. Though it's in the middle of the night, he isn't sleeping. He twists and turns as though his very body is uncomfortable. I close my eyes and try to repress the memory of that dark space in the refrigerator.

He finally manages to doze off just after four. I feel him relax, and draw closer to him. His body is warm and heavy and *real*.

I used to think that whatever happened between me and Michael in the future, my body would preserve the memory of us, and that would keep it alive for years. Long after he might have left me.

Our days together were like dialysis. They cleansed my body of loneliness and provided me with fresh, new blood; red and white blood cells of closeness and another warm body next to mine, of fantastic sex and sudden laughter and the way he looked at me when he smiled.

Outside the cabin, a blanket of fog hangs low over the meadow. The silver birches by the stream look delicate, as though they've lost their way and just paused for a moment to work out where they are heading. I can't see the mountains from here, but I tell myself that they are still out there, anchoring everything.

"About me coming back," I say. "I might have run into a slight problem..."

But I'll fix it, I think. *Somehow.* If it's not my body that's going to keep the memory of us going, maybe there's something else. Maybe there's something I've overlooked.

The sun rises eventually and chases away the fog. Michael smiles in his sleep. His eyelashes flutter. Even now, with everything going on, the sight of him sleeping still makes me feel better.

Then he opens his eyes. His gaze is warm and unfocused, as if he can still see whatever was going on in his dreams. Then he wakes properly, and it's as though the fog has seeped into the cabin instead. Everything turns gray and cold and warped. I don't know what his eyes are seeing now.

He rolls over onto his back. Squeezes his eyes shut. Presses his palms to his eyelids.

When he eventually manages to drag himself out of bed, he moves slowly and wearily, like a broken man. He doesn't bother about breakfast, but fetches a laundry cart from the motel, and then he spends the entire morning cleaning the cabin. I only just manage to jump out of the way as the rug from the living room comes flying toward me. He tears the sheets from the mattress, but leaves them lying in a heap at the foot of the bed. Then he wipes the coffee table and the chest of drawers and every other surface.

The entire cabin smells like cleaning products, and suddenly I hate that smell.

I spot Mr. Callahan's car before Michael does. His father pulls up outside and slams the door with far too much force. He does most things with too much force.

The noise makes Michael step outside. Mr. Callahan's eyes are drawn to the dishcloth in his hand. Michael blushes faintly and then looks irritated at having blushed. I move over beside him. For the first time, I notice how tense his body is. He has to make a real effort to keep his hands from balling into fists.

"You show up here after all this time and don't even bother to tell your own family?"

"Hi, Dad." Michael tries to sound nonchalant, but his jaw is clenched as he speaks.

"I had to hear it from someone in town, for God's sake. How do you think that makes me look?"

Mr. Callahan has an aura of aggressive disappointment. There's a threatening power to him that his civilized exterior can't quite hide. Though maybe I'm just biased.

"Like the loving father you are," Michael suggests.

"Don't talk back to me. You're not too old for a thrashing."

"No, I guess you never grow out of that," Michael courteously replies.

Mr. Callahan studies him, trying to work out whether the tone is meant as an insult. It is.

"So you're back, are you? Left all your pretty rocks behind?"

"For now."

"You'll soon get sick of Pine Creek again. After all your exciting travels. This is hardly the place for a bestselling author. Too good for your parents, too, I imagine."

Michael tenses his jaw to stop himself from saying anything.

"Dinner. This Friday. Your mother misses you."

"I don't know if I'll still be here then," Michael tells him.

If he leaves, he won't ever come back. I'm sure of that. I know him. Right now, even without Mr. Callahan's visit, it wouldn't take much to make him leave Pine Creek for good, and if he does that, he'll forget all about me.

He'll decide to put it all behind him just like he did when he left me the first time, and though I should be used to it by now, though I should have expected it again, the thought that I won't even exist in his mind fills me with panic.

"You can't leave before my funeral," I say in desperation.

Then I freeze.

My funeral.

I'm going to be *cremated*.

I can't let that happen.

CHAPTER 10

Never in the History of Mankind

I CLOSE MY EYES TIGHT AND THINK: *TOWN OR THE MOTEL?*

I'm sitting on the hill beyond the parking lot where MacKenzie and I used to watch the cars that slowed down at the crossroads.

Right turn signal: the motel. Left turn signal: the town.

A car that turned off meant something was about to happen. A customer, a delivery, anything.

The motel looks tired and abandoned in the sunshine. Everything is gray and empty. The only hint of color comes from the glossy red of an empty cola can blowing around in the breeze. I wrap my arms around my knees.

Something is worrying me.

I haven't seen any other ghosts.

What if I can't make it back inside my body before the funeral? I'm not saying I won't—I'm going to find a way, I'm sure of it. Only...*what if*? I might not be brave enough to go back to the funeral home, but I spent a few hours today wandering around our cemeteries. I visited new graves and old graves, the graves of strangers and the grave of my mother.

Nothing.

Not even a slight stirring or a silvery outline or any kind of sensed presence. Not even from Mom, and surely she would try to meet me if she could. If people are really allowed to stay behind, linger as I seem to be doing, wouldn't there be more of us?

I'm not sure exactly what happens when you're cremated, but I imagine fire and heat and flames. What could possibly remain after *that*?

I make a mental note to hang around Annie Smith's and try to find out what happens when you burst into flames, but for now I just sit here, thinking about what I've done with my life.

Planning a funeral can do that to a person, especially when it's your own.

I think there's something unique within all of us. A way of looking at the world, I suppose, a kind of inner core or soul, whatever you want to call it. I've spent my entire adult life working at the motel, which means I've met my fair share of unusual people. We're all much too weird to not be unique. No one is weird in quite the same way as anyone else.

Take MacKenzie. She can look at anything and see it as an adventure. Michael looks at the world and sees hundreds of millions of years. Alejandro sees life as a series of still images. If he were here right now, he would probably think the cola can was the most important thing. He must be the only motel worker who cleans rooms with a camera around his neck. He works part-time as a photographer, but refuses to quit the motel because he says it gives him so many images of human loneliness. Until now, I never really understood what that meant. We were always there, and surely you can't be lonely if you're among friends?

Or take Dolores. She can look at a person, any person, and see someone who is hungry, who needs to be fed.

So what did I do? Who was I? I can't think of a single way that the world will be poorer without me in it. All I know is that I'm going to miss the world.

None of the cars stop. It's three in the afternoon, and no one is stupid enough to stop here unless they have no other choice. Lunch is over, so even the restaurant is empty. The afternoon stretches out ahead of me. Then the evening. And night. That's how it'll continue until it all comes to an end.

Not that anything was guaranteed to happen just because a car stopped. Yes, it was exciting, but we could never be sure they would actually stay.

Some people studied the motel from their cars and decided they were better off trying to find somewhere better. Baker City—named after Edward D. Baker, the only senator in U.S. history to have been killed in combat—is just a few hours away. And nowadays, there's Airbnb and all kinds of other things, so sometimes people just sit in their cars while they go through their options.

The first real indication that someone was planning to stay came if they got out of the car. "If they've actually bothered to get out, there's a 70 percent chance they'll stay," Juan Esteban used to say, and MacKenzie repeats. "They've driven a long way. Once they're on their feet, they won't be able to stomach the thought of getting back in the car for another few hours of driving."

If they take their bags inside with them, the likelihood of checking in is almost 90 percent. "People hate carrying their bags back to the car. No one likes to feel dumb, and there's nothing dumber than hauling bags back and forth across a parking lot."

The only time that rule doesn't apply is if it's a married couple and the man is doing the carrying. "The wife doesn't care if the man feels stupid," MacKenzie always says. "And she can find fault in everything." MacKenzie doesn't trust married couples, particularly not married women. She's convinced that they try to take out their unhappiness on her motel.

Things married people argue about: whose fault it is that they didn't set off sooner, who was really in charge of reading the map, why he refuses to stop and ask for directions, why he's so cheap that he wants to stay at this motel, why they even have to visit her mom. There are never any arguments if they're going to visit his mother; the wife will be stoically resolute then, clutching the mother-in-law's gift tightly in her lap.

The parking lot in front of me is still empty. Even the cola can has blown away.

And then, suddenly, a car slows down and turns off the road.

I get up and run toward it, the way we used to do as kids, and for a few minutes, I'm caught up in the fantasy. MacKenzie is with me and we're sixteen again, with so much energy that we would rather run than walk. I sprint down the hill and out across the asphalt, empty parking spaces in front of me, trees and road on the horizon.

I come to an abrupt halt when the fantasy falters. I should be seeing MacKenzie's back by now. She was always faster than me.

Still, the Honda is real and has parked outside the motel. I notice that it has California plates, and when I peer in through the passenger-side window, I see all the usual signs of a long car journey: a half-eaten sandwich, hastily wrapped in brown paper, a Pepsi can, and an open bag of Doritos.

The woman is alone, and she hasn't made any movement to get out. Her hands are gripping the wheel, and she lowers her head toward it. She is wearing a fantastic red, wide-brimmed hat, and her long, dark hair hangs dramatically over her shoulders.

She lifts her head, still leaning toward the wheel, and her eyes scan the parking lot and the low motel building. Her face seems familiar. Not the red lipstick or the pronounced eyebrows, but something about the high cheekbones, the solid jawline...

I jolt upright. *Camila.*

As she climbs out of the car, I'm sure of it. Camila has come back.

She had a different name while we were growing up, but her new name feels so natural. She's Camila, as utterly and completely as though she always had been.

I tear my eyes away from her and run over to reception. I want to see MacKenzie's reaction when Camila comes through the door.

MacKenzie is sitting behind the reception desk, staring straight ahead. She doesn't even have the energy to be bored. She looks up when the door opens, but the sun is in her eyes, so she just smiles politely and makes a slight gesture to the space in front of the desk.

I don't think Camila has ever seen MacKenzie's polite smile. She never used to have one, but now it's the only one she ever uses.

For a second, I can see two MacKenzies. My MacKenzie, where all of the details are so familiar that I can barely take them in, and Camila's, a confused mix of new and old. The same stubborn lock of hair constantly getting in her eyes; the same instinctive, unconscious movement as she impatiently pushes it back. A tanned face that should look healthy but seems more tired than anything, a new and withdrawn confidence in everything she does. The kind of confidence that stems from no longer having to worry about proving anything to anyone. A tired cynicism that has etched itself into her face. I wonder whether Camila has noticed all of this, too.

One Mississippi, two Mississippi, three Mississippi, I count in my head, and then suddenly there it is: a real smile on MacKenzie's face.

She gets up, strides toward Camila, and lifts her up. Camila is much taller than MacKenzie, so she has to lean backward to get Camila off the ground, but she doesn't seem to care. She spins Camila around and around.

Camila laughs from sheer surprise, takes a deep breath, and breathes in the scent of MacKenzie, at once new and familiar. When she finally exhales, the sound is halting and jittery, somewhere between a sigh and a sob. She closes her eyes. I think I spotted tears welling up in them, but when she opens her eyes again, I'm no longer sure what I saw.

"I got your message," Camila says. "I had to come."

"I know," says MacKenzie.

Camila left Pine Creek just after Michael.

He was always talking about leaving town, so often that I wasn't sure it would ever actually happen.

Camila, on the other hand, had never even mentioned it. She was almost as quiet as I was, but while my silence was from having nothing to say, Camila's was a case of sheer self-control. She endured her work at the motel and the small-mindedness of the town in silence, never complaining that the work was boring. She never tried to make the town accept her. She had no hopes of anything changing while she was still there.

Camila never shared the love that MacKenzie and her uncle had for the motel. Juan Esteban always said that freedom was owning a property and running your own business. He had encountered far too much racism when he first arrived in the United States from El Salvador to believe it was possible to forge a career within an existing American business.

But Camila could never see the freedom in cleaning motel rooms. She watched Juan Esteban slowly wearing himself out, and she dreamed of a different life. I think she longed for the anonymity of the big city, a job you could leave behind when you went home for the day, never having to work in the service industry or smile at angry customers.

She wanted to make a life of her own, she said.

A few years after she moved to Los Angeles, we got a message saying that she had changed her name and pronoun, so she can't have forgotten us entirely. She still wanted us to know.

I replied, of course, and got the occasional message back from her. Talking about what she was doing. About how LA traffic was driving her crazy, but the nightlife was fantastic. She told me when she started to take hormones; she told me about her operations, the fact she was dating a woman doing a PhD on theater from a queer, postcolonial perspective; she told me when things ended between them, when she experienced a clear day with almost no smog. Big things like that.

Over time, her messages became more and more infrequent, and eventually they stopped altogether. The last time I wrote to her, the old email address no longer worked.

When Juan Esteban died and left her the motel, she didn't show up for the funeral. She didn't even bother to sell the motel. For several years, MacKenzie sent tax returns and profit statements to a PO box in LA, but she never got any response. The only document Camila ever sent us was a power of attorney that gave MacKenzie the right to do what she wanted with Camila's motel.

MacKenzie shows Camila to her room. "Beer at six," she says.

It's more of an order than an invitation, and at quarter to six I am in Camila's room, watching as she gets herself ready. Three quick buffs of powder and blush, followed by a new coat of mascara.

I like watching her movements. In a way, she's completely different: a new appearance, a new name. New breasts, too, I think, immediately feeling embarrassed. But in another sense, she's still the same as ever. She's herself. No, she's *more* herself now. Her movements are more natural, more self-assured.

After Camila finishes applying her makeup, she pulls on her boots and grabs her jacket, and with that, she is ready to go.

A sign on the door encourages guests to turn out the lights before they leave. One of Juan Esteban's many obsessions toward the end—every time the electricity bill arrived, he would be irritable for days. Camila shakes her head, turns out the light, and closes the door behind her.

I follow her down to reception. MacKenzie is waiting outside, and she waves enthusiastically. Camila's arrival seems to have given her a new lease on life. I can tell from the way she moves that she's decided to have fun tonight.

It's a delicate facade; I know how thin-skinned she really is. The only thing stopping her from reacting whenever her irritation, anger, or tiredness gets to be too much is a refusal to let others see her break down. Since I disappeared, though, even the smallest of things have cut her deeply.

Still, for one night, she can forget this mess and have fun. She'll drink beer and tell funny anecdotes, at least half of which are lies. Why let the truth get in the way of a good story? Sometimes she lies *even though* it doesn't even lead to a better story. *Imagination's a muscle, Henny. You have to use it. If you stop lying or telling fibs, you'll wake up one day and see the world exactly as it is. Terrible fate, huh?*

"You'll have to hold down the fort tonight," MacKenzie tells Alejandro. "We're going to get drunk."

Alejandro mutters something without looking up from the computer. It may or may not have been "about time."

MacKenzie turns to Camila and says, "We need to pick up Michael, too."

Camila seems nervous when Michael's name is mentioned. I guess things aren't *exactly* like normal. We've all changed. Some of us more than others. But it'll be fine. She wants to see Michael. I know that.

I jump up into the cargo bed as Camila climbs in beside MacKenzie, who starts the engine and flashes her a quick smile.

"To the Redwood Cabin!" I shout into the night.

MacKenzie pulls up outside the Redwood Cabin, winds down the window, and shouts, "Michael! Beer! Camila's here!"

Michael clearly also received the message about her new name and pronoun, because he takes in her new appearance without a word.

All he says is "You came back."

"You too." Camila sounds tense.

They glance at each other as they try to get used to being together again.

"When...?" Camila asks.

"Three days before."

Camila swallows. "I wish..."

"Yeah."

"God, I just can't believe she's gone. Not *Henny*. She can't be. She was always the best of us."

MacKenzie quickly interrupts. "Not tonight," she says. "We're not thinking about it tonight. I refuse. Tonight we're going to get drunk and think about absolutely nothing."

Michael and Camila's eyes meet in a newfound understanding that seems to surprise them both. I guess they're wondering whether it's really such a good idea not to talk about me at all. Not that they have a chance against MacKenzie when she's in this kind of mood.

"Come on," she says. "To town."

MacKenzie and Camila are sitting up front, with Michael and me in the bed of the truck. He has one arm draped over the edge, his legs outstretched in front of him. I lean against his shoulder and see stars and sudden flashes of tree trunks in the headlights.

Michael bravely attempts to make small talk from the truck bed, even though he has to shout to be heard over the engine. "So what are you doing these days?"

Camila's reply comes with the wind. "I'm an assistant. The boss runs a construction company, but his real dream is to write film scripts. I spend half my time reserving writing courses and harassing agents to read his latest incredible synopsis."

I rest my arm on Michael's leg. As we reach the edge of town, the stars are replaced by streetlamps, and when I see the outlines of the meager elms, I know we're almost there.

If I really make an effort, I can feel the wind on my face.

Never in the history of mankind has there been a friendship like ours, and as we walk into Timber Bar together, nothing has ever felt so right.

We're a conquering army, a cavalry regiment charging across the prairie, ready to capture the night. No, better. A *returning* army. Scarred, yes, but older and wiser. We've turned our setbacks into victories, returned when they thought we were defeated, and look at us now! Grown up, strong, free. Reunited.

The heat hits us as we step through the door. The tones of Bruce Springsteen's "Tunnel of Love," too.

"For God's sake, Buddy," MacKenzie says. "Put something happier on."

She is our commander, just as she always has been. Ready to lead us into adventure or battle, or both.

Buddy grins. He likes MacKenzie, so he swaps the *Tunnel of Love* CD for *Born in the USA*, and soon even Bruce Springsteen is refusing to retire or give up.

"No surrender!" I sing along with Bruce, standing a little taller as I walk alongside Michael, smiling at everyone we pass. Timber Bar has never been more inviting, its subdued lighting more cozy, and the dark tables more homey.

Michael goes over to the bar to buy the first round of drinks, and I look up at him in confusion when he returns with three beers.

Why only three?

Ah. Because I'm dead.

He could have bought me a beer all the same, I think. As a kind of tribute or something. "She's with us in spirit, and she wants a Pabst Blue Ribbon," he would say, "since she has zero taste and prefers her beers wishy-washy."

I toast with them anyway. "To us!" I say, high on friendship and expectation. "To all the days we spent together at the motel, to Michael and Camila being back, to all of us being together again, to tasteless beer, and—why not—to Bruce Springsteen!"

"So, uh, how do you like your job?" Michael asks.

It strikes me that Michael and Camila don't seem to be in quite as high spirits as MacKenzie and me. Camila has chosen a table in the back corner of the bar, as far away from everyone else as she can get. We're sitting in half darkness in the corner by the dartboard.

"Come on," says MacKenzie. "Talk about something fun!"

Michael glances anxiously around the room. Camilla uses her nail to scrape tiny pieces of the label from her beer. Silence settles over the table.

MacKenzie fills it with tales from the old days. Every time she opens her mouth, she says something like "Do you remember when...?" or "Can you remember the time we...?"

We shouldn't have gone our separate ways, I think. MacKenzie and I had each other, but we'd let Michael and Camila go off on their own.

"I never thought I'd be back here," Camila eventually says.

She looks skeptical as she says it, but that just reminds me that it really is a miracle. We might be shy and nervous, but we're also *together*.

If you'd asked me two weeks ago, I would have said that my life was going to go on like it always had. But now I've slept with Michael, and suddenly we're all here. I remembered us and missed us, but I'd also given up. I can see that now. I judged the future on how life had been up until that point. We hadn't been reunited before, and that meant we never would be.

It's a form of arrogance to think that life won't change.

Camila seems to be scrutinizing the bar. She looks out of place, but on a deeper level she also seems incredibly *right* here. Her bottle of beer belongs here, between Michael's and MacKenzie's; her long, slim fingers look right between Michael's strong digits and MacKenzie's practical hands.

I can't explain it in any other way but this: it suddenly feels inevitable that we're all here. Just two weeks ago, that was impossible.

"I can't believe everything is still the same," Camila says. "Shouldn't more have changed? Anyone who says that you can't go back has clearly never been to Pine Creek. I don't think I've even thought about it in ten years. It's like it stopped existing when I left. Like it's all just an old backdrop that's been dragged out again for the Christmas play."

"Nope, it's here year-round," MacKenzie tells her.

"It's the opposite for me," says Michael. "I think everything seems a bit too real. Like the town has just been waiting to grab hold of me and pull me in."

He turns the bottle in his hands. Even MacKenzie seems to be working off some kind of restless energy through small, pointless movements.

"Come on!" I say. "We need to have fun. We're back together!"

But they aren't listening, of course.

Michael leans in to MacKenzie. "You never thought about leaving?" he asks. Camila has picked off the last of the label. The remnants are heaped in front of her, and she seems unsure what to do with them.

MacKenzie shrugs. "Where would I go?"

Michael hesitates. "What about Henny? Didn't she ever want to move away?"

My name hangs over the table like a depressing reminder of why they are here. I wish he hadn't mentioned me, but I'm happy he's thinking about me.

"She never met anyone? Got married, had seventeen kids, bought a house on the same street as her dad?"

"We never talked about it," says MacKenzie. "But..."

"Yeah?"

"It was so tragic. A traveling salesman. He had charm, looks, a great body—poor Henny couldn't resist him."

"MacKenzie!" I protest. Both Michael and Camila seem fascinated by this new and completely false story about me.

"What happened?" Camila asks.

"Turned out he was already married. To four other women. I don't think he quite had seventeen kids, but it can't have been far off. But... sometimes I don't think it was his betrayal that hit her hardest, but the baby... Her dad made her give it up for adoption. She was never quite the same after that."

"MacKenzie!" Camila blurts out. "None of that's true, is it?"

"Of course not. But it's truer than your depressing idea of small-town life. Henny loved it here. Show some respect."

Michael looks troubled, but also relieved.

Over by the bar, an argument about "that damn Bruce" has flared up, but it's an easy victory for Buddy. Bruce can keep dancing in the darkness, and if that makes Stacey Callahan go completely fucking crazy, then so be it. That's all Buddy has to say on the matter.

Michael leans forward over the table. "Is that...?" he asks as Stacey staggers over to us.

"Stacey, Camila," says MacKenzie. Stacey doesn't even glance at Camila. No hint of recognition, not even a surprised remark. Camila relaxes. "And you know Michael."

Stacey leans against the table. "Welcome back," she says. "Your brother's an idiot."

"Uh, good to see you, too," says Michael.

She tries to focus on MacKenzie again. "Sorry about the whole Henny thing," she says. "Should've been my husband that died instead."

"It's an unfair world," MacKenzie agrees.

"And, uh, how're things with Derek?" Michael asks.

"Yeah, you know, he keeps himself busy. Managed to sleep with everything on two legs and almost everything on four."

Michael chokes on his beer. "You'll have to tell him I said hi," he pants once he eventually stops coughing.

"Do it yourself," Stacey says, staggering back over to the bar.

MacKenzie tells an anecdote about crashing Cheryl's brand-new Volvo the first time she borrowed it. *Do you remember, do you remember, do you remember.* "And then she always gave me bumper stickers saying stuff like 'Honk if you love Jesus' and 'I'm driving fast for Jesus.' Or my personal favorite: 'Next time you pray, ask Jesus for more driving lessons.'"

That's the second time she has told that anecdote this evening.

Michael buys another round of beer for MacKenzie and Camila. He has voluntarily taken on the role of designated driver. The new bottles jostle for space with the empty ones on the table.

Something catches my attention, and suddenly I can no longer see the half-empty bar or the dark wooden paneling. All I can see are flashing blue lights and gravel at the roadside, police tape flapping in the wind and the absolute silence after the shock.

The truck driver.

Paul. He is etched into my mind just like everything else from that Sunday afternoon, but right now he is sitting alone in a dark corner, with a full beer in front of him. I think it must have been his plaid shirtsleeve that caught my eye. I remember how he kept pulling at it.

I don't know what I feel. He's a reminder that I'm dead, but he's also the only person who really knows what I went through. We share that small stretch of road, only a hundred yards or so, where our lives changed forever. At least I wasn't alone.

I'm just about to get up and go over to him when Camila says, "I hate the motel," and I decide to stay where I am.

She says it in roughly the same tone anyone else would say, "What beautiful weather we're having today!"

"Do you know what my first thought was when I got to my room today?" she asks.

"What?" says MacKenzie.

"The walls need painting again. Juan Esteban worked there his whole life. The motel ate him up. It sucked out all his energy and personality, and the only proof of all his hard work is that the walls need repainting. It's like a never-ending story."

"Don't look at me," says Michael. "I already painted them once."

"I was the only person who saw it for what it really was. A run-down, tired, *lonely* place. Everyone else just saw Juan Esteban's enthusiasm. He was like an illusionist who pulled the wool over everyone's eyes. While he was talking, no one saw what it was *really* like. All those lonely men who stayed for one night and then went on with their miserable lives. Small, dark rooms. And the apartment we lived in! That was hardly any better. It barely even had a kitchen! No cooking, no kitchen table, nothing to make it into a home. It was just a waiting room. Thirty minutes or so until the bell rang and someone needed something, or the next thing had to be done, until finally you could go to bed. And Juan Esteban acted like the whole thing was completely normal. No, worse, like it was something *positive*. All I wanted was a home, and I got a motel. And now I'm back here."

"Cheers to that," MacKenzie says.

Camila takes a few swigs of beer. "Do you remember how he always used to go on about leisure time? 'Leisure time is the future. When you grow up, you can run your own motel.' As though that was the height of success in life. As though there was nothing I wanted more than to stay here forever and continue his life's work."

She shakes her bottle and seems surprised to realize that it's empty.

Michael gets up and buys her another. Unfortunately, the bartender also sends over some whiskey, which Camila immediately knocks back. She eventually empties Michael's untouched glass, too.

"He was like a magician in some cheap show. Standing there with his arms outspread, not realizing his tricks would never save the motel."

A new swig of beer. She pulls at this label, too, but it just peels away from the bottle, irritatingly intact. She scrunches it into a small ball instead.

"I'm only here for Henny's sake," she says. "I'm leaving after the funeral."

I glance over to the other corner, but the truck driver is gone. A half-empty beer is all that is left in his place.

On the way back to the motel, Camila sits in the bed of the truck, slumped against MacKenzie as Michael drives. I dithered between getting into the front seat or the truck bed, but eventually decided on the other side of Camila.

She is incredibly drunk and keeps mumbling to herself: "Henny is dead. Henny is dead. Henny is dead." It's like a melody. Her head droops onto MacKenzie's shoulder.

"Your message," she says, turning to face MacKenzie. "Those words have been going round and round in my head ever since. Message request from MacKenzie Jones."

She closes her eyes.

"I only came back for Henny."

"Of course you did," MacKenzie says wearily. All of her energy seems to be gone. She lifts her face to the edge of the truck so that she can feel the cool breeze on her cheeks. Her hair swirls around her face until eventually I can no longer see her expression.

Michael parks outside the motel. MacKenzie declines his offer of help and supports Camila, who is still humming to herself as she walks up the stairs. Fishes the key out of her jacket pocket. She waves it at Michael in a gesture that means *We're all good, everything's fine here.*

He lingers down below, watching as MacKenzie manages to open the door and get Camila inside.

She dumps Camila on the bed, on top of the floral covers. She does, at least, pull off Camila's boots.

Camila stares up at the ceiling, and raises her arms in a sweeping gesture. "Allow me to introduce the great, magnificent Juan Esteban Alvarez. For his next trick...nothing!"

She is still talking to herself as MacKenzie leaves the room. Saying, "Absolutely nothing is fine."

CHAPTER 11

Fault 1...

THE NEXT MORNING, I'M WAITING OUTSIDE CAMILA'S ROOM. When I hear the unmistakable sound of someone trying to open the broken blinds, I decide that she must be dressed and walk straight through the door.

She is standing with her back to me and spends several minutes fighting with the blinds. She swears quietly to herself. Stuck in eternal half darkness.

"Do you remember when you first came here?" I ask. "You were so much cooler than us."

I couldn't quite put my finger on what it was about her. She was wearing jeans and a T-shirt, just like the rest of us, but somehow it was clear that *her* jeans and T-shirt came from the big city. And like her clothes, she was also subtly different from us. There was something about the way she moved. She was tall and thin and graceful, and she always made me feel slightly countrified. She looked at the world as though she could see straight through it. In my world, everyone loved MacKenzie, but Camila would look at her with a strange, reserved expression. She studied her often, always completely openly, but without showing any emotion whatsoever.

"You hated the motel," I say.

In fact, she hated the whole of Pine Creek, and possibly even the state of Oregon. Not that she had been particularly fond of Los Angeles, either. It's not the kind of place you can love, she always said. It just *is*, but what it is is bigger and crazier and dirtier than any other city. You can learn all about life in LA.

"You can do that in Pine Creek, too," MacKenzie muttered.

Camila's seventeen-year-old self had never even considered that it might be possible to miss the traffic in LA, but she did. "The roads in Pine Creek don't even get busy," she said.

"There's a line of cars every time Dolores makes tamales," MacKenzie argued.

Camila had arrived in town roughly a month before summer break, and she walked around as though she refused to acknowledge she was actually here. *I'm not here*, her stubborn eyes said. *You can't force my body to exist here*, her tense posture screamed. Her body always seemed to be turned away from whoever she was talking to.

Back in the present, Camila lies down on the bed. All I can hear is the hum of the air-conditioning and the sound of her breathing. Louder when she breathes in, softer on her out breaths. *In.* Out. *In.* Out.

She stares up at the ceiling.

Says, "*Goddamn* it."

I guess she remembers.

Eventually, I think her need for caffeine forces her into action. She struggles up, checks that her clothes aren't creased, and leaves the safety of her room.

On her way downstairs, Camila studies the motel as though she is writing one of those angry TripAdvisor reviews where the guests seem to have spent their entire stay methodically and enthusiastically looking for faults.

Fault 1: Broken blinds.

She passes a woman in a poncho and dark sunglasses who is in the process of checking out, and pokes her head around the door to inspect the woman's room.

Fault 2: Peeling paint in several rooms.

The woman returns before Camila has time to check whether the blinds are working properly.

She tries to sneak into the restaurant, but she barely makes it inside before she is caught in a bear hug. She stands there, stooping uncomfortably, her arms pinned to her sides, as Dolores holds her tight and rocks her back and forth.

Fault 3: Enthusiastic staff who want to talk about the past.

Dolores makes a big deal of showing Camila over to the best table, by the window, with views out onto the empty parking lot and the overcast day outside. There isn't a single crumb on the tabletop, but Dolores wipes it all the same.

"I'm so glad you're back...Camila?" she says, slightly hesitant toward the end. Almost as though she is trying out the word in her mouth.

Camila smiles tensely. Beneath the table, she digs her nails into her thighs.

"I knew you'd come back," Dolores says. "Eventually. Do you remember—"

"Not now, please, Dolores," Camila says. "I need coffee. I can't deal with any memories right now."

Dolores looks wounded, but she quickly nods. "It's hard for all of us," she says compassionately. "I'll leave you be."

But not before she has straightened the pointless little tablecloth and swiped a plastic flower from beneath the nose of a surprised construction worker at the next table.

"I can tell you want to be alone for a while," she says as she sets the flower vase on Camila's table.

Dolores pats Camila on the shoulder and double-checks that the flower is standing straight. When she finally leaves, Camila closes her eyes in relief.

I don't think the flower is helping. Its plasticky orange petals can't compete with the compact grayness outside. An irritating, stubborn drizzle has started to fall, the kind you just can't escape.

After perking herself up with a cup of coffee, Camila finds MacKenzie in room 11.

She is standing on a stepladder, trying to fix the ceiling fan. She has a tool belt around her waist and is wearing a thick, red-plaid shirt.

Fault 4: Broken ceiling fan.

Camila stands in the doorway for some time, watching MacKenzie work. At first, I think she is including MacKenzie in her critical evaluation of the motel, but there's something else in her eyes, something I can't quite place.

"I'm sorry about yesterday," she suddenly says. "I hadn't exactly planned to go on a drunken rant."

MacKenzie keeps working.

"I guess it's just being back here," Camila continues. "I felt like a teenager again. And that's *not* something I appreciate."

MacKenzie smiles faintly.

"And everything with the motel. Nothing's changed. Juan Esteban wasted his whole life here, but what did he get out of it? Just work, work, work, and the motel is *still* run-down. So I..." She focuses on the fan. "Jesus Christ, is there *anything* that works like it's meant to around here? Do the coffee makers even work?"

"The one in room 7 is a bit temperamental," MacKenzie tells her. "But it'll survive a while yet."

"I never grieved for him, you know," Camila says.

"I did."

"I was too busy hating the motel to see him clearly, and he was definitely too busy with the motel to see *me*."

Camila's eyes are drawn to the floral curtains over the window. Whatever homey touch they might have brought to the room is canceled out by the gray walls and impersonal furniture.

MacKenzie follows her gaze. "Henny tried to make the place a bit cozier." Her voice is blunt. It almost seems as if she is trying to get Camila to say something critical, but Camila just smiles sadly. Silence spreads out between them.

"Anyway, I wanted to apologize for yesterday," Camila eventually says. "It wasn't exactly the first impression I wanted to make. So. Yeah. I'll get back to...doing something."

MacKenzie climbs down from the ladder and turns on the fan. It spins a few times, jolts, and then stops.

Luckily, Camila has already gone. MacKenzie shrugs and climbs back up. I head off to find Dad.

Pine Creek likes to boast about having more churches than bars, but as MacKenzie always says, that isn't much of an achievement considering the nightlife around here.

MacKenzie also says that we have more closet drinkers than real Christians.

Dad's church, like the majority of those in town, is on Church Street. At first glance, it's just a simple, redbrick building, but that's deliberately misleading—the same way old money shuns ostentatious displays of wealth.

The Pine Creek United Methodist Church looks small because it's one of Pine Creek's oldest buildings, but as you come closer, it's easy to be impressed by the pretty stained-glass windows and the gravestones in the "old churchyard"—where the town's old money is buried.

The pastor is wearing a light-blue shirt, and he looks strong and powerful behind his desk.

Dad shrinks in his presence. His skin looks so pale that it almost matches his white shirt, and his tall frame seems to be drowning amid all the black. Polished black shoes. Pressed black trousers, black tie, black jacket. There are a couple of stubborn grays sticking up from his otherwise manically neat hair, and it pains me to realize that he hasn't noticed.

Cheryl's T-shirt today reads *If you think you're so perfect, try walking on water*.

"So, this Saturday," says the pastor. "Have you given any thought to the service? Did she have any favorite songs, anything you want us to play?"

Dad has brought a list of hymns with him. We're going to sing "Abide with Me," "The Lord Is My Shepherd," and "When the Trumpet of the Lord Shall Sound."

"Sometimes, when someone so young dies..." the pastor begins. "What I'm trying to say is that it can be nice to include something a little more...modern."

"Modern?" Dad repeats in roughly the same tone he would use if the pastor had suggested smoking weed at the church's morning coffee.

"A pop song, perhaps? Something Henny liked?"

I don't actually think that's a good idea. Most of my favorite songs are country tracks, and it feels cruel to subject my friends to that when they're already feeling sad.

"'Bye, Bye, Baby' would be perfect if it hadn't already been used in *Love Actually*," I say, feeling like I should at least contribute to the discussion. "Or something by The Beatles. 'Hello, Goodbye.'"

"How about 'Fly on the Wings of Love'?" Cheryl suggests enthusiastically. "Or 'Somewhere Over the Rainbow'? You know, 'Sooommmeeewheeere, ooover the raaaiiinbooow'?" She stops singing when she notices Dad's expression. "Or 'Wind Beneath My Wings'?"

"I just want a normal, respectful, traditional funeral!" Dad snaps. "Is that so hard to understand? I want it to be dignified. No pop songs."

"Maybe people could wear white?" Cheryl says. "All white. White shoes, white trousers, white..."

"Black," says Dad. "Dignified."

The pastor scribbles something on the sheet of paper in front of him. It might say *black*. Or *dignified*. "Would you like to tell me a little about Henny? What she was like?"

Dad stares at him in confusion. "She was...well, perfectly normal."

"Okay, yes," says the pastor.

"A good girl. Always conscientious. Never caused any trouble."

The pastor scribbles away. I suppose he's written *perfectly normal*.

"And will her...*friend* want to say a few words?"

Dad storms down Church Street, his black jacket flapping in the wind.

Cheryl struggles to keep up. Her eyes are fixed on him, which means she has to move sideways, like some kind of stressed-out crab. She keeps opening her mouth to speak, but then she closes it and shakes her head as though she has tried out a few words in her head and decided not to say any of them.

"It's..." she begins, but when Dad turns to her, her voice trails off.

"*What*, Cheryl?"

"I just want you to know that if you need anything, I'm here. Anything at all."

"I'm going home. What could I possibly need right now?"

"I meant later. In general."

"You always follow me to these meetings, don't you? Whether I want you there or not."

"Yes, but if there's anything else I can do…"

"You've said that thirteen times already."

"Not that many," she protests.

"Thirteen. I counted. You're going to crash into something if you insist on walking like that."

"Yes, Robert," she says.

Dad looks tired, angry, and sad. Far too many feelings for him to be able to keep them completely hidden.

"Everyone will talk when she shows up at the funeral," he eventually mutters.

He is careful not to look at Cheryl.

"There's not an ounce of shame in her body! It makes no difference how well I plan the funeral. Henny was completely innocent. Everyone knows that, but people will still talk and whisper and gossip, all because of *her*. She stole my Henny from me, and now she's going to turn my funeral into a *spectacle*."

"Um, don't you mean Henny's funeral?"

"All my life, I've tried to do the right thing. I've never complained or moaned, unlike certain others. All I've asked is that people leave me in peace, that they respect me and don't gossip about me like they do about everyone else. Henny was a good child. No one had a bad word to say about her. She always said 'please' and 'thank you' and didn't bother anyone. But that won't matter when *she* turns up. All anyone will remember is *that* old story, and I guarantee she'll say something inappropriate, too. She'll give a speech or something. Say that Henny is named after a cognac or some other nonsense!"

"Jesus Christ, Dad," I say. "It was a *joke*."

"I just want a dignified funeral. Is that too much to ask? My daughter is dead. *My* daughter!"

I walk right back to the motel, but I don't go inside. Instead, I walk around the back, toward the river. I just have to get away from it all for a while.

"It's always darkest before the dawn," I say to myself. My voice sounds unsteady and oddly distant.

I swallow. "God doesn't give us more than we can manage."

I falter and lean against the silver birches. Close my eyes. Take a deep breath. When I open my eyes, the mountains are looming above me, and suddenly I know what I need to do.

I have to take this up with God.

I cross the river without pausing to think. The icy water comes up to my knees, but I don't feel any chill. I cross the neighbor's land and stride past chewing cows.

I'm going to be completely honest with God, I decide. I'll admit all my faults and shortcomings. If this is a punishment, I at least want to know what I'm being punished for. Unless…maybe there's some purpose to this test. Some lesson to be learned, and if I can just find the right argument to convince him, God will let me come back and then we can all be happy again. It can't be too late for *him* to fix this.

I walk and walk, my eyes fixed on the purplish-gray mountains in the background, *still* in the background, even though the sun has passed its highest point and has started to swing to the west. I'm going to get to those mountains, climbing so high that I can touch the clouds, and then I'm going to *force* him to fix this.

If that's his will, of course.

Don't demand anything. Be humble. Reasonable.

The mountains tower up in front of me, but they're still several miles away. I compromise and climb onto a small boulder instead, turning my face toward the cumulus clouds.

"Dear God," I begin.

But then I can't think of anything else. Everything I prepared is gone.

"I've never been interesting or exciting. Maybe that's one of my short-comings? I've been given every opportunity in life, but I haven't done anything with them. I haven't traveled. I've barely even left the state. Well, MacKenzie and I once went to Cottonwood, Idaho, to stay at the

Dog Bark Park Inn. I guess I can always say that I've slept in the world's biggest beagle. That's something, isn't it?"

I stubbornly continue. "I guess I should have given more money to charity. I've tried to help when I could, but I know I could have done so much more. I'm not going to make a secret of that. Is that the lesson I'm supposed to learn? Give more money, help my fellow men and women? Because I'd love to do that if I could just come back. Right now, I've got exactly 147 dollars and thirteen cents in my account, but I'll give it all away, the whole lot. It's not a problem.

"I...I haven't taken care of Dad the way I should have. I should've gone to see him more often. But I've spent every Christmas and Thanksgiving with him, despite MacKenzie celebrating alone with pizza at the motel. If I can just come back, I'll take better care of him. I'll eat dinner with him every weekend. Every day! At least!"

I don't know what to say about Michael. It's difficult, because I think God might be expecting some kind of sacrifice, and I can't give him up. Eventually, I tell the truth.

"I'm selfish, I know. I want Michael. But other people get to love without having to die for it, so I... No, I'm not going to apologize. I want him to stay here and be mine, and I don't care whether he would be happier somewhere else, because I'm not going to let him go again."

I glance around in search of some kind of sign that God has heard me. A flash of lightning or a choir of angels or a sea that has suddenly parted. Even some kind of divine wind that can pick me up and carry me back to that Sunday afternoon, so I can look up one minute earlier and not cross the road and turn up in reception, where MacKenzie will be slightly shocked that I am suddenly hugging her...

But I'm still just surrounded by cows.

"Come on, God," I say. "It's not exactly like you're entirely innocent yourself, is it? How's it going with all those wars and famines and followers who seem more interested in harassing LGBT people than anything else? All right, so I wasn't perfect, but do you really think this is a fair punishment? Whatever happened to 'Let he who is without sin cast the first stone'? Huh? *Huh?*"

I run my hand over my eyes. That wasn't what I had planned to say.

I've annoyed him now. But there still isn't any lightning, and honestly, what can he do to me that he hasn't already done?

I'm dead.

I'm going to be cremated.

Fire and heat. Then nothing.

CHAPTER 12

Fire and Heat

IT HAD BEEN EXQUISITE TORTURE TO SIT NEXT TO MICHAEL IN the car on Saturday morning. We had woken up twisted around the sheets and each other, and he had suggested a day trip. I didn't want to get out of bed, didn't want to stop touching him now that I had finally been given the chance, but as I sat next to him in the car, I felt good. I decided that I liked looking at him with his clothes on, too. It was fun being able to fantasize about taking them off.

His hand was on my thigh. It felt natural, as though we were an old couple out for a ride. We both smelled of the same shampoo. I had borrowed his deodorant, too, and every time I moved, I thought of his body. On top of me, inside me, not innocently sitting next to me in the car.

I was more awake than I had ever been before, but also so tired that my legs ached. I was relaxed and excited, and time had ceased to exist. I thought, *Michael is here*, and felt the kind of irresponsible happiness you only feel after having sex all night.

Michael turned to me, smiled, and shook his head. I didn't know if it was at me or himself.

I gazed out the window. "Tell me how everything began," I said.

The asphalt up ahead of us glittered in the sunlight, and the trees were like dark shadows on both sides of the road. I started the story for him: "Once upon a time, long ago," I said, "when all of the land on earth was gathered together in one big supercontinent called Pangaea..."

"You remember its name?"

I remember everything you told me, I thought.

"Yeah," I said.

"Well, this was a long, long time before that."

"Hundreds of millions of years ago?"

"Much longer than that. Four point five billion years ago."

"What existed back then?"

"Nothing. Just fire and lava and smoke. The earth was so hot, it didn't even have a crust, and it was constantly being bombarded by meteorites."

His voice was confident, calmly telling a story about the beginning of the earth. It transported me into a parallel world until we seemed to be driving backward through history, a few million years per mile. The straight road and the pines all around us transformed into a hellish inferno, but I was safe beside Michael. I already knew that water would soon cool the surface of the earth.

"Earlier than we thought, in fact," Michael said. "Maybe even as early as 150 million years after the earth was formed. But there was still no oxygen in the air. So we need to jump forward in time, to western Australia."

"One of your rocks was from Australia, wasn't it?"

"Australia is fantastic. There's so much of it that still hasn't been explored. There'll be enough work there for generations of geologists to come, finding answers to questions we haven't even asked ourselves yet. The entire continent is like a constant reminder of how small and insignificant we are, and how little we know. Just think of all the amazing things we still have left to explore. One weird thing that has already been discovered are the stromatolites in Shark Bay in western Australia."

"You've been there?"

"Yeah," he said eagerly. "Imagine a completely unforgiving landscape."

His eyes glittered with some kind of internal fervor, and the words started flowing more quickly. He even took his hand from my thigh so that he could use it to gesture.

"Scorching sun, red rocks, everything is dry and burned, and the shallow water in the cove is unbelievably salty—more than twice as salty as the sea beyond. But those relentless conditions are the reason the stromatolites are still there. They survive because nothing else does. At one point in time, they dominated all life on earth and fundamentally changed the planet's climate. They're the reason for most of the life that came after them, the reason we're here in Oregon in the twenty-first century, driving a car and thinking about how everything began. And they were definitely the reason for my work in Australia."

"What did they do?"

"They gave us oxygen. In the ocean at first, then in the air, until the conditions were right for the earth to explode into life. The stromatolites are one of the earliest examples of photosynthesis. They took light from the sun and created oxygen. Back then, the ocean was still full of iron. Iron and oxygen... I'll let you guess what happened next."

"Rust?"

"Yup. It rusted. Year after year for millions of years, layer upon layer at the bottom of the ocean. You can actually still see those deposits in certain places today. It's like being able to see the planet breathing. The first-ever breaths in the biosphere. That rust is why Australia has such enormous iron reserves. I spent a year working on Mount Whaleback as a result of that. I... Henny! You're laughing at me. You got me going on purpose, didn't you, so I'd go on and on about geology again?"

I smiled. "I've missed it."

Then I leaned back and closed my eyes and thought about how freedom is being able to drive a car without any idea where you're going. For this one short weekend, I wasn't working at the motel, and it felt amazing. Freedom was having Michael's body beside mine rather than cleaning rooms like usual. It was involuntary yawns as a result of too little sleep and a straight road through the forest.

I know that deep down, Michael does like Oregon, because he took me to Crater Lake, which was formed 7,700 years ago. The Native Americans saw it happen. I know that a place is geologically uninteresting to him if people were around to see it take shape. And he would never go anyplace uninteresting for himself.

That must mean he took me there for other reasons. Maybe because it's one of the most beautiful places on earth. Because the water is a completely clear and brilliant shade of blue, reflecting the sky above like a mirror, and it feels like you're standing above the clouds and looking down at heaven. Because he knows I love it there.

Crater Lake formed after Mount Mazama erupted, sending a cloud of ash as far as Canada, Wyoming, California, and Nevada. The volcano then collapsed, which created an enormous hole, a kind of cauldron that slowly filled with rain and meltwater. The lake is 1,942 feet deep, the deepest in the whole United States, and has no inlets or outlets. That's what makes the water so unbelievably beautiful.

"Not even eight thousand years old," I said. "You're losing your touch."

"I thought I'd probably showed you enough rocks in the middle of nowhere."

"Admit it. You come here because you think it's beautiful. You've *missed* Oregon."

"I've missed certain things in Oregon."

I laughed. I was trapped in my own bubble of happiness. We never stopped looking at each other. We never stopped smiling.

It wasn't as though I thought we would be together forever. I knew he might leave me again. The rocks might call to him, all those exciting, exotic places that were memories to him and empty words to me. Places like Shark Bay. It was just that the future didn't matter. Time had been knocked off-kilter. Maybe that moment at Crater Lake would last forever, or maybe it would be followed by several moments that were just as painfully beautiful, but I would take it on regardless. I wasn't afraid of pain borne out of love. There and then, life seemed as crystal clear as the water beneath us.

Just live, I thought. *Experience everything. Feel everything. Seconds count; several days are a miracle.*

CHAPTER 13

A Certain Amount of Happiness

I'M AWARE OF THE IRONY.

During our last weekend together, I tried to convince Michael to visit his family, but now that we're standing outside his parents' house, all I want is to take him away from here.

Michael is wasting my time. *Our* time. Just two short days from now, I'm going to be cremated. He is wearing jeans, a black T-shirt, and a jacket. He looks unbelievably handsome, but not even that can perk me up. He's going to waste an entire evening with his family.

"They don't even like you!" I say, though I instantly feel guilty. I should be supporting him. I should probably have put on a dress or something, but I'm stuck in these jeans and this damned polka-dot top, and there's nothing I can do about it because I also happen to be dead.

Michael is hovering by the front door. He still hasn't rung the bell.

"Okay, okay," I say. "It's fine. It's going to be okay."

Then I take a step back.

"What are we doing here, Michael?" I ask.

I can't waste my time at expensive houses with someone else's dysfunctional family.

"It's not too late," I plead. "We can still get out of here."

"So you came, did you?" Mr. Callahan grunts as he opens the door.

"Guess so."

He steps aside for Michael, and after hesitating for a moment, I follow them in. A couple of hours. I'll keep him company and suffer through this evening, and then I'll get to be alone with him. Relax next to him and forget all about my upcoming funeral.

The family has gathered in the living room for a drink before dinner:

Michael's mom, Joyce; his brother, Derek; and Stacey, who is already tipsy. I used to like Joyce. She's nice as long as you take her for what she is. But now she says "Michael" in a confused voice, as if she has just remembered she has another son.

Derek thumps him on the back, unnecessarily hard. *Of course he does.* He's an ex-football player, after all. Not that he's played in fifteen years, but I guess he needs to show that he's still got it. Stacey gives Michael a hug that lasts a little too long.

We're an odd bunch, even Joyce. She is wearing something pale and lavender, and it's almost as if she blends in with her surroundings. She drifts around, seemingly unaware of the conversations going on, and when she leaves the living room to check on dinner, Michael is the only one who notices. The faint, lingering scent of her perfume is the only sign she was ever there.

Mr. Callahan is chatting with Stacey, and Derek takes the opportunity to pull Michael to one side. I follow them.

"So how's it going with the rocks, Bro?" Derek asks. He has put on weight since he stopped playing football. There are still muscles beneath the fat, but they're well hidden. His shirt is crumpled and a size too small, one of the buttons struggling to hold it closed.

There's something else about him, about the way he keeps glancing at Michael. Derek used to look at the world with a kind of boyish charm. *Here I am. Come on, love me.* But now he seems surprised that life has moved on without him. *Here I am. Why don't you love me anymore?*

"The prodigal son returns," he says.

"Temporarily," Michael replies, forcing himself to look at his brother.

I can't tell what he is feeling. At one point in time, he used to worship Derek. Derek took care of him and occasionally let him tag along on his adventures, teasing him the way big brothers and demigods do, and if he expected a little worshipping in return, Michael was perfectly willing to give it to him.

"Worked down any interesting mines lately?" Derek asks.

"Arizona. Copper."

I wonder whether Michael has missed him. I wonder whether he still misses the old Derek.

"So you couldn't sneak out any gold with you? How's the price of gold doing these days?" Derek buys and sells things, each deal crazier than the last, but never anything as valuable as gold. "Still, the book must've brought in some money? *New York Times* bestseller and all that. Who would've thought it? My little brother, a celebrity."

"What do you want, Derek?"

"I've got an investment opportunity for you. It's a sure deal. I'd..."

"How much?" Michael interrupts him.

"Five hundred bucks. I'd do it myself, but I thought I'd give you a chance to make a killing."

From across the room, Stacey's eyes narrow as she studies her husband.

"Since you're my brother and all." Derek's eyes glitter. "And because I'm broke. My capital's a little tied up at the moment. Got a couple of other projects in the pipeline. So what do you say?"

There it is: the old Derek's smile. He is always so sure people will forgive him, even when he's begging for money from his brother—a man he hasn't seen in fifteen years. Almost no one can resist that smile.

I'm not surprised to hear Michael say, "All right. I'll transfer the money tomorrow."

Derek boxes him on the shoulder. "Welcome home, Bro," he says.

Stacey shakes her head as though she knows exactly what just happened.

Eventually, they all make their way into the dining room. It has dark wooden paneling and a large table set with pretty, delicate porcelain. I stick to the walls, suddenly embarrassed to be intruding like this. Maybe I should have stayed in the living room. I wonder how long they can take to eat. *Almost free, almost free*, I repeat to myself like a mantra.

Each of the plates is laden with an impressive slab of steak, mashed sweet potatoes, and peas.

"I guess you heard that the Canadians closed the sawmill," Mr. Callahan says. He pauses to chew on a chunk of meat. "Three years."

More chewing. His jaws grind in the same way as his voice when he continues: "That's how long they managed without me. I knew what would happen the minute I saw the manager they'd sent down to take over. That man had no idea what people here need or want. I could've taught him a thing or two, if he'd bothered to ask. But, you know, they paid well. I'm not complaining. I've managed to keep myself busy, I'll have you know. There's always something that needs fixing in this town. Bob does his best, I suppose, but you know what it's like. In the end, he's just a politician. He doesn't exactly live in the real world."

"But you do, Dad," Michael says drily.

Joyce impales the peas on her fork, one at a time.

"You bet your ass I did. I had to work hard for all this. I certainly never got anything for free. This piece of meat didn't just jump into my mouth." He waves his fork to prove his point.

"How about you, Mom?" Michael asks. "What's been going on in your life lately?"

Joyce misses the next pea, and her fork screeches against the plate. She looks up at her son in confusion.

"Going on?" says Mr. Callahan. "What could possibly be going on in her life? She doesn't do anything."

Joyce looks relieved. She manages to stab the pea on her next attempt.

After dinner, Michael escapes onto the porch. He leans his head against the wall and closes his eyes.

"We can go now, Michael," I say. "It can just be the two of us for the rest of the evening."

But no. He doesn't move.

Fine, I think bitterly. *Let's stay here a little longer.*

Stacey comes out with two glasses of whiskey. "I'm sorry about Henny," she says. "And for not talking about her at dinner. We're a bunch of self-centered assholes. You two were friends, right?"

Michael knocks back the whiskey. Stacey raises an eyebrow, but then heads back inside and returns with a refilled glass. And the bottle.

"Want to talk about it?" she asks, sitting down on one of the porch chairs.

Michael reluctantly slumps down in the chair next to her. "Dad hasn't changed, has he?" he says.

Stacey lights a cigarette. There is an old cola can on the table between them, and she uses it as an ashtray. "Did you think he would've?"

"I guess I'd hoped so."

"I just want everything to be like it was before. But Derek has definitely changed."

"How do you think Mom's doing?" Michael asks.

"Doing? Joyce? She's the picture of health."

"No, I mean... Is she happy?"

"As happy as anyone else. More than a lot of folks, I'd guess." Stacey blows a perfect smoke ring. "Did you know she's a vegetarian now? I caught her smuggling tofu into the house a couple weeks ago. She has it for lunch."

"You know you can eat tofu without being a vegetarian?"

"You think? This isn't Portland, you know."

"I just meant that maybe she..."

"Did you notice she managed not to eat a single bite of that incredible chateaubriand at dinner?"

"A vegetarian, huh. Keeping it a secret from Dad, I assume?"

"Clearly."

Stacey lights another cigarette and takes a long drag on it, closing her eyes and slowly blowing the smoke from one corner of her mouth. With the cigarette between her fingers, she takes a sip of whiskey, her eyes still shut.

"Do you remember what I looked like in high school?" she asks.

"Everyone remembers how you looked in high school," Michael replies. He empties his glass. Fills it again.

It's true. Perfect skin, as though her personality was too good for acne. Dimples, brilliantly white teeth. Long legs, always tanned. Full of life and youthful energy.

"No, I mean really. When I look at myself in the mirror now, I can't believe I was ever that young. Do you think we only get a certain amount of happiness in life? That you can use it all up over the space of a few years and then have none left?"

"Suffering seems to be limitless, in any case."

"I was happy in high school. *I was.* It made me forget all about my pathetic, white-trash parents and the trailer and the dirt. I even duped myself. I wish high school had never ended."

Stacey used to turn up at every game Derek played. People in town cheered on their relationship almost as much as they cheered on the team.

Her cigarette has burned down to the filter and singes her fingers. Swearing, she drops it into the can.

I was also happy in high school. Looking back now, it seems like only the idiots were. People who didn't know any better. Stacey tells a long anecdote from our time at school, but Michael doesn't speak. He just drinks whiskey.

"Dwelling on things is pointless," he eventually says.

"Why? It's one of my favorite pastimes. Cheers to dwelling!"

Cheers to that, I think.

More of her bright-coral lipstick transfers onto Mr. Callahan's expensive whiskey glass.

"Maybe you're right," she says after a while. "And you definitely did the right thing by leaving. I should've forced you to take me with you."

"I left the day after your wedding."

"Exactly. If I'd had any sense, I would've done the same."

There is something hard and cruel in her eye. She doesn't duck from the truth about herself, so why should she spare anyone else? Michael looks embarrassed, but I can't help but admire her. If she really had wanted to, she would've jumped into his car the day after her wedding and left with him.

When she gets to her feet, she is unsteady. She raises her voice when she next speaks: "If I'd had even an ounce of sense, I would've left *before* my wedding."

I hear a voice from the living room window: "If only my *wife* would spend a little more time on the house and a little less on booze."

"All I know about drinking, I learned from my *husband*."

Michael stays outside long enough to drink two more glasses before he gets up and walks toward his car. He has to take a sudden step to one side to avoid walking straight into the oak tree. He leans against the car and waits for the world to stop spinning. Then he kicks the tire and says, *"Goddamn it."* His voice echoes around the expensive houses and parked cars, each of which is probably worth more than the motel. He kicks his car one last time and slumps down to the pavement. He sends a text and covers his face with his hands, and then we sit there beneath the oak tree.

Twenty minutes later, MacKenzie's pickup pulls up in front of us. Michael staggers to his feet and slumps into the passenger seat. I jump up into the bed. Through the small window separating the cab from the bed, I can see their tired faces, momentarily illuminated by the cab light. I can see myself, too. Outside. In the bed of the truck. While *MacKenzie* sits there next to Michael.

"I drank too much" is all he says.

"That's what family does to you."

Michael turns away. "Thanks," he reluctantly says.

MacKenzie shrugs and drives away. "It's all included in the price," she says.

"I think I'm going crazy."

"Craziness is included, too. And I'm sure whiskey helps."

I can see his face in the rearview mirror. It looks dogged, blank, faintly lit by the dashboard and the headlights. I want to run a finger across his forehead and smooth out his frown.

"Can't get much worse, in any case," he says.

"You sure about that?" MacKenzie goes on: "Drinking is overrated. I'd try hitting something instead."

"I already tried that."

"You look like you've gone twelve rounds against yourself."

"And lost." Silence. "I was crazy to come back here. What did I think would happen? Everything would suddenly be great, and all of life's secrets would reveal themselves, and the past wouldn't matter anymore? Like I'd become someone new the minute I parked outside the motel?"

"That's not true," I say quietly. "You're crazy for staying away for so long."

"Sure," MacKenzie agrees. "You're crazy for coming back."

"It's not like I even made a conscious decision to do it. It was more like I woke up at check-in one day, and there she was. Everything felt right again. Like all the different parts of my life had suddenly come together. Past and future, reality and fantasy."

"It *was* right," I say stubbornly.

"And then?" MacKenzie asks. "What did you think would happen then?"

"I didn't think. And now it's too late." He runs a hand over his face.

MacKenzie parks outside his cabin. Michael struggles with the seat belt, and then he is free and out of the car. He stands with his back to her, to me.

But he continues to talk. Now that he's started, it seems like he needs to get it all out. "Do you know how many times I've cleaned that damn cabin?" he asks.

"No."

"Yes," I say.

"I've scrubbed the floor, cleaned the whole bathroom, washed the sheets three times, swapped out all the towels, wiped every surface—"

"You do know cleaning is included in the price of the room?"

"—but I can still smell her *everywhere*. When I go to bed, I can feel her body beside mine. Soft and warm and sexy and, goddamn it, just *there*. I've already been back too long, even though there's nothing for me here. But for some reason I can't leave. I keep hearing her voice. *Stay, don't go, stay.* I've always been strong enough to know what I want, but it's like she's taken over my head."

Michael turns back to the car, and as he throws open his arms, it feels as though the gesture is directed at me. "I left her once when she was *alive*, for God's sake. Why can't I leave her now? Why can't I just get out of here, move on, *stop smelling her everywhere*."

"Go to bed, Michael."

"I need to get out of here."

MacKenzie puts the truck into reverse, and I quickly jump down from the bed.

"Yeah, yeah," she says wearily through the open window. "But not tonight."

He waves half-heartedly. "Thanks. I guess. For the ride."

"Motel taxi service, that's me."

And with that, she is gone and we are suddenly alone.

He tried to clean me away.

He goes straight into the bathroom and starts throwing things into his toiletry bag with rash, angry movements. Toothbrush, toothpaste, razor. Everything piles up in an unsorted heap that just makes him angrier. The mess riles him up. The fact he is still here riles him up. As he grabs his backpack and starts throwing his clothes into it, he misses the bag practically every other time.

"Of course you can't leave me," I say to his back. "We belong together. We always have. And you can't leave here *now*. I haven't even been buried yet. Later, maybe, once I'm gone, but definitely not yet."

He snatches a T-shirt from the floor and shoves it into his bag. There are still a few left in the drawer, all neatly folded.

I put my hands on my hips. Move right in front of him. In his way. I'm not going to leave him in peace so he can carry on like this.

"You might think you can just go on with your life like none of this meant anything," I say. "But it did. Don't kid yourself otherwise. You're going to remember me, whether you want to or not. And you're going to miss me."

He moves over to his collection of rocks on the dresser. Picks up two from Oregon, takes them out onto the porch, and throws them away, one after the other.

"*Michael*," I say. "Stop!"

But he just goes back to the dresser and grabs the swirled piece of blueschist that I held in my hand.

His little piece of Oregon.

I think he's hesitating. I hope he is. But it must just be my imagination, because he readies himself and puts all his energy into sending the rock high into the air, into the forest.

CHAPTER 14

"What Do You Want from Me, Henny?"

DURING OUR WEEKEND TOGETHER, WE ONLY ONCE SPOKE ABOUT what we were doing.

It was Saturday night, and we grabbed some blankets and pillows and lay down on the grass by the river, the invisible mountains up ahead and Oregon's countless stars above.

His head was on my shoulder, and my fingers moved slowly over his back. I lingered on one of the three pale freckles on his shoulder blade and found myself thinking about how many other women must have touched him over the years.

I didn't know where the thought had come from, but it was definitely there. The world had caught up with me again, and I couldn't escape the feeling that our time was running out.

I had no idea how long he would be staying, but it was Saturday evening. My weekend would soon be over. I had to be back at the reception desk the next afternoon.

I must have shifted slightly, because he looked up at me and realized I was watching him.

"What are you thinking about?" he asked, his voice gruff with sleep.

I shook my head. "Nothing," I said.

And then: "All those years after you left, didn't you miss your family?"

I tried to keep the tone of my voice light, but what I really wanted to know was: Didn't you miss *me*?

Michael pulled away from me, rolling onto his back. He rubbed his eyes in an attempt to wake up. "You want to talk about my family?" he said.

"I just thought... You didn't even come back for Thanksgiving or Christmas, or..."

"Why would I come back? I don't understand people who spend the whole year moaning about their families and then still head home for Christmas. Why not celebrate with someone they actually like instead?"

Was that what you did? I wondered, though I didn't ask it aloud. Even in my head, it sounded jealous.

"And you never wondered how they were, or whether they missed you?"

Whether *I* had missed him. Why didn't he come home just as an excuse to see me? Did I really mean so little to him that he could leave me the same way he left his parents and the rest of town?

"Derek was there, and he was always the one who meant the most to them." Michael sounded deliberately indifferent, but a note of nostalgia had crept into his voice. "Do you remember when he played football? The whole town would show up. Every single game." He shook his head. "I thought he would get away from here."

That was how Michael always talked about Pine Creek. As something he had managed to escape. He was convinced that if you weren't careful, you would wake up one day twenty years later with a wife and four kids. And that would have been awful.

"How...how are they?" he asked. He seemed embarrassed by the fact that he still cared.

"I don't know," I said. We had never been close. I would say hello to Joyce if I saw her in town, but I had never liked Mr. Callahan. "Are you going to see them now that you're back?"

Michael shrugged. I could feel it beside me. He stubbornly stared up at the stars. I looked up, too, but moved imperceptibly closer to him until my hand was resting against his thigh.

"Maybe you have to move on," I said. "I don't know how long you're planning to stay. I'm sure you're busy and..."

I lost my trail of thought. "What are we doing, Michael?"

"What do you mean?"

"Am I going to wake up one day and see you packing your things?"

"Come on, Henny. Is that really what you think of me?"

That was what happened the last time.

From that very first summer we spent together, I knew that I wanted to spend the rest of my life with him. I never tried to fool myself. I loved him, and that was that.

I think he loved me, too, but we were so young. I still hadn't learned that love isn't always enough. He already had a plan. He wanted to leave Pine Creek, and that's precisely what he did.

I never found anyone I wanted as much as Michael, and after he left, I wasn't prepared to settle for any less. It's a special kind of curse to experience love like that at such a young age, and as I lay there and looked up at the dark night sky, I wondered what it had been like for him.

Maybe he had a woman in every corner of the world. One for every starry sky.

Michael propped himself up on one elbow and studied me intensely. I could see all kinds of emotions flickering through his eyes, but I had no idea what they meant: desire, longing, tenderness, loss, uncertainty. I thought I could see regret, but I didn't know whether it was over the past or the future.

"I have no idea what we're doing," he said. "This wasn't something I planned. Maybe I should have given it more thought, but I didn't. I definitely wasn't planning for you to kiss me."

"You kissed me, too!"

"I didn't plan that, either."

He took my hand. Hesitantly, as if he expected me to pull it back. He turned it over in his hand and followed the lines on my palm as though he was looking for the answers there.

"What do you want from me, Henny?" he asked.

PINE CREEK GAZETTE

OBITUARIES

John Richard Lewis

John "Johnnie" Richard Lewis has passed away after a long illness. Born February 17, 1945, he was the youngest of six handsome brothers. Sadly, he never had as much luck with the fish as his brothers, who always landed bigger catches, and though he tried valiantly, he was never quite as tall, strong, or handsome, either. He worked at all three sawmills in Pine Creek and insisted, right up until his death, that it was pure coincidence that every one had closed down. Aside from his unfortunate fondness for fishing, his passions in life were football, the Ducks, and the wife. In no particular order. He is survived by his wife, children, and grandchildren, and by his five older and more handsome brothers, who paid for this obituary.

Sarah Elizabeth Robinson

Sarah Elizabeth Robinson, born May 5, 1927, has left this earthly life in favor of the heavenly. She passed away peacefully at home, surrounded by her beloved family and her cats: Moe, Larry, and Curly. Sarah loved her cats, her family, Jesus, and her church; she was always there for those who needed her, a warm and attentive listener, a loyal friend, and a pillar of the community. A memorial will be held Tuesday at Sacred Faith Evangelical Church. The congregation will care for the cats.

Henny Broek

Henny was born July 23, 1983. She lived in Pine Creek, Oregon. She is survived by her father, Robert Broek. Her traditional and perfectly normal funeral will take place at 3:00 p.m. Friday at Pine Creek United Methodist Church.

CHAPTER 15

Half Sounds and Half Lives

SITTING ON CHERYL'S SOFA, MACKENZIE LOOKS INCREDIBLY young. She is peering around the room as though she can't quite work out how she ended up here.

There's a pretty simple explanation: Cheryl called MacKenzie an hour ago and asked her to stop by when she had a moment. It's the first time in fifteen years that we've been to Cheryl's place, and I can't decide what's so strange about it—the fact that we're here, or that we've stayed away for so long.

Neither MacKenzie nor I have any idea why Cheryl wanted to see her.

Cheryl hands MacKenzie a cup of coffee. "It should probably be hot chocolate," she says.

"With peanut butter and jelly sandwiches," says MacKenzie. "No crusts, obviously."

She glances around the room. "I can't believe it's so long since I was last here," she says. "Not since..." She self-consciously lets her voice trail off, and Cheryl looks embarrassed, too.

"I still drive like a madwoman," MacKenzie quickly adds.

Cheryl smiles. Seeing them together now, the fury that once separated them seems even more incomprehensible. I think they feel that, too.

We were sitting just like this the first time Cheryl saved us.

We were sixteen at the time, and MacKenzie's father was having a particularly intense episode. The first of many. MacKenzie's mere existence seemed to provoke him more and more the older she got.

On that particular day, she didn't want to go home until he had calmed down or passed out. She was afraid. My strong, brave, invincible MacKenzie's face was pale and uncertain. And so we sat on a bench on

Water Street, pretending everything was fine, pretending we were just hanging out like usual.

It's hard to pretend you want to be outside on a cold, damp evening in October, but we did our best. We sat there in the hazy glow of a streetlamp and saw the lights come on in the houses all around us, eventually going off again, one by one.

The last dog owners had long since passed by on their evening walks and were now back in the warmth of their houses. In a way, it was a relief not to have to pretend everything was fine to their curious faces.

I was already hopelessly late. I knew Dad would be furious, but I also couldn't leave MacKenzie on her own, so I stayed there with her. Neither of us had eaten dinner. We laughed in embarrassment whenever either of our stomachs rumbled.

MacKenzie pulled her hands into the sleeves of her thin denim jacket and refused to take my scarf. The damp chill had gotten under our skin, but we eventually stopped shivering out of sheer exhaustion.

"It could be worse," I said. "It could be snowing."

MacKenzie laughed. It was a weak laugh, but a victory all the same. Then she told me to go home. Again. Like before, I ignored her.

We never saw Cheryl approaching. Suddenly she was just there in front of us, wearing pale-pink sweatpants and her husband's oversize coat.

"What's going on here, girls?" she asked. She must have seen us from her kitchen window.

MacKenzie didn't reply.

Cheryl glanced from her to me.

"Nothing, Mrs. Stone," I eventually said.

I shifted closer to MacKenzie for support, but her body was stiff and cold against mine. She felt much smaller than usual.

"Henny?" Cheryl asked.

She isn't going to give in, I thought. She's going to insist on taking us back to Dad's, and I can't just turn up there with MacKenzie. Dad had clear rules about visitors and overnight stays.

I can't fix this on my own, I thought.

I didn't dare look at MacKenzie as I said, "MacKenzie can't go home."

Cheryl's eyes moved back and forth between us. MacKenzie tried to look brave, but she couldn't quite manage it like usual.

"Well, you can't sit here all night," Cheryl said. "Come with me, girls."

Cheryl's kitchen was wonderfully warm and much, much better than the park bench. I went to the bathroom, and by the time I got back, she had made hot chocolate. MacKenzie's frozen fingers were already wrapped around her steaming-hot mug, and there was another waiting for me.

Cheryl spread peanut butter and jelly onto slices of bread and then cut away the crusts, and it was the most delicious thing I had ever eaten. She made a whole mountain of them, and MacKenzie and I took as many as we dared, slowly thawing out. The worst desperation had disappeared from MacKenzie's eyes.

While we were eating, Cheryl went over to the phone in the hallway and called Dad, just like that, telling him that MacKenzie and I were staying at her house that night. "I don't think we'll bother calling your dad," she said, and MacKenzie laughed.

Cheryl Stone was the bravest person I had ever met.

Both MacKenzie and Cheryl are thinking back to that evening now.

The living room has barely changed over the years. It might be a little less chaotic now that Cheryl's sons are older, but the whole room is still practical and cozy. Durable fabric on all of the furniture, comfortable armchairs meant for curling up in, paintings that never seem to be hanging straight, flowers on every free surface.

It was Cheryl who taught MacKenzie to drive. Her dad was never sober long enough to care about her driver's license, so one day after that first evening, Cheryl simply took charge as if it were the most natural thing in the world. I'm sure she paid for some lessons for MacKenzie, too.

"So...how are you?" Cheryl asks. "Are you coping?"

MacKenzie shrugs. "It is what it is," she says.

"I...I'm sorry." She says it warmly and naturally: real sympathy, not something people force themselves to blurt out when they don't know what else to say.

MacKenzie nods.

"I'd like to ask you a favor," Cheryl says. "But I don't really know how to put it."

"It's normally easiest just to come out and say it."

"Do you think you could consider...*not* going to Henny's funeral?"

She shouldn't have just come out and said it, I think.

Cheryl continues before MacKenzie has time to reply: "It's not for my sake. It's Robert. He's afraid everyone would just focus on your...relationship, rather than the funeral."

"Our relationship," MacKenzie echoes. She puts down her cup.

"He's very upset about the whole thing. Not that you shouldn't be able to go to the funeral, of course, because obviously you should."

MacKenzie no longer looks young.

Cheryl continues. "I know we haven't always seen eye to eye on certain things—"

"True. You said I'd burn in hell. I didn't agree."

"—but it's for Robert's sake. I'm worried about him. He's lost everything, and now he's obsessed with the idea that people will talk. About... well, you and Henny."

"Jesus Christ, Cheryl. Even you must know there that was never anything going on between us. Or have you found some kind of Bible passage that forbids friendship?"

"But you can understand why people might wonder, can't you? It's not really that surprising, is it? You lived together, and you're, well, *you*, and you made such a big deal of it and..."

"*I* made a big deal of it?"

"Does it really mean that much to you?" Cheryl asks in desperation. "You don't even go to church anymore. What do a few psalms and a boring pastor matter?"

Begging now, she adds: "And just imagine how hard all this is for Robert. Yes, he's obsessing over the funeral, but he's always been like that. Proper, correct. Hates it when people talk about him. He just wants to be left in peace."

"He's not the only one."

"And now he's finding everything so difficult, it's such a hard time for him... If we can make things any easier for him, don't you think we should do our best to do that?"

MacKenzie slowly gets to her feet. "I'll think about it," she says.

MacKenzie drives straight back to the hotel and gets to work. She pretends that she just needs to start cleaning, and begins with room 3.

But the universe seems to have turned against her. The bag in the vacuum cleaner is full. She accidentally picks up two duvet covers instead of one sheet. The light bulb goes out.

"I can't believe she said all those things!" I shout when MacKenzie returns with a fresh vacuum bag. And a sheet. And a new bulb. "What right does she have to stick her nose into who comes to *my* funeral? And Dad! Who said he gets to decide everything? You should be choosing at least half of the songs. And giving a eulogy. I really hope you just turn up and tell them about our long, *close* friendship. *Very* close. Half the town thinks we're a couple anyway, so why disappoint them? You can bring champagne. Toast to me in the church and say that we drank it for breakfast every day."

MacKenzie bashes her toe as she changes the sheets. I grimace as a *goddamn it* flashes through her eyes. Her body tenses, more from irritation than pain.

Then she relaxes. With forced indifference, at first: *What does it matter? It's just a toe.* Then, slowly, genuine indifference takes over: *What does anything matter anymore?*

"I have an idea," I say. "You can offer people Hennessy cognac! And it'd be a great idea to dress all in white. Convince everyone else to do the same."

I want her to rant and rave and refuse to give in.

But she's tired. Everything is slow and sluggish. It's as if she is wading through water. When she finishes making the bed, she closes her eyes. Keeping them open seems completely beyond her.

"It's just a funeral," I say. "It doesn't matter."

She slumps down onto the freshly made bed. Hands on her knees, shoulders hunched, her face turned down toward the rug. Her breathing is suddenly rapid, and her eyes snap open. She can't get any air, and the room starts to spin all around her. She stares down at the floor as though it's the only thing keeping her alive while her breathing runs riot.

I drop to my knees in front of her and place my hands on top of hers, but I can't push the hair back out of her eyes.

"Shh," I say. "It's going to be fine. You're not alone anymore. Camila is here."

MacKenzie tips backward. Forces herself to hold her arms away from her body. Her cheeks lose some of their unnatural reddish tint, and her blond hair spreads out around her.

I lie down next to her and look up at the ceiling.

"It's going to be all right," I say. "You don't have to go through this alone. Camila is back."

MacKenzie's breathing gradually slows.

I whisper into her ear: "Camila is here. Camila is here. Camila is here."

Many hours later, MacKenzie heads down to the check-in desk and hangs up our homemade sign—*Back in fifteen minutes, ring the bell.* She grabs a couple of beers and fetches two chairs, setting them down outside Camila's room.

MacKenzie and I used to sit like that. A six-pack of beer between us, our feet on the metal railing, looking down at our kingdom below. I'm not sure whether the chair is for me or Camila.

MacKenzie doesn't knock on her door. She doesn't say anything. She just sits there in silence. I think she's sitting guard, but whether it's over me or Camila is unclear.

Once, MacKenzie told me that the thing she likes most about motels is that everyone in them is lonely. No one belongs. You both exist and don't exist. Between realities, she said.

"And we, Henny, get to live here full time."

It was a miracle that never ceased to amaze her.

I wonder what will happen now that I'm no longer here to help out. Will she be able to manage all of the work on her own? Will she even stay? It's impossible to imagine MacKenzie anywhere but here. And it's definitely impossible to imagine the motel without MacKenzie.

I glance anxiously at her in a way that would drive her crazy if she could see it. *Stop mollycoddling me*, she would say. But I'm a ghost, and that means I'm allowed to keep an eye on my best friend.

Camila's door opens.

"Beer?" MacKenzie says without turning around.

"It's raining."

MacKenzie looks up. "We're under a roof," she says.

"It's late, MacKenzie. Go to bed."

But MacKenzie just holds out a bottle of beer in Camila's direction.

"I don't feel like talking," says Camila.

"Good."

"No conversations."

"Suits me just fine," MacKenzie says firmly.

I get up from my chair. Camila hesitates, and then sits down on the very edge of it. MacKenzie waits a few seconds, her arm still outstretched, and then puts down the beer beside Camila.

I jump up onto the railing in front of them, and we sit there in silence, listening to the sound of rain and the moment.

Camila stretches her long, slim legs and lifts her feet onto the railing. Without seeming to think about it, she picks up the beer and takes a couple of swigs.

The neon light from the sign is hazy in the rain and barely reaches the trees on the other side of the road. The dark forest is only visible whenever a car passes by.

"God, I'd almost forgotten it could be *beautiful* around here," Camila says.

MacKenzie smiles. "It does happen."

"MacKenzie..." Camila sounds hesitant.

"Mmm?"

"How could you stay here? After the vote, I mean. In the six months after it, you hated this place even more than I did."

"Ah, I just hated the people. The roads and the motel weren't homophobic."

"Was it because I went away and left you to take care of everything?"

MacKenzie closes her eyes. "It wasn't your fault, Camila. It was my decision. I guess I... Who knows what I was thinking? Maybe I was an idiot."

Don't say that, MacKenzie, I think.

"I didn't actually hate the town after the vote," Camila says. "I was probably more thankful than anything, because I'd discovered there were other LGBT people here. I wonder if the Oregon Citizens Alliance knows how many gays and lesbians and trans people they brought together. The problem was that I knew I could never go through my transition here. Everyone would keep seeing me as a man and would keep using my old name and pronoun."

"Deliberately, I bet," MacKenzie says wearily. "Assholes."

I make a promise to myself never to use her old name again. But I do have to admit that I'm curious why she chose Camila. It must be so much fun to choose your own name as an adult.

"Do you know something I learned when I was still a kid?" Camila asks, continuing without waiting for a reply. "I learned that you can never turn back. The only way to survive is to always be willing to pack up your things and leave. That's where Juan Esteban was wrong. He thought freedom came from owning your own place. Working for yourself, all that crap. But that just traps you."

"So you left."

"Want to know something funny?"

"Tell me something funny."

"I got fired just before I left LA. The boss wanted someone with more 'power of persuasion,' someone who 'took initiative.' I spoke to hundreds of agents, begged them to give his manuscripts a chance. But I guess he thought someone else would be able to do more. So, I got the boot. And since I didn't have a job, I couldn't pay the rent for my room—I was sharing an apartment with three other women. I moved out before I left."

I'm still waiting for the funny part.

"Don't you see? I'm just like Juan Esteban. Everything I own is here, at the motel. I've got no life, no future. I might talk about leaving as soon as the funeral is over, but I don't actually have anywhere to go."

MacKenzie chuckles quietly. "You and me, Camila. You and me." Then she stretches with a new sense of determination. "I *chose* to stay," she says. "I wanted to. I love this old place. It's my home. And Henny was my *friend*. I'm not going to let them win."

"Dolores called me Camila."

MacKenzie rings the bell on Dad's door. Again. And again. It's ten o'clock at night, but she doesn't care. The shrill sound cuts through the quiet street. If the neighbors want to look, let them look. *My funeral is tomorrow.*

Eventually—and reluctantly—Dad opens the door. "Come in, then," he mutters. "Cup of coffee?"

It's hardly the right time for coffee, but it's a purely instinctive offer. I'm sure Dad would offer the grim reaper coffee if he came to visit. He's actually dressed like he was expecting him; I can barely make him out in the dark hallway.

"I spoke to Cheryl," MacKenzie says. "She said you don't want me at the funeral."

Dad refuses to meet her eye.

"Robert! It's Henny's *funeral*. We've been best friends since we were seven. *You've* known me since we were seven. She was my best friend."

"And she was my *daughter*! Mine. Not yours!"

"Uh, no," says MacKenzie.

"*We* were best friends until you came along and stole her from me. After that, Henny was never happy just being with me. I wasn't exciting enough. Not funny enough either, I suppose, not compared to you and your motel. She should have been living here with *me*. The house is definitely big enough. I worked hard to be able to keep it when I retired, but Henny moved to the motel the minute she got the chance, with *you*."

MacKenzie is staring at him with a shocked expression, but Dad doesn't seem to have noticed. It's like he has been collecting these accusations in his head, all higgledy-piggledy. Junk that has been building up in there for years. Big and small, true and false, it's all given the light of day. I can't think of a way to stop him.

"You said she was christened after a *cognac*. Henny is a beautiful old Dutch name, and my grandmother was a fantastic woman, and…"

"That was a joke! I was fifteen!"

"Dad!" I say as firmly as I can. "MacKenzie is my friend. She's always been there for me. I'm sorry if you feel like I abandoned you, but it wasn't her fault."

I feel like shaking him and forcing him to listen. They should be closer than ever now that they're both grieving for me. If the people I love have to be unhappy, they should at least be unhappy together.

But Dad's words keep coming, even faster now. "You made people talk about you. You were always so visible, which meant they talked about Henny, too. Why did the two of you have to live together? It's not natural. She never would have started working at that motel if it weren't for you. She never would have moved over there, and she never would have been on that road. What was she doing there?"

"Uh," I say. "I don't think you want any details, but it actually had nothing to do with work."

Not that Dad cares about logic or fairness. He has leaped from his perch, and now he's in free fall.

Then, all of a sudden, he notices the ground is right beneath him. It comes closer and closer as he falls faster and faster. For a brief second, he seems to regret it. He stares helplessly at MacKenzie as though he's trying to grasp hold of something in his fury, to stop himself.

But it's too late.

Almost involuntarily, he says, "She wouldn't have died if it weren't for you."

Everything becomes frighteningly quiet after that.

MacKenzie, Dad, and I just stand there in the dark hallway. Frozen in shock. His words are too spiteful even to hurt.

"Well, I'm glad we straightened that out." MacKenzie's voice sounds remarkably flat. "For a while, I thought Cheryl was exaggerating."

CHAPTER 16

Hundreds of Millions of Years Ago

THE CLOCK ON THE BEDSIDE TABLE READ 2:03 P.M. I HAD TO BE back at check-in by three.

Our bodies were so close that I no longer knew where my skin ended and his began.

I pulled away from him so that I could sit up in bed and study him properly. It was the middle of the day, but he was lying on his back, naked and drowsy. I leaned over him and explored the tanned skin on his arms and the pale areas his T-shirts had covered. He reached up to push my hair out of my eyes, but otherwise he lay still and let me touch him however I wanted.

"You know," he said. "I never doubted that I really wanted to go for my job. I love being a geologist. I'm happy with my life. But lately...I've felt like there's something missing."

I had been missing. I turned away to hide my smile, then returned to his body. I was amazed by how familiar it felt after such a short, eternally long weekend.

"It was okay while I was still struggling to make it, but the more successful I became, the emptier it felt. Does that sound stupid?"

I wondered whether he could see how hard my heart was beating. "You're a bestselling author," I said.

"I only wrote that so I had something to do when I wasn't working. And maybe... I guess the whole time I was thinking that I only talked about rocks with you."

"You didn't even dedicate it to me."

I lay down against his shoulder. Closed my eyes. He wrapped an arm around me and pulled me closer.

"Tell me about rocks," I said.

"Once upon a time, long ago," he began, smiling to himself. "Hundreds of millions of years ago, in fact. There was a fish known as the conodont."

I sat up and looked at him in surprise. "A fish?" I said. "You *have* changed."

"Patience. I'll get to the rocks."

I lay back down against his shoulder. His finger traced slow, meaningless patterns on my arm.

"There's actually nothing special about the fish itself. It looked like a kind of eel, with a soft, fragile body that hasn't survived very well. There are actually only two intact specimens in existence. Anyway, this fish had a lot of teeth, and those teeth are still here. When the fish died, they sank to the bottom of the ocean where they gradually disintegrated and disappeared—everything but their teeth. They stayed where they were, on the seabed, until the seabed became mountains and rocks. Fossilized teeth from those fish can now be found in the limestone at Grindstone Creek in the Blue Mountains—the oldest rocks in Oregon."

It was almost two thirty.

"But the most interesting thing is that because the fish lived for hundreds of millions of years and developed over time, we can use their teeth to date the rocks. Aha, their teeth looked like this, which means that the limestone in Grindstone Creek must be 380 million years old. Isn't that insane, Henny? A long-extinct fish whose teeth can date an immovable rock in an indestructible mountain range."

I buried my face in his neck and breathed in the scent of him. Memorized the feel of his skin. His rib cage rose and fell beneath my hand as silence spread out between us.

"Henny?" he said quietly.

I nodded against his neck.

"I haven't changed," he said.

CHAPTER 17

The Sun Still Rises

I'VE FAILED.

As I walk around in the darkness the last night before my funeral, I can't think of anything else left to do. I tried praying, but after a few hours, I just felt like a nagging child. *Please please pretty please.* Parents might give in to it; God apparently does not.

So I walk.

I walk around the motel, the parking lot, the cabins, Dolores's small kitchen garden in the back, the river. I peer into every vacant room. I even pause for a few minutes in the dark laundry room, just standing between the washing machines.

Maybe you don't get second chances in death. Maybe all I was supposed to do with this extra time was find a way to say goodbye to them. I wish I could be brave about it. Be strong, like Michael and Camila and MacKenzie always were. But it's hard to be brave when your friends are unhappy.

I used to think that I was bound to them by some kind of unbreakable bond. Something like thick, velvet ribbons. Tied loosely between us; a safety net rather than a shackle. But now I'm all caught up in that ribbon. I've twisted and turned until it is wound so tightly that I can no longer move, and the more I struggle, the tighter it becomes.

If only I knew they would be all right without me. I could leave them then, I think.

I hesitate about going back to Water Street. I can still remember MacKenzie's harrowingly pale face as she drove away. *She wouldn't have died if it weren't for you.*

But in the end I decide to go there anyway. He is my father, after all.

It's four in the morning, and he is sitting perfectly still in his armchair. Eyes closed. He's so still that I have to get up close to make sure he's still breathing. He is. He falls asleep while I'm there. Snoring gently.

I wonder whether I should say anything. Some kind of final message. *Stop being an idiot*, I could tell him. *Apologize to MacKenzie.* But his face is thin and furrowed, his skin like parchment, and I decide he has his own cross to bear. I hope his Jesus is watching over him. All I say is "Bye, Dad" before walking away.

MacKenzie is still awake. She is lying on her back, staring up at the ceiling. Eyes half-closed. Desperately empty. *Bye, MacKenzie.*

I reach Camila's door next. *Bye, Camila.*

I can't bring myself to say it to Michael. Instead, I curl up next to him for a while, but I'm afraid of wasting more time. Afraid that my thoughts will drift away, and I'll disappear without having made the most of what little time I have left here.

I want to be intensely here during my last few hours on earth. My last sunrise. *I'll have to find a good place to watch it from*, I think as I resume my walk around the motel. A faint grayness has already started to seep through the darkness. Dawn arrives so slowly that I have to turn between east and west to see the difference. To the west, jet-black night. To the east, a slight, slight hint of gray on the horizon.

Then I look up.

The roof.

It's not exactly like I can do any more damage to myself, I think as I climb onto the railing. I grab hold of the gutter and haul myself up, swinging my legs until I manage to hook a foot onto the roof and drag myself up.

To the east: fantastic grayness. The dark outlines of the mountains. To the west: *Pine Creek Motel and Cabins. Vacanci s.*

From the roof of the motel, I watch the sun rise for the very last time. A brand-new view for my last morning on earth. The last miracle of my life.

The way the sky explodes into orange and red behind the mountain is like an omen of what is to come. In just a few short hours, I'll be eaten up by fire, and then I'll disappear and that's it.

I walk over to the edge of the roof. I feel a sudden jolt of dizziness in my stomach, but I don't look away. I don't step back. I enjoy the fear. It's a sign that something within me is still alive. And when I look out at the bluish-purple mountains with their backdrop of fire, it's so beautiful that I feel an ache in my chest. The way I used to. A rushing sense of awe. Like feeling dizzy at the world.

All of this will still be here, I think. *It's just me who won't.*

I drop to my knees and grieve for myself with wild, furious despair.

I can't disappear yet. There's still so much I want to *do*.

I want to see the first spring flowers. The last autumn leaves. I want to wake up to the magical first day of snow. Breathe in the crisp, cold air after a snowfall.

I want to drink beer with MacKenzie after a long day at work. I want to enjoy the first sip of coffee on a crisp autumn morning. I want to enjoy the second sip, too. I want to kneel beside MacKenzie and swear as we try to work out how to remove a red wine stain, eventually deciding just to move the couch over it.

I want to eat a tomato that I've picked from the vegetable patch. Walk barefoot in the grass by the river. Fall asleep, exhausted, on the couch one rainy afternoon. I want to crack up with laughter at something meaningless with MacKenzie. It has to be meaningless.

I want to make out with Michael and fall asleep against his shoulder. And, you know, everything in between. We didn't get enough time together.

I wish I could make sure Camila wasn't lonely anymore. I think she has been. I want to see her laughing again, maybe at something MacKenzie said, maybe while working at the motel with her.

I mourn for the people we were and the people we were forced to become and everything we could be again, if only we had *more time*. I want to sit in our usual place out in back of the motel, on a line of chairs against the wall. I want to grow old with them. And most of all, I want them all to be happy. I want to see them strong and free and *together*.

Like we used to be.

Camila is the first to emerge, beautiful and composed in a dark jacket, skirt, and black boots. Her heels are high and thin, and they click against the asphalt. *Click, click.* Slowly, like some kind of challenge. *There's still time, MacKenzie*, her heels seem to be saying.

Come on, MacKenzie, I think.

Michael is next. Unbearably handsome in his dark suit. Grown-up. Newly familiar.

I turn away, but then I change my mind. This might be my last chance to look at him, so instead I try to memorize him so well that not even fire and heat and calcination can obliterate it. As 97 percent of me becomes liquid and then sand, the memory of Michael's body will live on.

I wish life had been different, I wish they had never left, I wish they had come back sooner. Regrets: possibly the ultimate example of how we humans refuse to accept our powerlessness. Even when faced with things that have already happened, we're unable to accept that there's nothing we can do about them.

"We can't leave without her," Michael says. The funeral begins in fifteen minutes.

"I knocked on her door. I shouted. I tried the handle; it was locked." Camila runs a hand over her face.

"Maybe she left already," Michael says.

Camila checks the time again.

Eventually, they get into the car, but they do it as slowly as they possibly can. Swinging their feet in. Closing the doors, hesitating with a hand on the ignition. I see them reflected in the windshield, faint and distorted, as though they're drifting away from life and not me.

I jump when I hear the engine start. Michael winds down the window and leans out, looking toward the motel. I see his face, one last time, as they slowly pull out of the parking lot.

This can't be it. Not already.

My legs move without me making a conscious decision for them to do so. Down from the roof, heading I have no idea where.

I'm thinking: *Michael.*

Then I hear a smashing sound.

It came from my bedroom.

I get there just in time to see MacKenzie hurling my favorite coffee mug across the room. It hits the wall with a dull thud. Old coffee sprays across my cheery, bright-yellow walls.

"MacKenzie!" I protest. "We painted those walls!"

There is a stifling, pungent scent of perfume hanging over the room; my bottle of perfume is smashed in one corner. Three different editions of Michael's book have been torn up next to it.

MacKenzie yanks my clothes from the wardrobe and then turns her attention to the bedsheets, the embroidered throw I was so proud of when I got it, my pretty blue cushions. She struggles to tear them in two, tugging, ripping, and biting until there are feathers floating through the air like snow.

"MacKenzie, stop!" I shout. "Stop this! You're destroying my *things*, for God's sake!"

But MacKenzie's eyes are fixed somewhere over my shoulder. I turn around and realize what she is looking at. My photos. Lovingly framed and neatly lined up on the dresser.

MacKenzie and me in front of the motel sign, sixteen years old and wearing ugly nineties jeans. She is wearing her flannel shirt, of course.

MacKenzie, Camila, Michael, and me on our way to prom. Me uncomfortable in my tuxedo and MacKenzie dressed, ironically, in a ball gown. I think we both wished that she had won the coin toss about who would wear a dress.

A picture from when the cabins were finished. I saved it purely because it was a picture of Michael and me, even though there are so many others in the shot that only my shoulder is visible. Still, I could see Michael and know I was standing right beside him, and every time I looked at that picture, I remembered our first summer together.

"No..." I say. "No, no, no."

The photos are in mismatched frames that I bought over the years. Minimal silver, flaking gold paint, black wood, sleek and elaborate; an odd mix that I thought looked homey. My very first home of my own.

I hold out my arms to protect them from MacKenzie, but she has made up her mind to destroy everything.

She hits the frames against the dresser, smashing the glass into huge, sharp shards, not caring that moments from my life are falling to the floor. Wooden frames snap into uneven pieces. A few of the photos tear with heartrending rips.

When she finally stops, the room is in chaos.

"Watch out for the glass," I say automatically, but I don't think I'd actually care if she cut herself right now. Half of the photos are ruined, and the others are in a sorry state beneath their broken frames.

I bend down and desperately try to pick them up, save them, put the pieces back together, but my fingers just grasp over and around and through them. MacKenzie has slumped down against the wall at the other side of the room. She is curled up with her arms around her knees and is rocking back and forth. She takes a deep, shaking breath, and then they finally appear: the tears.

I've never seen MacKenzie cry before. Not once. No matter what she's been through. Right now, a lifetime of tears is trying to escape. MacKenzie doesn't care that her nose is running. She doesn't even care that she's sobbing. Right now, she is as defenseless as a small child.

She says something, but her sobs are so violent and her breathing so unsteady that I only catch a few words.

"Never. You. Leave. Me. Never. Leave. Were."

She gasps for air. Squeezes her eyes shut. Wipes her nose with the back of her hand.

Says, "You weren't supposed to leave me."

This is how it ends.

A torrent of final memories. Chaotic, one on top of another, like pop-up windows that just keep on multiplying.

MacKenzie and I outside school on our first day. Her enormous coat. The way she had to shake her arm to get her hand free. Friends forever.

The scent of fresh wood and sawdust and warm grass. Michael and I, alone, back when being alone was a luxury. I'm going to call it the Redwood Cabin. A photograph in which only my arm is visible. One day, I'll leave all this behind.

Cheryl's smiling face, still tragically familiar but also terrifyingly distorted. A stand on Main Street, back when everything felt ridiculous. Pink sneakers.

MacKenzie's hard stare. MacKenzie, surviving. MacKenzie, finding her way back to herself. MacKenzie, taking me to the Dog Bark Park Inn. MacKenzie, never dreaming again.

We're all together, around the back of the motel. Michael and Camila are with us. One of those long summer days that never seem to end. The sun is on our arms and legs. We're tanned and covered in mosquito bites.

Together again.

CHAPTER 18

I Fly Like an Eagle

ONE MISSISSIPPI, TWO MISSISSIPPI, THREE MISSISSIPPI...

I'm still here.

As the streetlamps flicker to life, it all starts to feel like a bit of an anticlimax.

That's when I notice the lights on the road from town. They're like an uneven string of pearls: one first, then another, then a long dark stretch before the next light appears. They start appearing close together after that, in one long line.

Dolores's car is the first to pull in. She jumps out before Alejandro even has time to turn off the engine.

"Cookies!" she says. "How are people supposed to fill up on coffee and cookies! If they'd just asked, I could have prepared some food. It wouldn't have been any trouble."

"Maybe they didn't want..." Alejandro begins, but he immediately stops short.

"What? Is there something wrong with the food I make?"

"No, no."

"And wouldn't Henny want people to be full after her funeral? Do you think she'd want people to think that we're stingy? Or inhospitable?"

"No, no."

"Then stop talking and get frying! They'll be here any minute."

I stretch and lean toward the window. "MacKenzie? I think... It actually seems like I'm still here. Maybe we should go down and help out? If there are a whole load of people coming here, Dolores and Alejandro could probably do with a hand."

When Michael and Camila turn up in the parking lot, I can't hold back. I run down and follow them into the restaurant. MacKenzie will probably come down, too. I'm sure she will.

The kitchen is already a hive of activity. It seems perfectly natural that they're all so smartly dressed, as though Dolores always wears a black dress to press minced meat into burgers, and Alejandro would never dream of heating up the fryers if he wasn't in a suit, his camera around his neck. Camila pauses for a moment, then kicks off her boots and starts chopping onions in her stockinged feet. They're a team. They move around one another with the silent communication and instinctive understanding of dancers. A hand on a shoulder, a smooth movement behind a back, light footsteps, beauty in constant motion.

Then there's Michael. He is standing by the wall just inside the kitchen door, trying not to get in the way. He looks shell-shocked, slightly nauseated, as if barely surviving some kind of catastrophe.

His eyes are the only part of him that is moving. Beneath the sheer desperation, I can see something verging on warmth as he watches Camila, Dolores, and Alejandro move around the kitchen. It's a kind of goodbye, I think, and then he turns his back to all of them.

"Michael!" Camila shouts. She grabs his arm and drags him deeper into the kitchen. "They'll be here soon. Can you put on some coffee so we can serve that first, before everything else is ready? And when they get here, can you unlock the door? No point making them wait out in the parking lot." She pats him on the shoulder. "You might want to take off your jacket."

Before long, the others arrive. Acquaintances from the past, a couple of old teachers, people I haven't seen in years. Some I don't know at all.

I see Buddy and his friend Miguel, plus Miguel's wife, who I've never met. Two handymen who always eat lunch with us and whose names I don't know. They stick close to Buddy.

Clarence also shows up, with a couple of regulars from the bar. I hope they've brought their own hip flasks, because Clarence's doesn't usually last long.

They're here for my sake.

The psalms and uncomfortable black suits have left them depressed and subdued, and they breathe in the crisp autumn air as if they've just been released from prison. They relax when they realize that Dad isn't here, and I see several people undo the top buttons of their shirts and stuff their ties into their pockets.

The first few people in line hesitate, wallets in hands, but Dolores firmly waves away any offers of payment. She is still muttering "Cookies!" to herself.

The atmosphere in the restaurant soon becomes much cheerier. The aroma of Dolores's cooking drifts in from the kitchen, and Alejandro and Camila are running back and forth with plates.

"It was just how Henny would have wanted it," someone says ironically. "Especially the psalms."

"I'm sure Henny would have liked to hear something by Bruce," Buddy says, and by that point they can even laugh at the whole wretched state of affairs. Everyone but Buddy, that is. He was being serious.

Clarence pulls out his hip flask. *You drink, Clarence*, I think fondly.

Michael has rolled up his shirtsleeves and is walking around the room with the coffeepot. When it gets too hot inside, he goes outside and leans against the wall. The air out there is cool and crisp. His breath forms small clouds, and with no one looking at him, his face relaxes into tired hopelessness.

Camila follows him out.

"What are you going to do now?" she asks.

Michael shrugs. I don't think he can reply.

"Are you going to leave?"

"Henny loved this place," he says in spite of himself. "Not just the motel. This whole dumb town."

Camila nods. She waits in silence, but places a hand on his shoulder. I think what she really wants to say is that he isn't alone.

"I should leave," he eventually says. "There's really nothing worth staying for now. But I also can't get away from the feeling that I have some kind of unfinished business here. Like Henny still wants something from me. You probably think I sound like an idiot."

Camila slowly shakes her head. "No, I know what you mean. Sometimes I think I can feel her presence at the motel."

"So you're going to stay?"

"I don't have much choice. But yeah, I'm going to stay."

I smile. That's enough for me. And then I can't stay still any longer. I spread my arms and run around like I did when MacKenzie and I were kids, pretending we were eagles.

I'm trapped in rash, irresponsible happiness, a kind of quivering feeling in my chest; a spontaneous, swelling gratitude at everything there is to see and hear and smell in life.

I run around and around the parking lot. I circle the parked cars and do a lap of the whole motel. I'm still here, I'm free, and I gallop between the apple trees, the cucumber and tomato plants, eventually heading back to the parking lot.

MacKenzie should be here.

She has made her way down to the reception desk and is alone in the darkness. I stand next to her in front of the closed automatic doors, and we both peer over toward the restaurant.

"MacKenzie, you know you don't *have* to be alone like this, don't you?" I say. "And you definitely don't have to be standing in the dark. Okay, so you didn't go to my funeral. I don't know why you cared about Dad and Cheryl, but they're not even here tonight. Your friends are. At your motel, in your restaurant. Why aren't you over there with them?" I press my nose to the window.

But MacKenzie isn't listening. She is staring intently toward the restaurant, and when I follow her line of sight, I realize that Camila has come outside again. She wraps her arms around herself in the chilly air, and it's possible that she notices MacKenzie's presence, because she suddenly looks straight toward us in the dark reception area.

I glance back and forth between them.

Neither moves. Two women, both standing in darkness, watching each other.

Camila is first to look away. She takes a deep breath, as though something has just surprised her. There's an odd warmth in her eyes, a half smile on her lips. She is studying the motel with an understanding that seems to surprise even her, and looking at MacKenzie with something verging on tenderness. She doesn't seem to know what to do with these new feelings. She is frozen in the night, as unmoving as MacKenzie, though I suspect she is longing to keep her company.

MacKenzie's face says, *Don't ask. Don't even talk to me.*

So Camila doesn't. She just stays where she is, keeping her company from a distance.

CHAPTER 19

I Follow a Smile

I SWEAR THE SUN IS BRIGHTER, THE AIR CRISPER, THE AUTUMN colors more beautiful than ever. I'm pretty sure that never in the history of Oregon has there been a sunrise like this morning's.

And the most fantastic thing of all? There'll be another one tomorrow.

During breakfast, I stand with my nose in the coffee machine, breathing in the steam as the hot water hits the finely ground coffee. It's as close to a cup of coffee as I can get.

Dolores is alone in the kitchen, but she seems to be enjoying it. The funeral has set something inside her free. It's as if she is done with grieving and has given herself permission to get back to work. She whisks the pancake batter with strong, steady arms. Strips of bacon sizzle on the griddle. She cracks eggs to make scrambled eggs, adding salt, pepper, and a few handfuls of cheddar cheese—then another, just to be on the safe side.

I walk over to the griddle and breathe in the scent of the thick slices of ham keeping the bacon company. Perfect avocados become avocado butter. Huge containers of apple juice clink as ice cubes are added.

I might not be able to eat anymore, but isn't the smell of food almost as good as the taste?

Food I would like to eat: A sun-warmed tomato. A grilled cheese sandwich. Or a steak salad with dark, freshly grilled meat and crisp, fresh leaves. And nachos! A whole mountain of them, with chicken, I think, and jalapeños, sour cream, and cheese. Dolores's birthday breakfasts. I always looked forward to them with a certain sense of dread, because who can eat waffles and syrup, fried chicken, a breakfast burrito, scrambled eggs, bacon, roast tomatoes, toast, and cheap sparkling wine secretly blended with orange juice in a single sitting?

It was the most magnificent birthday of my life, the first one I celebrated after we started working at the motel. Juan Esteban warned that I had to eat everything myself, but it turned out that MacKenzie, Camila, Michael, and Derek were all more than happy to help out. Still, you should have seen my eyes when I thought I would have to eat it all on my own!

After breakfast, I walk into town. It's as if I want to reassure myself that it's still there. And it is!

There's the tasteful town sign, and there are the elms. All of the leaves are now brilliantly red, I discover. If I'm still here next year, I'll come over here every day to find out exactly when the first leaf changes color.

Pine Creek is so intertwined with my past that I almost manage to forget that I don't have a future. I see town the way it used to be: so big and confusing that every excursion became an adventure; somewhere it was perfectly possible for a ten-year-old girl and her best friend to get lost on one of its side streets. As children, we explored Pine Creek as though it was our very own kingdom. It grew with each new street we conquered, every shop we poked our heads into, every grown-up MacKenzie charmed.

As I pass the school, I can see myself and MacKenzie in the children playing in the sun. I think this kind of sunshine is the one I like most. Cold and bright and sharper than it is in summer. Like water in an icy stream. But then I start to doubt myself and make a mental list of my favorites:

A clear autumn day in late September. The first spring sun, when everything is pale and gray and the branches are bare, almost glittering in the sun. The confident July sun, one day after another, with the heat and light shimmering in the air. The sunlight that filters through a particularly big oak, the way it did when MacKenzie and I lay beneath Dad's tree, looking up at the clouds. The sunlight in winter is nice, too, I think, promising myself that I'll pay attention to it this winter.

I spend almost an hour on Elm Street, watching the people hurry by. Everyday life is like a play being acted out in front of me: harried mothers shopping with tired children, handymen grabbing an early lunch at Sally's Café, senior citizens moving slowly but surely along the street.

It's a little disappointing that the town's inhabitants don't seem to realize what a miracle it is to be alive, but maybe that's unfair of me. It's easy for me to say, being dead. I'm sure they have other things to think about.

I follow a smile all the way from Elm Street to Water Street. It starts with a seven-year-old girl who is out with her mother. The mother is half a step ahead of her, and the girl is constantly trying to catch up. I can see the mother going through the day's plans in her head, mentally rushing from one place to the next. The girl, on the other hand, is looking all around. Her eyes sweep over the people, the buildings, an empty plastic bag that needs to be investigated, a forgotten glove that has been carefully hung up on the branch of one of the elms. And, at some point in the middle of all of this, she smiles innocently and cheerily at an old woman with grandmotherly wrinkles, white hair, and a colorful knit hat.

I decide to follow that smile.

The woman passes it on to the young man packing bags at the supermarket, and he smiles genuinely, not just politely, at the next customer, a confused woman who is trying to keep track of her wallet, bags, and gloves. She is so focused on making sure she hasn't forgotten anything that she pays no notice to anyone around her, and I have to follow her for at least ten minutes. Then, just before she reaches Water Street, she looks up and beams at an elderly man with a dog.

That's where it dies out. The man grunts in response, looks down at the ground, and wanders off. He isn't going to look up and smile unnecessarily, I'm sure of that.

Dad is out in his yard. He's wearing a pair of pressed gray trousers, a pale-blue shirt, and a pullover. His movements are slow and dignified, letting everyone know that he is raking leaves in a sorrowful manner.

Cheryl and her husband are working in their garden, and Dad keeps trying to shield himself from her friendly offers of juice, coffee, or a warmer sweater.

He starts raking even harder.

Oh, Dad.

As I make my way back to the motel, all I can think about is the look in the smiling girl's eyes.

Wonder. That was what I saw. To her, the main street in Pine Creek is a big, exciting world, just like it once was for MacKenzie and me. I wonder when we stopped looking at the world with that kind of simple fascination.

Maybe we can learn to see things for the first time again, I think. Maybe we just need to pause and allow ourselves to remember how everything used to be.

So, when I get back to the motel I stand in the parking lot and look up at it. If I really focus, in this particular glittering sunlight, I can see it the way I did the very first time. Exciting. Enormous. The best thing ever to happen to us.

Pine Creek Motel. Vacancies.

The neon sign made everything new and exciting. And a tiny, tiny bit dangerous, even though it was the middle of the day and the motel was almost empty.

I had never stayed in a motel before. At sixteen years old, I had never even left Pine Creek.

It was a sunny afternoon in May, and MacKenzie had pulled up down the road from the motel, meaning we could look at it however much we wanted. She pushed a damp lock of hair out of her eyes.

"Look, Henny," she said.

There were only three cars parked outside, but MacKenzie studied them intently. Then she reached for a pen and paper from the glove compartment and wrote down: Montana. Washington, Idaho, and Iowa were already on her list.

"Cars from all over the country come to the motel," she said. "And we're going to work there."

Something new had appeared in MacKenzie's eyes, and looking back now, I know what it was: love at first sight.

This wasn't just another way for her not to have to go home at night; it wasn't just a fun part-time job. MacKenzie had fallen for this tired, horrible, weird place. Something completely new had appeared in her world, and I struggled to keep up.

But even MacKenzie hesitated as we stepped into the reception area.

After the bright sunlight, the room felt dark and drab. There was a lone fan struggling in vain against the heat, noisily pushing warm air around the room. I was painfully aware that we weren't here to check in and that we were only sixteen.

"We need to talk to the boss," MacKenzie said, and for some reason—maybe out of sheer curiosity at what this gangly teen with the confidence of an adult could want, maybe because MacKenzie had irresistible charm—the woman at the desk sent us up to Juan Esteban's office.

It wasn't like any other office I had ever seen. In my eyes, it was as big as a ballroom. The sunlight seemed to dance over the barely restrained chaos.

There were papers scattered across every free surface, and I could see a bucket of brushes and an unopened can of paint in one corner. On one of the bookcases, a tool belt lay ready to be worn. Juan Esteban was standing in the middle of it all.

He was short and thin and drowning in an old-fashioned suit with huge shoulder pads, but his personality filled the room.

His personality *was* the room.

Juan Esteban never stood still. During the minute or so that passed between us being shown into the room and him noticing us, he had picked up a piece of paper, given it a quick glance, put it to one side, picked up another, patted his jacket pocket. Then he swung around and saw us. His eyes were intensely dark, his hair thin and flecked with gray, sticking up in several different directions. His forehead was damp with sweat, but that was the only real sign he was feeling the heat.

"We want to work here," MacKenzie said. I think Juan Esteban must have been able to see something in her, because he instantly seemed to grow calm. That's the best way I can describe it. It was as if their restless energies spoke to each other.

MacKenzie looked him straight in the eye.

He nodded. "We'll give it a try. I'm assuming you want an after-school job? A few weekends a month? Just for the summer?"

"We both do," MacKenzie interrupted him.

Juan Esteban seemed surprised to see me, as if he had only just realized I was there. Then he waved a hand, as though I was a minor detail. One kid, two, it made no difference to him.

"Have you ever worked in a motel before?" he asked.

"No," said MacKenzie. I quickly shook my head.

"Neither had I when I bought this place. I promise you, it'll be the adventure of your lives. Absolutely anything can happen at a motel."

For a while, the evening sun colors everything a warm shade of golden orange, and as darkness falls, I'm still standing in the parking lot. I take three deep breaths and pretend that my chest is still rising and falling, that my lungs are still drawing in air. It feels like breaking the surface after you've been holding your breath underwater. I'm going to go in and see MacKenzie soon, keep her company while she works, and then I'll hang out with Camila. We can do whatever she wants, and after that I'll run over to the cabin to see Michael. It feels incredible to have time again.

I don't know why I'm still here, and I have no idea how long it will last, but I do know that I need to make the most of this second chance I've been given. The possibilities dance in the blue and red light of the parking lot.

I feel a stab of something, some kind of new energy, a purpose, perhaps. There has to be a reason why I'm still here, and I'll work it out sooner or later.

MacKenzie is alone at the reception desk. Her face is blank and exhausted. Her eyes are half-closed, her forehead creased, her cheeks hollow as though grief has taken up residence in her sinuses.

Things I *don't* like: blank faces.

"I wish I could make you see the world the way I do now," I say to her. She barely even looks up as Camila comes into the room.

Camila has prepared a speech. "Since I don't have anywhere else to be, I thought I could help out," she begins far too quickly, her voice trailing off when she notices MacKenzie's complete lack of interest.

She forces herself to continue. "But right now, I don't know how anything works. I assume things have changed since I worked here. I don't even know how our finances are doing."

"Pretty interesting."

"Or how the reservation system works."

"That's even more interesting."

I think Camila must be wondering whether MacKenzie is joking, but there isn't a hint of humor in MacKenzie's eyes.

"You must have a lot to do, now that Henny—"

MacKenzie interrupts her. "I can handle it," she says.

"But still..."

"Have you ever heard me complain? Did I ask for help?"

Camila looks away and then stubbornly decides to continue. "I'll do anything. Cleaning. The night shift."

"I don't need any help."

Things Michael and I will never do together: Go on a road trip. Argue about whose family we'll spend Christmas with. Move in together. We'll also never: Buy a dog together. Argue about whose turn it is to take it for a walk. Spontaneously surprise each other with flowers. Make a nice dinner for the other when they're tired after getting home from work. Decide to skip dinner and have sex instead.

The thought could depress me, but I decide to focus on the most important thing instead: I'm still here.

So, I move in with him.

It goes incredibly smoothly. I guess I thought it would be more difficult. More fighting about what should happen to one person's books and the other person's table and whose couch we should really keep.

But I just take my pretend box of pretend things and go over to the cabin and pretend to unpack.

I turn the whole thing into a kind of pantomime. Pick up the box. It's big, I imagine, even though I can't think what I would fill it with right now. Torn photographs, perhaps? In any case, I hold my arms wide apart, push the door open with my shoulder and shout: "Here's the first box!"

And then I stop dead in the living room with the pretend cardboard box in my arms.

Michael is moving restlessly around the cabin, as though he thinks that the answer to all of life's mysteries is in the next room. He kicks a pair of shoes out of the way by the front door, grabs two coffee cups from the living room, forgets what he's doing, and takes them with him into the bedroom.

I hurry after him. "Is it all right if I take one of the drawers?" I ask his back, unnecessarily cheerily.

Not that my imaginary clothes will take up much room. I'm stuck in my jeans and the blouse with the red polka dots, which I'm really starting to get sick of by now.

I sigh. I wonder if it counts as living together if one of us doesn't know about it.

Michael paces back and forth. The living room is the biggest room in the cabin, with the most floor space, but it's not big enough to be very satisfying to trudge around in. Michael has to swing around the sofa and dodge the little dining table on every loop. I stand by the window to keep out of the way. It's almost a relief when his phone starts ringing.

I can see that the name on the screen is *Julia*, and I have time to tense up before I hear the weary tone in his voice when he answers. Definitely not a girlfriend. His agent, it turns out.

"How are things with my favorite nerd?" she asks.

"I don't have time to chat right now," Michael lies. Time is all he does have. "Could we speak—" he begins, but Julia interrupts him.

"Why am I the only one who cares about your career?"

"I'm a geologist. My career is going fine, thanks. I don't need an agent."

"The fact you're even saying that shows how much you need me."

"What do you want, Julia?"

"I want you to write another book."

"I don't have any inspiration."

"Inspiration is for wimps. How hard can it be to find a couple of rocks to write about?"

"I...I just don't feel like talking about rocks right now."

I anxiously pat his arm.

"You need to strike while the iron is still hot," Julia continues. "Right now, people are interested in rocks. That's a fact, but it's not going to last forever. They'll move on and find some other obscure thing to obsess over. Maybe it'll be frogs, who knows? So you need to get a move on." Then, with a hopeful tone in her voice, she adds: "Where are you, anyway?"

"Oregon."

"That's not the right place for exotic rocks. Give me something *exciting*. I want you on some snow-covered mountain in South America or in the middle of the Canadian wilderness..."

"If there's snow on the ground, you can't see the rocks."

"You're going to make me age prematurely."

"Julia..."

"At least think up some interesting places? If you have a good enough idea, I can sort out a decent advance for you. Just write me a couple of pages. And whatever you do, don't fill it with a load of boring geological terms, all right? We want it to *sell*, don't we?"

With that, she hangs up. Michael stares irritably at the phone as if he wants to call her back and tell her what he thinks of *her* ideas.

Ultimately, that proves too much effort, and he takes out a notepad and obediently starts scribbling away: exotic places where you can find rocks.

He writes down the first place he can think of, along with everything he knows about it.

Aconcagua (Argentina, Andes). World's highest place of sacrifice. Subduction zone. Volcanic rocks: lava, breccia, pyroclastics.

Then he continues, sarcastically:

Brilliant idea! Travel to Saturn. Diamond rain. Guaranteed bestseller. NB: Explain to Julia that unfortunately the diamonds are uncut. Will that affect sales? Plan B: Become a diamond seller instead. Before leaving: Buy a sturdy umbrella. And rubber boots.

I smile. Michael once told me about the diamonds on Saturn. I was picturing glittering jewel raindrops before he explained that in actual fact, most of the rain there was rock.

"There's methane gas in Saturn's upper atmosphere, and the lightning storms transform it into soot particles. As the soot falls toward the hotter areas, the carbon becomes graphite."

"Pencil lead," I said. "You're telling me it rains lead?"

"Yeah, well, only for a while. After falling another 3,700 miles toward the gas planet, the graphite becomes diamond. They estimate that around a thousand tons of diamonds fall on Saturn every year."

"You'd need a pretty sturdy umbrella for that," I said thoughtfully. "Ours can barely even handle a light breeze, so they'd be no use against rocks."

"Uh," said Michael. "They actually don't know what happens to the diamonds as they near the core of the planet. The suspicion is that the conditions are so extreme that they can't keep their solid form and become liquid instead."

"And they say that diamonds are forever," I said, sounding disappointed.

"Not on Saturn. Maybe they've got a sea of liquid carbon up there."

"So you'd need a decent pair of rubber boots, too?" I said, and then he started telling me all about the problematic aspects of visiting one of the gas giants.

Michael tears out the sheet of paper, crumples it up with a clear sense of satisfaction, and sends it sailing into the air. Darkness has fallen outside, and when I peer out through the window, all I can see is his reflection. It breaks my heart to see him struggling on his own like this.

I turn my back to the window.

"Do you remember the first time we met?" I ask.

It was the summer I turned seventeen. If I could, I would have stopped time right there. I suppose that's what we like about memories. Looking back, we *can* stop time. The days don't move relentlessly forward, because all days have already been.

Others would probably say that nothing special happened that summer, and maybe they're right. It wasn't the summer of my first kiss. It wasn't the summer when I learned what love was, or the summer when I was teetering between childhood and adulthood. No one died. No dark family secrets were revealed, changing me forever. In fact, no one changed at all—myself excluded, possibly—and not even I can point to anything concrete and say: Look. Here. *This* happened, at the very least. Three perfectly ordinary cabins were the only clear sign that anything had happened.

I'm not even sure we were happy. It definitely wasn't complete happiness, if that even exists.

But there was a *promise* of happiness. Everything was new. Our hearts hadn't yet hardened. Everything was still possible.

The motel suddenly was buzzing with life and activity. Trees were felled and glades were cleared, and Camila, MacKenzie, and I battled with stumps and bushes and weeds until our hands were raw and our backs ached, and then the men arrived to build the cabins.

"I was terrified of those men," I say to Michael's back. "They had dirty nails and spat without warning and knocked back beers in under a minute, crumpling the cans afterward. But MacKenzie loved it. Of course she did. She got in among them until you could barely see her anymore—not surprising, given that everyone was a foot taller than she was. But she had enough balls to make them laugh. She asked them about fishing and hunting and made them tell increasingly unbelievable stories, until every one of them had caught a fish that was at least six feet long. Between the eyes. Caught it with their bare hands. Or their teeth."

It's as though I can see the air quivering in the heat. One of those heat waves where the asphalt burns beneath your feet and people worry about the old folks dropping like flies. Then there was the atmosphere. Something in the men's bodies. A frustration as tangible as their sweat.

They had already been forced to accept fewer hours at the sawmill, so it wasn't hard to convince some of them to swing by after work and build the cabins. When they weren't lying to MacKenzie, they were busy talking about past and future catastrophes. "There'll be more people laid off." "You don't mean that. What makes you think that?" "Maybe because this whole goddamn country is going down the drain."

The men were split into two camps. Those who thought everything was going downhill and would go to crap like it always did, and those who thought everything was going downhill and would go to crap in completely new, enormous ways. "No one will stay here once the sawmills are gone," one of them said. "People are stupid enough to stay anywhere," said a second. "People will always need wood," said a third. "Yeah, but they sure as hell don't need us."

"And then Juan Esteban hired Derek and 'a few other kids,'" I say to Michael. "And my life changed. Just like that. Do you remember?"

Derek Callahan.

A local legend. The football hero. The demigod. The natural focal point of every group, well known and celebrated wherever he went.

I don't say this aloud to Michael. I don't want him to hear the irritation in my voice. He always worshipped Derek. Instead, I say: "The news that Derek would be working here perked up the men better than beer."

He started one Monday or Tuesday in early July. I had already lost track of what day it was. At four in the afternoon, it was still unbearably hot, and everyone stuck to the shade. No one was working particularly hard. Dolores sent us iced tea and lemonade in sweating containers that clinked with ice cubes, and the men lowered their beers into the river to cool them down.

There were four high school kids tumbling out of Derek's bright-red pickup truck, but all eyes were on Derek. He was the stereotypical American teenager: sun-bleached hair, clichéd blue eyes, polite but cocky, with broad shoulders and a flat stomach and narrow hips that reminded the men that they had once looked like that. They were real men and had worked hard for their beer bellies, but even they had once been young and fit.

"Derek!"

"Derek Callahan."

"Yo, Callahan!"

That's what we heard the minute he climbed out of the truck.

They gathered around him, hitting him on the shoulder and thumping him on the back and saying that the Beavers would have to watch out, huh, with him on the team, the Ducks were sure to win, yeah, Derek, isn't that right, Derek?

"How did you decide which school to pick?" MacKenzie asked. She had secretly always cheered on the Beavers, but like everyone else in town, she was willing to change her mind. Derek thumped her on the back and said, "My little bro picked for me," and everyone laughed at the joke.

Juan Esteban knew nothing about football, but he understood people, and he knew how to transform his project into something great.

"Leisure time is the future," he said. "Leisure and football. That's the American dream, as close to freedom as most of us will come."

Derek nodded politely at Juan Esteban and hit one of his friends when the older man wasn't looking. Derek's friends were trying to stifle laughter, not that Juan Esteban cared, and I, well...I was looking at Michael.

He was tall and slim and could have been strong if he had been able to get his arms and legs under control. His hair was darker than Derek's and his eyes more reserved. They were the same shade of bluish-gray as the mountains at dusk, and there was something distant about them that also made me think of mountains. They could seem so close but still felt so far away, even as you moved closer. It was as if you could approach Michael for days without ever actually reaching him.

"Do you think that sounds ridiculous?" I ask him now. "Maybe. But that's how I felt. I couldn't stop looking at you, and I also couldn't explain why. With hindsight, I think it was just one of those rare moments in life when you know you've found your way home. You were like a clearing in the forest. You might not notice it at first, but you know it's been there all along. It was as if you'd been there, waiting for me. That's what it felt like. I'd been following a path, trudging along with no idea of where I was going, and suddenly I arrived."

Back then, there was nothing but pine needles and stubborn roots and piles of fresh timber where we're sitting now. People, too. A chaotic group of noisy men. Then there was me, who always ended up to one side. Suddenly, I could spend my time there watching Michael.

He didn't notice me. Not at first, anyway. He gazed admiringly at Derek, ignored Derek's friends, seemed interested in MacKenzie and fascinated by Juan Esteban.

"We're going to build cabins," Juan Esteban announced. "Fantastic cabins. People will come from all over the country to stay in these cabins. They're going to be the best cabins the world has ever seen."

Camila stood at the edge of the group with her arms folded. Michael looked at her, too. She shook her head at everything Juan Esteban said. She seemed ashamed of his enthusiasm, but MacKenzie loved it.

And then Michael's eyes moved on to me. He smiled, surprised, when he noticed me looking at him, and it struck me that he must be used to being in his big brother's shadow. Just as I was used to hiding behind MacKenzie. I wondered, in that drawn-out moment when his eyes met mine, whether he had chosen to live that way—as I had—or whether he actually longed to be seen.

Beside us, MacKenzie laughed at something Derek had said, and I looked away in embarrassment, suddenly aware of everyone around us. I knew that Michael was still looking at me. His gaze felt like a soft, cautious examination. It wasn't at all intrusive, not frightening, just surprisingly gentle. As if he wanted to suss me out without bothering me. As if he thought there was something worth approaching slowly and cautiously.

"Did you know that was the first time in my life I was grateful MacKenzie wasn't standing in front of me? And when you eventually looked away, I felt it immediately, like there was something missing from my skin. I wished I'd been more exciting or interesting. Enough so you would keep looking at me, at least."

That was another first in my life.

CHAPTER 20
The Dreams We Had

MACKENZIE IS ALONE IN ONE OF THE BOOTHS BY THE WINDOW when Camila slips into the seat opposite her.

"Tell me how the motel works," she says.

It's midmorning, and MacKenzie has a cold cup of coffee in front of her. The fluorescent lights on the ceiling make her skin look drab and her forehead creased. Maybe the coffee has given her a headache.

"You're not going to give in, are you?" she mutters irritably.

"Nope."

"I thought that working in a motel was pointless. Juan Esteban wasted his life. Nothing works. You hate this place."

Camila shrugs. A new determination has crept into her movements. "A woman can change her mind," she says.

MacKenzie sighs. "Fine, but don't come moaning to me when you're bored with it all." She leans back in her seat. "There are two ways to make money as a motel," she begins.

Camila leans forward.

"You can run it at such a high standard that people are prepared to pay more to stay with you. That means microwaves and coffee makers in every room. It's got to be spotless, with a nice check-in area, friendly staff. You employ people so you don't have to do everything yourself. If something breaks, you don't swear at it; you call someone to come and fix it. You could run a small, charming bed-and-breakfast, too—with individually decorated rooms, luxury breakfasts. The whole personal, charming thing."

"But why... I mean, what are the risks of that approach?"

MacKenzie almost smiles. "You mean why would anyone choose to run a cheap, shabby motel instead?"

"Uh, yeah."

MacKenzie glances around. The only other guest is a woman in her midsixties, with a bright-red sweater and a pair of glasses with thick, red frames. When she came in, she had said hello to Dolores in a clear, cheery voice.

"Excuse me, ma'am," MacKenzie says.

There are two plates of pie on the table in front of the woman. Life's too short to choose between apple and pecan, she had said as she ordered.

"Do you mind me asking you why you chose to stay at our motel?"

"I just needed to get a few hours' sleep. I set off a little late yesterday, and I saw you had vacancies as I was passing by."

"And if our rooms were twice the price?"

"Eighty dollars for a motel room?" The woman sounds indignant.

"Imagine it's a charming little bed-and-breakfast."

The woman looks embarrassed. "Honestly, honey, I probably would have slept in the car. I don't need a cutesy room. I'm on my way to see my granddaughter in Washington. She..."

This is followed by a half-hour pause in MacKenzie's lesson. The woman has a number of grandchildren scattered around the United States, it seems, and she eventually leaves the restaurant with a jolly wave.

MacKenzie continues. "Ultimately, there's a limit to how much people are willing to pay for a motel room. There's a limit to how much they can *afford* to spend on accommodations, period."

"You've never wanted to run a charming little bed-and-breakfast instead?" Camila asks. There is something that sounds like longing in her voice.

"What would I have done with the motel if I had? The other approach is to cut out any unnecessary expenses and compete by being as cheap as you can. People get what they're paying for, and that's what you can mutter if anyone complains. You only deal with the really urgent repairs. The bare minimum of general maintenance, too. If you can find relatives who are willing to work for room and board, that's a bonus. Otherwise, you do as much as you can yourself."

"Well, Juan Esteban managed to find one relative at the very least," Camila mutters, but so quietly that I don't think MacKenzie hears.

"Most of our guests just pass through. They need a place to stay for the night, nothing more. And then there are those who stay in a motel for weeks, because they have no place else to go. Some are new in the area, unable to find a place to rent long term before they've cashed a few paychecks. Staying in a motel is seldom cheaper than renting your own place, but we never require a deposit, and you can always check in right away. Juan Esteban never really liked those guests. Felt he was taking advantage of people's desperation. So we have a fixed, low-price option for people who need to stay here longer."

"Like Clarence?"

"Oh, he can afford it. Sold his house when the wife died. Has some sort of pension. Claims he saves money by living here, but I think he just doesn't like to be alone. Or possibly just likes to be able to drink full time without having to clean or cook for himself."

MacKenzie actually seems invigorated by the conversation. For a moment, I can see the old MacKenzie in her expressions and movements. The way she was before her defensive walls became so high, before I died, before all this. Somehow, Camila has managed to find the right thing to talk about. MacKenzie has always loved both the motel and the madness required to run it.

MacKenzie seems to be debating something with herself, but then she gets up and says, "Follow me."

"Where are we going?"

"You'll see."

They head upstairs. At the top of the stairs is a short, cramped corridor. On one side is the door into what used to be Juan Esteban's private apartment, where MacKenzie and I now live. Where I lived.

On the other is a door that has been closed for years.

"If you're going to stay, you'll need an office," says MacKenzie. She opens the door. "We haven't used it since Juan Esteban died."

"Jesus Christ," says Camila.

"You said you wanted to help. You can start by cleaning in here."

Juan Esteban's office has remained frozen in time, but it's unclear exactly which time that is.

An enormous computer screen dominates the desk, only marginally more modern than the typewriter. Brochures from the Cross Country Inn and other motel chains are spread out to one side of it, glossy and colorful, with convincing diagrams showing the benefits of joining the family. Everything is covered in a layer of dust.

Camila has changed into a pair of old jeans with holes in the knees and paint flecks on the thighs, plus a washed-out old T-shirt. She ties up her hair with a scarf and surveys the room in front of her.

She closes her eyes. Opens them again. The mess is still there.

"Right," she says. "I want you to know that you don't scare me. This is my office now."

I don't know if she's talking to the room or the spirit of Juan Esteban, but she immediately heads off to hunt for some cleaning products. That's one thing we have plenty of.

We keep everything in a large room beneath the office. None of the guests will ever set foot in there, so we haven't wasted any money making it look nice. The concrete floors are bare, and the shelves are made of untreated wood, barely even sanded.

Camila drags one of the cleaning carts up the stairs and swears quietly to herself. Then she heads back down for the vacuum cleaner.

The blinds in Juan Esteban's office work well enough, but the room looks even worse once she manages to open them.

A large faux-Persian rug covers most of the floor, possibly the only frivolous item in the entire motel. The bright reds and blues are dull with dust, even after she vacuums it.

It takes Camila several hours, but eventually the room is clean enough to be able to work in. The colors of the rug are visible again, and the big desk is gleaming in places.

The computer is a different story.

She grabs the huge screen and tries to haul it away, but it's heavy and wide and clearly evil. The cord keeps catching on things, the screen constantly threatening to slip through her fingers. She has to stop halfway down the stairs to wipe her palms on her jeans and readjust her grip. Her face turns redder and redder.

Outside, in the sun, MacKenzie is leaning nonchalantly against the wall. "If I were a gentleman, I'd offer to help you with that, wouldn't I?"

Camila's jaws are tense with effort. "Never. Thought. You. Were," she manages to mutter.

"That hurts! And I've just had a thought: Shouldn't I be worried that you're stealing motel property?"

"You said it yourself. It's my motel."

The computer screen slips out of Camila's hands and falls to the ground. "Crap," she says.

MacKenzie laughs and shakes her head. "Come on. Give it to me. I'll get rid of it for you."

Camila shakes her head, but she doesn't argue when MacKenzie takes one side of the screen.

"Where are we going?" MacKenzie asks.

"I don't know. Not too far. I guess we'll have to put it in my car until I can find somewhere to get rid of it."

"Put it in mine. There's a dumpster in town. I'll get rid of it later."

They haul the screen over the edge of the truck bed.

"Don't make me go back up to that office," Camila pleads.

"You're the one who said you wanted to help out."

"Did he never throw anything away?"

"Not during the last few years," MacKenzie tells her. "We vacuumed after he died, and his lawyer went through the papers we needed. But we just ignored the rest."

"Smart move."

MacKenzie leans in to Camila and runs a thumb across her cheek. Then she stops short. She freezes, her hand still right next to Camila's face.

Camila's eyes widen. MacKenzie's gaze keeps being drawn to her lips. The air around them seems to buzz with energy, as though they're surrounded by their own force field.

MacKenzie looks away first. "Dirt" is the only explanation she gives, taking a step back. She seems determined to put a reassuring distance between them.

Camila blinks in confusion and then heads back up to the office. As she walks, her fingertips brush the spot where the dirt was. MacKenzie watches her leave.

The office looks much better now that the computer is gone. Camila wipes down the rest of the desk, which leaves her with somewhere to work.

She sits down. The old desk chair creaks beneath her as if it's protesting at being used again after all these years.

"Right," she says to herself. "What the hell do I do now?"

MacKenzie is on her way to bed when she notices that the door into Juan Esteban's office is ajar. Moonlight streams in through the window, painting pale rectangles on the freshly scrubbed floor. The desk looks absurdly big now that it's empty. For a moment, she imagines she can see Juan Esteban in front of her, standing by the window like he used to, master of all the asphalt and concrete below. Then she spots Camila, who is sitting perfectly still in the middle of the floor.

I don't know how long she's been sitting there, but it must have been several hours—the sun set some time ago, but Camila hasn't bothered to turn on any lights. As I move closer, I can see that she has a book in her lap. I squint down at it, faintly illuminated in the moonlight.

The scrapbook, I think, moving closer. Yes, it is MacKenzie's old scrapbook that Camila is clutching.

The book is an old photo album someone left behind in one of the rooms. It's baby pink, with white lacelike patterns around the edges, and there was only one photo inside: a family portrait of a mother and two sons on a horrifying leopard-print sofa. The father is standing to one side, stiff and serious and wearing a Hawaiian shirt.

No one ever got in touch to ask for it back, so MacKenzie started using it herself. She left the picture where it was and made up fantastical stories about the family. She even imagined the adventures the Hawaiian shirt had been on before it found its current owner.

The rest of the album is now full of newspaper cuttings and yellowed leaflets advertising funny, unusual, or cool motels. Some have been neatly cut out, if there happened to be a pair of scissors at hand, but the rest have been torn. On some, parts of the neighboring articles have come along for the ride; on others, half the name of the motel is missing. Long-forgotten contexts and indecipherable half words. "We'll go here one day," she always said, but the only place we ever actually visited was Dog Bark Park Inn, and that isn't even featured in the album.

"Your old scrapbook," Camila says without looking up. "I remember you working on it the summer we built the cabins."

MacKenzie hesitantly sits down in front of her. "Why are you reading that old crap?"

"What happened to all the dreams we had?"

"The same thing that always happens with dreams," MacKenzie tells her. "We managed a few of them and forgot about the rest. People would go crazy if we weren't so good at repressing things."

"Did you ever go on your road trip?"

"It doesn't matter anymore."

"I wonder how many of these motels are still open."

MacKenzie takes the scrapbook from her and turns it over in her hands, with something that looks almost like tenderness. "Who knows," she eventually says.

"I've been thinking about Juan Esteban all day," Camila says.

MacKenzie nods, urging her on.

"It's strange, because I never let myself think about him after I left. I didn't think about anything relating to my teens. I thought I could just move on, but that's impossible, isn't it? Sooner or later, things catch up with you."

"I don't know," MacKenzie tells her.

"I wish I could have gotten to know him as an adult. Talked to him about life. Not that we ever talked when I was a kid; he was always too busy with the motel. But he moved all the way from El Salvador to Oregon and bought a motel in the middle of nowhere. I wish I could ask him how he managed to make a new life for himself like that. Didn't he ever look back?"

"'There's no point trying to fight fate. Better to save your energy for dealing with everything fate sends your way,'" MacKenzie quotes.

Juan Esteban was full of sayings like that. He was always eager to share his worldview, and MacKenzie was always eager to learn. Then again, he also said things like "Never work for the whites," and MacKenzie had to remind him that *she* was white. "No one's perfect," he replied with a wink.

Camila smiles faintly, but her eyes are worryingly glossy. "I...I didn't feel anything when I found out he'd died. I was *happy* about that. He was so far away, and I had my own life. And now it's like I'm grieving for both him and Henny. I should have come back sooner. I should've... I don't know. Cried when he died, I guess."

"It's never too late," MacKenzie tells her. "You grieve when you're ready. That's the good thing about grief. It's always there, waiting for you."

She doesn't sound especially grateful.

"I've cried more this week than I have in the rest of my life combined. I think maybe it's because of Henny. I can feel her presence here. Still." She swallows. "It's like she's daring me to feel things. But part of me *liked* not feeling things. This... MacKenzie, I don't know whether I like crying."

MacKenzie had tensed up when Camila mentioned my name, and now her face is irritatingly blank and closed off. But she surprises me by saying: "It's only because you've been crying alone. Cry away. There's always a shoulder here if you need it."

And so Camila cries. She buries her face in MacKenzie's neck and cries.

MacKenzie quietly takes a deep breath.

"It's all right," she says softly. "It's going to be fine. Everything will work out. I swear."

But I don't like the look in her eyes as she says it.

She doesn't think it applies to her.

I stay with MacKenzie that night. She lies on her back, staring up at the ceiling, and doesn't get any sleep.

"I can still remember exactly how you looked the first time we met," I say.

It was the first day of school. The building towered ominously, the enormous yard stretching out in front of it. I couldn't quite take in how many other children there were, and how terrifyingly confident they all seemed. They were running around, fighting, laughing, and being incredibly loud.

Then there was me, who still hadn't dared to leave Dad's side. I glanced up at him and realized, for the first time in my life, that he had no idea what we were meant to do, either.

MacKenzie was wearing jeans that were already dirty, even though the day had just begun, plus a gray T-shirt with holes in it and a coat two sizes too big. The cuffs hung way beyond her fingertips.

I stared at her, fascinated. In my world, clothes were never dirty or torn. I was smartly dressed in my purple leggings and clean sweater, and I stood obediently next to Dad while the others ran around.

MacKenzie walked straight up to us, shook her hand free from her cuff, and held it out to me. "MacKenzie Jones," she said.

I had never shaken anyone's hand before. "Henny," I said.

She shook Dad's hand, too. "Mr. Henny's dad," she said.

Then she grabbed my arm and dragged me off into the yard. "We're going to be friends," she announced. "I can feel it. I can do that sometimes. Feel things. Why isn't your mom here?"

"She's dead," I said, embarrassed.

"I don't have a mom, either, so we're a perfect match," MacKenzie continued. "We're going to be friends forever."

And we were. MacKenzie was like a force of nature, sweeping into my life and dragging me with her, whether I was ready for it or not. I was scared of everything, but MacKenzie didn't fear a thing. Or that's what I thought, anyway. I was shy and awkward, but MacKenzie could charm anyone. Even Dad liked her. Everything that happened in my life from that point on was, somehow, due to her.

"Sometimes, I think I probably would've stayed put at the edge of the yard if it hadn't been for you," I tell her now. "That lonely kid in purple leggings, her hair in bunches, while all the others ran toward their new lives. I think you were the engine that drove both our lives forward."

Aside from Michael, I think now. Michael was all mine.

"And no matter what happened, you could always make me laugh. Your laugh was always so fantastic. Deep and dark, like it started down in your gut and bubbled up out of you. I could listen to your laugh for weeks. It made me braver. *You* made me braver. Nothing bad could happen to me as long as you could laugh at it."

But MacKenzie doesn't laugh. I sigh.

I search for signs that she is starting to look tired. I hope she'll manage to get at least a few hours' sleep.

"I know you refuse to believe in any kind of higher plan, and you'd probably hit me if I came out and said that there might even be a meaning to my death. But that's just because you think that a meaning has to be something positive. You think I'm saying 'There is a meaning, so it's a good thing I died.' But I'm just as pissed off about the whole thing as you. What I'm trying to say is that if I *have to* be dead, and unfortunately it seems like that's the case, then...I want my death to mean something. I want it to shake the world to its core. Nothing should be the same afterward. You should be changed."

MacKenzie suddenly gets up. I do the same, and we stand side by side, each studying our reflection in the window.

"I know what you would say. You'd tell me that that's already the case. Your world has been shaken up. But that's precisely my point. Amid all the undeniably horrible things my death has done to you, I want there to be positives, too. One will do. Or maybe two. Right now, I think that the meaning of my death was to bring Camila back to us, so I hope you won't refuse to see anything positive in that. Because you can't imagine that anything meaningful or beautiful could come out of something so sad. There. I won't keep blabbering. Try...try to get some sleep, at least. I'll sit here until you do."

When I leave at dawn, she still hasn't quite dozed off, but she is at least in bed with her eyes closed. That might be as close as she gets these days.

I'm on my way over to see Michael when I hear a door slam in the Trembling Aspen cabin, and I pause and watch as a weary family with small children heads down to check out.

I stand in the glade around the cabin, thinking about how there used to be trees right here, and how one day, there will be again. We had to cut down so many of them to build the cabins, but nature is stubborn and has more time on its hands. Thin saplings have already started to grow, brushwood, too, plus a lone beech tree that suddenly found itself getting more sunlight once the pines came down.

It was MacKenzie who named the third cabin after the trembling aspen, and I think it was the drama of the colors and the movements that fascinated her. Camila named hers the Pine Cabin. And that was that.

The sun rises above the mountains, its light falling on the aspen trees growing down below. They're known as trembling aspens because their flat leaves quiver with even the lightest breath of air. Personally, I've always thought it looks like they're singing. There's something so frivolous about them that makes me think they could be cheerily humming to themselves in the autumn breeze. I think it's the bright colors. A whistling, burned-yellow sea in front of the sober gray mountains.

And then it's as though I catch the scent of fresh timber and sun-warmed grass. This is exactly where we were sitting, I think.

The work we did for Juan Esteban that summer was sporadic and irregular, but we didn't care. We carried the things he told us to carry; we kept out of the way if one of the adults told us to keep out of the way and spent the time in between chatting and eating.

Dolores sent out a never-ending stream of food: thick sandwiches full of ham and tomatoes and mayonnaise, fries, mountains of glossy red apples that only MacKenzie ever ate, coffee, lemonade, iced tea.

MacKenzie and I were sitting on the grass, waiting for something to do. The sun was beating down on us. MacKenzie picked blades of grass and tried to whistle with them, and Camila kept to herself. I still hadn't come up with a way to get closer to her, and MacKenzie didn't even try. Dolores was busy bringing the barbecue outside, so she could cook burgers in the middle of all the sawing and hammering, and Michael was standing next to Derek.

I couldn't stop myself from stealing glances at him. I was convinced everyone knew how I felt, but I still couldn't help it. I was unhappy when he wasn't nearby, and painfully nervous whenever he was. I wanted him to come over to us; I wished he had never shown up.

The sudden groundswell worried me. *Too many people*, I thought. It was easier when it was just MacKenzie and me.

When Derek started doing push-ups, Michael came over to me.

"Come with me, Henny," he said. "I feel like doing some work. We can carry a few planks of wood before lunch."

So, Michael and I started moving wood together, two planks at a time. The others had started to gather around the barbecue, leaving us alone by the foundations of one of the cabins. They would be named after types of trees, and Juan Esteban had promised that MacKenzie, Camila, and I could each name one. This was my cabin.

"Do you think you'll live here forever?" Michael asked. He looked at me as if he wanted to know everything I had ever thought.

"Yeah."

"There's nothing out there you want to see? Or, I don't know, achieve? It's a big world."

The planks were warm from the sun, and I carefully lowered my end to the ground. I didn't want it to get dirty.

"Do you know what I'm going to do after high school?" Michael asked.

I shook my head.

"I'm going to study geology. And then I'm going to travel. I'm going to explore the history of the world. I'm going to see rocks that are hundreds of millions of years old."

Michael made no move to head back to the others.

"Most people spend their whole lives in the place they were born," he said. "Like someone built invisible walls around their town or city. But the worst part is that there aren't any walls. There's nothing stopping us. We put up our own barriers."

"Are things always better somewhere else?" I asked.

"For some people here, they could hardly be any worse. But that's not the point. The point is that we don't know. Because we don't have the nerve to find out. Just look at all these men. Their hours at the sawmill have been cut back, but they're still here. They get fired, but they stay here. They get divorced, drink, suffer—and stay here."

The hamburgers were ready. The men always did everything with a hammer in one hand and a burger in the other. When Juan Esteban wasn't looking, they passed Derek a beer with a conspiratorial wink. "Just don't tell Coach Stevenson." I could hear them, but it felt like they were miles away.

"Not Derek, though," Michael continued. "He's going places. He starts preseason training in a few weeks, and then he'll be able to escape this town. College is only the beginning. He'll get to see the country. Experience things. Me too. I might not have football, but I'm going to get out of here. I want to see the world, Henny. I was born in Pine Creek, but no one is forcing me to stay put. I'm not going to serve a life sentence here."

I looked at him in surprise. "It's not a prison, Michael."

"Just look at the people here. It may as well be."

The air smelled like sawdust and dry grass, smoke from the barbecue and fresh timber, and I had no idea what he was talking about.

He can't mean it, I thought. *Not really. We had the river and the mountains behind us, and no one could look at all that and still want to leave.*

I gestured toward the half-finished cabin.

"I'm going to call it the Redwood Cabin," I said. No one else knew that, not even MacKenzie. "Do you know how redwood trees grow?"

"No."

"They can be over three hundred feet tall, almost thirty feet wide, and live for thousands of years."

"That much I do know," he said. Amused. He hit his hands against his thighs. Neither of us seemed to want to join the others. I tried to wipe my forehead on my arm when he wasn't looking.

"But they need very specific conditions to be able to grow," I said.

"You only find them along the coast, and they prefer to grow in valleys. Their roots are surprisingly shallow for such big trees, but they also interlink with other trees' roots. That's how they're able to withstand the weather."

I glanced at him to see whether he had understood what I meant. I couldn't read anything from his face; he could have been either skeptical or amused.

"They survive because they stick together," I explained. "I think people are the same. We can cope with a lot, but we're also surprisingly fragile. The only way to survive is to let your roots grow around other people's. Find a nice, sheltered valley and some other people to hunker down with. Why would that be any easier someplace else?"

"So you want to stay here because it's safe?"

I shook my head. That wasn't what I said. Not because it was safe, but because that was what we needed to grow and develop. We needed one another to be able to achieve things.

Michael wanted to go his own way, but I could tell, even then, that there was a longing within him that he didn't want to admit—even to himself. I could see it in the way he was constantly being pulled toward us, in the look in his eyes as he turned to us. He hungered for friendship. We all did. MacKenzie, Michael, and Camila—we would become friends and develop roots, and then none of us would ever want to leave Pine Creek.

I pause. That's it. We may have been torn apart by a hard, cruel world, but we've been reunited thanks to me. That must be the reason I'm still here. I've finally found my purpose. I have to make them happy again.

That's what *should* have happened. We should have stayed put and been happy together, and we *would* have been if it weren't for the town's narrow-mindedness. Then I think about Michael's determination to leave town long before the campaign even began. Maybe it wouldn't have changed a thing, but we would at least have had a *chance*. Maybe I would have been able to convince him to stay if it weren't for the Oregon Citizens Alliance.

But here we are, together again. And I'm going to make them happy.

MacKenzie, Camila, Michael. And maybe even Dad, I add out of duty. That's my list.

Four people. That doesn't sound unreasonable, does it? It's not like I'm demanding peace on earth or anything like that.

At one point in time, I knew them better than anyone. Better than they knew themselves. I'm sure of it. Not that they lacked self-awareness, but because they were so busy living that they couldn't see themselves.

But I could.

I wasn't distracted by life. I had no other dreams than to be right there with them, right then. I always just wanted what I already had, and maybe that did make me boring, but it also meant that I could *see*.

If I knew everything about them once, I can get to know them again, I think. Somehow, I have to work out what they need, and I know that the answer must be somewhere in our past. In the house of memories we built together and then let come crashing down.

Somehow, I need to make them remember how we were, and then I need to make them see what we could be. Maybe... I run back to the motel. I've got an idea.

I've tried talking to them while they're awake, and there have been moments when it almost felt like they were able to feel me there. But that's not enough. Maybe it'll be easier to get through to them while they're sleeping.

I start with MacKenzie, since I hope she will have dozed off for the last few hours before she has to get up. Whenever I've had trouble sleeping, I've always drifted off just before it's time to wake up.

She has actually fallen into an anxious, much-too-light sleep. Her eyelids are twitching, and there is a tense frown between her brows.

"MacKenzie," I whisper eagerly in her ear. "You're strong and free and invincible. You want to laugh and joke and go on adventures. You want to *live* again. You're tough and fantastic, and you can joke about anything."

I repeat those words to her, over and over again.

CHAPTER 21

MacKenzie "Jack Daniels" Jones

THE NEXT MORNING, MACKENZIE DOES SEEM TO HAVE A newfound sense of energy, but there is also a hint of something dangerous glittering in her eyes. Something as hard and brittle as glass.

She grabs her jacket in passing, strides across the parking lot, and walks straight over to...a trash can? She bends down, rummages through it, and pulls out an empty vodka bottle and six crumpled beer cans.

She doesn't look happy, not really, but her restless frustration does at least seem to have found a new outlet. I join her as she drives to the liquor store on the way into town.

When she emerges from the shop, she has a quart of extremely cheap whiskey in her hand.

She immediately pours half the bottle into the flower bed.

That doesn't surprise me; MacKenzie takes her whiskey seriously and would never drink that brand. No, what really surprises me is that she saves half. She is on her way back to the car with the bottle in her pocket when she stops dead and turns around. She heads back over to the row of shops.

The trash cans out back prove to be a veritable gold mine: another empty vodka bottle, seventeen beer cans, and a small bottle of gin. MacKenzie grabs a bag and drops her new finds inside.

What the hell are you up to, MacKenzie? I think to myself.

After that, we drive toward town. The car smells of stale beer and gin, and we both hum along with Bruce Springsteen. I stick my head out the window, and we both sing along, loudly and sincerely, about the promise we made to never retreat or surrender.

MacKenzie parks up on Water Street, carefully scanning all around before jumping out of the car and running over to Dad's trash can, into which she quickly empties all of the empty bottles and cans.

She throws herself back into the car, drums the wheel in time with the music—"blood brothers in the stormy night with a vow to defend"—and does a sharp U-turn off Water Street.

If she has a plan, I have no idea what it is, but she's clearly pleased with how this first step has gone.

By lunchtime, she is parked outside Hank's, ready to intercept Dad on his daily walk.

"Mr. Broek!" she shouts.

Dad looks uncertain. Uncertain and incredibly tense. He automatically straightens up, the way he always does when he doesn't know how to act.

"I just wanted to apologize for the other day," MacKenzie says. Her voice is warm and humble. "I don't think I showed enough understanding for your situation."

Dad looks even more troubled now, and for good reason. MacKenzie apologizing! When *he* was the one who said all those terrible words. I still haven't forgiven him for that.

"Aha, yes, well..." he says. He can't meet her eye. "I don't suppose any harm was done."

MacKenzie takes Dad's hand and shakes it enthusiastically. So hard that Dad's arm and coat flap around, and in the general confusion that ensues, she gently slips the half-empty bottle of whiskey into his pocket with her free hand.

She pats him on the shoulder and then heads back to the car.

I'm curious to find out what MacKenzie's plan is, so I spend a few hours just hanging around in town. Making my way over to Dad's house, I hear Cheryl's upset voice from her living room.

I pause for a second before tiptoeing over to her garden and pushing my way through the flower bed. I'm in the middle of a rhododendron bush, stooping beneath the open living-room window, and when I stand up straight, I see Cheryl pacing back and forth in front of her couch.

Her husband has a thick book open on his lap and doesn't quite seem to have given up the prospect of being able to continue reading. His entire face radiates a kind of gentle patience, from his deep-set eyes and tragically ugly glasses, and he wears his lopsided, homemade sweater with a refreshing lack of self-awareness.

"He stuck his hand into his pocket and pulled out a bottle of whiskey, right in front of everyone! Poor Harrison looked shocked, let me tell you. It was open, too! It was obvious that Robert had already taken a good few swigs from it. He pretended he had no idea where it was from. 'It's not mine,' he said as if a whiskey bottle could just appear in his coat pocket. He couldn't even come up with a better lie!"

Cheryl's husband closes his book, keeping a finger inside to mark his place. "What should he have said?" he asks. "'It's not mine; it's for a friend'?"

"Well, that would have been more believable than a whiskey bottle magically appearing in his pocket."

"Better than a rabbit in a hat," Cheryl's husband says. I've always suspected that he has a good sense of humor.

I raise my head a little higher.

"Whiskey! The man has never touched a drop in his life, I could have sworn on that, but grief does strange things to people. And he has been a little...overwrought lately."

"If you ask me, he's been overwrought his whole life," Cheryl's husband says, and Cheryl smiles reluctantly.

Oddly enough, MacKenzie devotes a lot of time to denying the rumors about Dad's alcoholism. She generally stays away from town, and she definitely avoids the people living there. After the vote, she reached a kind of cease-fire with them. It wasn't quite peace, and she hasn't forgiven them, but she learned to live with the townspeople by pretending they simply didn't exist. Her world was the motel. She might have gone to the bar or the grocery store or the post office from time to time, but that was all.

But now MacKenzie even stops to speak with Dad's neighbors when she runs into them outside Hank's Restaurant.

"You've heard about Robert?" the neighbor asks. "We're worried about him. We really are."

"Of course Robert doesn't have a drinking problem," MacKenzie says. Then, unfortunately, she adds: "Everyone enjoys a drink from time to time."

The next day, to a new neighbor: "Isn't it understandable that he might want a stiff drink every now and then? If people want to drink vodka out of coffee cups in their own homes, aren't they free to do that? Robert is the last person who'd have a drinking problem."

The neighbor's eyes glitter. "Vodka in coffee cups...?"

"Pfft, he wasn't even drunk." MacKenzie pauses for effect. "Slurring a little, maybe, but hardly *drunk*."

Cheryl is prepared to do whatever it takes to save Dad from himself. She knows her duty, and no one could ever accuse her of not giving her all to save a friend's body or soul. I can see her filling up with more and more Christian compassion with every bottle that mysteriously appears in Dad's life.

Eventually, she decides to confront him.

They're drinking coffee in his kitchen, and everything is perfectly normal until Cheryl says, "Robert—and I'm saying this as your friend, so don't take it the wrong way—we need to talk about your drinking."

Dad stares at her.

He isn't even angry, he's so shocked.

"My *what*?"

"Your drinking," Cheryl says firmly. "I know that Henny's death has hit you hard. I *understand* that, I really do. It must be so tempting to escape and avoid having to think about it, to be free and relaxed and have fun..."

Her voice trails off, and then she finishes firmly: "But drinking is not the solution. Believe me. It's part of the problem."

"I don't drink," Dad says. "I don't know where you've gotten this from. If it's about the bottle I found, I've already told you it wasn't mine. I was as surprised as you."

"But, Robert, there were three empty vodka bottles in your trash! Just this week!"

"Have you been going through my trash?"

Cheryl is too absorbed in her mission to feel any shame. "No, the trashman noticed the clinking, and he told Bill, who told... Look, it doesn't matter. The point is, you have a problem. You need to admit that to yourself."

"They weren't mine!"

"Those ones, too?" Cheryl says, her eyebrow slightly raised. "Denial," she whispers to herself, shaking her head.

It's only then that Cheryl's words really sink in. The color drains from Dad's face. His hands, clutching his coffee cup, start to shake. "The trash man and Bill and... They've *all* been talking about this? Is that why everyone has been giving me such strange looks? Because they think I've got a *drinking* problem?"

"We're worried about you."

"Just leave me alone."

"But, Robert!"

Dad glares at her.

"We can talk more about this later," Cheryl quickly says.

Once she has gone, Dad buries his face in his hands.

"The *trashman*," he mumbles to himself.

Dad is now refusing to leave the house.

He checks the trash every day to make sure no new bottles have appeared, but he does it in secret. Every time he goes outside, he checks the street to make sure none of his neighbors are nearby. Cheryl calls, but he doesn't pick up. When she knocks on the door, he refuses to answer.

Instead, he sits alone at the kitchen table, dwelling on the catastrophe that has struck him.

"Come on, Dad," I say. "It's just a joke."

Though when I really think about it, both MacKenzie and I know what Dad thinks about jokes.

Jokes are the reason Dad stopped liking MacKenzie in the first place.

We had just started high school, and it was time for one of the many introductory icebreakers where you talked about your name and what it meant. I obediently got up and explained that Henny was an old European name, a variant of Henrietta; I said that I was named after my father's grandmother, a woman he adored. She and her seven children had moved from the Netherlands in the late nineteenth century, and, as my grandmother always said, they didn't lose a single one along the way.

I had just finished when MacKenzie stood up and added: "Or at least that's what Mr. Broek claimed to get Mrs. Broek to go along with it."

Everyone looked up at MacKenzie in confusion. Even Buddy, who was the most disruptive boy in class.

"You might not be aware of this, but there's a famous cognac that people call Henny."

Buddy was definitely looking up at MacKenzie now.

"Hennessy, her dad's favorite. Mr. Broek thought that if he named his baby after it and sent them the birth certificate, they'd give him a lifetime supply in return. Or a couple of bottles, at the very least. Sure, he was pretty disappointed when he found out that wasn't true. But it was nothing compared to how *my* dad felt when he heard about the idea. 'Goddamn it,' he said. 'If I'd known that, I would've called you Jack Daniels.'"

Dad didn't appreciate *that* story when it eventually was relayed back to him. "Named after a cognac!" he cried in dismay. "How could she say such a thing?"

I tried to explain that MacKenzie hadn't meant any harm by it. Everyone knew it was just a joke. She wasn't even making fun of us—the joke was meant to be on her own father. But Dad never looked at her the same way after that.

And if he didn't appreciate a harmless joke in high school, I don't want to know how he feels right now.

Though, at the same time, another part of me thinks that maybe he shouldn't have been so awful to MacKenzie.

Eventually, he has no choice but to go out and buy food. He chooses a quiet afternoon when most people should be at work, but he still doesn't manage to avoid them entirely. The woman three houses down waves cheerily from her kitchen window as he passes.

She leans out through it, so that all he can see are her unbearable grinning face and her gray hair.

"Robert! I just wanted to say that I spoke to MacKenzie the other day, and she reassured me there was no way this rumor about you having a dri— Robert? Robert! Where are you going?"

Dad has already hurried off down the street.

There are two old men chatting outside the grocery store, and Dad recoils as though he is convinced they're gossiping about him.

He snatches a basket and throws things into it as he passes, without once pausing to check his list or compare prices or read the small print on the ingredients list, as he always does otherwise.

When he turns the corner to the vegetable section, he almost crashes straight into two women. They live one street over from him and immediately stop talking when they see him. Dad heads for the checkout without even remembering to buy milk.

He anxiously glances over his shoulder and throws money at the poor young teenager behind the till.

Freedom is within reach.

He'll be back in the safety of his own home soon enough.

Unfortunately, however, Clarence is in line right behind him, with a six-pack of beer in his hand. While Dad is waiting for his things to be packed up, Clarence turns to him and tries to be comradely by saying: "Sometimes you've just got to drink to cope with this life, am I right?"

Dad flees.

He doesn't even take his things. He hurries through the automatic doors and almost runs straight into an elderly woman making her way inside.

The boy from the till runs after him.

"Sir!" he shouts, holding up the two forgotten bags of food.

But Dad is already halfway down Elm Street.

CHAPTER 22

Nothing Works in This Place

MICHAEL AND I ARE SITTING OPPOSITE EACH OTHER IN THE restaurant. The breakfast rush is over, and he has an entire booth to himself. He has his computer and notepad with him, and I tell him all of the latest about Dad as he works.

It feels good just to be able to sit here and talk to him. This is exactly how it would have been if, well, if things were different. He would have been hard at work in the restaurant, and I would have interrupted him by stopping for a coffee.

I smile. I'm sure he wouldn't have minded.

Michael suddenly starts writing. I get up and move over to him so that I can read over his shoulder. *Remembering Henny*, he has written at the top of the page.

He pauses, the pen still in his hand. Over by the counter, Alejandro is trying to take a picture of one of Dolores's dishes, but Michael hasn't noticed. He stares out of the window as he thinks, and then he continues writing:

Get to know the person she became after I left.

See this dump of a town through her eyes.

"Uh, you might have a bit of work to do there," I say.

He hesitates before reluctantly adding one last point: *Get to know my family.*

It's hard to be sure, but I think Joyce feels more confused than anything when Michael goes over to their house. She doesn't show it, but something in her eyes makes them seem even emptier than usual.

Michael had wanted to start with Derek, but unfortunately neither he nor Stacey were home. They live in a separate apartment in his parents' house, and Michael felt like he didn't have any choice but to pop in and see his parents now that he was already there.

"I was just passing by," he says.

"How lovely," Joyce replies without any enthusiasm whatsoever. Still, she opens the door wide enough for him to step inside.

The kitchen is full of warm, rustic colors, but it's too big to feel either personal or cozy. There is a functional wooden table in the middle of the room, surrounded by what seems like an endless amount of counter space.

They sit down opposite each other, a sea of polished wood between them.

"How about a cup of coffee?" Michael eventually suggests.

"How lovely," Joyce says, but she doesn't move.

Michael gets up and searches the cupboards for some coffee. At least half of them are completely empty, and the rest contain roughly the same number of stainless-steel pots and Teflon-coated frying pans as we have at the motel. One of the cupboards contains enough canned food to survive an apocalypse.

Michael finds a pack of instant coffee and decides to make do with that.

"Okay, then," he says.

"How lovely," says Joyce.

"How are things, Mom?"

Joyce gives him a blank look.

"And Dad?"

"Your father is always fine."

Joyce is perched on the very edge of her chair. She is thin and slender-limbed and looks more like a deer than anything, always primed to run. Her hands are in her lap, but she doesn't seem relaxed. It actually feels more like she has no idea what to do with them. Her coffee is untouched on the table in front of her.

"Any plans for the fall? I still don't know how long I'll be staying."

"How lovely." Her voice is weaker now.

"Mom...have you always been sure what you wanted in life? You never doubted where you were headed or wondered whether you made the right decisions?"

"Oof," Joyce says. She is out of her chair before I even have time to process her getting up.

"I have to make lunch," she says, picking a door at random. Unfortunately, it leads into the living room.

Just a second later, the front door swings open. I hear Derek's heavy, energetic footsteps in the hallway. "Mom!" he shouts. "I just need to borrow..." He peers around the kitchen, taking in Michael and the two coffee cups. "Where's Mom?"

"I think she ran off into the living room," Michael says, confused.

"What did you do?"

"Nothing! I was just trying to get her to talk about her life."

"Nothing, you say," Derek mutters sarcastically, shaking his head. He takes Michael by the arm and pulls him over to the front door. "Michael and I are leaving now!" he shouts over his shoulder, shoving Michael outside.

I think I hear Joyce's voice before the door swings shut behind them. It sounded like she said "How lovely."

"Just so she knows it's safe to come out," Derek says.

"What did I do?"

"Mom doesn't like talking about herself." He pauses to think. "Mom doesn't like talking about anything."

He jumps into Michael's car, and Michael stares at him in confusion.

"Drive toward Elm Street," Derek tells him.

Michael seems much more relaxed with Derek than he was with his mother. He might hesitate for a second at being bossed around, but there is something so irresistible about falling back into the old childhood habit of following Derek. I sit down in the middle of the back seat so that I can rest my elbows on their seats and still be able to see them. Michael shakes his head at himself, but he is smiling, too, and I guess he must be thinking of all the times he followed his tough big brother on adventures.

"How long has Mom been switched off like that?" he asks.

"Has she ever liked reality? Why did you have to ask her about things? You know she doesn't like thinking."

"I guess I knew that at one point in time." Michael sounds hesitant. "But I don't remember it always being this way. Shouldn't we do something?"

I wonder whether he is thinking up a new point for his list. *Stop Mom from being so switched off.*

"Why?" Derek asks. "If you ask me, Mom's the happiest person in this family."

"She ran off into the living room!"

"What's wrong with running away from things? It's a talent. Mom's definitely the smartest of all of us, not that that's saying much."

Derek continues: "She might be switched off, and her social skills might leave a lot to be desired, but in her own little way, she manages to leave this town and reality and what the rest of us call life. She does it all the time. I've never done it, Dad's never done it, and I doubt you've had much luck with it, either. We've had far more opportunities than Mom to get away from here, but she's the only one who's really managed it, and it's all due to her internal resources."

"Internal resources?"

"You should come over here one day and see her staring straight ahead. She's the Mariota of escaping reality."

Typical Derek to use a football player as a sign of excellence.

"She should write books," Derek goes on. "Host a TV show. The art of not giving a damn and still smiling at everyone. If booze could switch me off like that, I'd never be sober."

"You think she secretly drinks?"

"Not Mom, no. But the rest of the family probably do."

"And you? How've you been? Are you, uh, happy with your life?"

"For God's sake, Bro," Derek begins, before changing tack. "Crap." He slumps as low as he can in his seat and hisses: "Just keep driving."

It's only once we reach the next intersection that he turns and looks back.

"You think he saw me?"

Michael glances in the rearview mirror. Coach Stevenson is standing on the sidewalk on Elm Street, shouting and shaking his fist in the air. We can't hear what he's saying, but his face is bright red and twisted in anger. As though we were some kind of idiotic referee in a football game.

"Think so," Michael says drily.

Derek shrugs philosophically and sits up straight again. "Oh well, we got away," he says.

Michael turns to his brother. "Since when do you have to hide from Coach Stevenson?"

"Since he started sharing how unhappy he was with an order he made through me. It should've been a good deal," he adds indifferently. "I ordered team shirts from a company in China. I double-checked the spelling of every name several times. The foreign companies aren't always great at American surnames. But everything was right!"

"So why's he so angry?"

"They were a little on the small side. To put it mildly." Derek can't help but laugh. "They probably would've fit the kids' team."

Michael doesn't see the funny side of the situation. "You can't keep hiding from him forever," he says.

"Are you kidding? That's exactly what I'm gonna do."

"But it's Coach Stevenson. He worshipped you."

"Yeah, well, times change."

"Never thought of getting a normal job?" Michael's voice is excessively nonchalant, and I can tell that he is shaken by what Derek has become. He didn't see it happen gradually like I did.

"And what kind of job would that be, huh? Stacey would be beside herself. She's been going on about it ever since we got married. I'm not going to give her the satisfaction. You can drop me off here."

They are driving by a small side road with no signs.

"How are you going to get home?"

"I'm sure Jim'll give me a ride. There are still a few people in town who like me."

Michael drives back to the cabin and immediately turns his attention to his project. He makes coffee, throws his notepad onto the table, grabs his pen, and gets to work. He writes, strikes through, tears out a whole page, thinks, starts over. I'm sure he's working on the list to avoid thinking about what Derek's life has become. Michael is still determined to take charge of life using lists.

I pat him on the shoulder and head off to the motel to see how MacKenzie is doing. I spot a cleaning cart outside one of the rooms and find her inside. Before long, Camila joins us.

She sits down on the bed while MacKenzie cleans the bathroom. She is wearing a white, low-cut shirt today, with jeans, boots, and a new sense of determination.

MacKenzie is wearing a hoodie, a loose pair of jeans, and tiredness. I think it's the scent of Camila's perfume that she notices first, spiced and strong and fresh, a kind of tough sexiness that mixes with the smell of bleach.

When MacKenzie emerges from the bathroom, Camila crosses her legs, leans forward, and eagerly says, "We can do more with the motel."

"Uh..." MacKenzie replies. Her eyes are drawn to Camila's low-cut top.

"We both know you're not as indifferent as you pretend to be. You *care*."

MacKenzie forces herself to look up. "Do I?"

"Yeah. You love this old place. You still care about the motel."

"Ah. The motel."

"So we should be able to do more. Redo things. Make it *ours*. It's not Juan Esteban's motel anymore." She looks out of the window and smiles. "We could even buy a new sign. Something more...uniform, maybe?"

MacKenzie isn't smiling. "Camila, you can do whatever you want," she says.

"Yeah, but I don't want to do it alone. I don't want to take over your motel. I want to do it with you."

For some reason, MacKenzie blushes.

"If you really want to do all that stuff, you should do it," she says. "I mean it when I say the motel is yours. No, let me finish. I'll try to help out, but I don't know if... I don't know if I can bring myself to be enthusiastic about it. I don't know if I have the energy to be enthusiastic about anything right now. I don't feel anything."

Some of the glow disappears from Camila's eyes. "I understand," she says, looking away.

Her words don't really seem to reassure MacKenzie. If anything, she looks disappointed. "All right," she says, as though they have agreed on something.

"I know that you don't want to feel anything," Camila says stubbornly. "And that's okay, of course. But if we have to work here, we may as well do it properly. Things are starting to happen. I can feel it. We should be able to do more. *I* can do more."

MacKenzie throws the dirty towels into the laundry basket and grabs some fresh ones from the folded pile on the cleaning cart.

Camila gets up and steps to one side so that MacKenzie can strip the bed. "I know I was only an assistant at the construction firm, but in reality I was left in charge of most things. When there weren't any on-site emergencies going on, my boss preferred to spend his time trying to write movie scripts. Administration really wasn't his thing. So I dealt with the accounting firm that looked after our books. I got them all the documents they needed, kept an eye on the cash flow, the accounts receivable and accounts payable, and I did most of the day-to-day discussion with clients and suppliers. Howard was a little...inconsistent. Unstructured."

"So you had to deal with everything?"

Camila shrugs. "Howard gave his staff really generous health insurance. It covered my transition, and he let me take time off when I had my operations. That creates a certain sense of loyalty. There are so few trans people who get that kind of support from their employers, so I was grateful. Howard is generous by nature, and he was friendly as long as it didn't require any personal effort from his side. I think he just thought it was easier to be cool."

The room is so small that they have to stand right next to one another, hemmed in by the chair in the corner, the bed, and the window out onto the parking lot. I'm on the other side of the bed, pressed up against the wall.

"Still, it must've been asking a lot of him to let you take time off," MacKenzie says. "If you looked after so much of the business."

Camila laughs. "I found my own temp and taught her how everything worked before I left. I'm not sure he even noticed I was gone. Maybe he just called her Camila the whole time. But the point of telling you all this is that I do actually know quite a lot about running a business. If I could take a look at our accounts, I can see whether I can come up with anything. Who knows? Maybe I'll have a few ideas."

"If you want to go through boring numbers, why not?"

"Only if it's all right with you."

"It's your motel. Knock yourself out."

Camila spreads out balance sheets and profit-and-loss statements on the desk in front of her. I'm perched on the one small corner that isn't covered in piles of old folders and printouts.

She starts methodically, twelve years back. Skims through the reports. Moves on to the next year. After making her way through all of the folders, she gets up, stretches, grabs another cup of coffee, and starts over. She finds a notepad in our unsorted pile of cheap office materials, plus a pen advertising some kind of salvage company, and starts going through the files properly. She jots down a word or a figure from time to time, chews on the pen, and then moves on.

Once she is finished, she finds MacKenzie in the parking lot. The hood of MacKenzie's car is up, and she is hunched over the engine. She stands up as Camila approaches, oil and dirt on her cheek. Camila reaches out and wipes it away with her thumb. "Dirt," she says with a smile.

MacKenzie bends back down to the engine, but I'm sure I saw a flash of red on her cheeks.

"Did you find anything in all the figures?" she asks.

Camila leans against the car. "What happened three years ago?"

"What do you mean?"

"You had unusually high staff costs. For eighteen months. Did we have an extra employee then?"

MacKenzie reappears from beneath the hood. "Worried I've been embezzling your money?"

"MacKenzie!"

"I mean, you *have* been away a long time. Maybe the temptation got to be too much for me. I raised my own wage and opened a bank account in the Cayman Islands so that I can retire in the sun..."

"The staff costs weren't *that* high."

"I should have taken more, is that what you're saying? But as you said, we have such small margins..."

Camila hits her on the arm. "Come on. I'm just curious about the reason. And just to be clear, I wouldn't have had anything against you taking the money and running off somewhere warm. You should have *something* to show for working so hard all this time. Though I guess I would've been annoyed if you hadn't taken me with you."

"You, me, a beach, some palms..."

"*Heat*," Camila continues. The sun is shining, but there is no warmth in it. She shivers in the cold air. MacKenzie nods toward her jacket, which has been slung onto the roof of the car. It's too small for Camila, but she drapes it over her shoulders.

"Well, I don't want to disappoint you," MacKenzie says, "but unfortunately I don't have an account in the Cayman Islands."

"I won't bother chatting you up, then," Camila mumbles under her breath.

"What did you say?"

"Nothing. So what did you do with the money?"

"Dolores was sick. She had to stop working for a while. Even with the health insurance we had, we weren't sure she would be able to keep the house."

"Jesus, was she all right?"

"She's back in top form, as I'm sure you've noticed. Still has the house, too."

"So you hired a temp to cover for her, or...?"

"We raised Dolores's wage."

"By how much?"

MacKenzie shrugs. "One hundred forty percent."

"But that... So much... How did you manage to break even? I know you increased your staff costs, but not with anything close to that much."

"Oh, Henny and I took a pay cut. It's like Henny said, she needed the money more than we did. And it all evens out in the end."

MacKenzie wipes her hands on an old handkerchief. She closes the hood of the car with a firm thud. "I know what you're thinking," she says.

"What?"

She pats the car. "Nothing works in this damn motel."

Camila gives MacKenzie a strange look. "Right," she says. "That's exactly what I was thinking."

By evening, a number of new points have appeared on Michael's list. There are several sheets of paper spread out across his table, and it looks like he has decided to get Derek's life in order. I guess he feels like someone has to. He has dismissed the idea of finding a job for his big brother but is determined to smooth things out between him and Coach Stevenson.

On another sheet of paper, Michael has made a list of people to speak to about me. MacKenzie, Camila—even though she's been away for so long—Dolores, Alejandro. Even Buddy and Clarence, mostly because he knows they hang around the motel and have plenty of time to spare. Dad is on the list, too, but with a question mark after his name. I suppose Michael has no idea of how to approach him. I could have told him that Dad didn't know me, either.

But Michael hasn't written anything about how he is going to learn to like Pine Creek.

CHAPTER 23

Normal and Proud

IT STARTED AS A JOKE DURING EARLY FALL IN OUR LAST YEAR OF high school. That's how I remember it, anyway.

It's hard to worry about things you can laugh at, and MacKenzie was better than most at seeing the funny side of things.

There were two key events that fall, taking place at roughly the same time. The first was a letter sent to the *Pine Creek Gazette*, complaining that teachers were free to spread homosexual propaganda in schools. Just imagine the author's surprise when he found out that *The Color Purple* was available in the school library. And that the students were free to borrow it!

The letter was signed *Normal and proud*.

"No one in Pine Creek is normal," MacKenzie said. "Though we're proud of that, of course."

The second event took place in town, or at least that's what Hank claimed. Two women who had come to his café for lunch suddenly—entirely without warning, and completely in the open—started kissing. Just leaned across the table and started it!

"Obviously I kicked them out," Hank told anyone who would listen. "You can't be carrying on like that while people are eating lunch. They kicked up a fuss, of course, claiming they'd been discriminated against and threatening to sue me. But old Hank here wouldn't give in. It's not about discrimination. You just can't sit there, kissing like that, right in front of everyone."

"Hank," said MacKenzie. "You know we're all on your side here. I just wish you could explain this to Derek and Stacey, too. That way, maybe I wouldn't have to watch him stick his tongue down her throat all the time."

"That's completely different," Hank said, but fondly. He liked MacKenzie.

"Of course," she said. "At least they're normal and proud."

"I can't believe I missed it," MacKenzie muttered later, once we were back at the motel. "Pine Creek's queer population doubled, and I wasn't there to see it."

That was how it began.

One afternoon a few weeks later, MacKenzie treated me to milkshakes and burgers at Hank's. She worked off the bill by working there, that is. She had done far fewer shifts at Hank's since she started at the motel, but she still enjoyed putting on her waitress uniform and going around, refilling people's cups with the coffeepot. The real waitresses were willing to tolerate her as long as they didn't have to share their tips.

MacKenzie and I drank our milkshakes, and three men sat at the bar complaining about the coffee and the gays.

"Even if you paid us to drink this goddamn coffee, it'd be daylight robbery," said one of them.

"I'm all for Measure Nine, because I've got two sons. The day someone tells my son that it's okay to be gay, I'll hit him in the jaw," said the other.

"Jesus, Hank, what century did you brew this coffee in?" said a third. And then: "You know what the problem with gays is? They don't reproduce, which means they need to recruit. They're gonna recruit 10 percent of our kids. They'll convince my grandkid to become a homosexual."

"It's not that I'm prejudiced," the first man reassured the others. "I've got nothing against anyone. I think everyone knows that. But it's not the same with gays and dykes."

One of the men nodded in agreement. The other pulled a face—he had just taken a sip of his coffee.

"Who cares what they think," MacKenzie muttered. "They're dumb enough to drink Hank's coffee."

But we left soon after that.

CHAPTER 24

Pine Creek Through My Eyes

INTERESTINGLY ENOUGH, TOWN IS STILL THE NEXT POINT Michael decides to grapple with.

I don't think he has any idea how to approach it, but he gets an unexpected hand from Camila. She sits down at his table in the restaurant—I think of it as his "usual" booth now—and bashfully tells him that she wants to do "something" with the rooms at the motel.

"But I need some moral support," she adds. Then she looks up at Michael, touchingly unsure of herself, as though she doesn't quite know where the limits of their friendship lie—nor how much she can ask of him.

"I thought you hated the motel," Michael tells her, surprised.

"I was drunk! It was just...weird to be back."

"And now you want to fix it up?"

Camila looks down at her coffee. "It's MacKenzie," she eventually says. "She had to run this place while I was away. And now she's all alone. I just want to do something to help her." A stubborn look has appeared on her face. "Whether she wants it or not."

Michael glances from her to the computer screen, and for a moment, I think he's about to get back to work or add something to his list. That's when he sees the point about viewing this dump of a town through my eyes.

"Shopping trip to Pine Creek?" he suggests, and Camila flashes him a grateful smile.

He packs up his things, and thirty minutes later, they are standing side by side on Elm Street. Michael's car is parked nearby; they decided to use his for their shopping trip because it has the bigger trunk.

They start at the most expensive home-decor shop, purely because it's on Elm Street. The canisters and jars are all gleaming white and invitingly arranged, so that we can really *feel* how empty our lives are without glass jars labeled *pasta* and *rice* and *grains*. Everything seems to be shouting: This could be your home! Your life could be organized and coordinated and full of artfully arranged blankets in tastefully contrasting colors!

The blond woman behind the counter was in our class at school. In terms of the hierarchy back then, Tiffany was right in the middle, but aiming squarely upward. I think she might even have dated Derek for a while before he moved on to Stacey—her fifteen minutes of high school fame. Now, she radiates the slightly superior self-confidence of someone who truly believes that she has a perfect home.

Michael and Camila don't recognize her. They're too focused on the cushions, in various shades of cream and lime green. But Tiffany is watching them with unconcealed curiosity. They're the only customers in the shop, so she has plenty of time to stare.

Michael picks up a small cushion that seems to have been made more for decoration than for comfort. "Do you want the motel to be one of those places with a billion cushions that you have to move off the bed before you can get in, and even then you can't find a proper pillow?" He looks down at the pile in front of them. "Because if you do, I'm not sure there are enough here. We'll need hundreds of cushions."

Camila studies the price tag. "Maybe not."

"There has to be *something* I can do..." she continues, though she doesn't get any further before Tiffany butts in, her curiosity getting the better of her.

"Sorry to interrupt, but aren't you Derek's little brother?" She gives Michael an admiring glance and then adds: "Tiffany. We were in the same class." She moves on to Camila as though she is trying to size up the competition, but a confused crease appears between her perfectly shaped brows. "Weren't you...? Your name was..."

"Camila," she says quickly. "I'm Camila now."

Tiffany looks as though she is about to argue, but there is so much she wants to know that she decides to move on. "Are you a couple? I always did think you were gay." She turns back to Camila. "You, too, of course."

She is clearly more interested in Michael than Camila. "So have you moved back to Pine Creek?" she asks, a hint of hope in her voice.

"We came back for Henny's funeral," Michael says, but if he thinks that respect for their grief will dampen her curiosity, he is very much mistaken. "We're staying at the motel," he adds.

"The motel! Right, of course. With MacKenzie Jones. *She's* a dyke, isn't she?"

Michael and Camila turn and leave the shop.

The last thing they hear is a desperate "Not that there's anything wrong with that, of course!"

"Well, that went well," Camila mutters. They don't stop until they are several blocks away, confident that Tiffany hasn't followed them. "I guess it was a dumb idea."

Michael rubs his eyes. "Not as dumb as mine," he says, though he doesn't explain what he means.

"Do you remember what we were like when we were kids?" Camila asks.

Michael's laugh is short and harsh. "A bunch of losers and outcasts," he says.

"God, yes, but also... You know how there's a really clear distinction between the popular kids and the losers at school? I never understood why *we* weren't the tough, popular ones. MacKenzie always made it feel like it was a conscious decision not to hang out with the others. Like being a loser or being popular was something you could *choose*. She created some kind of wild, free, crazy bubble around us, where absolutely anything could happen."

She did, I think.

"Not just MacKenzie," Michael adds. "Henny did it, too. She used to look at me like I was more interesting than Derek."

Camila nods. "She was the first person I came out to."

"What did she say?"

"Nothing. She just started to think of me as a woman, and that was that."

"You should've said something to us, too."

She shrugs. "I wasn't ready."

Michael nods.

"You saw her...before she died?" Camila asks.

"Yeah."

"I wish I had, too."

Michael is quiet.

"What was she like?"

"She was...perfect. Just...perfect."

I shake my head. "No one is perfect," I say.

"Had she changed?"

"Yes and no," Michael says. "In one sense, she was exactly the same as always. Like she had just been waiting for me here. I know she lived her own life and had her own experiences, but that was how it felt. She was like my rocks—timeless."

"Well, MacKenzie has definitely changed. Jesus, hanging out with her was like being caught up in a tornado."

That doesn't sound entirely positive, but I know what she means. Overwhelming. Intoxicating. Engulfing.

"She was always so tough and invincible," Michael adds.

"Exactly!" I eagerly agree.

But Camila shakes her head. "No. She was human, too. She was freer and braver and more open than anyone I'd ever met. But now she seems so resigned. All she does is work. I thought that if I could do something with the motel, she would get drawn into it. I just want the old MacKenzie back."

I do, too, Camila.

"I wish I could've protected her from life," she says. "She doesn't even want to talk about Henny, but I know she's thinking about her all the time."

Michael seems to strike "talk to MacKenzie" from his *Remembering Henny* list. It's probably just as well. MacKenzie can be pretty nasty when she doesn't want to do something.

"Come on," he says. "We just need a new plan. I don't think starting at some trendy home store was the right approach. What we need is a secondhand shop. We shouldn't try to make the motel into something it's not. We should...improve it slowly."

Camila still looks dejected.

"This time, we'll look in the window first," he continues. "And if we see anyone who seems even remotely near our age, we leave immediately, all right?"

Luckily, the first secondhand store they find is run by a friendly woman in her fifties. She looks just like the shop she runs: chaotic and covered in chintz-like fabric.

The shop is much bigger than it looks from the outside, or else the woman has just ignored the laws of physics by cramming in as much as she possibly can. One corner is dedicated to furniture, and dining tables and mismatched chairs jostle for space alongside old wingback armchairs and a huge black leather sofa. Another section is filled with hundreds of pictures. A chaotic mix of cross-stitch embroideries, framed nature prints, and portraits of long-dead people. Camila starts there and has soon jokingly bought three pieces of embroidery, all featuring uplifting phrases.

Now that she has bought something, she really lets loose. Shopping bags quickly fill up. Michael brings the car over, parking it outside, and patiently carries everything out to the trunk. The woman behind the counter looks incredibly pleased.

"You've taught him well," she says in a loud theatrical whisper, with Michael still in earshot. "*Exactly* how a man should be."

Camila buys a pile of white lace tablecloths, two mismatched vases, a couple of floor lamps, some table lamps, and a small walnut bedside table.

"Be careful with that," the woman warmly warns Michael.

Michael carefully packs everything into the car. The autumn sun is shining down on him, and there is a group of kids nearby, pretending to be football heroes. Three of them are wearing green Oregon Ducks shirts. On their backs, a huge number eight in yellow, and above it, the player's name: Mariota. The Oregon Ducks' legendary quarterback. Michael smiles to himself as he loads the furniture into the trunk, and then he pauses and watches them thoughtfully.

When he heads back inside to fetch the rest of Camila's shopping, he has an absent look on his face. He's mulling over an idea, I can tell.

Camila has already paid for everything when the woman says, "Maybe you could use this fantastic old bar counter, too. Traditional handiwork, and it's been given a good coat of white paint, as you can see. The man who bought it got married soon after, but unfortunately he and his wife had very different ideas about what was important in a home. The bar was the first thing to go. But just look at all of the beautiful detail!"

"I don't think we need a bar."

"It's actually an old bureau, so it would work wonderfully as a desk, too. For your office, perhaps?" The last part is directed at Michael, but it's Camila who is thinking about her big, impersonal office and the hulking great monstrosity of a desk currently in it. She looks longingly at the simple elegance of the piece in front of her.

"I'll give it to you for a great price."

Buying it would be a real extravagance. I'm sure Camila can hear Juan Esteban lecturing her on how unnecessary it is to waste money on things the guests won't even see.

"I'll take it," she says.

On the way back to the hotel, Michael is deep in thought about his new idea. He helps to carry everything up to the office while he waits for Camila to decide where she wants it, but it's clear that his mind is elsewhere. He quickly excuses himself, picks up Derek, and drives back into town. Derek talks constantly as they drive.

"Detergent. That's what I'd really like to find. Everyone needs detergent. And having the right brand name is less important than with stuff like shampoo or conditioner. I learned that the hard way."

They turn off by Elm Street. Derek doesn't need any encouragement to keep talking.

"I once got hold of a big consignment of detergent. A whole pallet. A few boxes of fabric softener, too. I worked my way through town, going house by house. And I did it during the day, you know, when the wives are grateful for a bit of company. *Coffee, Derek? Come in, Mr. Callahan.* That's all I heard. And they all bought it, too. I gave them a good price, and my margins were pretty decent. Fabric conditioner thrown in for free if you bought enough. Then the same guy I'd gotten the detergent from made me a new offer. Shampoo and conditioner. A pallet of each."

Derek shakes his head at the memory. "What a goddamn mistake that was. I should've known. None of those women..." He stiffens up. "Hold on. Where are we going?"

Michael parks outside our old high school. An ugly, pale-blue building. It doesn't seem to have changed since we were there, except that everything seems smaller now: the parking lot, the two-story main building, the entrance to the principal's office, and the teachers' lounge.

"What are you up to?"

"Derek, this is ridiculous. You can't hide from Coach Stevenson forever. You may as well get it over and done with. What's the worst that can happen? He yells at you a little?"

"*A little?* I can tell you never played football in school."

Michael climbs out of the car, opens Derek's door, and takes a firm hold of his arm. The football field and the gymnasium are to the right of the school, and as you approach, it quickly becomes clear that the school building itself is much less important.

The school may look the same as it did fifteen years ago, but the football field has kept up with the times. New floodlights. New bleachers—nothing more than stainless-steel benches with no roof, but that's all you really need. People turn up at the school's games regardless of the weather. The grass is freshly cut, the lines brilliantly white. No one has bothered to maintain the running track around the field.

Coach Stevenson's office is right next to the field.

"Derek Callahan Jr."

The voice surprises us, and both Michael and Derek jump. They look incredibly guilty as they slowly turn around.

"Don't you try to get away from me now," the voice says. "I might be older than you, but I'm in good shape."

"Hi, Coach Stevenson. Nice to see you after so many years."

"Don't distract me, Michael. I've got plenty to say to your good-for-nothing brother."

He still shakes Michael's hand when he holds it out to him.

"Come on, Coach. Say what's on your mind. I'm ready." Derek smiles disarmingly, but it doesn't work. Coach Stevenson has been training kids for thirty years, and there isn't a trick in the book that he hasn't seen before. He is immune to any attempt to escape his fury.

"Those shirts you sold me were worthless."

"They were great quality!" Derek protests. He throws his arms up in the air, as though he is offended by the very thought that he, Derek, would sell him something worthless. "I got you the right amount. The right names and numbers. All spelled correctly."

"That might be true. But it doesn't matter, does it? *Not when the sizes are all wrong!* You'd barely fit a twelve-year-old in those shirts. 'Pay in advance,' you said. 'Trust me,' you said. 'Am I not your best-ever player?' you said. 'Sure,' I said. 'That's right, Derek. Let me ignore the fact that you haven't achieved anything since then, that you're a worthless nobody who makes your sissy of a little brother look like a shining example of masculine integrity...' Sorry, Michael. I get a little carried away."

"Don't worry, I stopped listening when you started to insult my brother."

"Right. We're meant to be inclusive these days, and I try to keep up with the times, but..."

"Did you mean literally or figuratively?" Michael interrupts him.

"Huh?"

"The shirts. When you said they would fit twelve-year-olds."

"Should think so. But I don't coach twelve-year-olds, do I? I coach a *real* team, you know?"

With that, he is off again. Michael lets him talk for a while, then interrupts. "But there are twelve-year-olds at the school, right? And they're crazy about football, just like they were when I was a student? They worship your team."

"Of course they do. But what does that have to do with anything?"

"Make a thing of it. Invite the local paper down here, get your big, tough heroes to put an arm around some weedy twelve-year-old's shoulders and give him a shirt. Support the next generation, that kind of thing. Tell them that if they train as hard as they can, they could be here, too. Does Derek's record still stand?"

"If you think a stupid old record will make me..."

"It doesn't actually matter, just sounds better in the article. All sponsored by former football hero Derek Callahan, who'll be there to smile and shake hands and hope that one of those twelve-year-olds can break his record."

Coach Stevenson is about to argue, but he stops short. His mouth opens and closes like a goldfish.

"Sponsored?" Derek says. "Hold on a minute, little bro…"

"Sponsored," Michael repeats.

"And he'll be sober and presentable and wearing a suit like a grown man?"

"Even if I have to force him into it myself."

Derek remains composed until they are out of earshot of Coach Stevenson, but then he grabs Michael by the arm and says, "What the hell do you think you're doing?"

"You couldn't keep hiding from him like a baby," Michael stubbornly replies. "You used to be invincible. Everyone worshipped you. But look at you now. Happy to dupe people with crap they don't need, and on top of that, you have to run and hide every time you see Coach Stevenson. For God's sake, Derek."

"You had no right to try to sort this out without even talking to me. It's my life."

"So do something with it!"

They stare angrily at one another. Derek gives in first. "Done's done, I guess."

"For once in your life, could you show a little fight? Get angry. Stand your ground."

It looks like Derek is about to hit him, but then he crumples like a broken football. "You think you know everything, don't you? Just because you got out of here and went to college and lived in all kinds of weird places. Then you come back and think you've got the right to stick your nose into other people's business. What the hell do you know about real life?"

He sounds more whiny than cocky. Derek can hear it, too, and his face turns an angry shade of red.

Michael looks like he has just discovered himself kicking a puppy, but that makes him even angrier. This is Derek. He should be strong and tough enough to defend himself against his little brother.

I think Michael wishes Derek *had* hit him. "You can always use some of the money you borrowed," he said.

Derek stares wearily at him. "You can be a real asshole sometimes, you know that?"

CHAPTER 25

Illusions

I'VE ALWAYS CHOSEN TO BELIEVE THAT THERE IS SOME KIND OF fundamental justice in life.

Recent events might have given that belief a few knocks, but still. Some kind of, well, karma. If you're a good person, you'll benefit from that. If you're a bad person, it'll come back to bite you in the long run.

MacKenzie always laughed at what she called my "touching belief in divine justice." "Tell me, Henny," she said. "What is it about human history that makes you believe in 'justice'? The rich just get richer, the poor poorer. Nice people get punished, and the jerks get off scot-free."

So, I have to admit that I get a certain sense of satisfaction out of knowing that MacKenzie will soon discover that sin sometimes punishes itself.

Dad is on his way toward the reception area, and he is carrying a heavy suitcase.

It's so heavy that he is leaning to one side, and that's how he crosses the parking lot—lopsided and slightly jerkily. Every now and then, the case hits the ground, which means that his approach sounds like *step, thud, scrape, step, thud, scrape*. When he reaches reception, he seems relieved to put the suitcase down on the floor.

MacKenzie stares at him with a look of shock. Shock and guilt.

"Mr. Broek?" she says.

Dad's eyes are fixed somewhere above her head as he forces out the words he knows he has to say: "I may have misjudged you."

"I don't actually think so," MacKenzie mumbles.

"I heard that you didn't think..." Dad clenches his jaws. "That you didn't think I had a drinking problem."

"I know you don't have a drinking problem," she replies entirely truthfully.

"In that case, you're the only one. People keep *staring* at me. Cheryl has been going through my trash! There's no way I can stay at home."

MacKenzie glances back and forth between Dad and his suitcase. The concern on her face is actually quite funny. "You want to stay *here*?" she says, sounding dismayed.

"This is a motel, isn't it? You rent out rooms? Surely that's why you exist?"

"But...you want to stay *here*?"

"Yes. I'd like a room. Doesn't matter which, so long as I can get away. If Cheryl talks to me about *my problems* or *my nerves* once more, I won't be held responsible for my actions."

"Uh, welcome to the Pine Creek Motel."

"Just give me a damn key." Dad clutches his forehead. "Now look what you've done. You've made me start cursing."

MacKenzie has given Dad a room on the first floor.

He snorts disapprovingly at the drab room, but I suppose he must think it's better than staying put on the same street as his neighbors, because he starts to unpack. Carefully and deliberately, like everything else in life. Every item has its place.

He lifts his shirts from his suitcase, gives them a shake, and hangs them up in the wardrobe. He places two perfectly folded sweaters into a drawer, along with his socks (also folded) and underwear (ironed). He hangs up his three suits, too.

Next, he unpacks his toiletry bag, lining up everything on the shelf in the bathroom. A perfectly squeezed tube of toothpaste (he starts from the bottom, of course, and folds as he goes, avoiding any waste), a new toothbrush, reading glasses. There is something touching about the near-military precision with which he lines them up. It's as if he's waiting for an inspection.

Last of all, he bends down over the suitcase and carefully pulls out... Jesus Christ, an urn. Is that...*me*?

The lid is being held in place by a couple of strips of masking tape. No way that's just a jar of face cream or something. My ashes have clearly come along for the ride.

I'm touched by the fact that he's brought me back to where I belong.

He carefully peels off the tape, wipes the urn with the arm of his sweater, and places it next to the TV.

Oh, Dad.

Then he sits down at the foot of the bed with his hands neatly folded in his lap and his eyes fixed straight ahead.

He seems to be thinking: What do I do now?

"Did you know there's a man outside, *drinking* in front of your motel?"

MacKenzie doesn't even look up from the computer. Dad has been loitering in the check-in area for the past half hour, helpfully pointing out everything that is wrong with the motel.

"In broad daylight! From a hip flask!"

"I wouldn't be throwing rocks in your glass house if I were you," MacKenzie mutters. "Sorry, sorry, I know you don't drink. But that's just Clarence."

Dad is sitting on the uncomfortable sofa, and he has pushed a broken lamp and a few old brochures on the coffee table out of the way to make room for my urn. MacKenzie's eyes keep going back to it.

"And the blind in my room seems to be stuck. I was sure you'd want to know as soon as possible."

This is Dad's second visit to the reception desk. MacKenzie looks as though she is daydreaming of a happier time when she was left in peace.

"And how am I supposed to iron my shirts? There's no ironing board!"

MacKenzie mutters something to herself and then sets off to find one for him.

Camila takes over at the desk.

When MacKenzie gets back, Camila is deep in conversation on the phone. The person on the other end has clearly seen our sign.

"No, sir, unfortunately we don't have a bar. Or a pool. Yes, it's a little unfortunate that the sign says we do. It needs…updating. Measure Nine? That was a ballot in 2000, proposing to make it illegal to "propagandize" for homosexuality. Yes, it's crazy. Ah, you meant homosexuality. I thought you were talking about the measure. Do we have gays here? Of course we do. We ship in a busload every day. I'm sorry you feel like this isn't the motel for you. Have a good day, sir."

"He didn't make a reservation?" MacKenzie asks sarcastically.

"You've never thought of getting a new sign?" Camila replies. And then: "What's this?" She points to a scrap of paper that has been taped to the desk, only visible to anyone sitting behind it.

"A serenity prayer," MacKenzie explains. "I've needed it since Mr. Broek moved in."

"'God, give me the serenity to accept the things I can't change, the courage to change those I can, and the wisdom to know the difference,'" Camila reads aloud. "Very fitting."

A deep male voice interrupts them. "I use that every day," Sheriff Ed says, and both MacKenzie and Camila jump guiltily. The sheriff has that effect on people.

"Do you have a couple of minutes?" he asks Camila.

"Sorry?" she says. "You want to talk to me?"

"If you have time."

She casts an uncertain glance at MacKenzie. "Sure. I guess."

"Maybe over lunch?" the sheriff suggests, and Camila reluctantly follows him over to the restaurant. She glances back over her shoulder as though she is hoping someone will save her.

"Dolores!" the sheriff cries. "You look fantastic, as always."

"You're hungry. As always."

"Guilty."

The sheriff orders "the usual" and fills an enormous paper cup with Mountain Dew. Camila sticks to coffee.

Sheriff Ed sits down at a table, firmly pushes the plastic flower to one side, and says, "This is just an informal chat."

His words don't seem to make Camila any more comfortable. "So you're not going to arrest me, read me my rights, and drag me away in cuffs?"

"Not today. A couple of people from town asked if I would come over and talk to you about the sign, whether you could maybe do something about it. They, uh, think it gives a bit of an...unkempt impression."

"They wanted you to talk to *me*?"

"Yes, um, I heard in town that the motel is yours, strictly speaking, so..."

"You thought you'd have more success with me than MacKenzie?"

The sheriff tries to smile disarmingly. "She's a little sensitive when it comes to complaints from town."

"You get a lot?" Camila sounds surprised.

The sheriff is saved from having to answer by Dolores arriving with his food: an enormous hamburger that takes up half the plate, a mountain of golden-brown onion rings, and a lone slice of tomato. The sheriff pushes the tomato to one side.

"It's MacKenzie's motel," Camila tells him.

"Not legally. Onion ring?"

She shakes her head.

"They also think that the sign might not be...accurate. Maybe Mr. Alvarez got a little...enthusiastic toward the end? And, well...those signs MacKenzie added? Isn't it time we put the past behind us?"

"You said 'a couple of people from town.' Who, exactly?"

"You were living in Los Angeles until recently, weren't you?"

"What does that have to do with anything?"

"Police work in a town like this is a little different than in a big city like LA. My job here isn't primarily to solve crimes. I have a detective for that, and his job isn't all that hard. If a serious crime gets committed, we generally know who did it right away. Most of our time is actually spent keeping the peace. We prevent. We make sure we're visible in the community so that troublemakers behave and keep their mischief away from law-abiding citizens, so that ordinary folks feel safe and trust us. Do you know what my first job was as sheriff?"

Camila looks impatient, but she politely shakes her head.

"Organizing a Christmas collection for the children at the hospital.

Children donated old toys they no longer played with, and the sheriff's office organized a big summer picnic as thanks. Barbecue, patrol cars, happy kids. That's how you get to know people around here. And then you devote time to balancing various interests against one another. To being some kind of buffer between them. Old ladies who want silence after seven in the evening, teenagers who just want to have fun..."

"Homophobes who want to be left to hate in peace?"

"Oh, come on, folks around here are decent. Ninety percent, anyway. They just go a little crazy sometimes. But they also do plenty of good. You need to remember that."

"And now they're upset again?"

"A few are very upset. There aren't a lot of them, but they've been nagging Bob, and Bob talked to me. You know Bob Parker? Maybe not. Politician. He's the one who gets things done around here. That's how it works in a town like Pine Creek. You work together and diffuse any tensions before they have time to turn into real problems."

Camila looks out at the sign from their table by the window. I can't read her expression. Then she turns back to the sheriff. "How can you eat so much and still be so thin?"

"I burn a lot of calories worrying about the state of the world."

MacKenzie folds her arms as Camila explains why the sheriff wanted to talk to her. "You want to change the sign because *they* want us to?"

"Come on, you have to agree that it isn't exactly...true."

MacKenzie's eyes glitter against her will. "I wonder if they'd really want a true sign," she says to herself. Then, to Camila: "Well, it's your motel."

"Come on, it's a possibility. A new sign, to show that things are moving forward. I mean, it's the first thing people see, isn't it? Don't you think it would be better if it was a little more honest? And maybe more... uniform?"

"Honest, you say. I think I might have an idea."

"So you'll handle it? I have no idea how to order a new sign."

"Don't worry," MacKenzie tells her. "You'll get your new sign. And it'll be honest."

Something in the tone of her voice and the glimmer in her eye tells me that Camila should be worried. I think Camila must be able to sense that, too, because she says, "And no lies about having a pool or a bar or anything like that. Or an amusement park," she adds, in case MacKenzie is planning to come up with any new lies.

"It'll be the most honest motel sign ever," she says.

The next morning, Michael continues work on his list. I spent the night trying to make his subconscious decide to visit Derek so they could talk about what happened, but he went straight over to the restaurant when he woke, crossing out "Solve the Derek and Coach Stevenson problem" and moving on to the next point.

He has made it to "Get to know Henny," but he seems reluctant to get started. He spends the morning staring out the window, and the first person he talks to is Dolores, who comes over to force more coffee and pecan pie on him.

"I was away for so long," he says as she refills his cup.

"Too long," she agrees. He gestures to the seat opposite, and she sinks into it with the relieved sigh of someone who has spent her whole life on her feet.

"You and Camila," she says.

"Uh, yeah. I was wondering what Henny was like as an adult. What kind of person did she become? Now...or, well, after everything."

He seems nervous about how Dolores will react to his questions about me, and I am, too. The funeral should have drawn a line under this whole mess. I don't want them to have to go around being sad or remembering me all the time.

But Dolores looks *happy*. I think she *wants* to talk about me. I can't quite understand it, but it's nice all the same.

"Her favorite dessert was anything with chocolate," she says. "Every time her birthday came around, I would ask her what she wanted and she always said 'something with chocolate.' So, one year, I made her a Something with Chocolate cake. It had chocolate sponge, chocolate mousse, dark-chocolate icing, chocolate sprinkles on top, and chocolate-covered strawberries to decorate it. After that, she asked for the same thing every year."

She takes his empty plate and cup. "It's not *my* place to doubt the Lord," she says. "But I really hope He's doing the same for her up there in heaven."

On his way out of the restaurant, Michael sees Buddy and Clarence sitting in the sun on Clarence's usual bench, and he decides to go over and chat with them. They slide over to make room for him, and neither has anything against talking about me. There's no room for me on the bench, so I sit down on the ground beside them.

"A good woman, Henny," Clarence says, filling his coffee cup from his hip flask. "And I want you to know that I've forgiven her for what she said about my dead wife."

Michael and Buddy are staring at him. I feel pretty shaken up, too. Surely I never said anything bad about his wife?

"She said I would see her again in heaven!" Clarence's dignity deserts him, and he knocks back the contents of his cup.

"Wasn't that was nice of her?" Michael asks.

"Yeah, well, she couldn't know that it's the one thing I'm most scared of."

"Sorry?"

"Seeing her again! The wife'll have a thing or two to say to me, let me tell you, and she'll have had plenty of years to practice. That woman knew more about my sins than God."

He takes another sip from his cup. "So you're trying to get to know our Henny, are you?" he asks.

"Yeah."

"You won't manage it. No one knows anyone else. Not really. We just see our own image of them. We don't even know our damn selves."

"Do you know what Henny always said to me?" Buddy speaks up.

"Booze?" Clarence asks, holding out his hip flask.

"No. She said, 'Hi, Buddy. How's it going?' She always had time for you, and she was always happy. Things aren't the same now she's gone. It's those little things that make you feel welcome, you know? If you had a big problem or something that needed fixing, you'd go to MacKenzie. But it's possible to feel down without really wanting to be helped, if you know what I mean. And then it was Henny that you wanted to see. Not to talk about your feelings, just to be with her. She was like...home."

That's the most I've ever heard him say, and the most beautiful, too.

"Take the whole thing with the Christmas tree," he continues. Michael looks confused, but Clarence immediately knows what he is talking about. "I'd gotten hold of a Christmas tree. Thought it could be nice in the reception area, you know? But I'd, uh, misjudged the height."

"It was at least three feet too high," Clarence adds.

"Yeah, I was an idiot. And I said so, too. But MacKenzie just pulled out a saw and cut it in half. Henny insisted on putting up both halves in reception. It made it more unique, she said, because which other business in town had *two* Christmas trees? So MacKenzie might be good at fixing things, but it was Henny who made you *feel* good."

I don't know whether I agree. In my eyes, it was always MacKenzie who made people feel good. I just helped out.

There are two kinds of people who stay in cheap motels. Those who are only passing through, and those who don't have anywhere else to go. For both, it's a temporary thing. One just lasts a little longer than the other.

Over the years, a number of people from town have found a temporary home with us at the motel. We've been a kind of safety net over the abyss—something that's much closer than some would care to admit.

The majority eventually find somewhere else to go. Sooner or later, they all move on. But here's the interesting thing: sometimes, I think they were happier here. They were free. They enjoyed MacKenzie's gallows humor and Dolores's food; they started laughing again while they were here with us, possibly for the first time in a long while. The laughter always confused them, but once they had started, it came naturally. Deep down, their bodies still remembered what laughter felt like. They were able to rediscover it here, with us.

And then they thought: *This is only temporary*, and then they moved on. No one came back. Ultimately, we probably just reminded them of some of the worst moments of their lives. As they rebuilt themselves, they also built up defensive walls, and they didn't want to remember our particular brand of freedom, born as it was out of helplessness. The way the best freedom always is, if you ask me.

Throughout this whole conversation, Alejandro has been standing by the sign, taking pictures of it from different angles. He becomes Michael's natural next port of call.

"Henny?" he asks as he kneels down and snaps a picture of the dent in the sign where a drunk driver once...parked. "She was five years older than me, but I always thought of her like a little sister. There was something so innocent and vulnerable about her. She was so nice, I always thought that the world would gradually knock her down."

"Not the world," I say. "A truck."

"Did it?"

"No. At first, I thought, 'Typical white woman. They can go through their whole lives being naive, without reality ever dealing them any serious blows.' But then I thought that maybe kindness could be a self-defense strategy in and of itself. I assumed she was kind because she saw the world through rose-tinted lenses, and that her illusions would eventually be crushed. But she was nice because she didn't have any illusions to lose. She knew how horrible the world could be, and that's why she helped out whenever help was needed. You can be invincible if you don't have any illusions."

He squats down to take yet another photo. I think he needs the distance the camera provides him to be able to go on.

"She helped my mom when she got sick. Did you know that?" he says. "MacKenzie made sure I took a break from time to time, physically forcing me into the truck, throwing a bottle of whiskey into my lap, and driving me around while I cursed fate. Then she stopped the truck, looked me straight in the eye, and said, 'I swear, Dolores is going to be fine.' I can still remember it. It was like she was God and had power over life and death. And do you know the crazy part? I believed her." He shakes his head as though to get rid of the memory and then quickly finishes his story. "Henny went to see Mom every day, and when she found out that Mom was struggling to keep up with the payments on the house, she just raised Mom's wage."

He looks Michael straight in the eye. "There's nothing I wouldn't have done for Henny."

It sounds like he wants to warn Michael that he'll crush him if he breaks my heart, but it's a bit late for that.

"What about you?" Michael asks. "I take it you don't have any illusions, either. You see the world exactly as it is?"

The dogged expression on Alejandro's face is chased away by laughter. "Me? I'm the worst kind of romantic. Enough dreams to be stupid enough to try to realize them, but realistic enough to know that I never will. So, I take portraits of kids all day, and I'm grateful for that. And now: pictures of Mom's food. I started an Instagram account for the motel. Right now, there are only five pictures of different dishes from breakfast on there, plus one of the back of the motel—with the stream, the haze over the meadow, and the pale-purple mountains in the background."

"Sounds beautiful."

"Sentimental crap. But you can't take pictures of the rest of the motel. Everything just looks small and worn out."

"How many followers do you have?"

"Seventeen. If you include me."

"Alejandro is wrong," I tell Michael.

It's evening, and we are lying on our backs in bed. I can hear from his breathing that he isn't asleep; we're both just staring up at the ceiling.

"I used to have illusions," I say. "No one is born without them. It's like the opposite of clothes. We're born naked, and the older we get, the more clothes we put on, until eventually we're ancient and wrapped up in shawls and warm sweaters and layers of scarves and socks. With illusions, it's the other way around. We're born wrapped up in them, but life takes them away from us one at a time. I kept mine for longer than most people, because life was kind to me and I wasn't imaginative enough to think up things that I hadn't experienced.

"I didn't connect MacKenzie's bruises with Dad shaking his head, for example. 'Poor girl,' he said, and I always used to think, *MacKenzie?* There was no one stronger or braver than her. Then she broke her arm. She had been climbing a tree, she said, but Dad just shook his head again. Another day, she said, 'Let's do something. I don't want to go home. Dad won't have crashed yet.' I lost another illusion right then, when I realized that there were fathers who drank and were violent and that there were homes people didn't want to go back to."

I don't want to think about this. I want to stay in that blissful summer. But I've started to realize that it was just the beginning. I can't think about the story Michael and I share if I don't also think about what came next.

And I don't want to do that.

"Memories can be so unpredictable," I say.

Michael hasn't closed the curtains, and the moonlight is filtering in through the window, illuminating the cracks in the ceiling. I trace them with my eyes, as if I'm trying to unravel a ball of yarn, one crack at a time, but they quickly become a confusing tangle.

"The last year of high school," I say, "I lost a lot of my illusions then, too. But…I was also so happy. That's what I find so hard to understand. It's like there are two different stories in my head. The one about you and me, and the one about everything else. I've been thinking about us this whole time, but I've always refused to think about that campaign. It upset me too much. I couldn't have stayed here if I was thinking about it constantly. Can you understand that? But I guess it's just a story, isn't it? We met as a result of it, and we went our separate ways because of it, too."

PINE CREEK GAZETTE

FORMER SPORTS STAR SHARES THE LOVE WITH FOOTBALL TEAM

To date, no one has managed to break Derek Callahan's record, but if we're to believe the man himself, it's high time someone did. This is the team that may do just that.

The *Pine Creek Gazette* was present as Derek Callahan and Coach Stevenson, two legends from the world of Pine Creek football, joined the varsity team to visit our eager youngsters. Each junior player was given a shirt bearing the name and number of a varsity player, and that wasn't the only thing offered. There was plenty of solid advice, as well as jokes and fun.

Coach Stevenson is looking forward to seeing Derek Callahan's record broken, and Callahan himself thinks this might be the team to do it.

"I'm sure one of these heroes will manage it," he told the *Pine Creek Gazette.*

HISTORY TO BE TORN DOWN OR MADE

Some things in Pine Creek have been around for so long that they have become historical monuments. Whether they appeared by accident or design, they have, over the years, become a constant in our town. If the elms on Elm Street suddenly started to grow, many of us would surely miss the old trees. No one remembers who first made the decision to paint our high school baby blue, nor the decision not to repaint it when there was graffiti that needed to be covered up. Yet the town's patchy school building is now part of our collective memory.

Few historical monuments have been the source of such fierce debate as the sign—and the creative liberties taken with it—at Juan Esteban Alvarez's motel. To some, it is an example of the American dream. Seventeen-year-old Alvarez arrived in San Francisco and bought a dilapidated motel in the far north, soon setting to work on renovating and replenishing it. He managed to build his cabins, but never got around to the bar or the pool.

The most recent additions to the sign were not Juan Esteban's. Instead, they bear witness to the dark history of both our town and state. They are a reminder of the way our town was divided by forces that tried to play one group against another.

It is the *Gazette*'s hope that we continue to remember our history, even if—as sources suggest—the sign disappears tomorrow.

CHAPTER 26

Microwaves in Every Room!

MICROWAVE OVENS IN EVERY ROOM! HITS THE GROUND WITH A THUD, momentarily overpowering Bruce Springsteen's *Wrecking Ball*. It's a depressing but fitting CD for tearing down a monument.

The signs are so rusted together that they have to be sawed apart. Buddy is sitting calmly in the cherry picker, armed with a saw and pair of construction headphones, humming along with "Death to My Hometown" in an uncannily cheery way. *Hmm hmm hmm, DEATH TO MY HOMETOWN, hmm hmm hmm.* That's what it sounds like, and then he gets to work on the next part of the sign.

The restaurant is full of people wolfing down bacon and scrambled eggs, their eyes fixed on the spectacle. Several have taken their coffees outside so that they can watch from the parking lot. Others don't even bother buying anything. They just park and lean against the hoods of their cars, watching either the destruction of history or the march of progress, depending on who you ask.

A man with a rusty Toyota, a red cap, and slightly greasy hair mumbles, "I'll be damned if I'm not going to miss the wretched thing."

"Should be put in a museum," a man whose name I think is Jack agrees.

That seems to be the general consensus.

"It was unique, if nothing else," says another man. "Who knows what boring crap they'll put up now."

MacKenzie and Camila watch as the sign comes down. I guess they can't stay away as piece after piece of our history falls.

Clarence waves to them from his bench. "I wouldn't miss this for all the microbreweries in Portland!" he shouts cheerily.

"Come on," MacKenzie whispers, pulling Camila over to the window-less stretch of wall nearby, where they can be alone. A small tree and a couple of bushes separate them from the doors into check-in, shielding them almost completely from view as they watch the sign being dismantled. Both have their hands in their pockets and seem to be playing it cool, but their shoulders keep brushing together, and I can't help thinking that it looks deliberate.

"I had no idea it would feel so weird," Camila says.

"It's part of our history."

"I can't decide whether I want to watch or not."

"Same."

Forest views! is the next part of the sign to come crashing down. Several people start clapping; there's something quite liberating about being able to enjoy such wholehearted destruction.

I'm worried about Juan Esteban's spirit and keep stealing guilty glances toward his dark office. Maybe he's still up there, being forced to watch all this.

The men in the restaurant—and they are almost all men—have turned their chairs so they can see out through the window. Their fries lie cold and untouched in front of them. They drink their coffee, and Bruce sings about taking care of our own.

"I mean, I know the sign lied," someone out in the parking lot says, "but did it do any harm? Everyone knew there was no pool."

"Or bar."

MacKenzie and Camila glance at each other. MacKenzie's eyes glitter, and Camila smiles and shakes her head.

"It is a bit of a shame," someone else says, but he is interrupted by scattered cheers.

No to Measure 9 has just fallen.

Both MacKenzie and Camila look away.

The crowd thins out during the afternoon, but people come flooding back to the motel that evening to watch the new sign go up. Watching things being torn down may be more exciting than seeing things being built, but a new sign is still an event. It demands ritual.

"Cheers," Clarence says, taking a swig from his cup.

"Almost time," someone else says.

"It wouldn't surprise me if they're expecting a speech," MacKenzie tells Camila. "In which case, you'll have to do it."

"Me?" Camila blurts out.

"It's your motel."

"You know that's not true."

But MacKenzie just gives her a gentle shove toward the new sign.

"I hope the damn thing works," Camila mutters. She reluctantly makes her way toward it, and smiles stiffly at everyone she passes.

When Buddy hits Pause on his CD player, everyone knows that the time has come.

"As I'm sure you all agree, the old sign was something of an institution," Camila says in a loud, matter-of-fact voice. "But sometimes we have to move on and embrace change. We wanted a sign that would give a better idea of what we want the motel to be, and what the motel could mean for the town. We hope you'll like it."

A few people clap. Everyone looks up at the sign.

Everyone but MacKenzie. She is staring at Camila.

In the silence that follows, we hear the click of Miguel hitting the switch and the buzzing sound as the lights come on. Suddenly, the parking lot is illuminated. Yellow, blue, and red lights flicker onto the upturned faces.

A new sign. Uniform. Honest.

A few people laugh, and then there is more applause.

"Good choice," someone shouts.

"Definitely more accurate now."

"My family has been pining away here for generations," says someone else.

"Refreshingly honest," says Clarence.

PINE AWAY MOTEL AND CABINS

MacKenzie has treated herself to one small extra sign. A memory of sorts, or possibly a tribute:

Now with color TV!

There are three chairs lined up on the walkway outside Camila's room. Three pairs of shoes on the railing: Camila's boots, MacKenzie's worn-out sneakers, Michael's walking boots. Their faces are illuminated by the glow of the neon lights. None of them can tear their eyes from the sign.

There is an open six-pack of beer on the ground between them, and the sweet scent of the joint they are passing back and forth mixes with the damp evening air.

Michael had watched the old sign come down and the new one go up from the edge of the motel lot. He must have seen MacKenzie and Camila standing together, but he didn't go over to them. He seemed unsure whether they wanted to be alone. This is actually the first time the three of them have hung out since their drunken evening before the funeral. MacKenzie fetched both the beer and Michael once the crowd dispersed, and now they are finally sitting here, next to me.

Juan Esteban would have liked it.

They don't really have anything in common, I think. MacKenzie is wearing a patched denim jacket and a multicolored knit scarf. Camila is in a dark-red coat, with a stylish, expensive-looking beige scarf wrapped around her neck. Michael is in his usual windbreaker, simple and functional.

They are looking out at the parking lot and the new sign, but I'm sitting on the railing so that I can study them properly. I can't get enough of it. They're back where they are supposed to be. The world feels right now that they're here, next to one another. They've been lonely, but now they are home.

"The sign's fantastic," Michael says, raising his bottle of beer to MacKenzie in a toast. She clinks her own against it.

"I do my best," she says bashfully.

"I'm not sure the rest of town will be so keen on it," Camila says drily. "A couple of people complained about the old one," she explains to Michael. "That's why we changed it."

"They'll be angry no matter what we do," MacKenzie protests. "But they've *got* their new sign. As promised."

"I guess you'll be changing the name of the motel now?" Michael asks.

MacKenzie rocks back on her chair and leans against the wall. "Welcome to Pine Away Motel and Cabins," she says.

"I like it," says Michael.

"It's so nice sitting here like this," says Camila.

I nod in agreement.

"Like when we were kids," Michael adds.

"All our grand theories about life and love and the meaning of it all," Camila continues. "We thought we knew everything."

"Not Henny," says Michael. "She was always quiet. You always had to ask her what she thought."

"She was the smartest of all of us, too," he goes on.

MacKenzie takes a drag on the joint. "Though that's not saying much."

"Do you remember the time we talked about what we wanted to do when we were older?" Camila asks. "You said you were going to have a pea shooter, MacKenzie, so you could shoot peas at kids. You'd sit on our veranda—because you were sure we'd have a veranda at the motel by then—and mess with all the children who happened to pass by."

"I still will."

Her plan was to have white curly hair, like some innocent old woman. A sweet old grandmother, that's what she would look like. She would shoot peas at all the young kids she saw, and when they complained to their parents she could just sit there and innocently widen her eyes. *Who? Me?* she would say, confusedly waving her knitting. Her plans were incredibly detailed: the knitting would be done with some kind of fluffy, light-pink yarn for maximum camouflage.

"I think maybe the parents here know you a little too well for that," Michael says.

"How did it go again?" Camila continues. "Michael wanted to have experienced things, MacKenzie wanted to have had fun..."

"And you wanted to have been yourself," Michael interjects. "To have lived freely and honestly and bravely."

"I guess we actually got pretty close," Camila says.

"So we got what we wanted," MacKenzie says. "I can't see that it made us very happy."

I remember that conversation. For a moment, I can see us the way we used to be. This was after the cabins had been built, after the vote, during our last few months of high school.

They were so confident in what they wanted, but I was terrified they would ask me. I didn't know what I was going to say. I had never thought about life that way. Eventually, of course, they did ask. They always did.

"And Henny said, 'I don't think life cares about our plans,'" Michael says. "I still remember that."

"Henny was always the fatalist among us," Camila adds.

"And then she said, 'I just want us to sit in a row on our new veranda when we're old. In matching rocking chairs.'"

"And here we are."

"Not Henny," MacKenzie points out.

I smile. I might not have achieved my goal of having a veranda thirty or so years from now, but surely this is pretty close.

Michael takes the joint from MacKenzie. Takes a drag. Holds his breath. Lets the smoke slowly escape. "We had some good times together, didn't we?"

"We managed to get a rainbow flag up on the school, if nothing else," Camila says.

"For exactly thirty minutes," says MacKenzie. "Before it fell down."

"Yeah," Michael agrees. "Duct tape probably wasn't the best idea." He takes another drag on the joint and passes it back to Camila. "But I know what Juan Esteban would have done right now."

"What?" asks Camila.

MacKenzie thinks, then she smiles appreciatively. "He would've put up a new sign," she says.

In unison, both she and Michael say: "Pine Away Motel and Cabins—now with new sign!"

CHAPTER 27

Limits to What Duct Tape Can Do

THE THING I REMEMBER MOST CLEARLY FROM THE TIME JUST before the Measure Nine campaign was how gray and meaningless everything was.

I didn't know why. Yes, the summer break was over. School had started again. But those things had never been a problem before; I had always liked school. It felt comfortable.

Suddenly, though, I was filled by a sense of unhappiness.

The feeling was so new that it took me several weeks to work out what the creeping restlessness was. I found myself getting annoyed on my quiet nights at home with Dad. Nothing ever *happened* there. And class? What was the point of sitting still while the teachers talked my life away?

Then I saw Michael in the yard or in the corridors, and everything felt new and exciting again. He was always alone, always in a hurry, always with his arms full of geology books rather than the ones he actually had to read.

I was sure MacKenzie could hear my heart racing every time he was nearby. *Just act normal*, I thought, my cheeks turning red.

Nothing else ever felt as real. I was only alive during those brief, endless moments when I saw him. Or, even better, when MacKenzie got him to stop and chat for a while. She always asked about Derek. Everyone did.

Maybe that's why, looking back now, I can't remember all that much about Measure Nine. Not that early on, anyway.

I've searched my memory for some sign that I was actually worried about all the madness that was going on, but I can't find anything.

It all happened so slowly. It's hard to realize that everything is going downhill when everyday life goes on the same as ever.

Measure Nine was the second campaign with that name run by an organization called the Oregon Citizens Alliance, a conservative Christian group which, in the early nineties, decided that homosexuality was the root of all evil. It was led by Lon Mabon and had a number of controversial members. Scott Lively was one of them, known for writing a book called *The Pink Swastika*, which argued that the Holocaust and the Nazis were actually the fault of homosexuality.

In 1992, they managed to force a popular vote on their first proposal. They wanted to amend Oregon's constitution to forbid "special rights" for LGBT people by adding a provision that said the state recognized "homosexuality, pedophilia, sadism, and masochism as abnormal, wrong, unnatural, and perverse." It was defeated by a slim majority.

They *were* crazy. It should have worried me. The first vote had been before our time, of course, but still. Their second proposal, another Measure Nine, wasn't much better. In just three months' time, Oregon's citizens would be given the opportunity to ban the state's schools from providing education about, encouraging, or sanctioning homosexuality or bisexuality.

"Yeah, because that's what schools here spend their time doing," MacKenzie muttered. "Constant homo propaganda!"

She decided to start a No to Measure Nine campaign at school, and she and I spent several days making posters ahead of our first meeting. I wrote the words, and MacKenzie "made them a little funnier" with color, illustrations, and slogans. We put them up all over the school, and then MacKenzie waited eagerly to lead the campaign.

We had been given permission to use one of the classrooms for our meeting, and somehow it looked different once class was over. Maybe it was just because MacKenzie had moved the furniture around. The desks were all pushed up against the wall, and the chairs were arranged in a circle. She had heard it was good to arrange them like that. It would make the meeting more open and less hierarchical, apparently. But since I was the only other person there, it was hard to tell whether it had worked. We had a rainbow flag stretched across the back of two chairs, and MacKenzie sat down at the teacher's desk by the board—*that* definitely made things feel different. She belonged up there. She was the leader, and I was her audience.

But we were also the only people in the room.

Until the door opened and Michael came in.

He just strode inside, dumped his pile of books on the floor, and sat down in the chair next to mine. I'm pretty sure I stopped breathing.

I forced myself to look at MacKenzie, but from the corner of one eye, I was constantly aware of every slight change in Michael's expression. I tried to sit up straight so that my posture would be better, and regretted that I wasn't wearing a cuter top. Or makeup. Anything that would make him look at me.

I had gone to the meeting for MacKenzie's sake, but in that moment, I felt almost worryingly grateful for the homophobic proposals that had brought Michael and me together again. It suddenly felt like absolutely anything could happen. The usual classroom smells around me—chalk dust, stuffiness, teenage angst—suddenly smelled like freedom and adventure.

I was so focused on Michael, but I still looked up when Camila came in. I don't know who was more surprised to see her there, me or MacKenzie. Though we went to the same school and worked at the same motel, she had always managed to avoid us.

Until now.

She glanced at the circle of chairs and then sat down at the far side.

"The measure is crazy," she said firmly.

MacKenzie looked down at her notes. I already knew what she had written there: (1) Open the meeting. (2) The crazy measure.

"We're not on that point yet."

I have to take a break here and go for a walk around the cabin.

How could I be so self-absorbed? How could I have been so focused on my insignificant infatuation? How could I have been so blind to everything that was at stake?

I reassured myself that the measure would be defeated, of course. MacKenzie was convinced we would win. And I would work extra hard with Michael by my side. It was great that more people had decided to get involved.

But looking back now, that doesn't reassure me. What is it about having a crush that causes such tunnel vision, such an inability to be present in any other parts of our lives? Ultimately, why would anyone want to be infatuated?

I liked my life before Michael came along. Afterward, he was the only thing that mattered.

MacKenzie came out to us during that meeting, but I don't even remember my reaction to it. I do, at least, remember what she said. Like so much else with MacKenzie, it was unforgettable.

She said, "I had a much more exciting idea about how to tell you this, but it didn't work out, so I guess I'll just tell you."

"All right," we said.

"I'm gay!"

"Okay," said Michael. I nodded. Camila was the only one who seemed interested. She leaned forward in her chair.

MacKenzie looked unhappy. "I *knew* the first idea was better. I wanted to write it on a cake, and then Ellen DeGeneres could've jumped out waving a rainbow flag. Or maybe she'd have a banner."

Camila actually smiled. "But it didn't work out?"

"She was busy, unfortunately. But she did write and wish me luck."

"That would've been interesting," Michael said.

"We can pretend it happened like that," I said. Then I glanced at Michael. Again.

Michael and Camila's presence had injected a new energy into the meeting. I wasn't the only one who felt it. MacKenzie was also invigorated by having new people there. Our conversation mostly revolved around how we could get others involved.

"We need to do something to make ourselves more visible," Michael said.

"We tried putting up posters." MacKenzie glanced at the rainbow flag. "Maybe we should put the flag up somewhere. Someplace it'll be really visible."

"We'd need a ladder."

"The motel has one."

I'm not sure whether they had a plan or whether it was more an outlet for their energy, but we went out to Michael's car in the parking lot. MacKenzie was just happy that something was finally happening. She felt freer outside the classroom. Michael was on board with anything, and Camila and I... Well, we just tagged along. I don't know what Camila was thinking, but I was just grateful to be near Michael. I wanted the meeting, that evening, to go on forever. We got into the car and suddenly it was summer again, even though it was September. MacKenzie drove, putting on her favorite CD—the one she played constantly back then—and we listened to the Indigo Girls' "Get Out the Map" on repeat.

"All right, we have our ladder," MacKenzie said once she had fetched it from the motel. "What else do we need?"

"Rope? Duct tape? Somewhere to hang it?"

"I can get duct tape."

The drive back to school was frustratingly short. It felt like we had barely turned around before we were there again. Michael jumped straight out of the car. Somewhere along the way, he and MacKenzie had decided to hang the flag on the end of the school building.

The two of them climbed up the ladder. It was the kind that folded in the middle, which meant they could climb from both sides, raising the flag together.

It worked. For a while, it was an incredible sight. They had covered each corner of the flag in duct tape, finishing it off with several strips across the middle. They climbed back down, folded up the ladder, and came over to where Camila and I were waiting. We stood in a line, leaning against Michael's car, and looked up at our rainbow flag on the wall of the school.

In that moment, I really did think that life was an adventure in which anything could happen. The rainbow flag on the wall of the school was proof of that.

And then it fell down. Of course it did. Slowly sailed down to the ground.

"I guess there are limits to what duct tape can do," MacKenzie muttered.

Camila laughed. An instinctive, completely open laugh that transformed her face and body and surprised her just as much as us. I think it was the first time I had ever heard her laugh. MacKenzie studied her with far more interest than she ever had before.

"Say what you like, but it's never boring when you're around, MacKenzie Jones," Camila said.

"We just need a bit more tape," MacKenzie replied.

CHAPTER 28

A New Ronald Reagan

I KNOW THAT CAMILA HOPES THE NEW SIGN WILL LEAD TO things changing around here. For her, MacKenzie, and the motel. But the biggest changes taking place actually seem to involve Derek.

I've come into town to kill time while the others are working. When I left, Michael was in the restaurant with his computer and phone, in the middle of an incredibly technical conversation with a colleague from British Columbia. MacKenzie and Camila were soldiering on as usual. New sign or not, there are always rooms that need to be cleaned.

So, I decided to walk into town, and as I passed Sandy's Café, I noticed Bob Parker's Cadillac parked outside. That's where I am now.

If it was possible for a local politician to be loved, Bob would be wildly popular, but he would be the first to admit that it's a contradiction in terms. Bob is more like an institution. People can complain all they like, but no one would ever dream of changing him.

Sally's Café functions as Bob's unofficial office, but he doesn't have any fixed hours there. If his car is outside, you know he's inside, and if you have any complaints or suggestions, it's just a matter of taking them in to him. Ditto if you just feel like a coffee.

It could be a fun way to pass an hour, I think. A bit like reading the letters sent in to the *Gazette*.

I have an awful lot of time to kill these days.

But I'm still not used to the fact that people can no longer see me. I feel awkward the minute I step inside. I even try to smooth out my blouse and stand up straight, pretending I have some reason to be there.

There are two folding tables against one wall, barely covered by a tiny red-and-white-checked tablecloth. Awaiting any particularly engaged citizens—or hungry passersby—are a huge plate of doughnuts and greasy sandwiches and a couple of thermoses of coffee. There are three men sitting by the wall, each drinking coffee. I can't work out whether they're here to see Bob, because he just keeps glancing up at the clock, as though he is waiting for someone else.

That's when Derek arrives.

He looks almost as nervous as I do, and it makes me think more of him than I have in some time. Even he seems to have no idea what he's doing here.

Bob strides straight over to him and says "Derek, come in" in a confident, friendly voice. "Great you could swing by."

The men by the wall look up from their coffee and doughnuts. Derek studies them as if he's trying to remember whether he sold them something at some point.

It quickly transpires that they've read the article in the *Gazette*. They thump his back, shake his hand, and talk enthusiastically about his former triumphs and the current team's prospects. It's only when they move on to the Ducks' future after Mariota that the atmosphere changes, but they quickly recover: back to high school football.

"I'm sure your record will stand," says a stocky, ruddy man who thumps Derek so hard on the back that coffee sloshes out of his mug.

"I don't know, Roy," Derek says. "A few of the kids looked pretty dangerous during practice. One of these days, they'll show what a has-been I am."

Everyone laughs politely. No, more than politely. Fondly. The article has reminded them that they used to like him.

After a while, Bob places a hand on Derek's arm and leads him over to a quiet corner. Probably about time: a calculating glimmer had just appeared in Derek's eye. I'm sure he was trying to work out what he could palm off on them now that they seem to worship him again. Curious to hear what Bob has to say, I follow them over so I can eavesdrop more easily.

"It's like I thought," Bob says, sounding pleased. "Sales? You've been wasting your talents."

"I'm good at selling stuff." Derek seems to want to go back to the men to prove it, right here and now.

"Sure you are," says Bob. "Just not as good at finding shirts that fit. But you look good in pictures, you shake hands like a pro, and you're good at dealing with weird people. What I'm trying to say is you should be a politician."

"I still have some pride!"

"Shame. You need to get rid of that. People don't become politicians because they're proud. Here, take a vanilla doughnut."

Derek takes two. He has to balance one of them on top of his mug.

"So that's why you wanted me to come by. Politician! You must be losing it, Bob. Dad says hi, by the way." He finishes off his first doughnut. "I'm not even a member."

"Oregon isn't like other states. We do things our own way. The party? It's always weak. It's personal campaigns that matter here."

I know more about Oregon's political system than I'd like. The big difference here, compared to many of the other states, isn't that we're more person-centric. It's that we have more popular votes. At every election, our poor citizens also have to make up their minds about dozens of other proposals.

But that isn't something Bob is thinking about right now.

"Trust me," he says. "You could win. Unless you've already sold too much crap to people around here. We just need to find you the right role."

"What? You need an old quarterback at your meetings? I don't know a thing about politics. I don't even know what a politician does. You read stuff? Go to meetings?"

"A lot of talking and listening. Mostly listening. That's what I need you for. You can do that, can't you?"

"I'm not deaf yet, if that's what you mean."

"Plenty of folks are good at reading proposals and paragraphs and small print until they go cross-eyed, but we'll never win if we can't listen to people. Find out what they want. What they dream about. What makes them angry. What stops from moving forward in their lives. Take that guy over there." Bob nods to a man walking by outside. "You could spend half an hour talking to him and find out all that stuff, right?"

"And?"

"Solve a single problem for him, and he'll vote for you the rest of his life. That's what politics is all about. Wheeling and dealing and problem solving."

Derek shrugs. He has already lost interest. "So what do I get out of it?"

Bob looks Derek straight in the eye. "You'd be respected again."

Derek's mug pauses halfway up to his mouth. That's the only thing that gives him away. Then he takes a sip of his coffee with deliberate nonchalance. They're just two men drinking coffee on a perfectly ordinary Monday.

"You'd be respected for who you are now, not who you used to be."

"Why the hell would I want that?"

He doesn't sound entirely convinced.

"Thanks for the doughnuts," he says with a nod to Bob and the three men.

"No worries," Bob says with no hint of disappointment in his voice.

He'll be back, Bob thinks. I know it from the way he smiles as he watches the door slam behind Derek as he leaves.

The next day, I can't say I'm entirely surprised to see Derek heading toward Bob Parker's real office. I have all the time in the world, and I'm interested in seeing what Derek is going to make of Bob's offer. I told myself I was just going to take a walk into town, but deep down, I knew I was hoping to run into Derek.

He isn't on my list, but you can't follow lists all the time, I tell myself. Plus, he's linked to Michael. Maybe being a politician is the real job Michael wants Derek to get.

Though you'd have to be incredibly optimistic to see being a politician as a real job.

I follow Derek like a pro. For several blocks, I pretend to be looking in shop windows; I dodge down alleyways, hide behind other pedestrians, and then—with excessive nonchalance—follow him openly.

It's incredibly satisfying to tail people as a ghost.

Derek hesitates outside the ugly salmon-colored building on the edge of town. Bob's real office is inside. I pretend to be completely absorbed by the nearest shop window. Unfortunately, it belongs to a funeral parlor, so I'm staring straight at a tasteful yet depressing wreath.

Eventually, he mutters "What the hell" and walks up to reception, where an indifferent secretary is killing time by reading the *Gazette*.

"Derek Callahan," he says, flashing her a blinding smile. The secretary is at least thirty years older than him, and wearing an ugly knit sweater, but charm is something that comes naturally to Derek. "Is Bob in? No, I don't have an appointment."

The secretary wearily reaches for the phone, presses a button, and says that Derek Callahan is here. She waits for an answer. Derek almost has time to change his mind before she blankly conveys the wonderful news that yes, Bob Parker has time to see him. Through the door and to the left.

The corridor is dark and narrow, and leads to a nondescript door with one of those nameplates that can easily be changed.

"Come in, come in," Bob says.

The cheap carpet in the corridor continues into his office. Inside, he has a number of dull-gray metal archival cupboards, a cheap bookcase full of reference books, and several volumes of state and local law. Framed, signed documents and a personal letter of thanks from the former governor. There is a sofa against one wall, or at least it looks like a sofa beneath the piles of papers and brown folders.

"I guess people don't become politicians for the money," Derek says.

Bob bends down and moves a pile of newspapers from the visitor's chair. "Very true," he says. "But some things are better than money. Power. Recognition. Getting things done your own way."

"Sounds a damn sight like work if you ask me," Derek replies.

Bob looks around the room. Eventually, he dumps the newspapers on the sofa. The piles collapse as they land. About half of them fall to the floor. "Sit yourself down," he says, gesturing to the now-clear chair.

Derek stays on his feet in front of a framed portrait of Ronald Reagan.

Bob shrugs and sits down behind the desk. Pushes a stack of paper to one side. Contentedly leans back.

"Ronald Reagan," he says. "The fortieth president of the United States of America. Did you know people often called him a lazy president? But so what? He got other people to do stuff for him. Do you know what Reagan's secret was? He understood that politics is an *idea*, and that the idea was more important than facts. He sold a story. Probably because he was an actor before he became a politician. The United States was a country of heroes. People hated us for our freedom. We were prepared to work hard, sacrifice ourselves for our country, and achieve success the hard way, without the help of any intrusive, incompetent state. Americans were different from everyone else. Back then, you were allowed to say that kind of thing."

Derek nods. Why not? It isn't particularly hard for him to believe that Americans are the best people on earth.

"But do you know what the funny part is? These days, we're all nostalgic for Reagan. But *his* idea built on nostalgia for the past."

Bob gets up. "We could really do with a new Reagan." He pats Derek on the shoulder. "Who knows? Maybe that could be you. A football player instead of an actor. Both sell dreams, which is what you have to do if you want to succeed as a politician."

"I haven't said yes yet," Derek tells him, though his protest is pretty half-hearted.

"The politics itself is easy. You're against taxes and the federal government, and you're for business, the nation, and God. In that order. It's really all about personality. Go to church, dress well, and stop sleeping around."

"How do you know I'm sleeping around?"

Bob doesn't bother to answer.

"I'm not sure politics is worth that."

Bob seems to realize that it's an unreasonable demand. "Okay, but be discreet about it. Stay away from other men's wives." He frowns. "You know, you're going to run into problems there. The wives will expect you to flirt with them, but the men will be offended if you do—and they'll be offended if you don't, too."

Derek laughs. "Bob, I've managed that balancing act since I was sixteen. Wives have always flirted with me."

"Speaking of wives... What does Stacey make of all this?"

"I haven't even made up my mind yet. I definitely haven't mentioned it to her."

Bob ignores him. "God, the two of you are going to work so well together."

"I haven't said yes."

"No, no. But later, when you do, you'll be the king and queen of politics. You could go all the way if you wanted to, I'm sure of it. Jesus, I remember when you were just kids! She came to every game, didn't she?"

"So what? The whole town did."

"Yeah, yeah, but still. You married your childhood sweetheart. A happy ending for the whole town. Always by your side! Always proud and supportive!"

"Uh, yeah..."

Bob also seems to be thinking about the current version of Stacey Callahan. "Maybe you could buy her some new clothes," he says. "You're a team now. The voters will want to see her standing by your side."

"The voters don't know my wife."

"No, but they're going to want to see her. Talk to her. All women like new clothes, don't they? Buy yourself a new suit. A couple of nice jackets, too. Oregon's a pretty informal state, so people don't expect you to go around in a suit the whole time, but remember that Pine Creek's a conservative town. A jacket never hurt anyone. Don't forget you're a Republican."

"That's one thing I can remember," Derek mutters.

"You're a natural. Trust me. If you just listen to what I say, you'll be a better politician than you ever were a football player, and that's saying a lot. You'll definitely have a longer career."

"For God's sake, Bob. It was my knee that was the problem."

"Football players are natural winners. That self-confidence you have, it'll take you far in politics. It's a game, a show, like everything else in life. Do you remember the feeling of having an innate talent? Instinctively being able to do things that others have to fight for?"

"Vaguely."

"You're going to feel it again. You'll have to work hard—I won't lie about that—but it'll be like your football training. The more you work, the more you'll feel like everything is just ticking along nicely. Everything will fall into place. People will praise you for doing things that come naturally to you. You'll be invincible. I'll book a few lunch meetings for you right away. With all the most important people in town. Before long, you'll be one of them yourself."

Derek relaxes. When Bob brings up Stacey's clothes for a second time, he doesn't even protest.

Back at the motel, the biggest change—new sign not included—is that some of the town's wilder teenagers have started hanging out on the hill beyond the parking lot. I guess they feel like the sign says something about their lives.

They aren't exactly doing any harm, but their presence, combined with their idleness, teenage drama, and hormones, gives off a slightly downbeat impression. The third time they show up after school, MacKenzie calls the sheriff to ask whether there is anything he can do.

"It isn't motel property, so I can't ask them to leave," he says. "If they start drinking or getting too rowdy, I guess I can send a car over to have a word, but I doubt it'll do much good. They'll find someplace new soon."

As a result, the teenagers are still there when Cheryl arrives at the motel that evening.

The sun is setting, and it *should* be beautiful, but suddenly I see everything through her eyes. The idle teenagers and their shrill, loud voices become ominous. The new sign shines fatefully over the tired concrete and asphalt, and through the restaurant window, Dad's lonely figure looks even more tragic than usual.

Cheryl shudders.

Even Clarence's friendly smile seems intrusive and potentially dangerous. She clutches her handbag tightly.

"It's just Clarence," I say.

Unfortunately, he cheerily asks if she wants a swig from his hip flask as she passes. With that, all of her suspicions are confirmed and any lingering doubt about what Dad is doing here is gone.

As are any thoughts she might have had about being calm and reasonable. The minute she reaches Dad's table, she says, "Oh, *Robert*! How *could* you?"

Cheryl throws her arms around him in an attempt to provide some comfort, but he stiffens in horror.

The other guests in the restaurant—two old men and MacKenzie, who was chatting to them when Cheryl came in—turn to watch. It would have been funny if Dad didn't look so tortured. MacKenzie and the two old men don't have any such scruples. They find the whole thing incredibly amusing.

Cheryl doesn't care. "How could you leave your friends and neighbors—your own home?"

"For pity's sake, woman, pull yourself together," Dad says.

"Everyone knows you shouldn't surround yourself with people who'll lead you to temptation when you're trying to stop drinking. You're supposed to stop spending time with them. You don't *move in* with them!"

"I'm not trying to stop drinking!"

Cheryl gasps. "But you have to! You can't go on like this. Who knows how far the drink can drag you down?"

"A man can have a bit of fun, can't he?" one of the old men says, and the other laughs in agreement.

Dad looks around in panic. "Cheryl, I can't talk about this right now."

"Don't you miss your home? How long are you planning to stay here? Why don't you come back with me now, and I can make us all a nice dinner. Everyone on the street is wondering how you're doing."

I don't know whether Dad was considering going home, but her last sentence definitely makes him stubbornly clench his jaws. "So they can keep gossiping, no doubt. Going through my trash and talking about me? No thank you. I won't be coming back. At least I get left in peace here."

MacKenzie follows Cheryl out into the parking lot. "Cheryl!" she says, trying to flash her a disarming smile. It falters as Cheryl spins around.

"You!" she spits at MacKenzie. Cheryl's voice is unsteady with righteous anger.

"I just wanted you to know that it wasn't my idea for him to move in here. If it was up to me, he would have stayed at home."

"It's all your fault!" Cheryl snaps. "And you don't even care!"

MacKenzie folds her arms. "You can think what you like," she says.

All that gives away her real feelings are her trembling fingers. She digs them deeper into her arm and smiles, purely because she knows it will irritate Cheryl more.

"That's the problem with you, MacKenzie Jones. You never take anything seriously. Everything's a joke to you, isn't it? Like your new sign. Not to mention the old one! You accused the whole town of being homophobes!"

"Not the whole town. But if you feel accused…"

"I'm proud of my work with the church. At least I have something that means something to me. And it's the *Bible* that says it's a sin. Not me."

"The Bible says all kinds of crap, unless my memory is wrong."

"I doubt the Bible says anything to *you*. You've always had a bad influence on people. You always did while you were at school, and you still have it over the town's kids."

MacKenzie instinctively glances over to the hill. There are even more teenagers there now. "They're only hanging out here because they have nowhere else to go," she says. Then she smiles, looking exaggeratedly friendly. "But you're right, of course. I've tried to get rid of them, but maybe I should be helping them instead. They're stuck in boring classrooms all day. Not just boring, but dirty, too. I *should* try to perk them up a little."

"You leave our school alone! You caused enough trouble while you were there."

"I wasn't thinking about the school, but maybe you have a point…"

"This isn't over yet. Believe me," Cheryl says as she climbs into her car. She slams the door and drives away.

That dangerous glimmer is back in MacKenzie's eyes.

I turn to her. "No more empty bottles," I plead. "Remember what happened last time. Imagine if Cheryl moves in, too!"

MacKenzie watches the teenagers over on the hill. Then she goes into the restaurant and reemerges with an apple pie for them.

"I'm not sure you should be feeding them," Alejandro mumbles.

"Hold the fort here tonight, okay?" MacKenzie tells him. "I've got a few things to do in Baker City."

The sound of a car horn cuts through the night.

I sit up in bed, confused, almost as drowsy as Michael. I had allowed my thoughts to drift, not quite asleep, but almost, when I suddenly heard...

There's that irritating sound again. Loud and impatient. The display on the clock radio reads 02:47.

"What the hell..." Michael mutters to himself as he pulls on a pair of jeans and a T-shirt. He doesn't seem any the wiser when he opens the door. MacKenzie's pickup is parked outside, and in the darkness beyond her headlights, I can make out the shape of the motel's longest ladder. The end is hanging perilously over the roof of the car.

MacKenzie looks unashamedly alert. She is warmly dressed in a thick coat, cut-off gloves, and a colorful scarf and seems to be radiating energy.

"Get in," she says. "We're going for a ride."

Michael looks down at his bare feet. "Give me a minute," he says, disappearing into the cabin.

Before long, he is back. Dressed but sleepy. His hair is sticking up in all directions, and his eyes are squinting at the world around him. But the cold night air seems to perk him up.

Camila is already in the truck, but she shuffles over to make room for Michael. She seems to be suffering patiently, with no idea what is going on.

I glance back and forth between the full car and the cold truck bed where the ladder is resting, then I climb inside and sit on Michael's lap with my head pressed against the windowpane. It isn't dignified, but it's better than being alone, beneath a ladder, in the bed of the truck. I don't need any more bad luck.

"What's going on?" Michael asks. He isn't questioning MacKenzie; he barely even sounds curious. It's more like he has just noticed that he's in a car in the middle of the night.

Camila tries to shrug, but she is so hemmed in between the others that she can't quite manage. "Don't ask me," she mumbles.

"You'll have to wait and see," MacKenzie says.

At three in the morning, the town is deserted. The shops, cafés, and bars have all been closed for hours. The streetlamps illuminate empty streets, and as we drive through a residential area, all of the windows are dark.

The school is definitely empty at this time of night. There are a couple of lights on over by the football field, as though to suggest that football never sleeps, but the school itself is bathed in darkness.

MacKenzie parks by the windowless end of the building, the truck's headlights shining onto the wall. She leaves them on, walks around to the back of the truck, and climbs up into the bed. Michael and Camila help her to unfold the ladder and take everything she passes down from the truck.

Before long, there are a number of cans of paint, a bag of rollers, and a long handle on the ground.

Michael watches skeptically as MacKenzie starts opening the cans of paint.

"Christ," he says quietly to Camila. "She's going to paint a rainbow flag."

"What do we do if someone comes?" Camila whispers.

"Run, I guess. We've got the getaway truck ready, in any case. But we're definitely leaving the ladder."

I move away from them to keep a lookout, but it's pointless. My eyes are constantly being drawn back to MacKenzie.

She pushes the first roller onto the handle, clamps it beneath her arm, grabs the can of bright-red paint, and quickly and confidently climbs the ladder. It stretches at least halfway up the school building, and with the long handle, she has an even bigger reach. She dips the entire roller into the can of paint and then rolls it along the wall several times, until she has a broad horizontal strip measuring roughly two feet in length.

"Are you sure you should be doing this?" I ask nervously. She's very high up. And the ladder seems a little unstable.

Once MacKenzie is happy with the first color, she climbs down, grabs a new roller and the can of orange paint. She climbs back up again. Michael grabs the first roller and drops it into a plastic bag so that it can be reused, then moves back over to Camila, who is leaning against the hood of the truck.

"When I said I wanted the old MacKenzie back, I didn't necessarily mean literally," Camila says. "They're going to be so pissed."

Michael laughs. "I think that's the point."

"They'll just paint over it."

"Maybe. But no matter how many coats they cover it with, we'll know it's under there."

"She's incredible, isn't she?" Camila says quietly.

"Yeah."

And she is. MacKenzie moves the roller back and forth in long, powerful strokes. I'm sure she has paint on her nose, and there's definitely some in her hair. She is humming to herself the whole time, as the enormous rainbow flag takes shape above us.

MacKenzie paints the last few inches of the bottom purple stripe, and climbs down to the ground.

It's as though her body has suddenly realized how tired it is. She stands in the glow of the headlights, totally confused, not seeming to know what to do next.

Michael and Camila tidy up for her. They lift the ladder into the bed of the truck and make sure it's secured in place. They clear away the paint, and then Michael kindly but firmly takes the keys from MacKenzie.

She crawls into the passenger seat and leans her head against Camila's shoulder. Michael and Camila are still on an adrenaline high, relieved at having gotten away with it. The whole way home, they talk about how they would love to see the kids' faces when they get to school tomorrow, about the statistical likelihood that there must be several LGBT people among the students, about the revenge of the duct tape... and then Camila glances at MacKenzie and realizes she has fallen asleep.

MacKenzie is sleeping! Real, deep, relaxed sleep!

Camila cautiously points to her, and Michael nods. They drive on in silence. All I can hear is the sound of the engine and MacKenzie's gentle snoring. As they approach the motel, Michael slows down.

"Let her sleep," Camila says quietly. She tries to look at MacKenzie, but it's difficult with her resting against her shoulder. "I don't think she's had a proper night's sleep in a long time."

And so Michael drives straight past the motel. We drive all the way to Baker City, until the sun comes up, when Michael turns around. On the way back, we pass the early-morning drivers lining up outside the McDonald's drive-through, but other than the rear lights of a truck in the distance, I-84 is empty ahead of us.

Michael drives, Camila is a pillow, and I remember.

All the while, MacKenzie sleeps.

CHAPTER 29

More of Us

NONE OF THE OTHER STUDENTS CARED ABOUT THE PROPOSED measure, despite the fact that it centered around schools. We might have been the battlefield the two sides were fighting over, but none of our schoolmates seemed to think the war affected them.

It was our last year in high school, but it felt like it was never going to end. Like nothing would ever happen. Most of our classmates weren't going on to college, and few had any idea what they were going to do instead. We were caught between the safety of our former lives and an uncertain future that would, at the very least, allow us to get away from the classroom.

Looming in the distance was the school prom. What did a proposed change in the law mean in comparison? We weren't old enough to vote, and the majority wouldn't have bothered even if we had been.

Still, we weren't the only ones in town who were against the measure. Some of the adults formed a working group, and notes were put up in the post office. MacKenzie forced the whole school group to attend their first meeting. We met on Broadway, at a house belonging to two of the women. They lived right next door to Michael.

I think we were all pretty nervous about going over there, but once we arrived, we realized the women were just as nervous as us. There were ten or so of them, most in their forties, all looking acutely uncomfortable as they sat on the sofa and in the armchairs and chairs that had been brought in from the kitchen.

MacKenzie was the only one who wasn't nervous.

"Hi, I'm MacKenzie," she said. "And I'm gay. This is Henny. She's heterosexual, but she's here because she's my friend. Michael, also heterosexual, and Camila, hetero too."

Or so we thought at the time. I suddenly wonder how Camila remembers those days. MacKenzie felt so liberated now that she had finally come out, and I was focused on Michael. But Camila didn't argue. She just looked from MacKenzie to the others with sarcastically raised eyebrows, as though she knew exactly what they were thinking.

They were thinking that she didn't look especially macho.

MacKenzie turned expectantly to the women gathered there. The ice cubes in their glasses clinked as they rushed to reassure everyone that they were perfectly straight but that they were, of course, against the measure, which was possible even if you were heterosexual. Very heterosexual. Married. Their husbands were against the measure, too. Because they were married. Every one of them.

All but the two women whose house it was. They glanced at each other and then shrugged as if they had already made up their minds and were just waiting for the right moment. "Actually..." said one of them.

"We're not just friends."

"We're not married, either. We were, but then we met."

"We got together and moved here a few years back. No one seemed to care that two women were living together. I guess they thought we were only doing it so we could afford a house. I know that a few people knew, but no one talked about it. Until now."

"Until now," the first one repeated.

"I don't know why they're suddenly so obsessed about gay people," MacKenzie said. "And why they're suddenly all talking about it. We've avoided talking about things for generations. Why change a winning concept? But I guess now we have to stop people around here from acting like complete idiots."

Carol and Pat.

Those were their names. I remember their names, but when I think back now, everything else is oddly hazy. I'm almost unsure they even existed. Did we just make them up because we needed them, or were they really so similar to all the other fortysomething women in town that I can't remember a single feature from their faces? What color was their hair? Who knows. Light brown, maybe. Warm smiles, like all the others.

I remember their home as a series of short clips. My brain zooms in on the random things it has saved all these years. The kitchen window: white lace curtains and the brightest red geraniums I'd ever seen. A fridge magnet: *Home is where the heart is*. Embroidered cushions on a beige sofa. A dark hallway. Rubber boots. A garden spade and a pair of forgotten gloves outside. A...cat? Old, grumpy, fussed over.

We stayed behind afterward to help clear up. MacKenzie and Camila even helped with the dishes. Once that was done, MacKenzie volunteered to do the drying, gazing with fascination at Carol and Pat. *She* probably memorized their faces.

To her, they were unique and unforgettable. Their very existence seemed magnetic to MacKenzie. Every time one of them came into the kitchen—to check how it was going or to return a forgotten coffee cup or to repeat that we *really* didn't have to do the washing up—she would look at them as though she expected them to perform miracles at any moment.

Once there was absolutely nothing left for us to do, and MacKenzie had offered to come back and cut their lawn, we headed home together. MacKenzie practically skipped along beside Camila, and Michael and I ended up behind.

"There are *more* of us!" MacKenzie said. "I always thought I was the only dyke in town. How is that possible? And another thing: If I missed them, how many others have I missed? There could be a whole load of us out there! See, something good has already come out of this madness."

Camila didn't speak, but I think she had also been inspired by Carol and Pat. Though she had been accused of being heterosexual, she seemed to be looking at MacKenzie with something very much like admiration.

CHAPTER 30

"Take a Cookie, Mr. Broek"

WE GET BACK TO THE MOTEL JUST IN TIME FOR BREAKFAST. I'M enjoying the new color in MacKenzie's cheeks and the new sense of camaraderie that seems to have developed between her, Michael, and Camila.

They're onto their third cup of coffee when MacKenzie suddenly says, "I wish I could see their faces."

Michael and Camila quickly make her promise that she won't drive over to the school, not even to innocently ask who decorated their wall. MacKenzie mutters to herself, steals some of Camila's scrambled eggs, and reluctantly agrees that it would be undiplomatic to annoy them any further.

Not until she's managed to get the paint out of her hair, anyway.

That's probably smart, I think, but it doesn't mean *I* can't go over there. I've been neglecting my duties as a ghost.

I leave them in the restaurant, smiling as Camila half-heartedly tries to save the last of her eggs, and head off toward town.

By the time I get to the school, classes have already begun, but there are still plenty of kids milling around outside. A few teachers too, I think. Maybe the sudden arrival of the rainbow flag has disrupted their lesson plans.

There are a couple of upset parents, of course, but the teenagers seem to think it's funny. I wonder whether that's because times have changed or because they just appreciate something new happening.

A young girl with pink hair laughs and takes a selfie in front of the rainbow flag. Her friends are waiting nearby, and as I move closer, I notice that one of them is wearing a *Basic Rights Oregon* pin on their jacket.

So. Things *do* seem to have gotten better. The mothers' upset voices don't concern me.

On my way back to the motel, I almost run straight into Bob and Derek. Bob seems to be dragging Derek around town, introducing him to everyone they pass, and I decide to follow them for a while.

Derek smiles and shakes hands and struggles valiantly to look as if he understands everything. People are friendly, but they're also a little standoffish: they size him up, remembering his football career. It seems like most still haven't decided whether it counts as a merit.

"I guess he knows what it's like to win," one of them says before Derek is quite out of earshot.

"And to fail," says another. "He came back from college pretty quick, didn't he? And what's he done since?"

Derek's jaw tenses.

Next up is a fiftysomething couple who show all the signs of being comfortably well-off. The man's jacket is well cut, and the woman's hair is professionally dyed a natural-looking shade of honey blond. Derek's smile widens even further to show that he is taking in everything they say.

"I don't know whether I trust a politician who smiles that much," the man says afterward. Derek hears this, too.

Cheryl and another woman intercept Bob and Derek on Elm Street. The other woman has a toddler balanced on her hip, and both have the air of being someone who knows she has Jesus on her side.

"Right at the top, Bob Parker," Cheryl says. The other woman nods so violently that the child bobs up and down and laughs in amusement. The women's dogged faces look even more frightening in contrast to the laughing child.

"How are we going to paint over it?"

"I told you I'll deal with it," Bob begins. "Don't you worry, we'll fix it."

"It's MacKenzie Jones who did it, I'm telling you," Cheryl says.

"Of course it was MacKenzie," Bob agrees.

"Must've taken a whole load of brushes," Derek chips in, an admiring tone in his voice. "But painting over it will be easy enough. Why not just paint the whole school?"

Bob pulls him off to one side and mutters: "Money. You'll hear that answer pretty often, let me tell you. There's no money. Ned from the paint shop usually donates a can or two when the graffiti gets a bit too… interesting. The school board has been nagging me to paint it for years, but there's no money for it. And it isn't just the paint. It's the labor, too."

"There was enough money for the new football field. Looked pretty good."

"Football isn't an ugly, old school building," Bob says quietly. He turns back to Cheryl and the woman.

"We want to know what you're going to do about this," Cheryl says.

Bob holds up his hands. "All right, ladies. All right. The school district will take care of it. Do you know Derek? Fantastic football player, and he'll be an even better politician."

They give Derek an uninterested glance, nod almost impolitely, and then turn their attention back to Bob.

"The school is already a mess!" the other woman says. "Many of the parents are upset about this. I hope you realize that. Sheer homo propaganda!"

Something in their quick dismissal of him, in only speaking to Bob, seems to spur Derek into action.

He excuses himself and pulls out his phone, taking a couple of steps away from the women and leaving Bob to drum up every ounce of charm he has.

"Ned!" Derek says. "Do you have a minute? Dad says hi, by the way. No, haven't managed to fit in much golf lately. The knee's been playing up again, you know how it is. Yeah, we're all getting older. Listen, you couldn't do me a favor, could you? No, I don't want to sell you anything. I'm trying to get hold of some paint. Outdoor paint. For the school. Yeah, of course it was MacKenzie. One of her jokes. No, no, not funny at all. Of course not. Ah, you've got a can of the pale-blue paint left. But I was thinking we should be a little more ambitious this time. If I can get together a team of guys for the painting itself, do you think you'd be able to sponsor the paint and a couple of brushes? I was thinking the football team could help out. As a personal favor to me. Would look good for you in the *Gazette*. You promise to think about it? Great. Say hi to the wife."

Derek hangs up. Everyone is staring at him.

"He'll go along with it," Derek tells them. "He just needs a little time to convince himself it was his idea."

The woman with the child allows herself an appreciative smile before she sets off to continue her chores. Bob seems to be hoping that Cheryl will leave, too, but she is still lingering.

"Derek," she says eagerly. "What do you think of the motel?"

"I, uh, don't really have an opinion."

"I have an idea," Cheryl continues. "And it strikes me that you could be the perfect person to do it. I need someone who can make things happen and who has the right ambitions. *Someone* has to do something about that darn motel."

"Excuse me, Cheryl," Bob quickly butts in. "We're already late for another meeting. Now that Derek seems to have solved the problem with the school..."

"But that's precisely why I want to talk to him about—"

"Gotta dash!" Bob practically drags Derek away with him.

"Why didn't you want to listen to what she was saying? Wasn't that the whole point of politics? Listening to people's problems and seeing how you can fix them? I managed pretty well with the school."

"I know what she wanted to say. She's already talked to me about it."

"So...? Did you fix it already?"

"It's unfixable."

"Maybe you just need some new ideas."

"Let me tell you about... Let's call them special interests. People can be very convincing. And very, very enthusiastic. It's easy to get drawn in, but if something goes wrong, it's you who's left with a whole street of shrunken elms."

"What if they have a point, though?"

"They always do. From *their* point of view. The problem is that they've got no sense of proportion or perspective, no idea that someone might see things different from them. They've got their ideals, and they aren't interested in meeting or compromising or even discussing the problem."

"Yeah, we couldn't possibly bring ideals into politics," Derek mutters. "How would that look?"

"What I'm trying to say is that there are a lot of folks with a lot of different ideals, but we all have to live together. And they want *their* issue to dominate everything."

"So what's *her* issue?"

"The motel."

"MacKenzie's motel? Because of the rainbow flag?"

"That just gave her fuel for the fire. What she's really upset about is the fact the motel tempts the town's kids—and older people—into ruin. She sees it as an entry point into alcohol, drugs, and bad morals."

"I had no idea the motel was so exciting. Maybe I should move in there myself."

"Don't joke about it when Cheryl's around. That's what happens when you have strong convictions. Your sense of humor's the first thing to go." He smiles as he says it. He is relieved that Derek doesn't seem to have been infected by Cheryl's enthusiasm. "I told you, didn't I?" he adds. "Mad obsessions!"

Derek shrugs. He has already lost interest. He is still thinking about his first political victory.

"At least they didn't complain about my smile this time," he says, thumping Bob on the back.

"Yeah, but you've got to paint the whole school," Bob reminds him. Still, he sounds impressed. He sizes Derek up. "Talk to Stacey. I've got a couple of dinners I thought you could tag along to. Purely social. With the most important people in town. You'll need their support if you're going to make it as a politician."

Exactly twenty-four hours later, Stacey storms into check-in with two canvas bags over her shoulder.

"Do you know what he *said*?" is her opening phrase.

MacKenzie is busy showing Camila how to do something on the computer, and both look up at the same time. Camila's hand is resting gently on MacKenzie's shoulder.

Stacey throws her hands up in the air, clearly grateful to have an audience.

"Uh, who?" MacKenzie asks.

"Derek! My good-for-nothing, alcoholic, cheating husband. He said that *I* should dress differently."

"He's dumber than I thought," MacKenzie reluctantly whispers to Camila. "And braver." Then, to Stacey, she says, "Is he still alive?"

"Yeah, which is more than he deserves. He thought I should be more 'representative.' Me! All because he wants to be a politician. What about what I want? I asked him. What am I meant to do? Be some politician's wife? Like hell, I still have some pride!"

Stacey drops her bags with a loud thud.

"So you want a room?" Camila asks.

"Why else would I be here? This is a motel, isn't it? Very fitting name, by the way. Sums up my life."

MacKenzie rolls back in her chair so that Camila can get to the computer, and she points out where things need to be filled in. Name, license plate, room number.

Stacey continues her monologue as they work.

"You're probably not even registered to vote, I told him, but he just went on and on about how he could learn and how he wanted to make something of his life. To be respected again; do you hear that, huh?"

She looks a little defensive. "I'm not saying there's anything wrong with wanting to do something, you know? People would respect him if he just stopped selling crap. But turning up at home and announcing that I need to buy new clothes—*boring* clothes. All because I'll have to stand there next to him, smiling and nodding like an idiot? No, that crosses the line."

"We hope you'll enjoy your stay here," Camila says, handing her the key.

"Ah, I'll probably just pine away," Stacey says, hauling her bags back onto her shoulder.

MacKenzie has given Stacey the room next to Dad's, and despite the stubborn drizzle outside, Stacey's door is wide open. I don't know what she's thinking right now, but I doubt it's anything nice.

She is standing in the middle of the room, hemmed in between the bed and the desk, glaring at her surroundings. As she makes her way into the bathroom, she stubs her toe on the bed and swears loudly to herself.

"Goddamn piece-of-crap bed."

When she decides to unpack, she opens the first bag and pulls out something at random. A makeup bag, I think. It ends up on the desk. She finds a dried-out mascara in her handbag, and throws that onto the bedside table. She also finds: three old napkins, an open box of throat lozenges that have spilled out into her bag, lipstick, receipts, and around three dollars in small change.

She picks up her suitcase and shakes it out onto the bed. Two pairs of jeans, five T-shirts, a strange orange dress, two pairs of tights, an unsorted jumble of socks, and two summer jackets tumble onto the bedspread.

Dad, who is passing by, pauses long enough to snort disapprovingly.

Stacey stares at him. Then she grabs the pile of clothes in her arms and throws it up in the air. Her things land all over the floor, and Dad hurries off to the restaurant in indignation.

The smell of chocolate chip cookies drifts out across the restaurant. Dolores is baking again. Despite the gray weather, the smell makes me think of sunny childhood afternoons, getting home from school, and seeing Dad in his neat apron with a tray of cookies in the oven. I find myself smiling as I step into the restaurant, just like everyone else in there.

Everyone but Stacey. She pulls a face as she notices the comforting scent. She pauses in the doorway, letting in a gust of chilly autumn air that makes Dad shiver in his too-thin suit.

She spots him sitting alone in a booth and walks over and slips into the seat opposite.

He gives her a disapproving look, as though to remind her that he didn't invite her to sit down.

"So what've you done?" she asks.

"Pardon?"

"To end up here."

"I haven't done anything!"

"Innocent, huh?" Stacey says. It's like they're in some kind of terrible prison movie. "I've heard that one before."

Dolores comes out and serves her a cup of coffee. "Cookies in ten minutes."

"Like one big, happy family," Stacey mutters sarcastically once Dolores is out of earshot.

"What's the problem with that?" Dad asks. "Surely you can't have anything against families?"

"No? What the hell has family ever done for me?"

"You know, cursing makes a very bad impression," Dad says almost automatically.

Stacey blushes.

"And family is the very foundation of our society!"

Stacey is glaring at him now. Dad notices and continues, "What's wrong with family, order, rules, and traditions? They make life easier. Family is the foundation of our society, and the trouble with this country is that people don't respect that."

"What a goddamn shame," Stacey says. "You old idiot."

With that, she storms out of the restaurant.

"Another harmonious day at the Pine Away Motel," MacKenzie says cheerily. She snatches a cookie from the tray before Dolores has time to bat away her hand.

"They need to cool down!" Dolores says, but she puts a couple onto plates, pushes one toward MacKenzie, and takes the other over to Dad.

He is still at his table, completely confused. "What did I do wrong?" he moans.

"Do you really want me to answer that?" MacKenzie asks. She takes her plate and walks away before Dolores has time to say anything.

"Surely there's nothing wrong with telling someone to behave like a civilized person? Some things are just right. When did common decency become something ugly? It can't be wrong to point out that it makes a more polite, decent impression if you aren't swearing all the time, can it?"

"Take a cookie, Mr. Broek," Dolores tells him.

CHAPTER 31
Michael's Memories

THE PRETTY PURPLE BOUQUET IS FROM MICHAEL. IT LOOKS SO sad in front of my gravestone.

"This is the first time you've ever given me flowers," I tell him, but he doesn't seem to be in the mood for jokes.

He spent the whole morning moving restlessly around the cabin, unable to focus on anything. He tried to wash the dishes, but he spent more time wandering around with the brush in his hand than actually cleaning anything. Eventually, he paused by the table and stared down at a dirty coffee cup as though he was trying to work out what to do with it. *Coffee cup. Dirty. I'm holding a brush. What am I supposed to do here?*

And then he just left the cup there.

I think the weather is making things worse. A thick layer of clouds has settled over town, and the sky itself seems to be bearing down on us. Michael stared at the walls as if they were closing in on him.

He needs me; that much was worryingly clear. I would have been able to make him relax. I don't think too much. If there's a dirty coffee cup, I'll wash it. Life isn't a list to be ticked off, one point at a time.

Suddenly he got up, grabbed his coat and car keys, and set off to deal with the next item on his *Remembering Henny* list.

Michael's flowers are competing for space with roses, lilies, and a sad little Tupperware box of enchiladas. Clearly Dolores is worried that I'm not getting enough to eat in heaven.

Grief is a strange thing, I think to myself. I could have sworn that Michael was happy with MacKenzie and Camila, but now he seems to be refusing to let himself feel like that. As though grief has to be experienced in a particular way. Unhappily. Alone.

In the rain. A heavy drop of water lands just inside Michael's collar, but he doesn't react.

I don't know what he thinks he's going to find here in the churchyard. If he's looking for memories of me, he would be better off going for a beer with MacKenzie and Camila.

But maybe I just have to leave him alone here to be lonely and unhappy.

Maybe people need to be sad from time to time.

The other headstones look abandoned in the grayness surrounding us, though the cemetery as a whole seems well cared for: neat grass, carefully planted flower beds, small bouquets in front of some of the headstones, and not a single weed as far as the eye can see. The cloud cover is so low that the church spire looks as if it might pierce right through it.

I walk a little uncertainly down the neat gravel paths between the graves, wondering again why I haven't seen any other ghosts. Surely I can't be the only person who can't bear to leave their loved ones?

Maybe we just can't see one another, the same way Michael and Camila and MacKenzie can no longer see me. Maybe we all move on eventually, disappearing to...someplace else.

"Michael," I begin, but when I turn toward him, I see that he is already walking away.

I have to run to catch up with him.

The schoolyard is deserted in the drizzle.

We stand together, staring at the asphalt and the basketball hoop and the doors into school. It's the middle of the afternoon, but we're still the only people here.

I know what we're doing. We're hunting memories together. Now that he has talked to others about me, he's searching for the people we once were.

If I really make an effort, I can see the outlines of a young Michael and Henny up ahead. We're in the middle of the schoolyard, chatting eagerly about geology or the Measure Nine campaign or something. The clouds seem to break right before me, the sun like a spotlight on my memories of us.

Then I make the mistake of looking at the real Michael, and the sunlight dissolves into rain.

I can tell that he's trying to see us, but his face is hard and lifeless. There's no way he could see the ghosts of us and not smile.

He doesn't even go over to the gymnasium where we danced together at prom. Something in his expression or in the grayness all around us must have infected me, because I'm thankful for that.

I don't want to think about that evening, either. My superstitious mind manages to avoid the happy memory of the only time we ever danced together. I suppose it's because that dance was the end of our story. I don't want to think about what happened next, but my brain knows. He left me. He came back. I died.

As he returns to his car, I'm as relieved as he is.

When he gets to Broadway, he doesn't even get out. Through steamed-up windows, we see the house where Pat and Carol lived and remember the sign that stood outside his father's house. *Yes to Measure 9.* Signs in front of all the other houses, too. Proud and open.

On Elm Street, he wanders around for several blocks before he finally manages to find the place where the candy shop once was. It takes him some time to realize that it has become the ice-cream parlor he and Camila were standing outside of just the other day. He pulls a face when it dawns on him.

That has to be enough now, I think. I can accept that he needs to grieve in peace, but why is he using his memories of us to torture himself? It's like picking at a wound. He is welcoming the pain. No, worse: he's actively looking for it. He is using our past to flog himself, and I wonder whether he thinks it's going to make him stronger.

He doesn't even go to *our* place! A guided tour of our memories, and he can't even be bothered to go to the place we kissed for the first time, the place where my indignation led us that day.

"Michael," I say. "You don't need to fight so hard to remember me. You're grieving enough as it is. It's okay to relax from time to time. Let yourself have a bit of fun."

I glance at the tragic figure beside me and realize that "have a bit of fun" is probably too much to ask.

"Maybe you should try to do something instead," I say. "Sometimes it's better not to think too much. Just do something. Anything. Like Camila's work at the motel, or MacKenzie's rainbow flag. Okay, so we probably don't need any more rainbow flags. It would've been funny to paint them all over town, but I think Cheryl is upset enough as it is."

I sigh. I don't think anything I'm saying is getting through. I think he's trapped between two conflicting impulses—grieving me and being a part of life here—and he doesn't even realize that the two aren't incompatible. They belong together. He will learn more about Pine Creek and me by hanging out with MacKenzie and Camila, or even with Derek, than he will by loitering on Elm Street in the rain.

I think he feels guilty every time he has even the slightest bit of fun, and I'm worried that if he continues to put pressure on himself like this, he'll give up and run before long.

There's also nothing I can do about it.

"I guess we'll have to do it your way," I say, but I make a promise to myself to tell him happy stories every night.

We go to the Timber Bar next, somewhere the two of us never went. Michael slumps wearily onto the barstool next to Clarence.

"You look a bit the worse for wear," Clarence says warmly. "What's the world done to you today?"

"Memories."

"Ah." Clarence gestures to the bartender. "This man needs a beer. Well, you've come to the right place," he adds to Michael. "Most folks who come here have something they want to forget."

"I was trying to remember."

"Is that so? There's no point trying to remember, if you ask me. No point trying to forget, either. Memories do what they want with us."

"I have to remember. I *have* to..."

"Have to. That's what people say when they're trying to convince themselves we control our lives, when in actual fact it's life that beats the pulp out of us. The best thing to do is just give in. That's what I've always done. The simple truth is that the whole of human history—and the whole of its future, for that matter—can be boiled down to a bit of oxygen, hydrogen, and carbon. A little nitrogen, calcium, and phosphorous, too, if we're being accurate, but they're almost negligible. We're 65 percent oxygen, 20 percent carbon, and 10 percent hydrogen, if I remember the numbers right. And then a few percent nitrogen, phosphorous, and calcium for the proteins, DNA, skeleton, and teeth. That's all we are."

"I know, I know," Michael says wearily. "We're just cucumbers with anxiety."

"You fight too much," Clarence tells him. "Pointless waste of energy. And if I knew Henny right, she'd tell you to relax. Henny wasn't someone who fought fate for no reason."

He should see me now, I think sullenly.

"But you're right about the anxiety." Clarence nods toward a dark corner of the bar. "We've got someone else struggling over there."

Paul. The truck driver.

He seems to have lost at least twenty pounds over the past few weeks. His cheeks are sunken, his skin taut and gray, his face all dark shadows. His eyes are black, still, and bottomless.

"Did you know Henny?" Michael asks Paul.

Clarence frantically shakes his head.

"I killed her," Paul replies.

"You've set him off again now," Clarence mutters. "Why did you have to mention her? Okay, okay, I guess you couldn't know."

"I keep seeing her everywhere. She looked so nice. She didn't even have time to be scared. If I'd just taken ten minutes longer at lunch, that's what I keep thinking. Or if I'd called in sick that day. I've never been sick in my life, but I could've taken one day off, couldn't I? And then she'd still be here. I wouldn't have even driven along that road."

I guess my life wasn't the only one that ended that day.

Michael studies Paul's tragic figure. "Or just hadn't gotten drunk," he mutters.

"He was sober," I protest, but Paul doesn't even seem to have heard.

"And I guess you're going to keep drinking until the bar runs out?"

"Come on, be nice to him," Clarence says. "He's not very good at drinking, either. There's plenty of booze for everyone here."

"That's not what I meant. If he's so sad or regrets it so much, why doesn't he do something useful instead? Does he think that sitting here all day would've made Henny happier?"

"So what do you suggest?"

"I don't know. But he could start by putting down that beer."

"Michael..." I say.

"Do something! Anything! If Henny had to die, her death should at least mean something. And that's *not* you becoming a complete wreck who spends your days in here. It was Henny who died, not you. You should be able to pull yourself out of it. If *I* can, then..."

"Michael!" I interrupt. "I don't think it's that simple. He was there with me when it happened. I was never alone. Surely that has to mean something? I think he's probably been alone ever since."

"He can't hear anything you're saying," Clarence interjects. "I tried to buy him a drink, but he's in his own little world."

Paul gets up. He staggers, but I'm not sure whether it's due to the alcohol or exhaustion.

One of the regulars shouts "Timber!" the way they always do when someone gets too drunk.

Paul doesn't hear that, either. He pushes a twenty-dollar bill across the bar, but he doesn't say a word. As he walks toward the door, he is just a gray silhouette against the rain outside. I blink, but he's still there when I open my eyes.

"Should he be driving?" Michael asks. "Hasn't he caused enough trouble already?"

"He's not driving anywhere. Walks here, walks home. Poor bastard."

"Jesus Christ," Michael mutters, getting up and heading out to his car. Paul hasn't even made it across the parking lot. Michael leans the passenger seat and opens the door. "Get in," he says, and Paul automatically does as he is told.

It turns out that Paul lives in a small apartment ten or so minutes out of town, in the opposite direction from the motel.

"All right, we're here," Michael says. Paul doesn't move.

"For God's sake." Michael gets out, opens the door, and drags Paul out of the car. "Give me your keys," he says. Paul obediently rummages through his pockets, but when Michael tries the door, it is already unlocked.

There are old clothes scattered around the living room, and the blind in the bedroom is still down. The apartment feels dark and claustrophobic. I feel an urge to roll up the blind and open the window. A bit of light and fresh air, that's what this place needs.

The kitchen smells sour, like old milk. There are dirty coffee cups and half-empty cans of beer all over the countertop. A messy pile of unopened letters on the table. Several have angry red stamps on them.

The worst part is that it's so obvious Paul used to care. This is a carefully decorated home. There's even a rug in the living room. The kitchen shelves are clearly marked. The few jars of herbs are lined up with their labels facing out. Homemade shelves in the living room, and a neat extension to the kitchen countertop. Beneath the pile of mail on the kitchen table is a small tablecloth.

Paul slumps onto the sofa, landing on top of a pile of clothes.

"Michael," I say. "I don't think we should leave him alone."

"If you get bored of your meaningless drinking, I'm at the motel," Michael says. He sounds irritated and reluctant, but he says it all the same.

"The motel! That's a fantastic idea. You can take him there now..."

Michael turns and leaves without even looking back at Paul.

I'm left alone in the depressing apartment.

"Okay, God," I whisper. "I could do with some help right now. What should I say? What am I even doing here?"

I hesitate. "Are you...okay?" I ask Paul.

I cautiously sit down next to him on the arm of the couch.

"You might not even want me here," I say. I clasp my hands in my lap and continue uncertainly. "Sorry if I'm intruding. I just thought you might want some company. I don't know what you want."

His eyes are closed, but his breathing is quick and shallow. I don't know what images are playing out in front of his eyes, but I can guess.

"Paul!" I say helplessly, moving closer. "Are you okay? I mean, obviously you're not, but is there anything I can do?"

Of course there isn't.

"You shouldn't be alone. Is there no one you can call? A friend? Your boss?"

Then I hear the welcome sound of a car outside, and when Michael reappears, I run over to him in relief. I'm no longer alone.

"You have to do something," I say.

He stares at Paul, who is still sitting on the couch, and seems to be thinking the same thing.

"Come on," Michael says. "You can't live like this. I'll give you a ride to the motel."

Paul looks up in confusion, but then obediently follows Michael out to the car. I can't tell whether it's because he wants company or because it's more effort to argue.

I jump out of the car the minute they pull up outside the motel and reach reception just before them. MacKenzie yawns and stretches behind the desk. It's ten in the evening. She looks up as Michael and Paul come in.

Paul has such a lack of presence right now that it actually takes her a few seconds to realize he is standing behind Michael.

"You made a friend?" she asks, and Michael grimaces.

"Not...exactly," he says. It just seems to have dawned on him that the motel might not be the best place for the man who was driving the truck that killed me. He glances back over his shoulder in surprise as Paul sways and faints.

MacKenzie gets up and walks over to Michael, and the two of them peer down at Paul. "Right," she says.

"You should probably know he was the one who...was driving the truck."

MacKenzie doesn't speak. I can't read her face. But she knows which truck Michael means.

"Maybe I shouldn't have brought him here," Michael goes on. "But I didn't know what else to do. He shouldn't be alone. I understand if you don't want him here, though. Just say the word, and I'll take him someplace else." He pauses. "I guess he can always sleep on the couch in the cabin."

"He can stay."

Right then, Camila comes into reception.

"Our latest guest," MacKenzie announces, gesturing toward Paul on the floor. She bends over him. When he comes around, her face is only inches from his. He blinks slowly.

"I keep seeing her," he says.

"Sure you do," MacKenzie replies. She looks up at Michael. "It's okay, I'll sort out the rest."

"Do you need help getting him to a room?"

She shakes her head. "He can sleep in the office tonight. Camila and I will manage."

Michael runs a hand through his hair in confusion. "I'll come back tomorrow," he says, and MacKenzie nods. Her eyes are still fixed on Paul.

She and Camila each grab an arm and pull him to his feet, and the three of them stagger over to the office, his arms around their shoulders. They manage to get him onto the couch.

"Who is he?" Camila whispers.

"You know, I have no idea what his name is."

"But..."

MacKenzie leans down over him again. "Excuse me, sir, I didn't catch your name."

"Paul Jackson."

"Nice to meet you. I'm MacKenzie Jones, and this is Camila Alvarez. Welcome to Pine Away Motel and Cabins. We hope you'll enjoy your stay here."

She's joking, but there is a forced cheeriness to her voice.

She drags Camila out of the office and pulls the door closed behind them, making sure to leave it slightly ajar. Wide enough for the lights and sounds of the reception area to seep inside.

Camila frowns in confusion. "But who is he?" she asks quietly. I'm pretty sure Paul can hear them, but when I peer in through the crack in the door, he is on his back, staring up at the ceiling.

"You heard him. Paul Jackson."

"Yeah, but what's he doing *here*?"

When MacKenzie replies, her voice is completely emotionless. In a conscious, deliberately flat tone, she says, "He was driving the truck that..." There is a lump in her throat now. "That was involved in Henny's accident."

Camila touches her arm. "But..." she says. "How can you let him stay here at the motel?"

"It wasn't his fault," MacKenzie replies. "It wasn't anyone's fault. And I don't think he's had a good night's sleep in a long time."

"Okay, but should we really leave him in the office? Can't we give him a proper room? We've got plenty."

"Yeah..." MacKenzie sounds hesitant. She turns toward the half-closed door, a thoughtful look on her face. "You know, I think just having other people around him will do the most good."

"In the office?"

"In general. I don't think being alone is doing him any favors." A frown appears on her forehead. "But I don't think there's much we can do for him tonight. Unless..."

"Unless what?"

"Do you know the best night's sleep I've had lately? It was with you and Michael in the truck after we painted the rainbow. Maybe that's what he needs."

"You want to put him in a car? Now?"

"I don't really think a car is the best idea," I say nervously.

"Not a car," says MacKenzie. "But maybe he could do with a bit of noise around him. Maybe it's time for us to give reception a spring clean. That way, he can lie there and be distracted by the hard couch and the light from out here and the reassuring sound of people working."

Camila hesitates. "Cleaning *is* more fun when there are two of you," she says.

MacKenzie doesn't argue. She just fetches the vacuum cleaner, and when the cord gets caught on the desk, Camila bends down and pulls it free. They even move the couch so that MacKenzie can vacuum behind it.

It quickly transpires that MacKenzie was right. By the time they finish vacuuming, they can hear Paul's irregular snores from inside the office, the sound of a body twisting and turning in its sleep. Camila shakes her head, but they spend the next few hours making more reassuring noise all the same.

They are still hard at work when the clock strikes midnight. There's something about the light in check-in that completely changes people's appearances at night. They look wearier, more worn out. It's unforgiving on wrinkles and bags beneath eyes. It makes skin look like sandpaper. But, oddly enough, MacKenzie and Camila seem to get more beautiful the later it gets.

Camila fetches coffee while MacKenzie sorts through papers. Her fingers brush MacKenzie's hand as she passes her the cup, and both smile unconsciously. No task is too much work: they even fetch window cleaner to spruce up the doors in the darkness.

"I can't even see the dirt." Camila laughs, shaking her head. It has, at least, stopped raining, and the clouds are slowly breaking up.

MacKenzie places a hand at the base of Camila's spine as she stretches to reach another section of the glass. It lingers there for an unnecessarily long time. I don't know whether she's even aware she is doing it. Maybe she just can't stop herself.

"That's the best time for cleaning windows," she says. "You can see the dirt too well in the daylight. Even when you're finished."

The smell of ammonia drifts through the office. I wonder whether it will help Paul sleep. The new sign glows above the parking lot, and everything is still out there in our little world.

"All right, I have to ask," Camila suddenly says. "How have you managed to date in Pine Creek?"

MacKenzie pauses midmovement. "If I'd tried to date in Pine Creek, I never would have gotten any," she says.

"So what do you do?"

"I go to Eugene."

"Ah."

"University town," MacKenzie explains. "Plenty of dykes. But most of them just want to discuss academic theories. Being drunk helps."

"And...are you seeing anyone right now?"

MacKenzie cleans the rest of the door, and Camila stands beside her, nonchalantly leaning against the wall as they both pretend that this is just a perfectly ordinary conversation between friends.

"I haven't been seeing anyone seriously for a long time. You?"

"Same."

"Because you haven't met the right person or...?"

"I don't know. I think lesbian bars are tricky. It's like I'm never enough of a woman for them. Sometimes I think they see the butch girls as more feminine than me. I always feel much more welcome in gay bars. Maybe it would've been easier if I was interested in men."

MacKenzie turns to her. "But you're not?"

"I'm not."

MacKenzie runs the squeegee down a section of glass she has already cleaned. She laughs awkwardly. "I think the doors are clean now," she says.

Camila leans in closer to her. "We can always tidy the brochure stand."

"Cleaning *is* more fun when there are two of you."

"I'm sure you always say that to women."

"Only the really special ones."

"What do you think of femmes?"

"I prefer my women to be made up and wearing heels while they clean."

Camila laughs. A deep, surprised, and genuine laugh. "Jesus, I've missed you," she says.

And then she stops laughing. Their eyes meet over their squeegees. MacKenzie is about to say something jokey, but she loses her trail of thought. Instead, she just faces Camila in the unforgiving light, late at night after a very long day, and looks more beautiful than ever. Camila too.

MacKenzie slowly moves her hand to Camila's hip. Surely not even she can tell herself that they're just cleaning now. Slowly, inch by inch, they move closer, until they are standing far too close to be nothing but childhood friends. The tension between them is almost painful. I want to tell MacKenzie to do it, to *kiss her* for God's sake, make out with her like you've wanted to ever since that moment out in the parking lot, possibly since she first came back.

But then, suddenly, they both look away. It happens so quickly that I can't tell who broke eye contact first.

MacKenzie takes a shaky breath. "The brochure stand," she says.
Camila clears her throat. "The brochure stand," she agrees.

I decide to leave them in peace after that.

I'm on my way toward Michael's cabin when I pause and look up at the clouds. I shake my head and smile.

"Okay, God. So you want me to save five people, huh? I'll do it—this time. But that's where I draw the line."

I can't stop smiling. I take two skipping steps, pause, look up again. "But I haven't forgiven you yet, if that's what you were thinking."

Two more steps. It really is a fantastic evening. "It was nice of you to make sure Paul came over here. Now you just need to get MacKenzie to kiss Camila."

CHAPTER 32
Nod If It Helps

I DON'T KNOW HOW WELL PAUL SLEPT—EITHER DESPITE OR thanks to last night's cleaning frenzy—but he does seem less worn out this morning. He does his best to erase all traces of himself from the office, but after pulling on his boots and straightening the cushions, there isn't much else he can do.

He stares at the door to reception as though there are unspeakable horrors awaiting him on the other side, but eventually he finds the courage to tiptoe out.

Dad is sitting on the couch. My urn is next to him, but Paul doesn't notice that. He sneaks past as quickly as he can, pausing and blinking in confusion at the bright sunlight outside.

I suppose it's asking too much of the motel to be able to fix everything, because Paul goes straight back to his old, ineffective plan of getting drunk. He walks to the liquor store and buys a six-pack of Budweiser, then sits down on the bench outside the restaurant, seemingly unable to bring himself to open any of the cans.

Clarence gives him a horrified glance as he passes on his way to breakfast. "Jesus, man, what are you doing?"

"Getting drunk," Paul replies, honest and indifferent.

Clarence shivers. "No commitment! No routines! How are you going to manage that if you aren't willing to *work* for it? Getting drunk is a full-time job. Or do I mean a calling? Either way, it's not for amateurs. Your body might pack in completely if you don't do it right. Breakfast first, then sun and booze."

Paul doesn't have the energy to stand up to Clarence, so he allows himself to be led into the restaurant. Before long, he is eating scrambled eggs, bacon, and toast. He drinks coffee and polishes off two slices of apple pie. He doesn't even argue when Dolores forces the second slice on him.

Back outside, on the bench, he listens patiently as Clarence tries to teach him everything he knows.

"People think they can do anything. So long as they want something, it'll come to them automatically. I blame all those self-help books. Positive thinking and that kind of crap. That's the problem with this country—no one is prepared to *work* for anything. Just take me. Do you think I ended up here by chance? No, I worked hard to be this much of a wreck. It took years. But the kids these days, they take drugs and get further than I've ever been in just a few short months. They don't even know whether it's what they want. They think it might be, but since they've never had to work for it, they've never been forced to really ask themselves: Do I want to spend all day drinking on a park bench? Do I have what it takes?

"Look at you. I'm guessing you woke up one day and thought, 'I want to start drinking.' Just like that. No preparation at all." He gives the cans of beer a disgusted glance. "No commitment."

Paul has closed his eyes. I don't know whether he's even listening. His face is raised toward the sun, and he is leaning back against the rough concrete wall behind him.

"Discipline. Routine. That's what it takes," Clarence says.

He turns to Paul.

"You look awful," Clarence says.

"How do you live with the knowledge that you've killed someone?"

"Booze?"

Paul shakes his head. "It doesn't work."

"Then I don't know."

"I can't sleep. When it's quiet, all I can hear is the sound of the truck hitting her. And when I close my eyes, I can picture her face right in front of me. It was so strange, the way she appeared like that. One second to the next, she was just there. I remember the sound of the brakes screeching, but I don't even remember whether her eyes widened. She must've just had a shower, because her hair was still damp. She'd tried to comb it, but the wind had messed it up. I remember thinking I was about to ruin her hair. Isn't that weird? I did, as well. Jesus Christ, I did. It was all matted with blood, and…"

"Okay, okay. I get it," Clarence interrupts. "Maybe you should try to think about something else."

"I tried to do the washing up the other day. But as I stood there, I couldn't see the water anymore. All I could see was blood. Bubbling red blood. I emptied the sink, but the blood just kept on bubbling up. Gurgling, almost. There wasn't even *that* much blood. She was just lying there on the road."

"Jesus, I need a drink," Clarence says. He gets up and walks away, but Paul remains where he is.

Clarence returns after an hour or so. He pats down his pockets and pulls out a folded napkin. On it, he has scrawled down a few lines of comfort. "All right," he says. "I spoke to the guys at the bar. Nod if any of this helps. Shake your head if it doesn't. Okay?"

Paul nods.

"Don't worry about it?"

Paul shakes his head, but he also manages a faint smile.

"It's all going to be okay."

A shake of the head.

"Time heals all wounds."

Another shake of the head.

"Try not to think about it so much."

A third weary shake of the head.

"She's with God now." Not even Clarence can manage that one without pulling a face. Paul shakes his head. "Didn't think so, but you never know. Everything happens for a reason?"

Paul doesn't even bother shaking his head this time.

"Michael!" Clarence says, desperately grabbing his arm as he walks by. "We need help!"

"He's just sitting there," Clarence continues. "But nothing I say seems to help."

He waves his hand in front of Paul's face, but there is no reaction. Paul just continues to stare blankly ahead.

"All right," Michael says. "I'll take over. You go off and...do whatever you usually do."

"I usually sit here," Clarence protests.

Michael runs a hand over his face. "Okay. So sit down. We'll go."

He grips Paul's arm and leads him around the back of the motel. I assume he's just trying to avoid the nosy stares of the lunch guests, but I also think Paul starts to feel slightly better when he sees the mountains. I always do.

Michael leans Paul against the wall and stands beside him.

Silence. Paul has nothing against that. He just stands there.

Michael sighs. "Henny loved it here," he says.

My name cuts through the haze. Paul turns toward Michael's voice.

"Of all the mountains, she chose that one. There's absolutely nothing special about it. There are higher mountains, more beautiful mountains, more geologically interesting mountains, but no. She wanted this particular view, to see this exact mountain every morning."

"It's a nice mountain."

Michael laughs. For the first time since I died, the hardness in his eyes disappears. "Damn nice," he says. "Henny dreamed of building a veranda here."

"The veranda wasn't the most important part," I say quietly.

"And we'd all sit here on it. Me, MacKenzie—her best friend—and Camila. Henny too, of course. We'd grow old together."

A smile lingers in Michael's eyes, and he shakes his head at himself.

"She looked so surprised when she died," Paul says. "Suddenly she was just there, in the middle of the road."

Michael pulls a face. "Let's try to focus on Henny while she was alive, can we? No more moments of death, all right?"

"I didn't know her while she was alive."

"I don't know if I did, either. But I hope I can get to know her now. And I guess you can, too."

Michael temporarily hands responsibility for Paul back to Clarence, and while the two men go for an early dinner at the restaurant, he tracks down Camila.

"I've got kind of a weird question," he says. "What do you think about me and Paul building a veranda? At the back of the motel."

"A veranda for Henny?" she asks.

"I know, it's a stupid idea, but it would give Paul something to do, and…"

"I think it's a great idea. And I think Henny would've loved it." She pauses. "This might sound strange, but sometimes I think I can feel her presence here at the motel. I think she wants us to be here. Maybe she always did."

I eagerly place a hand on her arm. "You *can* feel it! I'm still here. And you're right. You belong here."

"If that's the case, I wasted a lot of time," Michael says.

I shake my head impatiently.

"I thought you said you were happy while you were working," Camila says.

"I was, but…"

"Then it's hardly wasted, is it?"

Michael gives her a faint smile. "That's what Henny said, too."

"Maybe you should try listening to her," Camila suggests.

I love this woman, I think.

"I think she's happy with us now," she continues. "I think she likes the fact that we're all hanging out at the motel again."

Michael hesitates. "You know how you wanted to freshen up the rooms?" he says.

"Don't remind me. No matter what I try, I can't get them to feel cozy. Everything we bought just feels wrong."

"It's not my place to be giving you advice, but…"

"Please do!"

"When I was traveling with work, I stayed in a lot of motels. Often for several weeks at a time, months even. I never bothered to find an apartment if I didn't know I would be there for at least a year. I never needed the places to be fantastic."

"Not fantastic, no, but *a little* cozier?"

"Yeah, but is it really the rooms you should be focusing on? I never spent any longer in my room than I had to. The best places were the ones with some kind of shared space you could hang out in, so you could be around other people in the evening. Not that you did much there, but you could watch a little TV or talk about the news or drink coffee. You didn't just sit alone in your room, bored."

"How did you manage it?" Camila asks. "Traveling around like that. Never having a place of your own."

Michael seems surprised. "I had fun," he says. "My advice is to put more effort into the shared spaces where your guests can people watch. The restaurant, for example, or Clarence's bench, or..."

"There's not much I can do about the restaurant." Camila sounds thoughtful. "It's already cozy enough. Dolores's personality guarantees that. But I wonder... Michael, where did you put the leftover paint from the flag?"

"In the cabin."

"Bring it over."

Camila heads for reception, grabbing hold of Alejandro on her way over.

"All right," she says firmly. "Sorry, but everyone needs to leave reception. Please take any furniture you can carry."

Dad stands up, confused. He decides that she must have been joking about the furniture, but he does at least take my urn with him to the restaurant. MacKenzie looks up at Camila in surprise.

As it happens, she wasn't joking about the furniture. Camila convinces Buddy to help out, and he and Alejandro carry everything into the parking lot: the floor lamp, the old brochure stand, the coffee table— even the couch.

Clarence waves for Buddy and Alejandro to put the old couch beneath the sign, and then he sits down on it, crosses his legs, and waves for Paul to join him. "'I like work; it fascinates me,'" he quotes. "'I can sit and look at it for hours.'"

Alejandro temporarily pauses his lifting work to take a photo.

Dad and Stacey are the only guests who stay put in the restaurant. Sitting as far away from each other as they can get.

Buddy, Alejandro, and Michael drag the reception desk outside. They position the bulky old thing around the corner, out of sight from the restaurant. Camila has moved the computer, phone, and papers into the office.

She and MacKenzie glance around the empty room. The furniture has worn holes in the carpet, and though they vacuumed yesterday, they can still see the dirty, dusty outline of where the couch once was. In one corner, they find a lone cigarette butt. The room seems much bigger without all the furniture.

"You really take your cleaning seriously," MacKenzie tells her.

"Cleaning is just the beginning."

Michael fetches the cans of paint and the bag of rollers, and before long the painting is in full swing. Camila and MacKenzie are hard at work, and I sit down on one of the chairs outside and watch the cozy chaos unfolding. The floor lamp is next to the chairs, as though someone could sit down out here to read. The brochures, however, are fluttering away in the breeze. No one bothers to chase them, and before long, they are scattered around the parking lot.

The bright autumn sun bathes everything in a warm, sepia-tinged light, and the floor lamp and chairs and brochure stand cast long, dramatic shadows across the ground.

Paul is lying on the couch.

He's asleep again! This time, he is perfectly still in the middle of the parking lot, snoring in the glow of the neon sign. His face is relaxed. MacKenzie must have been right about it being easier to sleep somewhere bustling and noisy.

On the surface, Michael doesn't seem to be doing much, but something about him has changed. He's involved again. A part of something. When Alejandro snaps a picture of Paul sleeping beneath the sign, Michael even goes over to him and says, "You know, I've been thinking about your Instagram account. The one you set up for the motel."

257

Alejandro takes several pictures rather than responding.

"If I were you, I wouldn't try to present some polished image of this place," Michael tells him. "Why not take the pictures you want to take? Nothing about the motel pretends to be anything it's not."

Alejandro suddenly stands tall. "The honest motel," he says to himself.

"Somewhere you can pine away in peace and quiet," Michael agrees.

Suddenly, it strikes me that I don't just have a few people to help. I've got a whole flock. And right now, they're all gathered here. Dad and Stacey are in the restaurant; Alejandro has already started to take pictures and is currently interviewing Clarence; Michael and Buddy are ready to help out; MacKenzie and Camila are painting in reception. And Paul is snoring away.

There is nothing more beautiful than seeing the people you love suddenly doing things again. It's pure joy, an intoxicating mix of relief and freedom. The sun seems brighter, the colors sharper and the air fresher—all because Michael wants to build a veranda and Camila is repainting reception.

Somehow, we all belong together, and the motel is the center of everything again. The strange objects out in the parking lot make everything seem as magical as it used to be, as it should be now.

I walk around, catching snatches of conversation—"No, I don't want a goddamn refill" (Stacey); "Now we just need to paint the restaurant pink, too" (Clarence); "Yeah, and build Henny's veranda" (Michael)—and enjoying the beautiful evening.

Things are finally starting to happen. I can feel it. They aren't alone anymore. At first glance, it might look as though Dad and Stacey are alone, but they aren't. They're fondly irritated by each other. Sometimes we need a little irritation in our lives, just so we have something to cling to.

Not even Paul is truly alone. After he fell asleep, Clarence went in and fetched a blanket, dumping it unceremoniously on top of him. Michael came along later and straightened it out. Now that the sun is setting, he fetches another.

And Paul keeps sleeping.

Once the painting is done, everyone who is still awake gathers in reception. Curiosity even convinces Dad and Stacey to leave the restaurant.

"It's, uh...very colorful," Michael says. He knew which colors they had to choose from, but he still seems...taken aback by the first impression.

"No one can take that away from us," Clarence says.

It really *is* colorful. Camila has given up any thought of minimalist perfection: colorful freedom is all that matters now. She and MacKenzie have used up the paint by working in blocks. The wall behind the desk is blue and yellow, with both colors continuing past the corners and onto opposite walls. This is followed by a block of red on one side and green on the other, and the slightly trickier orange and purple paint on the wall around the automatic doors.

The whole thing is more or less symmetrical, and though Juan Esteban would have had a heart attack, it works.

The overall impression is charmingly chaotic; a warm, almost childish welcome.

"It's...multicolored," says Dad. "Who paints a reception area several different colors? This can't be right."

"At least it's not prim and proper," Stacey says approvingly.

After that, they help to carry the furniture back inside. Camila fetches cushions and blankets from her storeroom, and Buddy and Michael bring down the bureau she bought. It looks fantastic against all the bright colors.

"What do we do with the couch?" Michael asks.

"I guess we just bring it back in."

So, that's what they do. It's still the same boring, brown sofa, but it looks much cozier against the bright-red wall. Camila spreads out a couple of fluffy white blankets, and gently places a new decorative cushion beneath Paul's head.

A sleeping man on a couch always looks cozy, after all.

"Staaaaaaaaaaaaacey!"

I get up from my chair in reception. It's one in the morning, but I still haven't managed to tear myself away. I step into the hallway just as Stacey's door opens.

She has her padded jacket pulled tight around herself.

"Derek." She sounds shocked. She quickly runs a finger beneath her eyes to get rid of any stray mascara, ruffles her hair to make it look more evenly wild and curly, and heads down to the parking lot, where Derek is waiting.

He staggers and grabs the car door to stop himself from falling over.

"You're drunk," she says.

"Not drunk enough," Derek tells her. "I was trying to forget that my damn wife left me, but I haven't managed it yet."

"Don't swear." Stacey smiles at her own joke.

"What the hell's going on with you? Come on, Stacey, we might not always have seen eye to eye..."

"Ha!"

"But we've always stuck together, haven't we?"

I think Stacey is starting to doubt herself. Her eyes seem warmer somehow.

"How are people ever going to respect me if my wife is living at a *motel*? No one's going to take me seriously as a politician."

Stacey's face hardens. "What a shame."

"If that's how you want it. I'm not going to beg, if that's what you were thinking."

"You're the one who came over here."

"I just wanted to tell you not to come crawling back once you get sick of this place. And don't think I'll be footing the bill. You've lived a comfortable life until now, haven't you? No job. You've never even cleaned or cooked. All you've had to do is complain that I don't have a real job."

"Then it shouldn't make any difference that I'm here," Stacey mutters wearily.

"You're damn right. It's just more peaceful. I don't even know why I'm here. I guess it just felt weird to have peace and quiet after all your screaming."

"Enjoy it, because it's going to last."

"Until I find someone else. Shouldn't be too hard. There are still plenty of women who appreciate me around here."

Stacey launches herself at him. "Go to hell!" she shouts. "I swear, if I see your pathetic face around here again, I'll..."

Derek grabs her hands and pulls her toward him. Neither of them moves. I can see Stacey's rib cage rising and falling. Derek leans in over her.

"Stacey..." he eventually says, and she swallows.

Dad sticks his head around his door, ready to quickly close it and turn the key if he needs to. "Who's making such a racket?" he shouts. "I want you to know that I've called the police!"

"Crap," Derek says, jumping into his car. He is gone before Stacey even has time to work out what just happened.

She runs a hand over her face. "Did you really have to stick your nose into something that has nothing to do with you?" she asks.

"You were shouting and screaming. No one could get any sleep with you two carrying on."

"And you couldn't have just asked if everything was all right? Maybe talked to me before you called the police? For once in your life, maybe just been cool and let something go?"

She sighs quietly. *To herself*, I think. "No, of course you couldn't."

After that, she calls MacKenzie to warn her that the cops are on their way.

MacKenzie comes down to reception and promises to take care of it. When a young, tired deputy eventually turns up, he is met by the news that two strangers pulled up in the parking lot and started to fight. Both have gone, so unfortunately he's come in vain, but maybe she can offer him a cup of coffee.

"You're telling me two strangers parked just to start yelling at each other?" he asks.

"Yeah, you know what driving vacations do to people."

The deputy shudders as though he knows all too well. He says no to coffee.

CHAPTER 33

Just the Beginning

"LISTEN TO THIS CRAP," MACKENZIE CHEERILY EXCLAIMED FROM the depths of Pat and Carol's couch. It was a few weeks after our first meeting, and MacKenzie had already made herself at home. All I could see of her were the unruly curls hanging over the back of the couch and her feet on the armrest, bobbing in time with a tune only she could hear. The *Gazette* rustled as she waved it in the air.

Pat and Carol smiled at me. We were in the kitchen, washing up after an informal planning dinner.

Michael wasn't there. He was busy with college applications, though he still helped out with the campaign whenever he had time.

"The Sacred Faith Evangelical Church has written in, and my God, I never knew homosexuals were so powerful!" MacKenzie read aloud to us, in a haughty, affected voice: "'To present homosexuality as something normal, natural, or accepted is to teach children that they can break God's laws without consequence. It is to attack the morals our society—and schools—has upheld for the past two hundred years. School should not be a recruitment ground for homosexuals!'"

"I admire her," Carol whispered to me. "I never would've been brave enough to come out in high school. I'm barely brave enough now. I hope she's careful, that she'll take care of herself."

"Yup, we're all recruiting here," MacKenzie continued. "But the *Gazette* has actually distanced itself from their madness. There's an editorial in here somewhere." More rustling as MacKenzie searched for the right page.

Pat and Carol suddenly seem very clear to me again. I can remember how carefully I washed their cups. I was afraid of breaking them, even though they were all old and chipped. Their whole home was a little rough around the edges, and maybe they were, too. They wore comfortable but unflattering jeans. They loved their garden. There were always muddy footprints just inside the kitchen door, discarded gardening gloves and the occasional pair of shears, and everything was bathed in the fresh, earthy scent of a home in which the doors and windows are always open to the garden outside.

"Here it is," MacKenzie announced. "Oregon's Parent Teacher Association has already explained that teaching methods in the state do not 'encourage or promote homosexuality'—no, they're right there. 'The measure is fundamentally unnecessary. A teacher's role in the classroom is to meet their students' needs and to support their development—not to single out a particular group or emphasize the differences between people. Teachers also have a duty to encourage tolerance and respect.' Exciting reading, this, isn't it?"

Pat had big, deep-set eyes and fine lines and wrinkles from a long, intensive life. Her brown hair was the same color as the leaves in November. Carol's expressive mouth usually showed so much happiness, but in that moment, all I could see were doubt and uncertainty.

"We've never been political," Pat said to me. "We're just like everyone else. We vote Republican, we putter about in the garden, we make cookies for church bake sales."

"We're not anywhere near as tough as MacKenzie thinks we are," Carol agreed. All the while, MacKenzie continued to read aloud, giving her opinion on the *Gazette*'s argument and journalistic style.

"We just want to live our lives together," said Carol. She leaned in closer to me. "The *Gazette* got in touch and asked if they could interview us. I doubt anyone will care, but what do you think? We're just two women."

"I'm sure it'll be fine," I said. "I think it's great that the *Gazette* wants to interview you."

"Yes..." said Pat. "And we thought we should put up a sign. There should be *someone* on this street showing that they're against the measure."

Yes to Measure 9 signs had already begun to pop up along Broadway. MacKenzie had shaken her head when she saw them before the first meeting, but since we didn't really know or care about anyone living there, they didn't matter too much to us.

Pat and Carol hesitated in the hallway. "Are you ready?" Pat asked.

Carol squeezed her hand. Her face was pale against the light pink of her shirt. "Guess so," she said. "If you are?"

"Might as well get it over and done with."

"Stick it to them!" MacKenzie shouted. Carol smiled weakly.

"It's just politics, isn't it? We're allowed to have different opinions. Surely no one will care?"

"I hope they care!" said MacKenzie. "Who knows? Maybe you'll start a new trend along the street."

"We'll survive," said Pat. She took a deep breath. "All right. Let's do it."

And then, there it was. A lone sign reading *No to Measure 9*, followed by the Basic Rights Oregon logo.

"I'll put one up at the motel, too!" MacKenzie yelled.

"It's good that we've finally done something," Pat said.

"You know, it *feels* good that we've finally done something," said Carol.

"This is just the beginning," MacKenzie told them.

CHAPTER 34

Jesus on the Beach

IT'S SHEER COINCIDENCE THAT I'M THERE WHEN DEREK COMES to see Cheryl the next day.

I wanted to check that everything was all right with Dad's house. I don't know why. Some sense of responsibility, I guess, now that he's staying at the motel. So, I walked over to Water Street, arriving just as Derek pulled up on Cheryl's driveway.

It's Sunday, and the sun is glittering on the parked cars. People are streaming out of their houses in their best clothes, ready to head off to church. You get the impression that the street itself, the houses and the trees, are standing that little bit taller today in all their piety.

Derek glances around to make sure he has the right house, and I move closer so that I can eavesdrop on their conversation.

He looks tired and hungover, but he also seems to have a newfound determination that I've never seen in him before. He strides up to the door and barely even grimaces as he hears the shrill sound of the bell.

Cheryl and her husband are dressed for church. Cheryl is wearing a pretty blouse with jeans and pink sneakers, and her husband has on a navy-blue cotton shirt that looks like it might even have been ironed.

"You said you wanted to do something about the motel," Derek says. "I'm here to listen."

Cheryl glances at her watch.

"Derek," she says. "Do you go to church?"

"I've been using one of these for ten years now," the pastor says as he struggles with his headset, "but no one has ever been able to teach me how to put it on. I want you to know that they've done their best. Lord knows, Cheryl has tried." He pauses briefly as he tries to tuck it behind his ear. "She went through it with me just half an hour ago." Another pause. "Three times, in fact."

The pastor's gray hair is sticking up in all directions after his struggle with the headset, but he doesn't bother trying to smooth it out. His eyes are warm and amused, inviting us to laugh both with him and at him. He radiates humble plainness: his jacket is crumpled and one size too big and doesn't quite match his pants. There are more important things in life than clothes; that's what he seems to be saying.

I am standing by the door at the very back of the room. The notice board to one side of me is covered in various notes about activities within the church. One, written in huge red letters, informs me about a twelve-step program of some kind. Another talks about Bible study, and there are several posters for the dance evening in October and the senior citizens' Knit for Jesus campaign. In the brochure stand, leaflets for truck stops with chapels and religious services (all faiths welcome!) compete for space with brochures for the Holy Land Experience (vacations to bring your kids closer to God: performances every day at eleven and three!).

"This actually illustrates what I'd like to talk to you about today," the pastor continues. "None of us is perfect."

From where I'm standing, I can see only Derek and Cheryl's backs. Derek looks uncomfortable. His back is unnaturally straight, and he keeps stealing glances around the room, as if wondering what he is doing there.

"We want to be perfect. We try. At times, it's easy to think that God only loves us when we're as good as we think we have to be for His sake. As though God's love is something we earn. *So long as I do this. If I just stop doing that.*"

As he looks out at the congregation, he seems to be staring straight at Derek.

"*If I stop drinking,*" the pastor continues. "*Start going to church. If I can just become a better person, then he'll love me.* I myself was drunk for large chunks of my daughter's childhood. I did things that I'm now ashamed of. Things I still haven't forgiven myself for. These days, I'm sober. I'm a pastor. It's easy to think: *now* God loves him. But God loved me then, too—even when I didn't deserve His love. Jesus loved me at my very lowest point, at a time when I didn't even love *myself*."

Derek's back seems to relax. His shoulders drop, and his posture looks more natural. When Cheryl pats him on the knee, he gives her a grateful glance. For a brief moment, I can see his face in profile. It's still weary and drunk, but it's also calm. His eyes never leave the pastor.

I know how he feels, because the pastor's deep voice and the church have the same effect on me. Despite everything I know about them, it's hard to resist the uncomplicated warmth and joy that surrounds the congregation. If you've made your way here, you're welcome; that's how simple it seems to be. The church hall itself is unpretentious, and it's completely packed. People have squeezed into the pews along the walls, and they have to keep twisting to be able to see the pastor.

"There's a modern parable about Jesus that I've always liked. A man is walking along the beach, with Jesus by his side. All his life, there have been two pairs of footprints in the sand. Until the time comes when he falls. He suffers. He is alone, and he starts to doubt. He is as low as he has ever been, and when he looks back at that stretch of beach, he can only see one pair of footprints. 'God,' he asks, 'why have you deserted me? Why am I alone now, when I need you most?'"

The pastor looks out at the congregation again. "I think we've all felt that way from time to time, haven't we?"

Derek nods.

"And Jesus replies, 'Don't you see? That was where I was carrying you.'"

The pastor pauses briefly before continuing. "We suffer from a spiritual hunger in this beautiful country of ours. We're materially richer than ever before, but we've also realized that isn't enough. We have food and clothes and more gadgets than we can find the remote controls for, but we hunger and thirst for something more. Man needs more than the latest cell phone, and I think part of it is down to us searching for those two pairs of footprints in the sand. For meaning. A sign that we're not alone."

A weary-looking woman is sitting on one of the pews closest to me, and I notice that she has tears in her eyes.

"Evangelical faith is *practical*. We walk along the beach with Jesus by our side every single day. Every week. We think about Jesus on Sundays and then forget him for the rest of the week. When the Bible tells us to 'love thy neighbor,' that's what we do. We take care of one another. We take Jesus to work with us. We don't cheat in order to earn a few extra dollars. We take pride in what we do. We love and care for one another. We *forgive* one another, just as God forgives us. And we aren't alone. There are more of us than ever. This land was founded by Christians, though few remember that now."

I don't feel as relaxed as before. A knot has appeared in my stomach. The pastor's voice is louder, stronger.

"We are needed, now more than ever. Our traditions are needed. Our beliefs. But our way of life is under attack, and God knows we don't get any help from Hollywood or the mainstream media. We've moved from life-long marriages to single-sex marriages, from Clint Eastwood to *Brokeback Mountain*."

Derek laughs. No one else does.

"We are fighting a cultural war, and we are losing!"

The congregation is really fired up now. Several members glance at one another and nod. A few people clap.

"And we are constantly being told not to fight. Simply to give in. We're allowed to fight for union rights or for stricter environmental regulations, things that have an impact on ordinary folks, small business owners who are already on their knees as a result of federal laws. But if you dare fight for morals, for Christian values, suddenly you're criticized, mocked, shunned—prosecuted, even."

The pastor runs a hand through his hair. It is still sticking up in every direction, as if he has been electrified by his message. When he next speaks, his voice sounds completely different. Calm. Even warmer. Consciously nonjudgmental, in sharp contrast to the words leaving his mouth.

"I would like to talk to you about a business. You know the one I mean. Yes, the motel."

I peer around, as though everyone is about to turn and point at me.

"Lost souls are drawn to the motel, and to the false comfort of drugs, alcohol, cynicism, and an apathetic irresponsibility that tells them to joke about everything and take nothing seriously. These are people who could find a real home here."

Cheryl nods eagerly. Derek leans forward in his seat.

"The motel could have been an important part of town, a home for those passing through, part of our tourism industry, a place to look up to, a source of pride. But they have allowed it to fall into decay. Considering the owners, that isn't so surprising. It is run by people with no respect whatsoever for Jesus or the church. They take nothing seriously. Not our young people, not our school, our elderly, our town, our way of life. In their eyes, we are all pining away in this place we call home, this town that has given us so much. *That* is the image of Pine Creek they want to project to anyone visiting.

"None of us is perfect. Not them, not us. That isn't the point here. The point is that *we* are trying. We're doing our best. We welcome Jesus into our lives—we don't mock him! We can make a difference. Never doubt what faith can achieve—both in your life and in your community. Don't listen to those false voices in your head, or to the people around you, to the media, telling you that it is pointless even to try. There are so many of us walking alongside Jesus on the beach."

Once the service is over, people linger in the church. I suppose they want to spend a little longer basking in the beautiful image he conjured up for them. They feel acknowledged, forgiven, loved. Several want to speak to the pastor, either to thank him or because they hope that he might rub off on them. They have sat in silence, but now they want to speak; they want to talk about fate, to show him that they understand and agree. He greets them all with simple warmth. He has spoken, and now he will listen.

I watch the scene from a distance with stubbornly folded arms.

Outside, the sun is shining, as though to prove God's greatness, and when the congregation eventually starts to file out, the air fills with electricity. It feels as if someone has taken a balloon and rubbed it over their lives, and now everything is on end.

Derek can feel it too, but as he steps out into the crisp fall air, the powerful impression the pastor's sermon made on him fades. He pauses and seems lost, unsure whether he should leave or stay.

The pastor sees him and comes over. Cheryl is by his side.

He pats Derek on the shoulder. "Good to see you here."

"Great sermon, pastor," Derek says politely.

An informal group has gathered around them, lured in by the pastor's presence.

"Derek was the one who organized the much-needed painting work at the school," the pastor announces. Everyone smiles and nods.

"I used to follow all of your games, of course. But—if you'll excuse me saying so—I think you can make an even more important contribution here than you ever did on the field."

"Yeah..." Derek sounds hesitant.

"I assume you've also noticed the damaging impact the motel has on our town?"

"That dam...darned motel. They've definitely warped my wife's mind. But if she thinks I'm going to chase after her, she's wrong. I mean, she's only there temporarily, but..."

"Separating a man from his wife," one of the congregation members murmurs, shaking his head.

"*I* would never stay there," says another.

I feel a sudden, unreasonable anger at all of them.

"But where do we start?" Derek asks. "It's a motel. What the heck can we do?"

The pastor smiles. "I think you'll find that the answer is: a whole lot. And we'll start with a petition."

"We always start with a petition," Cheryl cheerily agrees.

"Do you know why I married Derek?"

Stacey is sprawled across the couch at check-in, her legs outstretched in front of her.

"No!" Dad says, sounding horrified. He is squeezed up against the armrest. "And I don't want to."

"It was because of my mother-in-law. I know it's stupid, but she had a husband who didn't drink or do drugs, and she lived in that incredible house. As much space as you like, and her clothes were always neat and tidy and perfect for the occasion. The food she served was perfect, too. Salmon, baby carrots, tender meat. *Peas*, for God's sake. And she eats them with a fork! My folks wouldn't have been able to eat peas if you'd given them a bib and a spoon."

"That's no way to talk about your parents."

"I didn't want to *be* like Joyce—I wanted her as a mother. I imagined us together in her enormous kitchen. Jesus, it seemed so big to me. You never bumped into the table while you were putting something in the microwave. She would teach me to cook, I thought. Something other than mac and cheese. And she would appreciate my help. A bit of company during the day. Maybe we would even bake together—apple pie, the kind with the lattice top—and we'd drink coffee, and there would be pretty, delicate white lace curtains, and the sun would be shining in through them. Don't laugh."

Dad isn't laughing. He still looks horrified at the intimacy of the conversation.

"I grew up in a trailer. You couldn't move without bumping into something. Mom and Dad were almost always drunk. Drunk or absent. They would disappear for days at a time. One of them, both of them, suddenly they just wouldn't be there, and I was left alone with my little sister. I actually used to feel guilty that life was easier when they weren't around. I made dinner for the two of us. Mac and cheese. Hot dogs. Do you know how sick a kid can get of hot dogs?"

"You don't need to tell me any of this!" Dad protests.

"No, I guess not even you deserve to have to listen to pathetic childhood memories. But the point is: when I was ten, I swore to myself that one day, I'd have a normal, happy family. I daydreamed about finding out I was adopted, and my real parents coming back to rescue me. But then I met Derek, and for a while I thought I could actually fit in."

Dad is staring straight ahead to avoid looking her in the eye.

"But it's impossible. People in this town never forget who you were. And everyone talks so much. I just can't bear the thought of people talking about me, laughing, and..."

Dad straightens up. "Exactly!" he says.

"Don't they have anything better to do? Why can't they worry about their own lives instead?"

"Did you ever learn to cook?" Dad asks. "Because it isn't so hard. You just follow the instructions, and then..."

Stacey runs her hands over her face. "Sure, sure," she says wearily. "That's exactly what I was talking about."

Dad gives her a surprised glance. He's thinking, *What did I do wrong now?*

CHAPTER 35

A Veranda for Henny

ALEJANDRO THROWS HIMSELF INTO THE PROJECT OF REVIVING his Instagram account. All afternoon, I see him walking around the motel with his camera in tow. He stops several times to interview guests about their opinions of the motel and life in general. I'm sure he must have gotten some interesting answers. Eventually, he tracks down Camila and asks whether he can have a chat with her.

"You know I made an Instagram account for the motel? There hasn't been much activity on it because, well, it's just not possible to take all that many flattering pictures of this place."

"A challenge," Camila agrees with a smile. "But at least now we have a rainbow-colored reception area."

"Uh, yeah. And that's definitely on there. But Michael came up with the idea of me taking *honest* pictures instead. You know, like the new sign. Truthful. With a bit of humor. To show we can laugh at ourselves."

I think Alejandro has been practicing this argument.

"All right," Camila sounds hesitant.

"So I've, uh, been uploading some more honest pictures."

"Could I see?"

He quickly flicks through his posts and shows her a couple of them. He wasn't kidding about the honesty part. Several of the photos are of the sign, of course, but he has also continued the theme of pining away in the others. In one of them, Dad is sitting unhappily at check-in. His face isn't in focus, meaning he is unrecognizable to anyone but us. Instead, the focus is on the bright-yellow wall behind him, and the gleaming urn to one side. The caption beneath consists of the list of complaints he reeled off yesterday, including his views on the frivolous, colorful paint that's now on the walls. The majority of portraits are blurry, the people impossible to identify, aside from one picture of Clarence, who is staring straight at the camera with his coffee cup raised in a toast. You can't tell that his cup is full of booze, but the caption beneath is a long quote from him. It's a bit like something from *Humans of New York*, except Clarence is talking about how liquor built this state. Liquor and constitutional racism. In another picture, a hungover group from Vermont is proud to be in focus. Alejandro hasn't edited their views on town, either.

The rest of the posts are beautiful, artistic shots of forgotten items and abandoned objects. A lone coffee cup with lipstick on the rim, an empty packet of potato chips on the ground beneath a trash can, and several genuinely beautiful shots of the mountains—but even they have a lonely, melancholic feel to them.

Then, of course, there is a picture of Paul asleep on the couch beneath the sign. Alejandro has written *#vacancies* beneath that one.

I glance nervously at Camila. I doubt this is what she was expecting. But all she says is: "And you think this will make people want to stay here?"

"It's just an Instagram account," Alejandro mumbles. "No one books a motel on the basis of its Instagram posts. Our home page and the entries on Booking.com and TripAdvisor are still perfectly normal. This just a bit of...fun."

I don't agree with him. He might have convinced himself that he was doing it for fun, but the pictures radiate honesty. They're fantastic, and surprisingly revealing. For a moment, I can really see the world through his eyes.

"I just wanted to check it was all right with you."

"Yeah..." Camila sounds hesitant. "I guess."

It's possible that Camila didn't give Alejandro her full attention, because as she walks away, her mind is definitely elsewhere. She fetches a basket from her room and takes it down to reception.

"Come on, MacKenzie," she says. "We're celebrating."

"Celebrating what?"

Camila shrugs as she drags MacKenzie toward the car. "Pick something," she says. "The new paint. The couch turning ten."

"I think it might actually be older than that." But she obediently follows Camila all the same, and they drive to a spot by the river, where they can be alone.

Camila spreads a blanket on the grass, brushing away a couple of dry leaves. MacKenzie stands beside her, gazing over to the edge of the forest. She closes her eyes and breathes in the timeless scent of cool, damp air and freedom. The hum of the road behind us mixes with the noise of the river, making it sound even more powerful. The passing trucks sound like the roar of waves.

There are a number of small birch trees clinging to the edge of the beach and one particularly fearless pine that's practically *in* the water. Three rocks form a kind of bridge out into the water. On the other side, there is a break in the pines, making the world feel bigger here.

Camila holds up a bottle of champagne and two coffee cups. "It's not really a celebration without some bubbly."

I lie down on my back in the grass. Up above, the sun and the wind play in the trees. A lone leaf swirls down to the ground as a gust of wind takes hold of it, making it spin through the air in lazy circles.

MacKenzie sits down next to Camila on the blanket. Camila pops the cork, and MacKenzie smiles when it foams over.

"Can I ask you something?" Camila asks.

MacKenzie takes the cup from her, immediately spilling a little champagne on her hand. "Ask away," she says.

"Why haven't you kissed me yet?" Camila calmly continues in the silence that follows. "I mean, we've been flirting long enough. *Do* you want to kiss me?"

I sit bolt upright, shocked by the bluntness of her question.

Not as shocked as MacKenzie, though. "For God's sake, Camila." She sounds panicked.

Camila slowly stretches out her legs in front of her. Sips from her cup. "It's not a difficult question. A yes or no will do."

"Why haven't you kissed *me*?"

"I wanted to. But then I thought it might be fun to see how long you would tiptoe around, flirting with me and not doing anything about it."

"Yeah, I can see you waited patiently."

"I got bored."

"I don't do that kind of thing anymore."

"So you're going to live the rest of your life as a celibate?"

"You're not a one-night stand, Camila. And I'm not getting into feelings. I don't feel anything anymore. I can't even remember how a heart works."

"Oh, MacKenzie," she says. "You feel so much you're about to break."

MacKenzie moves to stand up, but Camila grabs her arm and pulls her back down onto the blanket. "Are you ever going to stop talking and make out with me, or do I have to do everything around here?"

MacKenzie doesn't speak. I don't think she can.

"Does foreplay always last this long with you?" Camila goes on. "Because if it does, I'm surprised you don't spend months in Eugene before you get la..."

MacKenzie pulls Camila to her and kisses her before she has time to finish her sentence. I prudishly look away, get up, and start walking.

I'll have to walk back to the motel, I think. *But it's worth it.*

Amazing things in life: MacKenzie in shock, MacKenzie feeling nervous, MacKenzie in love.

They'll be a perfect couple. It wouldn't surprise me if MacKenzie proposes before fall is out.

Okay. Calm down, Henny. No expectations. MacKenzie can be incredibly slow at times.

Let's say before Christmas.

It's funny how much satisfaction men seem to get from measuring things. I know that Paul and Michael can't just get straight to work on building my veranda, but they're walking around with their strings and sticks and measuring tapes, checking lengths, widths and depths with focused contentment. Next, they double-check everything, and after that they double-check all of the angles. Not once do they throw down their tools in frustration. They actually seem to enjoy having to make the odd adjustment.

Neither of them speaks while they work. I guess they're communicating on some deeper level. Some kind of manly, carpentry-based telepathy.

It's the day after MacKenzie and Camila's excursion, and I'm still in an incredibly good mood.

"Are you sure this is the right time of year to be building a veranda?" I cheerily ask.

Michael shakes his head. Paul nods and moves the string a fraction of an inch.

"I think it looks straight," I say, just to mess with them.

Michael had turned up at Paul's bench earlier that day, and Paul had obediently followed him back to the car. He paused for a moment before climbing in, tensing up every time they passed a truck heading in the opposite direction, but he didn't put up any kind of fight. He actually didn't say anything at all.

"You any good at woodwork?" Michael asked once they were on their way.

"Okay, I guess."

For the first time, it dawned on Paul to ask: "Where are we going?"

"To buy wood."

Back at the motel, they had managed to spend almost an hour working on the measurements in peace and quiet, but the minute they start unloading the wood, everyone at the motel gathers around Michael's car.

"Well, well, well," MacKenzie says in a deep, authoritative voice. "What's going on here?"

Michael and Paul freeze.

"We're building a veranda," Michael tells her. "Out the back. Camila said it was all right." He looks a little sheepish at having to justify himself—or pass the blame on to someone else.

Everyone follows him around the corner. Michael and Paul have prepared a space for the wood, and there are already six boards stacked and waiting. They have marked out the shape of the veranda using string.

"My tomato plants!" Dolores cries out.

Unfortunately, her tomatoes are growing right in the middle of the marked out area.

"We're going to replant them," Michael quickly explains.

"Replant them!"

"We're building a veranda for Henny," Paul says. "This was her favorite spot."

"Aha," says Dolores. "A veranda for Henny. Well, that changes things. My tomato plants will probably be just as happy against that wall over there."

MacKenzie and Alejandro get to work carrying wood, Dolores returns to the kitchen, and Michael and Paul move one of the strings a few inches to one side.

"What did she look like?" Paul asks.

"Henny? She was the most beautiful woman I ever saw."

"Michael!" I protest. "Don't lie to poor Paul. He might actually believe you."

"Maybe not in a conventional sense, but Henny was really beautiful. She made all other women seem bland and boring."

"Good," I say, but then I stop short. "You can start dating again, though. Eventually."

"In a while," I add. But I don't believe it. Not now that he has finally found his way home. We're going to be together forever, that's how it feels.

The conversation trails off as MacKenzie and Alejandro dump another couple of planks onto the pile. Once they leave, Michael goes on. "I think it was the way she looked at you. She could always convince me of anything. Her eyes seemed to radiate some kind of easy confidence. *She* knew it was true, and if she knew, then how could I doubt it? Everything will be fine, people are fundamentally nice, the earth is flat—it made no difference what she said when she was looking at you with those blue eyes of hers. Bright blue, like the water in Crater Lake." He falls silent. "I must sound ridiculous. Let's keep digging."

They carefully move the tomato plants over to their new spot by the wall. Michael keeps talking without really seeming to be aware of it. "They say that the Inuit have hundreds of words for snow," he says.

Paul continues to dig.

"I should have at least one hundred words for Henny's different smiles. She could communicate absolutely anything with a smile—laughter, love, consideration, compassion, even the fact that she didn't agree with you. I actually think that if you got everyone who knew her to describe her smile, you'd find out she had a special smile for each of them. It meant it was impossible to argue with her. Don't get me wrong; I tried—when I was young and dumb. I tried to resist her, too. I knew I would be leaving, and I didn't need anything to make that harder. But then she smiled, and suddenly I was willing to do anything for her again. I've always been prepared to do anything she asked of me."

"That sounds nice," I say. "But you did actually leave town. I don't want to be petty, but that's *not* what I wanted."

I smile, to show that I'm not annoyed, but then I realize what I'm doing and laugh. I force my face into a *very* serious expression, the corners of my mouth firmly downturned and my forehead creased, but it's so ridiculous that I start laughing again after just a few seconds.

"I was an idiot," Michael goes on. "I thought I could realize all of my dreams and then find someone like Henny once I was ready."

"I don't think life gives us things when we're ready for them," I say.

"But I never met anyone else like her."

Alejandro and Camila come out with coffee, and Michael seems relieved by the interruption.

"We're talking about what Henny looked like," Paul explains. Michael seems embarrassed.

"She looked kind," Alejandro immediately pipes up. "You could tell her anything. She was the best listener I ever met. She had no preconceived notions about anything, so she listened to what you were really saying, not what she thought she should be hearing."

Dolores arrives with pie. "Helpful," she states firmly. "That's how she looked. She always let you know she had time to help whenever you needed it."

"You know, Paul," I say once they get back to work, "I'm getting a little worried about the image they're painting of me. It might actually be quite nice for someone to tell you how awful my hair looked in the mornings, or how grumpy I got when it rained for days in a row."

The only person who doesn't say anything about me is MacKenzie. She arrived in the middle of the conversation, tensed up, and left.

Camila watched the emotion drain from her face and ran after her. I turn the corner just in time to see MacKenzie shaking off Camila's comforting hand.

"I can't do this," MacKenzie tells her. She refuses to look Camila in the eye. "I'm just going to make you sad."

Camila looks wounded, but she quickly manages to hide it. "I'm willing to take that risk," she says.

"But I'm not. I don't want a relationship."

"I didn't say anything about a relationship," Camila argues. "But we could have fun together, MacKenzie. Before I came back here, do you know how long it was since I laughed properly? So don't tell me you can't make me laugh."

MacKenzie's eyes are drawn to Camila's lips, but she desperately says, "I'm not going to change my mind. This isn't some romantic comedy where the guy who doesn't want to get tied down falls for the girl in the end. I can't handle the expectation. One day, I'll let you down and then I'll break your heart, and I *refuse* to do that."

"Okay," says Camila. "No feelings. No expectations. Broken heart in the near future."

MacKenzie nods slowly.

"Good," Camila continues. "Glad we've straightened that out."

With that, she pulls MacKenzie close and kisses her again.

I walk away, shaking my head. That might be what MacKenzie wants, but it isn't what she needs.

CHAPTER 36

G-A-

THE INTERVIEW WITH PAT AND CAROL WAS THE FIRST TIME THE *Gazette* had featured a couple of real-life homosexuals. Everyone was talking about it. Michael, MacKenzie, Camila, and I headed over to their place after school to talk about how fantastic the article was. It was like MacKenzie was floating on the wind of change. She practically skipped down Broadway.

I kept glancing at Michael as we walked. I tried to look normal, but I had forgotten what people looked like when they weren't infatuated, when they weren't deliriously happy just to be walking alongside someone. *Don't smile so much*, I told myself. But it was impossible.

How could I *not* smile with the sun shining, the pretty trees bathing Broadway in shade, and the warm, soapy water trickling toward us over the dry asphalt. I jumped to avoid it, and thought that someone had definitely chosen a lovely afternoon to wash their car. I took another skipping step, just because I could, even though the water was no longer anywhere near my sneakers.

But Pat wasn't home, and Carol wasn't washing the car.

She was on her driveway, frantically scrubbing the garage door. Someone had scrawled *GA* across it in huge red letters. The *Y* was nothing but a faint shadow by that point.

"I don't understand who could have done this!" Carol said. "Which of our neighbors would come over here at night with spray paint?"

She continued to scrub furiously. Soap bubbles swirled through the air. There were tears in Carol's eyes, but she tried to blink them away. "This wasn't how it was meant to be. This wasn't why Pat and I moved here. We just wanted a normal life in a nice little town. We were working as waitresses when we met. Did Pat tell you that? Both of us were married. And then we moved. We wanted a fresh start. To settle down somewhere. A calm, boring life together. We would only argue about the other one never doing the dishes, or because we couldn't decide on what to have for dinner. But now here I am, trying to scrub graffiti from our garage door before Pat gets home!"

While Michael coaxed the sponge out of her hand and took over the scrubbing, Camila and I led her over to the steps. MacKenzie grabbed another sponge from the bucket and took out her anger on the red paint.

"It's just some idiot," she said. "Don't worry about them. Idiots don't count. There are plenty of decent people here, and they aren't going to tolerate this!"

I patted Carol's hand. I couldn't think of anything to say.

"Do you want me to spray *hetero* on all the other doors on the street?" MacKenzie offered. "Because I will. Or *Heterosexual*. That's longer. It'll take them ages to scrub off."

Carol laughed a little then.

"We're definitely going to ramp up the fight now," MacKenzie swore.

Looking back now, I wonder whether this was when it really all began. But if there's one thing life and death have taught me, it's that the beginning and the end are relative. You never know quite which is which when you're in the middle of it all.

CHAPTER 37

A Warning

DAD HAS DEVELOPED A NUMBER OF FIXED ROUTINES DURING his time here with us.

Every morning, he eats breakfast at seven thirty on the dot. Coffee, a bagel, and a light dusting of cream cheese. Another coffee once the dishes have been cleared away.

He spends the rest of his mornings in the reception area, eats lunch in the restaurant, and then goes on his daily walk, just like he used to at home. Now, of course, he just walks around and around the motel. Five laps. Always five laps. Even today, in the rain and the biting wind, despite the fact that his clothes are more suited to sunny strolls through town. His shoes are pretty flimsy, his coat too thin for the time of year. None of it is much good against the depressing, chilly rain.

Still, he doesn't let that stop him. He walks around in his suit, his shirt, and his too-thin coat, without either a scarf or gloves. He tries to keep his hands warm by pushing them into his pockets, and huddles down beneath the collar of his coat, but neither helps. His sunken cheeks turn red, and his nose starts to run.

After his walk, he goes back to the restaurant for his post-lunch coffee. Even there, he can't quite get warm; he just sits quietly, shivering away. It's not that we're stingy with the heating, but the doors are constantly opening and closing, so the cold air inevitably finds its way inside. The insulation isn't especially good, and the windows are drafty.

Stacey notices all of this from the next table.

"Why don't you just dress for the weather?" she asks Dad.

"My winter clothes are back at the house," he says with as much dignity as he can for a grown man who has just admitted that he doesn't dare go home.

"For God's sake," Stacey mutters. "This is ridiculous."

With that, she gets up and storms out.

Dad watches her leave in confusion. "What did I do this time?" he asks no one in particular.

But after only an hour or so, Stacey is back with two parcels, hastily wrapped up in brown paper.

"Here," she says, throwing them down onto the table in front of him. "You can't go around being cold the whole time."

Dad hesitantly unwraps the parcels. Inside one is an enormous red padded jacket, and in the other is a pair of colorful knitted mittens and a matching scarf.

"You're always freezing," Stacey explains. "It makes me cold just looking at you. Come on, try them on."

Dad picks up the mittens. He seems confused. They have reindeer on them, and lopsided snowflakes, plus a blue and green pattern that I can't quite make out.

"Maybe later," Dad says.

Stacey looks hurt, but she does her best to hide it. "Sometimes it's okay to wear fun clothes, you know. You don't have to be so goddamn proper all the time."

"Don't swe..." Dad begins, but he has enough sense to look ashamed. "Thanks," he reluctantly adds.

"Sure, sure," Stacey mutters indifferently. "You keep freezing, then."

It takes real commitment to collect names for a petition on a rainy Wednesday afternoon, but if there's one thing Cheryl has, it's commitment. She and another woman from the congregation—who was more enthusiastic than helpful—have set up a small gazebo in the middle of Elm Street, but the rain still keeps blowing in, forming small puddles beneath the cover.

I took shelter in the gazebo after being caught out by a sudden downpour. I don't like being reminded that the weather no longer affects me. It makes me feel like an outsider when everyone else runs for cover and I'm left alone in the rain. So, I rushed in after them, and now I'm standing here, watching the alarming spectacle going on around me.

The other woman is wearing a bright-yellow raincoat, and she hurls herself out of the tent, armed with her faith, a cheery disposition, and an armful of leaflets. "Stop sin!" she shouts. "Down with the motel!"

Derek sneaks in just behind me and tries to hide in one corner. He looks embarrassed and anxious. Cheryl holds out a cup of coffee to him.

Out on the street, people with umbrellas and upturned collars rush by.

"I have no idea how you do this," he says.

"You learn. It isn't so hard. It's just a case of talking to as many people as possible. Try to work out which argument works on which people, and stick to the message. It isn't a discussion. Think of it more as a test. A few people will try to outwit you and pick holes in your argument, trying to make you feel stupid…"

"That's not hard," Derek mutters.

"But just stick to the message. Think of them as tools who've come here to test you. They aren't interested in having a dialogue with you; they just want to convince you that you're wrong."

"I didn't only mean this, I meant…everything."

"Everything?"

"This whole Christian way of life. I mean, I believe in Jesus—of course," he hurries to add. "It's just that I think I've always been better at sin. It's not something I'm proud of, it's just who I am."

"Not who you are, who you were."

Derek gives her a blank look.

"Let me tell you something," Cheryl says. "I left home when I was fourteen. By the time I was twenty, I was working as a waitress and had been doing just fine on my own for years. I thought I was so tough. But I mistook my cynicism for wisdom. I didn't care about anything or anyone, I told myself, and I dulled my feelings with alcohol. Then, one day, on my way to work, I drove past a church with a billboard outside. They must have had that sign there for months, but I had never noticed it before. It had to be a sign, right? God reveals himself to us when we're ready for

Him. The billboard read *Jesus has a plan for YOU*. And something inside me... I just broke down. Sat in my car and cried. I had to park until I calmed down. I changed my life after that day. Started going to church again. Read the Bible—and I mean *really* read it as God's word. Then I met my husband and ended up here."

"But nothing we do is actually going to change anything, is it? What's the point of standing out here, freezing our asses off?"

"You know, Derek, the world isn't changed by a small number of great people. Many ordinary people, that's who really make a difference. And the world is never saved once and for all. We constantly have to save it anew. I think we have to save ourselves over and over, too. But it feels good to do something for someone other than yourself, doesn't it? To be a part of something bigger."

Derek shifts his weight from one foot to the other, either to keep warm or because he feels claustrophobic in the cramped gazebo. "Right now it just feels godda...gosh darn cold."

Cheryl laughs. "I know who I was back then. I don't try to hide it. But I also know who I've become, and I know who made that possible."

"Who?"

"Jesus, of course!"

"Do you think he can do anything about this weather?"

"You can always ask, Derek." She pats him on the shoulder. "You can always ask," she repeats quietly to herself.

Bob Parker is one of the many people rushing by in the rain. His eyes are fixed on his car, which is parked two blocks away, but he casts an indifferent glance into the gazebo as he hurries past. When he spots Derek inside, he stops dead and heads inside.

"Sign here if you'd like to see a more moral approach to business!" the other woman from the congregation chirps.

Bob flashes her a tense smile and takes a leaflet, shaking Derek's hand. "Can I have a word?" he hisses through his dogged smile, dragging Derek outside into the rain and over to the half shelter of an awning. The two men stand with their backs to the display window behind them.

"What are you doing?" Bob asks. He skim-reads the leaflet. "What is this rubbish? "A moral approach to business?" That almost sounds communist."

Derek looks away and mutters a hesitant "A few of us are worried about…"

"Oh, for God's sake. They've gotten to you, haven't they? I told you not to…"

"Stacey *left* me. All because of that damn motel. And your great advice didn't exactly help."

"Jake isn't going to like this. It's all well and good going to church, but business is something entirely different."

I have no idea who Jake is, and Derek doesn't seem to care about what he might or might not think.

"Maybe that's part of the problem," he says. "If more people actually cared about Jesus in their everyday lives…" He makes a face, embarrassed. Words like *God* and *Jesus* still don't feel natural in his mouth. "We're just interested in the motel," he finishes. It sounds defensive, even to him.

"All I wanted you to do was nod and smile and shake a few hands. But now you're caught up in this whole mess." Bob thinks on his feet. "All right, this is what we're going to do. We tell everyone that you just wanted to get to know the different churches. Next week, I'll take you to the Methodist church, that's where Jake and the other big business owners go, and you can explain that you believe in free markets and God—in that order. I'll go through exactly what you need to say, and then…"

"You know, Bob," Derek begins. "Some people actually acknowledge that I can think for myself and contribute more than just nodding and smiling."

"Of course, of course," Bob sounds impatient. "But you need to learn first."

"Some people think I already know how to do it."

With that, Derek walks straight out into the rain, grabs a handful of leaflets, and tells the first cold, damp person who passes: "Are *you* worried about our kids drinking outside the motel? Sign here for a more moral approach to business!"

I run all the way back to the motel, but I'm not even out of breath when I get there. The others are all in the reception area. Camila is frowning at the computer screen, clicking repeatedly on something. Dad is on the couch, like usual, and MacKenzie and Michael are in the doorway, watching the rain drum down on the asphalt.

"They've started a petition against the motel!" I shout.

"Strange," says Camila. "The website seems to be down."

Alejandro comes into reception, and both Michael and MacKenzie step back from the doors as a gust of wind carries the rain inside.

"The Sacred Faith Evangelical Church!" I say. "A petition! Against the motel!"

"Do any of you know what's up with the website?" Camila asks.

I jump up and down in front of them in the mistaken belief that one of them will notice me. *This isn't the right moment to be talking about technical problems*, I think irritably.

Alejandro looks incredibly guilty. "You know my new Instagram account?" he says.

Camila nods expectantly; MacKenzie shakes her head. Alejandro quickly summarizes the idea for her.

"The honest motel," MacKenzie says. "I like it!"

"Good, because we might have started to get a little attention."

I notice Camila tense up. "How much attention?"

"Oh, 137,000 new followers, give or take."

That stops my jumping.

"I think I'm starting to realize what the problem could be with the website," MacKenzie says, amused.

"What happened?" Camila asks.

Alejandro looks troubled. "Well, it all started when *BuzzFeed* picked it up. And then, uh, George Takei shared a link. That's when it really took off. It seems like people think honest businesses are refreshing."

MacKenzie laughs. "We're an internet sensation!" she says. Right then, the phone starts ringing.

MacKenzie and Camila are holed up behind the desk, taking turns responding to the requests for interviews and comments that have started flooding in. People are asking for honest appraisals of all kinds of things, and one of the newspapers wants them to pen honest answers to reader questions. All hope I had of somehow being able to get through to them is gone.

"We're not interested, I'm afraid," Camila says. "We run a motel. That's all."

"No comment," MacKenzie tells the next caller. "But don't quote me on that."

She looks up at Alejandro: "Have you ever considered adding a few cats to our Instagram account? That really would've got the ball rolling. You've got to think of the fans."

Alejandro makes a face. Michael shakes his head. Sitting in his usual spot on the couch, Dad looks more confused than anything, watching the chaos unfold around him.

Without warning, the automatic doors swing open and everyone turns toward the slim figure in the doorway. She has a huge scarf covering her head, and half of her face is hidden beneath a pair of dark sunglasses.

Jesus, I think. *It's...*

"Mom?" Michael asks, sounding confused.

The sudden warmth of reception has made her sunglasses fog up, and Joyce takes them off and starts polishing the lenses. Her eyes sweep across the colorful room. Michael stares at her with an idiotic, gaping expression.

"I've come to warn you," she says, smiling in the direction of the couch. "Is that an urn?"

CHAPTER 38

Would Jesus Check In Here?

ALEJANDRO HOLDS DOWN THE FORT BEHIND THE DESK WHILE MacKenzie, Camila, Michael, and Joyce regroup in the restaurant. Joyce has chosen the table furthest from the window, but she has at least taken off her scarf and sunglasses.

"They're out for the *motel*?" Camila asks, her voice incredulous.

"For a more moral approach to business," Joyce confirms. A cup of coffee appears in front of her, and she picks it up and sips from it.

"But...we're a motel," says Camila. "Surely they can't have any Bible passages that forbid people from checking into motels?"

"It wouldn't surprise me if they did," MacKenzie mutters.

"Who are they?" Michael asks.

"The Sacred Faith Evangelical Church."

"Cheryl?" MacKenzie asks.

Joyce gives her a blank look.

"Pink sneakers? T-shirts with Biblical quotes? Crazy?"

Nothing. Joyce has no idea. MacKenzie shrugs.

"How did you find out about this, Mom?" Michael asks her.

"I...saw them in town," Joyce is vague.

I notice with interest that she doesn't mention Derek. How long does she think it will be before Michael finds out that his brother is one of the people behind this?

Michael still seems more confused than anything. "But why are you here? You've never cared before."

Joyce doesn't seem the least bit upset by the implicit accusation. "I thought you should know. I wrote down what they're saying about you, so I wouldn't forget."

She opens her handbag and methodically rifles through the neatly organized compartments, pulling out a small notepad and a pair of reading glasses.

"Teenagers drinking on a hill," she reads aloud. "I don't know which hill. It was a little confusing."

Camila and MacKenzie exchange an odd glance.

"Rainbow flag on the school," Joyce continues, ticking off another point on her list. Did Michael get his love of lists from her? I wonder. "The new sign. You're leading the town's old people into sin."

"We're doing *what*?"

She double-checks her notes. "I think they mean Mr. Broek," she says.

MacKenzie actually laughs at that.

Joyce sighs quietly. "This is going to make life uncomfortable for me," she says. "*Just* like last time."

"Uncomfortable for you?" Michael sounds astounded.

"Extremely uncomfortable. I don't know why everyone can't just relax. And now you're all going to get involved, too."

She gathers her things and stands up. She seems relieved that the conversation is over. Her eyes seem strangely absent again, as though she has just survived something unpleasant but necessary—a trip to the dentist—and now she can retreat back into herself. She dismisses Michael's offer to walk her out to the car with a weak wave of her hand.

"Does Dad know about this?" he asks.

He should have asked whether Derek knows, I think.

Joyce pauses. "Why would I get your father involved in my life?" she asks. She wraps her scarf around her head, puts on her sunglasses, and steps out into the rain.

Michael shakes his head. "I think I should probably give up trying to understand my family," he says.

"What the hell's going on?" Camila asks.

"They've gone crazy," MacKenzie replies. "Again. That's what's going on."

The demonstrations begin the very next day.

There are only seven protesters, but they are armed with Bibles, placards, and religious conviction. A tragic, stubborn group on the other side of the road.

Derek and Cheryl aren't among them, but I think I recognize the woman in the yellow raincoat. She doesn't need it today: instead, she is practically drowning in an enormous puffer jacket. Her sweet, grandmotherly face radiates religious zeal as she waves a placard reading *Would Jesus Check In Here?*

They manage to make all work at the motel grind to a halt. Everyone gathers in the parking lot to follow the spectacle.

"That's actually a pretty interesting question," Clarence murmurs. "If Jesus *was* alive today, what kind of place would he check in to?"

"You're going to burn in hell!" one of the protesters shouts across at us. Any follow-up is drowned out by the sound of a passing truck.

"He wouldn't always be able to find a manger," Clarence goes on. "And it doesn't seem likely that he'd check into some luxury hotel. If we can translate the parable with the donkey to the modern day, it doesn't seem too much of a stretch to say that he'd pull up to a cheap motel in an old car."

"Why don't you go over there and discuss that with them?" Michael drily suggests.

"Do we know anyone with a water cannon?" MacKenzie asks. "Or a really long hose. A sudden rain shower could wash them away."

"Promise me you won't do anything stupid to annoy them," Camila begs her.

"Is that how it's going to be from now on?" MacKenzie protests. "I'm not allowed to do anything fun."

"There's no reason to stoop to their level. I think we should try to see this as an opportunity. We can let the town get to know us and show them that there's no war going on. That we're *good* for this town."

"Oh, there's definitely a war," MacKenzie says. "One side refusing to fight won't change that. It'll just change who wins."

Michael had driven into town earlier that day to pick up one of their leaflets, but we're none the wiser for it. The headline reads *Stop the immorality at Pine Away Motel*, and beneath it: *No-tell motels are often a breeding ground for crime, prostitution, violence, and drugs. Add your name to support regulation for a more moral approach to business.*

Alejandro takes a picture of the protesters. "I don't even know what a 'no-tell motel' *is*," he says.

"I regret making breakfast for them all these years," Dolores shouts angrily. "I'll, I'll..."

"Start with lunch," Camila says firmly. "Did you know that in Chinese, the word for 'crisis' is the same as—"

"The word for 'unimaginative consultant,'" MacKenzie interjects.

She pulls out her phone and calls the cops. Sheriff Ed himself drives over, but not even his cool competence can calm the protesters. If anything, they seem invigorated by his presence. They start chanting even more loudly when he shows up. In their eyes, they're Christian martyrs, valiantly enduring persecution from the police.

Sheriff Ed crosses the road and the parking lot. "There's not much I can do," he says. "If it gets any worse, I can force them to leave on grounds of disturbing the peace, but I'd rather not do that unless I really have to. There's a risk it'll just lead to more trouble. Have you thought about trying to reach a compromise with them?"

"How?" asks Michael. "By going to hell?"

That same day, a group of right-wing Christians picks up on this madness. *BuzzFeed* publishes a piece covering their craziness, and with that, it has begun. The right-wing Christians launch a campaign to lower our rating on TripAdvisor, and within just a few hours, our page fills up with negative reviews talking about sin and immorality. A number of liberal groups start a countercampaign, giving us only five-star reviews. In their eyes, we're the brave defenders of freedom and liberal values. None of them have ever even been here.

MacKenzie is looking after the phones. She cares less about the threats than Camila. Alejandro is tackling the in-box.

"How many calls about burning in hell?" he asks.

"I've lost count. How's it looking in the emails?"

"I've been deleting them all afternoon."

"I can help out," Michael says. "I have some savings, if the motel needs money. Just let me know. We can't let them get away with this."

"You're already helping us by building the veranda," Camila says. He and Paul head back out again, squelching over the still-damp ground. Before long, the sound of hammers starts echoing across the grass and the meadow on the other side of the river.

"Henny would say that I should forgive them," Michael says. "Or she'd remind me that they're just a tiny minority, at the very least. She had a weird ability to believe in people. Even when they let her down."

"There are some things that can't be forgiven," Paul says. "Not even by God."

"Not their God, in any case," Michael mutters.

"Do you represent another motel or a travel agency, or...?" MacKenzie asks on the line. She has started to get creative in her responses to all of the phone calls about burning in hell. "Either way, I have a few questions. If I'm going to end up in hell, what are the rooms like? I'd prefer a double bed to two singles. Because I'm assuming my incredibly lesbian girlfriend is going to end up there with me? My next question is about the pillows. They're very important, don't you agree? Can't be too firm, or... Hello? Hello?"

MacKenzie looks up at Camila. "She hung up without confirming my reservation in hell. I don't even know *when* I'm going."

"Okay, no more phones for you," Camila says. Then she raises an eyebrow. "'My incredibly lesbian girlfriend'?"

"I was improvising."

"I Googled no-tell motels," Camila tells her. She seems to be rearranging the brochures in the stand. "I had no idea what they were, either. But I found a website full of information from the cops. 'Crime in budget motels' or something like that. Anyway, a no-tell motel is a really cheap place that doesn't care who checks in or how long they stay. The anonymity and the low prices lead to all kinds of dubious behavior."

"I can guess," MacKenzie says.

"But the interesting thing is that they claimed 80 percent of the guests at a no-tell motel are from the local area. People use them for all kinds of illegal activities. Drugs, prostitution, criminal deals, violence, parties...that kind of thing."

"Just like here," MacKenzie says drily.

"Right? Who knows what Clarence gets up to in the afternoon. But it actually gave me a few ideas."

"Camila, have you been *inspired* by police warnings about dive motels?"

"Yeah, when you put it like that, I guess I have."

MacKenzie gives her an admiring glance. "That'll really give Cheryl fuel for her fire. But you're right. If we could get Dolores to follow up lunch by pushing some drugs, we could really improve our margins. Do you think Mr. Broek would be willing to help out?"

"That wasn't exactly what I had in mind."

"Now that I think about it, maybe Stacey would be better suited. That woman knows how to stand up for herself."

"I just meant that we could strengthen our local ties. So that's what I've done. Look." She holds up a leaflet, and MacKenzie moves closer to take a look at it.

"Ten percent discount for relatives of Pine Creek residents," MacKenzie reads aloud. "You should've added that no relative is too crazy for us. We'll even take parents-in-law."

"I've got some other ideas, too," Camila goes on. "Do you remember Juan Esteban's Christmas greetings? We could send out real cards, not digital ones, to all our favorite guests, and..."

MacKenzie raises her hands and softly cups Camila's face. Camila blinks, as though she has forgotten what they were talking about.

"You know it's not going to work, don't you?" MacKenzie asks.

"I know, I know. No expectations. You're going to break my heart."

"That wasn't actually what I meant. I was talking about the motel. You'll never win them over. Deep down, you must know that. They've got all the time in the world, and it's easier to fling crap than it is to defend yourself against it."

"Things are different now."

"I haven't been involved in any campaigns since Measure Nine."

"It's not the same," says Camila. "And we have to try, at the very least."

MacKenzie kisses her as though she is trying to make the whole world disappear. "I just don't want you to be disappointed," she says.

Camila looks away.

"Let's make sure we don't lose, then," she says.

CHAPTER 39

I Corinthians 6:9–10

I DON'T KNOW WHETHER I EVER GAVE MUCH THOUGHT TO GOD before I died, but I did grow up with him.

There were so many evenings when MacKenzie needed to avoid her dad, and she and I soon felt more at home in the town's many churches than she ever did in her actual home. No one cared that we attended several different churches, either. All the Catholic church asked of us was that we didn't take Communion. The priest even allowed MacKenzie to confess, but that might just have been because he liked listening to her stories.

MacKenzie was adamant that we should keep going to church after the campaign began. The proposal had split the congregations down the middle: both the Methodists and the Catholics distanced themselves from the measure, but the Sacred Faith Evangelical Church was in favor. MacKenzie didn't care about that. She was convinced they would change their minds. Hadn't they welcomed us for coffee and cookies all these years? And didn't they have the most entertaining services? None of the others put as much feeling into their singing.

Still, I couldn't help but glance at her and wonder whether she regretted that decision as we sat on the uncomfortable pews and listened to the pastor speak.

"My question for you is: Do you follow God's message, or do you defy it? Do you live by the rules that have existed for thousands of years, or do you live by your own rules?

"I had a worrying call today, from Mr. Lou Mabon at the Oregon Citizens Alliance. 'Did you know that homosexuals are taking over our schools?' he asked me. He wanted to know whether I—whether this congregation—would be brave enough to take up the fight against this development. That is the question I put to you today: Are we brave enough? Will we put up a fight? Will we stand up for the Bible and our children, or will we give in to sin? San Francisco has already fallen. Naked men walk shamelessly down its streets. Unless we take a stand now, our town will be next."

"Honestly, I seriously doubt Pine Creek is going to be the new Castro," MacKenzie whispered to me. "We'll never be able to compete with San Francisco's gay district."

But her face was worryingly pale.

"And if we permit homosexuality, what next? Sadism? Pedophilia? I say to you now: if we as a society decide that homosexuality is normal, we will have no choice but to say the same about pedophilia. Is that the road we want to go down? Are we willing to accept that our politicians have chosen this direction for us?"

The woman sitting next to us shook her head eagerly.

"The Bible is clear. The first epistle to the Corinthians in the English Standard Version tells us 'Do not be deceived: neither the sexually immoral, nor idolaters, nor adulterers, nor men who practice homosexuality...will inherit the kingdom of God.'"

MacKenzie attempted to smile, but it was stiff and forced and came nowhere close to her eyes. "At least I'm safe," she said.

"Homosexuality is deviant behavior; it is abnormal, perverse, and it will be punished. God says that they will die, and die they shall. They will then burn in hell."

"Okay, maybe not."

"God created our bodies, he created us, and he knows what works. He knew what would happen if a man lay with another man the way he lays with a woman. He knew that AIDs would emerge. Homosexuality is a perverse, dangerous way to live."

MacKenzie leaped up and left the church in the middle of the sermon. Heads turned to watch as I hurried out after her with our coats in my arms.

Cheryl followed her out, too, but as she placed a pleading hand on MacKenzie's arm, she shook it off and continued on her way. Only once we were several blocks away from the church did she slow down. Cheryl had stayed behind. I guess she wanted to hear the end of the sermon.

"How can they *believe* that stuff, Henny?" MacKenzie asked me. I had never seen her so upset before. Angry red patches had flared up on her cheeks, her voice was trembling, and her eyes were watery. "They know me. They've taken care of me my whole life. When Dad was drunk, I could always go there. And Cheryl! She just sat there and listened to that crap. But I guess…not everyone knows me. They've probably never met a gay person before. I shouldn't have brushed off Cheryl's hand like that. I know she means well. She does, doesn't she?"

I quickly nodded, unsure of what else I could do.

"They'll change their minds," MacKenzie said stubbornly. She still believed it then.

By that point, the campaign had finally made its way into the corridors of school. One of the teachers had started wearing a *No to Measure 9* badge and had been reported to the board. After that, all of the teachers were officially neutral. In the halls, however, *Yes to Measure 9* badges started to appear on our classmates' jackets. It was as if everyone had developed an interest in politics overnight.

MacKenzie was much braver than I was. When one of the tough kids loomed over us and accused us of being gay lovers, she walked straight toward him. I hid behind her. I'm not proud of it, but that's what happened.

I don't think I had ever felt as relieved as I did when Buddy intervened. "Pick on someone your own size," he yelled, and the tough kid suddenly seemed much less tough. Faced with Buddy's barely repressed aggression, he quickly walked away.

"Damn fag," Buddy muttered, but then he glanced over his shoulder, embarrassed. "Uh, sorry, MacKenzie. Old habit."

Still, the worst part about the campaign was the adults' reaction to it. They had always been so comforting and reasonable and kind, but they suddenly seemed to have been blinded by hate.

They gathered around a stand in town, yelling their message to passersby, their body language aggressive and their faces twisted.

"Do you think homosexuals should have special rights?"

"Do you want homosexuals, pedophiles, and sadists teaching your children?"

"Did you know that 90 percent of homosexuals are pedophiles?"

Many people simply walked on by, but quite a few stopped, and no one argued with them. MacKenzie and I watched them from further down the street. I don't know why. Maybe we wanted to torture ourselves.

"Why should homosexuals have special protection? There are people here in town—decent, God-fearing people—who can't find a job. There are old folks who are all on their own, with no one to care for them. Poor people, right here in our town. And we're supposed to protect homosexuals? Do you think they should have special rights just because they've chosen to live unnatural, sinful lives? They're rich, too. Don't let anyone tell you otherwise. Fact: they earn far more than the average American."

I pulled MacKenzie's arm to lead her away, but she wouldn't budge. I don't think she could understand how people who claimed to believe in their ideals had no problem lying for them, and she definitely couldn't understand how anyone could fall for those lies.

MacKenzie was brave. She was magnificent. She marched straight over to their stand and started debating with them. I hesitated for half a second, and by the time I made it over to her, she was surrounded by a group of agitated adults, all much bigger and older than her, fervently arguing with everything she said.

"God doesn't hate the sinner; he hates the sin," one of them said, their face far too close to MacKenzie's.

"I just don't believe in special rights for homosexuals," said another.

"It's for their own good. We can't let them think that what they're doing is natural or right."

I tried to push over to her, but a man kept getting in my way. He angled his body so that the others wouldn't be able to see, and then he grabbed MacKenzie's arm—hard, so hard that it left a mark—and hissed, "Fag-loving bitch."

MacKenzie grimaced.

"You're going to burn in hell."

I finally managed to get over to her, and she tore her arm away from him. I grabbed her other arm and gently led her away. The marks on her skin had started to turn reddish-blue. Clear impressions of five adult fingers.

MacKenzie rubbed her arm. "If they want to hurt me, they'll have to try harder than that," she said. "I guess they've forgotten how well my dad raised me."

But *I* was fighting back tears. Me, who hadn't even done anything.

Then MacKenzie froze. I was walking so close to her that I felt her body tense. I anxiously glanced back, and then relaxed. Cheryl was the only person walking toward us.

I can still remember the relief I felt when I saw her. I was blinking frantically. Oddly enough, the relief made me want to cry even more. I was desperately longing for an adult to come and save us, someone kind who could fix everything, stop the campaign, make the world normal again.

But Cheryl was making her way over to the stand. Her T-shirt that day read *Yes to Measure 9.*

I instinctively moved in front of MacKenzie to shield her from the sight. It was no use, of course. Cheryl was walking toward us. MacKenzie saw the T-shirt only moments later.

"She...she can...*go to hell*," I said.

CHAPTER 40

A Break-In Under Cover of Darkness

FOR THE FIRST FEW DAYS, THE PROTESTERS OUTSIDE THE MOTEL don't have any real impact on business. If anything, we actually have more people in the restaurant than usual, as people from town come over here to watch them. The parking lot fills up with cars, and the guests in the restaurant look more like a theater audience, their faces turned toward the road and the show on the other side.

The protest doesn't seem to be stopping people from checking in, either. Most of our guests arrive in the evening, when the protesters have gone home for the day. For several nights now, we've had ten to fifteen rooms filled, which is good for this time of year. If any of the guests are still here when the Sacred Faith Evangelical Church members arrive the next morning, they don't seem to care. They're mostly truck drivers and weary businessmen who have driven many, many miles, and being faced with Christian fanatics before breakfast doesn't seem to faze them.

The only real difference is that Michael and I are sleeping on the couch in the office now. It was his idea, but MacKenzie and Camila are happy to have him there. I guess the threats have had an impact on us after all.

We spend several days in a kind of tense balance of terror. Rooms are cleaned and keys are handed over as usual. Alejandro helps out in the restaurant, keeping the hungry public fed, and the protesters chant their slogans and eat their packed lunches, heading home once the sun goes down.

But then, one week after they first arrived, they finally come back at night.

I notice the headlights first. It's two in the morning when they slowly pull up on the edge of the road with their hazard lights flashing. Shadowy figures climb out of the cars, find their flashlights, and start lifting objects out of the trunks. Something catches the light, but I can't tell what it is from where I'm standing, and I don't want to leave the safety of check-in to go over there alone.

"Michael!" I shout over my shoulder as another car slows down and comes to a halt. "Wake up!"

I guess he hears them, too, because in the office, Michael stirs. A moment later, he is standing beside me in the gloom by the automatic doors, squinting out at the silent, ominous figures. They line up, dark and serious, like the first wave of an army.

He instinctively reaches for the phone and dials MacKenzie's number. "I think we've got a problem," he says. Before long, both MacKenzie and Camila have joined him in reception.

"Have you called the cops?" is the first thing MacKenzie asks.

"I didn't know what you would want to do."

"Well, I'm damn sure not going over there to talk to them."

Again, I see something catch the light. It's big and metallic and... round.

Michael squints toward it. "Is that...a *pan lid*?"

Suddenly, a wall of noise hits us: pan lids, ladles, even a couple of real cymbals. They must have borrowed those from the church choir.

"What the hell?" MacKenzie mutters.

One by one, the lights come on in the rooms. Doors start to open.

"Shut up!" one man shouts, sounding drowsy. He hasn't bothered to get dressed and is standing in the doorway in all his naked glory, dramatically lit from behind. Even from a distance, his hairy body is enough to make the protesters fall silent.

Dad sticks his head around his door and says, "I've called the police." For once, that is the right thing to do.

The noise starts up again with renewed strength, and anything else he has to say is drowned out by the banging and rattling. I glance toward the trucks and cars in the parking lot and hope that none of our guests are armed. A few have gotten dressed and are now outside; MacKenzie and Michael are desperately trying to stop them from crossing the road to fight with the protesters. Camila calls the police again.

From one side of the road, the swearing comes thick and fast. From the other, Bible quotes and noise. It sounds much worse out here in the parking lot. Even *I* can feel the noise starting to get on my nerves, and I don't even *have* nerves anymore.

The sheriff arrives after half an hour, flanked by three patrol cars. One pulls into our parking lot, and the others park by the protesters. Our side makes do with muttering about those idiots over there, and the guests cast a last few murderous glances over the road before allowing MacKenzie to herd them back into their rooms.

The protesters aren't anywhere near as compliant. They continue to bang their pots and pans in poor Sheriff Ed's face, until eventually he shrugs and tells the deputies to round them up.

We stand in silence in the parking lot, watching blankly. It *should* be funny. One of the deputies tries to get a woman in her fifties to drop a pan lid; another is hit by a ladle being brandished by a scrawny fifteen-year-old boy. The deputy's thick jacket takes the brunt of the blow, but it annoys him all the same. Eventually, he just grabs the boy and forces him into the back of his car. The last I see of him are two skinny, flailing legs.

But we still aren't laughing. Not even when two deputies have to work together to disarm a housewife clutching a pair of cymbals. She runs around and around the patrol car, smashing them together, until eventually the deputies close in on her from both sides.

There is something ominous about the furious commitment the protesters are displaying, a sense that something is being stepped up right before our eyes, something we might already have lost control of. It's unnerving to watch a farce that no one is laughing at.

Sheriff Ed crosses the road and comes over to talk to us. "I'll release them as soon as they've calmed down. Even though they *did* technically resist arrest and attack a police officer."

"With a ladle," MacKenzie murmurs blankly.

"Damn it, this isn't funny."

"No," she agrees.

"No good will come from us charging them. We'll just end up creating more martyrs."

MacKenzie looks over at the packed police cars on the other side of the road. "I think we already have," she says.

"We appreciate it, Sheriff," Camila quickly adds.

The sheriff wearily rubs his face. "Don't thank me yet. This isn't over."

But the night is, at least, quiet again. We look at one another in surprise as that dawns on us. In the rooms behind us, the lights go out one by one, and once the police cars have driven away, we stay where we are in the sudden silence.

No one seems quite sure what we should do now.

The next morning, I decide to pay the Sacred Faith Evangelical Church a visit. It's a chance to spy on the enemy. I stand across the road, on Church Street, watching the feverish activity. The parking lot is full of cars, many with license plates from Montana, the Dakotas, Idaho, and Wyoming. One of them has come all the way from Arkansas.

Bob and Derek are standing just a few yards away from me.

As yet, Bob hasn't taken an official stance either for or against the campaign. He has been a politician long enough to know that he just needs to wait out the storm. But unlike Derek, he lets his real feelings show.

"Christ, looks like we're importing loonies again," he says. "Don't we have enough of our own?"

"Brothers and sisters from other congregations," Derek finds himself saying. Then he adds: "How were we meant to know it would lead to such a fuss? Seems like people are really inspired by it, though, and surely all publicity is good publicity... Damn it, all hell's broken loose, hasn't it?"

"That's just what the pastor wants."

"They're not even from around here. And they think they have the right to criticize *our* motel? That almost makes me question this whole thing. What does some guy from Idaho know about our town?"

Bob raises an eyebrow.

Derek glances at him and then, with deliberate nonchalance, says, "Have you been over to the motel lately?"

"So people can tell me I'm going to burn in hell? No thank you."

"Ah."

"Why don't you just go see Stacey?"

"I doubt these folks would appreciate me creeping around at the motel."

"You could call her. You know, the telephone. Great invention."

"Seems like the whole country has taken an interest," Derek continues. "All the big TV channels and papers have called."

Bob turns to Derek. "Tell me you didn't say yes. Tell me you haven't agreed to go on national TV and become a celebrity madman."

"The pastor is doing all the interviews. Besides, we don't trust the mainstream media. It's all biased."

"You sound like a parrot," Bob sighs.

"What you mean is that I don't sound like *your* parrot," Derek tells him. For once, Bob has no comeback.

I decide to go for a quick walk around the church itself. Inside, there are people making signs, compiling petitions, brewing coffee, and photocopying leaflets. Laughing, too—the atmosphere is relaxed and festive. It's an opportunity for them to see friends and acquaintances from conferences, online forums, and Christian holidays. A few seem to be staying with members of the congregation, but others have brought air mattresses and sleeping bags and are camping out in the church building. Cheryl is rushing around, in her element, her organizational skills being put to the test. Today's T-shirt reads *The Motel Should Pine Away!*

There and then, I come as close to hating someone as I ever have. She's actually *enjoying* this.

Back at the motel, the protesters are chanting away like always.

"You're going to burn in hell!" they shout.

"Ah, home sweet home!" MacKenzie replies as she pushes the cleaning cart in front of her.

"Repent your sins before it's too late!" they yell after her as she strips the sheets in room 12.

"My sins are the one thing I don't regret!" she shouts back, her arms full of laundry.

They even shout at Dolores when she steps outside for some fresh air.

"No pancakes for you!" she tells them, indignant, storming back inside.

Alejandro has been snapping pictures from every possible angle. He prefers to capture absurd, humorous moments, like a protester holding a placard bearing righteous Bible quotations taking a bite of cheese sandwich, or one trying to juggle a placard, thermos flask, and coffee cup. But even his camera is powerless to avoid the ugly, frightening side of the protest: ordinary faces twisted in collective fury.

The tragic thing is that they're wearing us down. There must be at least a hundred people out there now, and no one wants to eat with a Christian mob screaming outside. Watching them is no longer amusing; they've now become a serious threat to a person's digestion. No one wants to be told that they're going to hell, and certainly not on an empty stomach.

"How long am I supposed to keep cooking food that no one is eating?" Dolores complains.

"Just hold out a little longer," Camila pleads. "They'll get bored eventually."

Dolores pats her on the shoulder. "Don't you worry, I'm not someone who gives in. But it's a waste of my talents; that's all I'm saying."

The only diner who isn't staying at the motel is Buddy. Out of sheer solidarity, he starts eating breakfast, lunch, and dinner with us. Aside from him, Dad, Paul, and Stacey are the only others. Paul just shakes his head and works on his veranda, Stacey shouts back at them—of course—and Dad has stopped going on his walks, taking refuge in the restaurant instead. He still hasn't started wearing Stacey's red coat, but he does keep giving her thoughtful glances, and he even goes as far as to nod approvingly when she shouts something deeply inappropriate at the protesters. But then he seems to realize what he is doing and makes sure his face is suitably blank when she looks in his direction. The two of them are alone in the restaurant. Even Clarence has started to sneak off to the pub as early as he can.

People have stopped checking in, too. Every evening, the protesters are there with their flashlights and placards, though they no longer have their pan lids. One of the deputies keeps an eye on them, but what is he supposed to do? No cars stop. The protesters keep coming, more every day.

Over in check-in, Michael, Camila, and MacKenzie have nothing to do. I'm doing my best to keep their morale up. "It's not the same as last time," I say. "These people aren't even from town. They'll get bored eventually."

Camila is sitting primly behind the desk, ready for someone to check in. MacKenzie is stretched out on the couch, staring up at the strip lights on the ceiling.

"The main thing is that we're here together," I say. "We were already becoming happier. This is just a temporary disruption. We'll have to...uh, come up with something."

Michael walks over to the doors. "How long can we survive?" he asks.

"We've had dead periods before," MacKenzie tells him from the couch.

"We can hold out a while yet," says Camila. "But I really hope we get some paying guests soon. And that they stay all night."

"I've been thinking about that," MacKenzie announces. "We'll just have to start drugging them. We can ask Dolores to slip some sleeping pills into their dinner, and then they'll be out like a light all night."

"We need to get them to stop here first," says Michael.

The strip lights hum. The protesters outside start up a chant. Cars drive by.

Suddenly, the phone rings.

Camila jolts and stares at it. I don't think she can bring herself to have yet another unpleasant conversation.

MacKenzie jumps up from the couch and moves over to her, places a hand on her shoulder, and answers.

"Welcome to Pine Away Motel," she says, winking at Camila. "For death threats, please press one. For general messages about burning in hell, press two. For prank calls, press three. To make a reservation at the motel that never sleeps, press four."

Camila shakes her head, but she smiles all the same.

"Weird," says MacKenzie. "They hung up."

The phone rings again almost immediately. "Okay, okay," she says before Camila even has time to speak. This time, she answers normally.

MacKenzie stands up straight, practically to attention. "Yes, ma'am," she says once the woman on the phone finally stops speaking. "No, ma'am. Of course not. Yes, ma'am. I'm sorry about that. *How many* people? No, no, that's no problem at all. When? Don't worry, I'll take care of everything. It'll be an honor. I just need to take your name and contact details, and a credit card number to process the reservation." She types everything into the reservation system with the phone clamped between her shoulder and her ear.

When she eventually hangs up, she says, "Someone called Mrs. Davies just booked nineteen rooms. For twenty-three people. Including dinner. The day after tomorrow."

"Nineteen rooms!" Camila blurts out. "That should keep us afloat. And Dolores will be happy to get cooking again."

"Do you think… Could it have been a prank call?" Michael asks.

"If it was, it's the best one I ever heard. She sounded exactly like a tough, lively old woman. *Not* someone who would lower herself to joking." MacKenzie makes a face. "She actually had quite a bit to say about *my* joke."

"I don't want to be the pessimist here," says Michael. "But what should we do about the protesters?"

"Damn it," MacKenzie mutters. She peers out through the window as though she's hoping they will have magically disappeared. They haven't. "Maybe we can drug *them* instead? Take them some coffee laced with sleeping pills? Because Mrs. Davies is going to have a perfect stay with us."

"They won't have gone by then."

"You can barely even hear them anymore."

Unfortunately, just as the words leave her lips, they start chanting "Jesus! Jesus! Jesus!" in unison, like some kind of Christian cheer squad.

Camila looks resigned. "We'll have to warn her, at the very least. They can't turn up here expecting a calm, peaceful stay."

MacKenzie still looks bullishly stubborn, but she eventually reaches for the phone.

"Mrs. Davies—" She starts so pluckily, but is quickly interrupted. "No, no, there's no problem with the reservation. Or rather..." She sighs. "I need to be completely honest with you. We're having some problems with protesters at the moment. Protesters, yes. They're much quieter now, and the sheriff has told them they need to leave by nine every evening, and... Yes, of course. I understand. Very good. Well, all right, then."

She hangs up and blinks in confusion. "She already knew about them. She said she'd read the articles."

"And? What did she say?"

"She said that if you start listening to crazy people, you'll be in trouble. She never lets anyone dictate what she can or can't do. She said she stopped listening to people several years ago."

"So...?"

"She's coming. Her and twenty or so of her closest relatives."

At four in the morning, the motel is completely deserted. The lonely streetlights cast a faint glow over their limited territory, but that makes everything around them seem even more desolate. The protesters are long gone for the night.

Aren't they...?

I freeze. A faint beam of light suddenly spills out of the restaurant.

At first, I'm not even sure what I'm seeing. The restaurant is still dark and empty, but the darkness inside is different, grayer than the night outside. It's the kitchen, I think. Someone has turned on one of the lights in the kitchen, but not the restaurant itself.

They're back!

My first instinct is to try to wake Michael, but once I've dismissed that, I feel surprisingly calm. I'll investigate on my own, and if it's the protesters, I'll come up with some way of stopping them or warning the others.

I creep through the walls and down the narrow corridor behind the restaurant. The radiators and pipes are clanking, but I don't notice any unusual sounds, not until I come closer to the kitchen door.

As I approach, I hear quiet footsteps slowly moving forward. They belong to someone trying not to be heard.

All right, Henny, I think as I press myself against the wall. *It's not like they can do anything to you. You're dead, remember.*

With that, I throw myself through the door.

I stop dead.

"Dad?" I blurt out, like an idiot.

It is actually, unbelievably, him. He is wearing a pair of freshly pressed suit pants and his old apron. One of his favorite recipe books is on the otherwise empty countertop. He's had it all my life.

"What are you doing?" I ask as he turns and tiptoes back out of the kitchen. He leaves the door unlocked, and looks incredibly guilty as he does so. He glances over his shoulder before sneaking up the stairs toward the rooms.

It's cold, dark, and damp. The frost on the metal railing glitters in the dim glow of the night lights outside the rooms. But Dad is warm. Before stepping out, he puts on Stacey's bright-red coat and the crazy knitted mittens. He wraps the scarf she gave him around his neck, before sneaking outside toward the rooms. He glances around again, listening for signs that someone is awake. Then he leans in to Stacey's door and knocks quietly.

So quietly that Stacey doesn't even hear. *It's four in the morning. She's asleep, for God's sake*, I think.

Dad hesitates. Knocks again. Leans in even closer to the door. "Mrs. Callahan?" he says. "Excuse me, Mrs. Callahan?"

He casts panicked glances all around him. We don't have any other guests right now, so I'm not sure who he thinks is going to hear him.

Dad looks increasingly nervous, but then the door opens.

"What the hell?" Stacey mumbles. She is wearing a huge T-shirt that reaches almost all the way to her knees. And then, sounding drowsy and confused, she says, "You're wearing my coat."

"Mrs. Callahan?"

"Stacey. Mrs. Callahan is my mother-in-law."

"Come with me."

She frowns. Pained. "What time is it?" she asks in a flat voice.

"Four. You need to come now."

Stacey is too tired to protest. She opens the door and takes two disoriented steps out into the night. "Jesus, it's cold!" she says.

"Uh..." Dad looks away. "Maybe you should get dressed first?"

Stacey looks down at her bare legs, then turns around and reappears five minutes later, wearing jeans and boots and a coat, not that she seems much happier for it. Dad walks ahead of her with quick, silent footsteps, and Stacey mutters to herself.

"This better be really damn important," she says. "To get me up at this ungodly hour. Who wakes someone up at four in the morning?"

"*Shh!*" Dad whispers desperately. "Just follow me. And be quiet."

"Why do we have to tiptoe around? What have you done?"

"I haven't done anything," Dad snaps.

They take the back route into the kitchen.

"Surely the restaurant's closed?" Stacey asks.

Dad doesn't reply. He cautiously opens the door and pushes Stacey inside. He tries to pretend that everything is normal, but it still takes him several seconds to turn on the light, and as the fluorescent bulb hums and clicks into life, he winces guiltily.

"Mr. Broek, did you *break in* to the kitchen?"

"Of course I didn't!"

"Did you steal the keys?"

"I borrowed them."

Stacey laughs, suddenly looking much more alert. "I underestimated you, Mr. Broek."

"Call me Robert. And keep your voice down."

On one of the kitchen tables, I can see number of items. Flour, sugar, cinnamon. A glass pie dish. Eight glossy Granny Smith apples. A rolling pin and a knife.

"It's time for you to learn how to make an apple pie," Dad tells her. "A traditional American apple pie. All we need to do is follow the instructions in this book. I took the liberty of sneaking ba...of going home to pick up my apron and my old recipe book. We can't fail with that."

Stacey seems frozen to the spot in front of the counter. To me, the ingredients look lonely and abandoned, but Stacey is staring at them as if she wants to make sure it isn't all a mirage.

"It... I..." she stutters.

"No, no, don't cry!" Dad sounds horrified.

"I never cry," Stacey says, stubbornly raising her chin. But her eyes do look suspiciously glossy. "It's just that no one has ever done anything like this for me before. That's all I'm saying."

"Coffee?" Dad asks, pointing to a thermos.

"You've thought of everything."

"Planning is important," he tells her, looking very pleased with himself. Stacey steps forward and wraps both arms around him.

"Thank you, Mr. Broek," she says.

"Do you want to bake or not?" Dad mutters. His cheeks are flushed.

Dad provides Stacey with a constant stream of instructions—peel and core the apples, cut them into inch-thick slices; make sure they're even, otherwise they won't cook at the same speed—and Stacey follows them all with heart-warming care. She doesn't even mind him leaning over her shoulder, correcting everything she does.

"Aren't you going to help?" she jokes at one point, but Dad is deadly serious when he answers:

"How are you ever supposed to learn if you don't do the job yourself?"

With that, he gives her more instructions. "Turn on the oven. Mix the flour, sugar, and butter. Now we'll put it in the refrigerator for a while, to rest. At least thirty minutes. We could really have done this in advance, but it doesn't hurt if it rests a little longer."

Stacey yawns. Dad pours two cups of coffee and then continues his lecture: "You want firm apples; otherwise, they go mushy. Slightly acidic, too. As you can see, it's all right here in the recipe book. It's just a case of following the instructions."

"How do you know how to bake?"

"I had to learn when Henny's mother died."

"I'm sorry," Stacey says. "About your wife, I mean. And Henny. I'm sorry I didn't say anything sooner. I never know what you're supposed to say in situations like that."

"No one does."

"It must've been hard. Suddenly having to do everything on your own."

"You deal with the things you have to deal with."

"And you dealt with them fantastically," I reassure him.

"Maybe," Stacey says. "But it can still feel hard."

"As long as you follow the rules, you survive. It's just like cooking." He bends down to see whether the oven is starting to heat up.

Dad might never have been someone who knew how to express his love, I think, but he showed it in other ways. I never wanted for anything while I was growing up. And he taught me how to make apple pie.

"I've never noticed that," Stacey says. She pops a slice of apple into her mouth when Dad isn't looking.

"What do you mean?"

"That you survive if you follow the rules. It might work with a recipe book, but the rules in life are so vague. And contradictory. No one tells you about them in advance. You just hear about them once you've broken them."

"But then you know for the next time!"

"Maybe. Unless they've changed. And it makes no difference whether you do everything right. People won't forget who you were."

Talking about his favorite subject seems to have reinvigorated him. "It isn't about doing everything right! It's about not doing things wrong!"

"It's impossible never to do things wrong."

Dad looks like his entire worldview has just been questioned. "But..." he says. "It must be possible. What do people have to strive for otherwise?"

"I don't know. I guess maybe you could try to be happy?"

"Happy! How are you supposed to know if you're happy?"

"I think the idea is that you feel it," Stacey hesitantly replies. I'm not convinced she believes in happiness, either.

"That seems incredibly naive," Dad says. "And then what? You're happy. That just means a new catastrophe is going to hit you soon, and what are you going to cling to then? No. Order. Rules and instructions. Never do anything wrong. Those are the constants in life. Cut the other end of the pastry now. In long strips, roughly two inches wide."

Stacey leans forward over the bench and slowly but surely cuts the pastry.

"Add the apple. More in the middle, so it's like a little mound. Add some butter, that'll make it juicier. And then we cover it with the strips. A cross pattern, a lattice...under, then over."

As I watch Dad with Stacey, I realize for the first time how lonely it must have been for him when I moved to the motel. I never thought about it at the time. He was so stuck in his ways and focused on everything being done just how he liked it that I occasionally thought he might actually have been relieved when I moved out. It meant he could do the washing up the way he wanted, if nothing else, and there would never be any plates in the wrong place on the dining table.

But the more pedantic he became, the more I should have been there to disrupt him. People can get caught up in their own minds if they aren't careful. And if there is one thing that death has taught me, it's that life doesn't care about how desperately we try to control it. You can do everything perfectly and still collide with a truck.

Though maybe I was much too orderly myself to really shake him up.

I smile. Stacey will probably do the job.

Right now, she is deep in concentration. She carefully lifts a strip of pastry dough and plaits it with the next one. "You've never thought about just...not trying?" she asks. "Ignoring their unwritten rules and regulations?"

"Society needs rules and norms."

"But they still talk about you, even though you've done everything right. Aren't you tempted to just ignore people's expectations? I think there's a sense of freedom in already having disappointed everyone. After that, there's nothing they can do to you. Be a little crazy. Tell people what you really think of them. Shock them."

"But I don't know how to shock someone," Dad confesses.

Stacey pats him on the arm. "*That's* something I can teach you," she says. "I actually don't know how to do anything else. When do we get to eat the pie?"

"It needs about an hour in the oven, but we'll have to lower the temperature after thirty minutes."

"An hour!"

But Stacey doesn't seem to have anything against waiting. Her nose is practically pressed against the oven door. "That there's my pie!" she says. "I made it!"

"Of course you did."

"Is it almost ready?"

While the pie bakes, they clean up after themselves. Wash up. Dry off. Put away. Then they sit in the dark restaurant, drinking coffee and eating apple pie in comfortable silence. Outside, dawn breaks—another fantastic sunrise to add to my collection. Light slowly conquers the road and the parking lot, until eventually the restaurant is bathed in sunlight.

Dolores is a little late, I think. She should have started preparing by now, though I suppose she has plenty of time to do it during the day at the moment.

A car pulls up in the parking lot. A weary man climbs out and stretches with a yawn. He looks like he has been driving all night. He must have spotted Dad and Stacey in the restaurant and assumed we were already open. The protesters haven't even showed up yet.

"Is that...?" Stacey asks.

"What will they think when they see us sitting here with the lights out, ignoring them and eating pie?" Dad asks. "What will *Dolores* think when she finds out?"

He seems to be wondering whether his dignity can handle hiding beneath the table.

"Right," Stacey says firmly. "We'll have to deal with this ourselves. Can you make bacon and scrambled eggs?"

"But..."

"I can make coffee, if nothing else. And we *do* have apple pie."

It takes Stacey a moment or two to work out how to open the door, but after that, the preparations take no time at all. She turns on the lights and makes coffee, while Dad rummages through the refrigerator on the hunt for bacon and eggs.

Stacey grabs one of the order pads from behind the counter and walks confidently toward the first customer.

"Coffee, please," he says.

"Coming up." She pushes the pad into her back pocket and pours him a cup from the thermos while the fresh batch brews.

"Apple pie?" she asks.

"Sure, why not?"

Stacey is a natural.

"I didn't know you knew how to work a register," Dad says admiringly.

"Pfft, who cares about that? The coffee and pie is on us!" she shouts out to their only guest.

By the time the second customer arrives, they are ready.

"We've got a limited menu today, and unfortunately we're only taking cash," Stacey tells him.

The construction worker shrugs.

"Coffee, bacon, scrambled eggs, and apple pie. For...five dollars?"

"Sounds good."

Unfortunately, the protesters turn up before our early-morning diners have time to wolf down their food. They knock back their coffee, grab their slices of pie, and leave.

Stacey waves a dollar bill in the air. "Look!" she says. "A tip!"

Dolores walks straight into one of the customers on her way into the restaurant. "What is going on here?" she asks, sounding confused.

Stacey and Dad freeze.

"Nothing, Dolores," Stacey quickly tells her.

Dad takes off his apron, and they both slowly back up toward the rear entrance.

"Just a couple of early customers," Stacey continues.

With that, they hurry away.

CHAPTER 41

Freedom

THE BARE BRANCHES OF THE TREES LINING ELM STREET GLITTER in the cold sunlight. People have wrapped themselves up in scarves, hats, and winter coats, but they seem relaxed as they walk down the sidewalk, as if the cool air doesn't bother them. Camila and Alejandro are standing side by side next to her car, smiling in confusion as people say hello to them—as though nothing unusual is going on in town.

"Do they even know about the protests?" Alejandro asks.

"Maybe they just don't care."

Camila had tracked him down in the restaurant thirty minutes earlier and asked if he could come with her for a while. "Bring your camera," she said.

I squeezed into the car with them, of course, and now we are all on our way to the secondhand shop where she and Michael bought the reception desk.

"Take some pictures from different angles," she tells Alejandro once we arrive. "Make them as appealing as possible. Try to make it look like this is the most charming antique shop God ever created."

Alejandro shrugs and gets to work. He takes sunlit images of the shopfront, of the old lettering above the window—which, in the right light, looks almost golden. He zooms in for more artsy shots of objects in the window, things that, with a little goodwill, could be mistaken for antiques. After that, he does the same inside.

The same woman is behind the counter, huddled in three thick sweaters and a pair of gloves. "You're welcome to take as many pictures as you like," she says. "But if you want me in any of them, I need to fix my hair."

She gives them a hopeful glance.

"I hope you don't mind," Camila says to her. "I wanted to take some pictures so I could talk to you about an idea I had." She pulls out a leaflet advertising the motel and places it on the counter. It's very simple, minimal and appealing, with one of Alejandro's images in extravagant color.

"We're making new brochures for the motel," she says.

"And you want to leave a couple here?" the woman asks drily.

"No, no. We want to do the same thing for you. I went through all of the brochures we have at the motel, and I realized they're all really old. We didn't even have one for your incredible shop! So I was thinking I would make some new ones, to give our guests tips and inspiration about things they can do in our beautiful town."

Alejandro holds out his camera and flicks through some of the images he has just taken.

"Imagine my little shop looking so charming!" the woman exclaims. "I've had it for thirty years, but I can hardly recognize it in those pictures." Then, with a cynical note in her voice, she asks: "What's all this going to cost me?"

"Nothing," Camila reassures her. "We're going to print off a few for the motel, and if you want any for your own use, I'm happy to send you the file so that you can have some printed, or copy them, or just print them out on an ordinary printer. It's entirely up to you."

"Hmm," the woman says. "If you want to leave some of your leaflets here, I suppose it's all right."

"So are we making free leaflets for the whole town now?" Alejandro asks on the way back to the motel. They have already taken pictures of several shops.

"If that's what it takes."

"But what do we get out of it? It feels like a lot of work just to get them to display a few of our own leaflets."

"That's not why. People around here are proud and stubborn. No one wants to think of themselves as immoral or linked to a den of sin, so if they *are* linked to us..."

"We can't be anywhere near as bad as the Sacred Faith Evangelical Church claims?"

"Exactly."

"Worth a try, I guess." Alejandro sounds doubtful.

"My next idea is to organize a party. I don't think people around here have been out to the motel for years. If we can show them that we're an ordinary, family-friendly place…"

"Do you really think anyone will come?"

"Everyone likes a party, don't they? Plus, you saw how friendly everyone in town was when they greeted us. It's just a loud minority that are in favor of the proposal."

"Very loud," Alejandro mutters.

When they get back to the motel, they see MacKenzie walking by with three sheets in her arms. Her eyes are fixed on the restaurant, but she stops to talk to them.

"Mrs. Davies has been calling all day," she says. "*And* several of the others from her group. At least five of them have offered to pay extra if we put them in a room as far away from hers as we can. Oh, and I've had an idea about the protesters."

With that, she disappears into the restaurant, humming as she walks.

"She seems to be in a good mood," Camila remarks.

"MacKenzie has never been able to resist a challenge. Plus, this Mrs. Davies lady sounds crazy. And you know what MacKenzie is like around crazy women."

"What's she like around crazy women?"

"She can't resist them."

The motel is a hive of activity again.

The doors are all open, airing out the rooms and making cleaning easier. Michael and Camila are both pushing cleaning carts, each taking one floor. In the kitchen, Dolores is already happily at work preparing for dinner the next day. Alejandro has had to put down his camera to help out.

MacKenzie is busy with her own project. She has spread out three sheets on the floor in the restaurant, fixed them together with a staple gun, and tied them to three wooden poles. She has already written something on the other side, though I couldn't see what. On this side, at least, it reads *WELCOME, MRS. DAVIES* in huge letters. She fills them in with the last of the red paint.

Dad and Stacey walk past the cozy chaos. Dad is wearing his warm, red coat again, and Stacey has an enormous scarf wrapped around her neck, covering practically her whole face. They walk around and around the motel, so deep in conversation that they don't even notice the protesters shouting that prayer is the best weapon.

"I'm not saying I'm going to move back in with him," Stacey says. "He probably doesn't even miss me. I'm sure he's moved on to some other slut by now."

"Of course he hasn't. You're married!"

"That's never stopped him before," Stacey mutters. "But just because I've moved in here, that's no reason for him to act like things are over between us! And now he wants to be a politician."

"That's a laudable ambition."

"Well, he's trying, at the very least. That must mean something. I guess."

She glances at Dad for support, and he nods gravely.

"Yeah... I guess maybe he would be doing better if I was there by his side," she continues. "He might look confident, but Derek doesn't like doing things on his own. He's used to having a whole team around him. And if I don't know what *I* want, maybe I might as well do what *he* wants. Don't you think?"

They have reached the back of the motel again. Michael and Paul have taken a break from cleaning to work on the veranda while the sun is still up. Stacey walks by without even looking up, but Dad slows down and watches their movements.

Stacey notices and says, "Michael there, he dated Henny."

"My Henny? When?"

"When they were kids. Last year of high school, after Derek went off to college. But I think they were seeing one another more recently, too. Before..."

"But what's he doing with that sick man who used to sleep in MacKenzie's office?"

"Building a veranda. For Henny."

"Henny wanted a veranda?"

"I think so. This was her favorite place. Building it seems to have helped Paul, anyway. Apparently he's completely traumatized. No wonder. Poor guy."

"Traumatized?"

Stacey gives him a surprised glance. "He's the one who hit her."

"Who...hit my Henny?"

"I'm sorry, Robert. Maybe I shouldn't have said anything."

They have already passed the veranda, but Dad turns to look back. For once, he doesn't know how to react.

"Are you all right?" Stacey asks.

"Of course I'm all right," he snaps.

They arrive in a long line, all nine cars. One by one, they slow down, blinkers indicating left, and turn off toward the motel. The protesters seem unsettled by their sudden arrival. People climb out of the cars and swarm across the parking lot, relieved to be outside. At least three teenagers and two adults sneak around the corner to smoke.

Clarence, Buddy, and Paul come rushing out with MacKenzie's banner. Each holding a pole, they stretch it out in front of the protesters. Buddy bends down to turn on the stereo, and Bruce Springsteen's voice drowns out the unhappy shouts from the other side of the road.

A father and his thirteen-year-old son are the first to step into reception. The man irritably scans the room. "This is just an ordinary motel," he complains.

The protesters have raised their voices to overpower Bruce, and for a while their shouts of "Repent your sins before it's too late!" mix with *Born in the USA*.

"We'd already booked a motel in Bend. It was a much better location for us. We had to set off a day earlier because my aunt decided she wanted to stay here. Then we arrive and find out it's just an ordinary motel."

"We're perfectly normal," MacKenzie agrees in the rainbow-colored reception area.

"She's not even my real aunt. That's what we call her, but she married into the family. I can't understand what my uncle was thinking. If he really *had* to marry her, he had some nerve dying on us after just a few years. Though by that point, I guess he was probably desperate."

He glances nervously over his shoulder again. When he speaks again, his voice is much quieter.

"Anyway, we're here now. Since she wanted to stay here of all places, I hope you can keep her amused. If you can keep her entertained for a whole day, you can have my firstborn son."

"Dad!" the man's son protests.

"At least you'd get out of these family gatherings," the father tells him.

The son can't argue with that.

"About our room," the father begins, but the automatic doors open and he trails off.

Considering the effect Mrs. Davies seems to have on those around her, she is almost laughably short. She is wearing a knee-length skirt, comfortable shoes, thick tights, a cream-colored blouse, a beige cardigan, and a light-brown coat. Her skin is wrinkled and as dry as parchment, and the glimmer in her eye suggests that her sense of humor is even drier. This is a woman who doesn't try to hide what she thinks about the world.

She raises an eyebrow at the father and son—a miniscule movement—and they both move to one side, practically cowering against the wall.

"I think it's best if I handle the checking in," she says.

The father and son nod eagerly and then scamper away.

"Susan," she says. For the first time, I notice the young woman behind her. Could be a daughter or a niece, I think, in that difficult age between childhood and adulthood. She has a tablet computer, a folder, and a list ready to be ticked off. It would have been easy to assume she was being browbeaten into helping Mrs. Davies if she didn't seem so relaxed in her company.

"I brought a list," Mrs. Davies tells MacKenzie. "Since everyone is paying separately, I thought it would be easiest to let them check in themselves. That way, we can cross them off against my list. This shouldn't take all evening, should it?"

"Of course not," MacKenzie replies. "And just to be on the safe side, I've got a list, too."

"Are you ready, Susan?"

"Yes, Aunty."

"Then let's get going."

Mrs. Davies raises an eyebrow, and Susan whistles. Within just a few minutes, the reception fills with people and a sense of organized chaos: group by group, they check in, each one being checked off both Mrs. Davies's and MacKenzie's lists. Alejandro and Michael help with their bags, and the air fills with "Welcome" (MacKenzie) and "Next!" (Mrs. Davies).

Just forty minutes later, only Mrs. Davies and Susan are left.

MacKenzie smiles. "We'll start serving dinner in a few hours, but I thought you might be hungry after your journey. Once you're settled in, just come down to the restaurant for some coffee and pie. It's on us."

"Hmm," says Mrs. Davies.

I'm sure she's impressed.

We're still busy setting the long table in the restaurant, but we've left a small table right by the window. Camila has spread out one of the lace tablecloths she bought, plus a vase of delicate red roses, and when Mrs. Davies and Susan appear, there is a pot of coffee, a small apple pie, and a number of cups and saucers ready and waiting for them.

MacKenzie guides them over to the table with an welcoming arm movement.

"Do you have to work, or would you like to join us?" Mrs. Davies asks.

"I'd be honored," MacKenzie tells her. She means it.

Susan pours each of them a coffee. Mrs. Davies takes hers with two sugars and a dash of milk, but MacKenzie shakes her head when Susan raises the little milk jug and sugar bowl. Mrs. Davies's eyes glitter: she definitely knows that our restaurant isn't normally set up like a sweet little tearoom.

"Do you want to know why my darling husband's—may he rest in peace—family is so scared of me?"

"I think I'll refrain from guessing," MacKenzie replies.

"Smart. You probably think I'm an old cow who bosses everyone around."

"The thought never even occurred to me."

Susan gives MacKenzie a shy, fascinated glance. This might be the first time she has ever met anyone who isn't afraid of her aunt. Still, she doesn't speak. Her eyes just dart back and forth between Mrs. Davies and MacKenzie as she nibbles her apple pie. It's like she can't quite decide whether MacKenzie is inspirational or terrifying.

"Clear-sightedness," Mrs. Davies announces. "I see the world as it is. That's what scares them. Most people spend the majority of their waking hours trying to deceive themselves, so the minute anyone looks at them—really looks at them—they're terrified. They think they can protect themselves by refusing to see the truth, but nothing could be more wrong. Seeing the world as it really is—that's the solution."

"Do you often like what you see?"

"It doesn't take much intelligence to be clear-sighted. In theory, it's perfectly possible to see the world as it is *and* be stupid enough to like it. But in my experience, that's incredibly rare. Either way, the question is irrelevant. Like, don't like, those are just judgments. *Facts* are what really matter. We've decided, once and for all, that the family will meet every other year. That's a fact. We'll also need to travel to the meeting place, and we'll need to eat and sleep en route. It's utterly pointless trying to tell yourself that the family will be better if we only have to spend a few days together."

"So it's not just clear-sightedness," MacKenzie says. "Logic and cogency, too."

Mrs. Davies allows herself a brief nod. "If you can handle it," she says.

Susan laughs. She can't stop herself from adding: "Aunty, you know perfectly well that humor's important, too. Don't try to trick her into thinking that you don't like to laugh at them."

She glances nervously at MacKenzie and seems to regret ever speaking.

Mrs. Davies smiles indulgently. "Youth," she says to MacKenzie. "They still think that being able to laugh at everything is the most important thing. The older you get, the more you realize that people aren't particularly funny. Humor depends on things being *new*, but human nature doesn't change all that much."

"*I* still think a lot of things are funny," MacKenzie tells her, winking at Susan.

"This coffee is very good," says Mrs. Davies. "The apple pie is exceptional. The protesters are...interesting."

"We like to think of them as part of our entertainment program."

"Can't be good for business?"

"The opposite. Sooner or later, all their shouting will make them hungry. I'm sure they'll stop by the restaurant any day now."

"Clear-sightedness, Miss Jones. That's the key to making it through life."

"More apple pie?" MacKenzie asks. Susan quickly nods.

When they leave the restaurant, MacKenzie stays behind to help out with the last few preparations for dinner. I'm curious, so I follow them. I still haven't decided whether I think Mrs. Davies is fantastic or terrifying—or both.

They have barely set foot outside before Susan grabs Mrs. Davies's arm. She peers around, lowers her voice, and says quietly but firmly, "I *like* them, Aunty."

Mrs. Davies gives her a surprised glance.

"You're not going to write one of your horrible columns about them, are you?" Susan asks. "So the place isn't exactly great, but it's...nice. Remember what happened with that hotel owner in Santa Monica."

I freeze.

"I didn't write anything that wasn't true," Mrs. Davies calmly replies.

"You had to get a restraining order against the poor man!"

"I did him a favor. Someone with such fragile nerves shouldn't be working in the service industry."

"Can't you just not write something this time? They've made an effort for us. What if they're upset?"

"I can't be held responsible for their feelings. I would never be able to write anything if I was." She turns to Susan and seems to soften slightly. "I promise you that everything I write will be true. I won't make up or twist anything."

Susan doesn't seem particularly reassured, and I'm not convinced, either. I have a strong suspicion that her promise won't be worth all that much. Up ahead, Clarence has decided that he has been sober long enough. The banner sags slightly as he abandons Paul and Buddy to head back to his usual bench.

"A little to the right, boys," he says, taking out his hip flask.

Mrs. Davies pulls a notepad from her pocket. Susan gives her a pleading look. "It's just one person," she says. "I'm sure everyone else here is nice and normal..."

Her voice trails off.

Right at that moment, Dad walks by, clutching my urn.

I can't think of a way to warn them about Mrs. Davies. I have no idea what kind of columns she writes, but if she managed to drive a perfectly ordinary hotel owner from Santa Monica to the verge of madness, I don't want to know what she's going to write about us.

The nerve of the woman! After they've made such an effort for her sake. She pretends to come here because she doesn't care what people say about us, but in actual fact she is here to look for faults. I wish MacKenzie hadn't made the banner. Or treated her to apple pie. She doesn't deserve it. She should be grateful she's even getting dinner.

I might not be able to do anything to stop her, but there's no way I'm going to leave her alone. I spend all afternoon following her. On at least one occasion, she glances back over her shoulder as though she can sense my presence. I hope she's afraid of ghosts.

The first person she talks to is Paul. He is alone, working on the veranda. His face has taken on a new, healthier color from being outdoors, and there is something peaceful about watching him work in the afternoon sun. He moves slowly, almost tenderly, around the wood that will eventually become a handrail, carefully sanding away a slight bump. He is so lost in his own little world that, at first, he doesn't notice that Mrs. Davies has appeared around the corner.

"Do you mind me asking what you're doing?" she says. Her notepad is back in her pocket. Paul looks up in surprise, the sandpaper in his hand.

"I'm building a veranda," he says. "For Henny."

"Does she work here at the motel?"

"Henny's dead. I killed her. She just appeared right in front of me. I don't want to talk about it, but...I didn't have anywhere else to go after it happened. So I came here. And now I'm building a veranda."

"For Henny."

Paul nods. "I need to do something," he says.

Stacey is the next person Mrs. Davies meets. She has just come back from town and is carrying several shopping bags as Mrs. Davies intercepts her. "Could I ask what you think about the motel?"

"It's okay, I guess."

I blink, suddenly emotional. What praise! Then I realize that Mrs. Davies doesn't know Stacey and has no idea what a compliment that is.

"And why are you staying here?"

"Because my good-for-nothing, cheating husband wants to be a politician," she replies, heading off to her room. Her phone starts ringing as she walks, but she doesn't immediately pick up. Instead, she pauses on the stairs and stares down at the phone. I move over to her and peer over her shoulder. *Derek*, I see on the screen.

Eventually, she answers, but she doesn't speak.

"Stacey? Stacey?" Derek says. "You there?"

"Yeah."

More silence.

"Have you seen the latest edition of the *Gazette*?" he asks after a moment. His voice sounds strained, but that might just be because it feels strange to talk to Stacey.

She doesn't make things any easier for him.

"No," she says before falling silent again.

"They're saying I'm an idiot! They're criticizing our new proposal. No, they're *mocking* us, like it's crazy to want to make this town better. And they're saying that I'm even more of a failure as a politician then I was as a quarterback. Stacey? You still there?"

Stacey nods. Then she realizes what she is doing and replies: "Yeah."

I glance down at the parking lot, where Mrs. Davies is making her way to reception. I want to keep an eye on everything she gets up to, but I also want to know more about this article in the *Gazette*.

"It's lies and slander!" Derek continues. "I was never a failure as a football player."

Stacey laughs. The sound seems to surprise her. "You were fantastic," she says, something that surprises them both.

This time, it's Derek who pauses. "I'm supposed to give a talk at a meeting for local businesses," he says uncertainly. "That's what the article was about. Bob says half the town will be there, especially after the *Gazette* wrote about it. You don't think you could... Would you come along, too? It's tomorrow evening."

"I don't know, Derek."

"Just for support. I need someone by my side. They...they're gonna *laugh* at me, Stacey."

"I'll think about it," she promises.

Mrs. Davies has managed to find Dad and his urn in reception. By the time I get over there, he is sitting stiffly on the sofa and staring straight ahead. She has to speak to him three times before he even hears her. He looks up at her and says—as though continuing some kind of inner monologue—"I don't know what to do anymore. There's no sense of order in this place. I made apple pie in the middle of the night. That's not like me. Not like me at all. You bake pies during the day. Yes, I think early afternoon is the right time for baking pies."

He raises an arm. "What do you think of this coat?"

"Very...colorful."

Dad nods in confusion. "Not like me at all."

"How did you end up here? Did you also have nowhere else to go?"

"I have my own house, I'll have you know. Paid off and everything. I've worked hard and been sensible all my life. But they all gossip so much! Those liquor bottles weren't even mine!"

Mrs. Davies nods at the urn. "And that there, it's...a friend?" She is using the kind of exaggeratedly calm voice that people usually reserve for someone crazy and potentially dangerous.

Dad raises his chin. "It's my daughter," he says with dignity.

My only comfort comes from the fact that Mrs. Davies doesn't manage to talk to Clarence. She is making her way over to him when he suddenly leaps up and says, "Excuse me, time and alcohol wait for no man," before hurrying off to the pub.

She scribbles something down in her notepad. Buddy is still struggling with the banner, but since he has been left to hold it up alone, it's impossible to read what it says. The protesters seem to have gained a second wind now that things have calmed down at the motel. Mrs. Davies actually tries to talk to them, but I don't think she gets very far. They know that she's staying with us, after all.

After that, thankfully, she goes off to get ready for dinner.

I don't relax until she is back in her room.

Dinner is a success, at least considering the vast majority don't want to be there. Their long table takes up almost the whole of the restaurant. Mrs. Davies is at the head, of course, with the others sitting down in the order they arrived: those who came first are furthest away, and the poor people who arrived last are right next to her. Dolores has outdone herself with the food, and I don't think anyone has even noticed the frozen protesters on the other side of the road. In the warmth of the restaurant, surrounded by the aroma of Dolores's food, it's easy to be generous. Even Mrs. Davies's terrifying personality becomes easier to handle when accompanied by good food. Dad and Stacey are wise enough to stay away; Dad is in his room, and Stacey has gone into town.

Once dinner is over, Mrs. Davies tracks down MacKenzie. She is leaning against the wall in the half-light, smoking a cigarette that she bummed from one of the teenagers.

The deputy is just trying to organize the protesters' departure for the night. They wave their signs one last time at the glow of MacKenzie's cigarette.

"It's just a motel," Mrs. Davies says.

MacKenzie sucks on her cigarette. "Yup," she agrees.

"There are thousands of motels just like this."

"But the question is: Do they have their own Christian mob?"

"There were probably too many motels before you were even born, and things have only gotten worse since. So why do you do it? Why not just sell and move away?"

"And let them win?"

It's a more honest answer than MacKenzie meant to give. She makes a face.

"I read about your motel," Mrs. Davies continues. "That's why I wanted to visit. You have all kinds of liberal groups supporting you, right-wing Christians threatening you. I read debate pieces and Facebook posts and lots of excessively positive reviews. Then I got here and… Well, it's just an ordinary motel, with barely a hundred protesters. Seventeen thousand people have reviewed your motel during the last week alone."

"I never read our reviews," MacKenzie lies.

"Does this say something about modern society? We're interlinked, connected, easily upset, but we lack the ability to prioritize which issues or problems deserve our attention. There are real problems out there, but people are arguing about your motel?"

"I'm not. But you seem just as interested as anyone else."

"Do you think it's reasonable?"

"We don't write any debate pieces. We haven't written a single

Facebook post. We don't share links; we don't make statements in the media. All she—I mean, we—want to do is run a motel."

The last few protesters drive away, and the deputy pulls out after them with his blue lights flashing. It looks like they have a police escort.

MacKenzie stubs out her cigarette. "Freedom," she says.

"That's what the motel means to you?"

"No. That's why people stay here. It's not because they don't have anywhere else to go. Or not the only reason, anyway. It's because they're free here."

With that, she heads back into the restaurant and gets started on the dishes.

For God's sake, I think irritably as I see Stacey sneaking out of her room at four in the morning. Now is not the right moment for a break-in.

But she doesn't care. She knocks firmly on Dad's door with her free hand. The other is clutching four bags from a clothing shop.

Dad opens his door ten minutes later, wearing his suit trousers, a shirt, and a cardigan. His hair is the only thing he hasn't had time to fix, but he uses his hands to try to smooth it out.

"It's four o'clock," he points out. Then he notices the bags in Stacey's hand. "I don't need any more clothes!" he quickly blurts out.

"They're not for you. They're for me. I need your help."

"Apple pie?"

"Cherry. And that's not what I need help with."

This time, it's Stacey who has planned ahead in the restaurant. The ingredients for a cherry pie are ready and waiting on the small section of countertop that isn't still full of dishes from the previous evening's dinner.

"It's an evening for local business, whatever *that* means," Stacey explains. Dad carefully measures out coffee. "Derek is giving a speech. That's all I know. So I need to be...dressed appropriately. Stay here."

She tiptoes off to the bathroom and gets changed. She reemerges five minutes later. Dad has already started with the pastry.

"Don't laugh," Stacey tells him.

But she looks good. Jeans and boots might not be what Dad would call appropriate, but her blouse is really nice.

"It's four in the morning," Dad says. "Why are you trying on clothes now? Why didn't you just ask the clothing store for help? I don't know anything about fashion."

"And have them laugh and talk about me behind my back? No thanks. All right, next outfit."

Dad ends up making most of the pie himself, because Stacey is constantly running back and forth to the bathroom to try on another outfit. "What do you think about this? Does it radiate boring politician's wife?"

"Very fitting."

"Don't go anywhere."

Each new outfit comes with another pained comment from Dad, until finally they make up their minds. Not that it makes Stacey any calmer. "The clothes are just one part of it," she says. "I'll have to talk to people, too. Ideally without making a fool of myself. But how the hell do I do that?"

"Say as little as possible. Don't swear. And no jokes!"

"Sounds like a goddamn blast. Sorry, that was a joke." Stacey sighs. "I hope all this is worth it. The new clothes, not swearing, no joking—I'm not going to be myself at all!"

"I thought you wanted to learn how to behave properly."

"I do."

"Then I don't know what 'being yourself' has to do with it. You can be yourself some other time."

Stacey laughs. Dad looks surprised.

That's when a handful of flour hits him.

Dad stares at Stacey in shock as the flour rains down on him. It gets everywhere: in his hair, on his neat gray pullover, on the floor all around him, and on the countertop he just cleaned.

"Stacey, I don't know whether Dad is quite ready for..." I begin.

"What are you *doing*?" Dad asks. He runs a hand through his hair and shakes his head to try to get rid of the flour, but that just makes it spread even more. Some of it lands on his cheek.

Stacey gives him an expectant look. "Come on!" she says.

"I've got flour in my hair," Dad moans. He automatically hits his hands against his trousers. "And now I've got it on my pants, too."

"You have to throw it back!"

Dad stands stiffly in front of her.

"Who knows? Maybe you'll like being young and reckless," Stacey tells him.

He does actually glance at the flour. Stacey nods encouragingly, and Dad reaches out. He quickly pulls back his hand.

"I can't!" he shouts. He laughs nervously. Maybe he's worried about having come so close to relaxing and having fun.

"With scruples like that, you're never going to win a food fight," Stacey says. She grabs a fistful of flour and threateningly raises her arm.

"It'll make a mess!"

"We can clean up. We've got plenty of time. Come on. Live a little."

For a brief moment, I think I can see Mrs. Davies's face in the window, but when I look again, she's gone. It must have been my imagination, I think. I hope.

Stacey throws the flour. Most of it hits his hair, but a little of it sticks to his forehead. When he blinks, there is flour in his eyelashes.

But this time, he doesn't brush it away. No. Instead, he grabs some flour and throws it at her before he has time to reconsider. It hits her square in the face, making her look just as ridiculous as him.

"Oops," Dad blurts out. "I didn't mean to... Sorry, sorry. Here, take some paper towels. Or a tissue?"

Stacey shakes her head and laughs. "Perfect shot!" she says. Then, before he has time to defend himself, she launches another fistful at him.

This time, they leave the restaurant before breakfast, and it's probably just as well. I would have thought that most of the guests would still be full after Dolores's dinner, but they all show up. I watch as scrambled eggs, bacon, and fried bread are shoveled into hungry mouths, followed by gallons of coffee and orange juice, all while everyone does their best to avoid Mrs. Davies.

She herself has an egg sandwich and two cups of coffee, and she actually leaves people in peace. The only time she speaks is to remind one of the fathers about his cholesterol levels, but she says it kindly, without any hope that he is going to abstain from the mountain of bacon on his plate.

Everyone helps out with breakfast, too. Alejandro follows Dolores's orders in the kitchen, Michael refills coffee cups and juice glasses, Camila runs back and forth with overloaded plates that are quickly scraped clean, and I amuse myself by shouting out orders wherever they arise. "More coffee here!" "More eggs." "Cream and sugar!"

Thanks to Mrs. Davies's presence, checkout is surprisingly swift and painless. People pack up, load their bags into their cars, and are ready to drive off in no time at all.

Mrs. Davies climbs into the back seat of one of the cars, and then she winds down the window and turns to MacKenzie. "I do have to admit, it's never boring at your motel."

"We do our best."

Clarence, Buddy, and Paul are still struggling with the banner, but this time they have the wrong side facing us. Mrs. Davies smiles and shakes her head, but her face quickly turns serious.

"You're never going to win," she says. "There are more of them than you, and they have less to lose."

With that, she drives away. MacKenzie watches her leave from the parking lot. I can't read the look in her eye.

Not long after, we all gather in reception. Camila is high on their success. "We did it!" she shouts. "Not one of them asked for their money back!"

Michael smiles. "But they didn't leave the firstborn son. We kept her distracted all day. She was actually pretty easily entertained; she seemed to enjoy chatting to people. Mr. Broek didn't get upset and Stacey didn't swear, so she can't have been that bad."

"This is just the beginning," Camila continues. "We know how to beat them now. I want to throw a party and invite the whole town. They'll see that we're just an ordinary motel."

"A party's not a bad idea," Michael says. "Just tell me what you want me to do. We should at least be able to show those idiots that they don't have the whole town on their side."

"I've already made a few leaflets for some of the shops," Camila tells him. "I should just make some posters for the party and ask the shopkeepers to put them up, too."

MacKenzie doesn't say anything, and after a while, Michael and Camila also stop talking.

In the sudden silence, we can hear the chanting again. For several days, we almost managed to forget about it.

"You're going to burn in hell!"

"Repent your sins before it's too late!"

"Let Pine Away pine away!"

"So we've still got some work to do," Camila admits. She glances at MacKenzie. "What did Mrs. Davies say just before she left?"

"She just wanted to thank us for a nice stay," MacKenzie lies without even pausing to think.

We stand together, looking out at her banner. On this side, it reads *Are You Jesus? 10 Percent Discount on Our Fantastic Cabins!*

Beneath it, in smaller text: *Offer applies Thursday through Sunday all fall. Cannot be combined with any other offer.*

CHAPTER 42

"Maybe It's Me Who'll Save You"

TWO WEEKS BEFORE THE VOTE ON MEASURE NINE, MICHAEL AND I offered to hand out leaflets together. I remember it being one of those bright, sunny days that almost make you forget it's November. But both winter and the vote were coming.

We started on Broadway, making our way along the rows of expensive houses with *Yes to Measure 9* signs outside, leaving leaflets in every mailbox. Michael put two in his parents'. We passed Pat and Carol and waved cheerily.

By the time we made it to Main Street, Michael suggested taking a break. "How about an ice cream?" he said, and I glanced around as though MacKenzie was about to jump out and accuse us of slacking. "We can leave some leaflets there, too," he suggested.

I laughed. We settled on coffee, but we dutifully placed a few leaflets on the bench all the same. When Joe, the man who owned the place, brought out our drinks, I gave him a leaflet, too. I had known Joe forever. He used to give MacKenzie and me free candy on Saturdays. MacKenzie would show up with her pathetic dollar and fifty cents, or however much she had managed to save up, and somehow it was always enough for a lollipop and a chocolate cookie and a juice—and if it was warm, he would also throw in an ice cream for being loyal customers.

MacKenzie offered to work for the ice creams, of course, but for some reason Joe didn't think he would benefit from having her in his shop.

"Joe," I said. "You're going to vote for us, aren't you?"

"Anything for you, sweetie," he said. He had thin white hair and a pink apron, and looked exactly as happy as someone surrounded by candy and ice cream should look. He glanced down at the leaflet. "Uh, what am I voting for?" he added.

"No to Measure Nine, of course!"

"Aha, that," he said, handing back the leaflet. "I don't really care about politics, but I think I'll probably vote yes. Can't hurt, if you ask me."

"You can't vote yes!" I blurted out. "You used to give us candy! You... you, you were so *kind*!"

"Take it easy, it's just politics. No one's going to care about a little vote, are they? It won't make any difference; you'll see."

Right then, I started to cry. Just like that. Joe looked about as horrified as I felt, but I couldn't help it. I cried hot, angry tears, and Joe's face grew paler and paler.

"How can you say that? Things have already changed for us!" I said. "It means something to us! And we can't even vote. I'm never going to come here again. I'm never going to eat *candy* again. I'm..."

And then I sobbed and cried even harder, until Michael led me away. Joe called after us, trying to comfort me by offering ice cream, or how about a juice if I was giving up candy.

I hurried toward Michael's car. "Why don't they care about us? And don't tell me it doesn't matter!"

"Never even crossed my mind."

"Or for me to calm down."

"You keep shouting."

I took an unsteady breath. "I wish I hadn't started crying. I should've just looked him straight in the eye and told him to go to hell."

"I don't know, Henny. That doesn't really sound like you."

"I'm tired of being me. I'm tired of being so nice, such a pushover."

"You care. You see the good in people. You even like this dump of a town. Those are great qualities. Come on, get in."

"Where are we going?"

"Does it matter?"

I shrugged and climbed into the car. "I'm not sad, if that's what you were thinking," I said. "I'm angry."

"I know."

I focused on the sound of the engine and the asphalt beneath the tires, and with every mile we put between ourselves and Pine Creek, the pressure on my chest became lighter. Yet...it felt wrong. It shouldn't have felt liberating to leave town. It was my home. Those people knew us. I had always thought they liked us.

Michael's eyes were fixed on the road up ahead, but he was clutching the wheel so tightly that I wondered whether he was imagining it was Joe's neck.

"I thought I knew everything about this town. I grew up here. People smiled at me and said hello, and..."

"Gave you candy."

I shook my head, but I smiled as I did it, and then I leaned against the cool window. "I don't have the energy for this world anymore," I said. "It always just ends up with me getting hurt. I should stop caring."

Michael parked, walked around the car, and opened the door for me.

"Where are we going?"

"You'll see."

We walked for an hour, uphill all the way, until the physical effort burned beneath my wounded feelings, until my lungs ached and I was no longer thinking about Joe. As the world opened up in front of us, I gasped.

"It's beautiful," I said.

Michael took hold of my shoulders and guided me forward so I was looking down at the stream below. His grip was firm, as if he wanted to force me to see what he could see.

"That used to be a coral reef," he said. "Once upon a time, hundreds of millions of years ago, the ground here formed in a tropical climate. You can still see traces of the volcanic islands that once made up Oregon. It took millions of years for them to move this far north."

I blinked. All I could see were ordinary rocks and pine trees and the sluggish river down below.

"The continents will keep on moving, and mountains will be broken down and rise again. One day, there won't be any archaeologists who can make out the traces left by the people who lived here, but there'll still be mountains and water. All this—our lives, the campaign, the whole of Pine Creek and the idiots living in it—is just a speck of dust in the history of the earth. None of it means a thing."

Michael let go of my shoulders and ran a hand through his hair.

"That wasn't quite what I planned to say," he said. "I'm not very good at this. But my point is: I've always known what this town is. I know that the people here are idiots. I can't come up with any way to make you think that they're great and that they love you and everything is okay, however much I want to. If I could, Henny, I would."

The look he gave me was so intense that I wondered whether he was finally about to kiss me. But he let go and backed away. The sudden distance between us felt strange.

"They're not all idiots," I said. "And MacKenzie will change their minds eventually. Just wait."

Michael shoved his hands into his pockets. He seemed stiff and unyielding, a whole foot away from me. "It's going to get worse," he said. "You know that, don't you? They're not going to change their minds. More people will end up on their side before this is all over."

"No. *No.* That's not what's going to happen at all. People will wake up one day and realize how stupid they've been, and then they'll apologize. They won't ever vote for such an awful measure. Besides, there are people who are committed to opposing it, too. Don't forget that. We would never have met Pat and Carol otherwise. And it got us, the four of us, to become friends. MacKenzie thinks we'll be friends forever."

Michael gave me a strange look. "Is that what you want?"

I looked away. "Yes," I said. Then I gave him an uneasy smile. "You don't need..." I began, but he stepped toward me and placed his hands on my cheeks, as if he could no longer hold back. He looked me straight in the eye and lied for my sake:

"It's all going to be fine. They'll realize that they're idiots, and they'll stop what they're doing. The measure will never be voted through. Nothing will ever hurt you again."

I swallowed.

He pulled me close and held my body against his as though he could protect me from all of life's sorrows, every last meaningless disappointment, and then he kissed me as if he wanted to save the entire world just for me.

"Michael," I said. "You know you don't need to save me, don't you?"

"Yeah." He sounded unconvinced.

But he had *kissed* me. He might have tried to convince himself that he didn't care about anything here, but we were standing so close that I could feel his heart drumming against my rib cage. Wild and intense.

My hands explored the warm skin beneath his sweater, and then I kissed him. All that existed were us and the mountains, and they didn't care at all. In that moment, I was invincible. Nothing could ever defeat me.

"Who knows?" I said. "Maybe it's me who'll save you."

He took a deep breath. "Henny, I don't think there's anything you can't do."

CHAPTER 43

Summer Rain

THE TOWN COUNCIL HOLDS MEETINGS ON A REGULAR BASIS TO discuss any issues affecting the local business community, but they are open to anyone. Tonight, it feels like most of town is here, and the only issue on the agenda is the campaign for a more moral approach to business.

Cheryl has put up posters all over town, but I think it's the *Gazette's* critical, rallying coverage of the campaign that is really behind the high turnout. We had all read the article, but by the time I left the motel, MacKenzie, Camila, and Michael still hadn't decided whether to attend. *One of us needs to hear what they've got to say*, I thought as I headed over here.

I didn't think many people would care, but the biggest hall in town is virtually full—and there are still another thirty minutes until the meeting begins.

I stare in disbelief as people continue to flood in. They leave their raincoats and umbrellas by the door, and before long, the whole room smells of coffee and damp gloves. I move among them, eavesdropping on conversations. The majority seem pretty skeptical. *They're* as God-fearing and moral as the next person, and if the folks from Sacred Faith Evangelical Church think they can come along and butt into *their* lives, they're going to be disappointed.

The woman from the secondhand shop is there, talking agitatedly with the person sitting next to her: "Immoral business? Well! Who are they to accuse *us* of immorality? I've been going to church since I was born! Since before I was born, even, because my mother was there every Sunday while she was pregnant! If this is about us being open on

Sundays, I've got a good mind to reveal just how many of them pop in after their service."

She cranes her neck and glares at Derek, who is pacing back and forth to one side of the stage. He looks stiff and uncomfortable in his shirt and jacket. All his usual charm is gone. His lips are moving, but no sound is coming out.

The fact that his parents are sitting in the front row doesn't seem to reassure him. Mr. Callahan looks tense ahead of his son's political debut, but Joyce keeps smiling warmly at everyone and no one. "How lovely," I hear her say, but I think her absent gaze seems a little more strained than usual. Maybe her life has already become uncomfortable.

"Just try not to say too much about this motel business," Bob reminds Derek. "It's not really something you want to be associated with, and it's definitely not the *only* thing you want to be associated with. Remember your long-term projects."

"All you need to remember is that you have Jesus on your side," Cheryl says into his other ear. "You're doing something big and good, and that's the important thing. If they laugh at you, let them laugh."

Derek looks like he is going to be sick.

When Dad and Stacey turn up together, I don't know whether Derek or Cheryl is more surprised.

"Robert!" Cheryl cries.

"Stacey!" says Derek. He glances around and pulls her over to one side. "You're here! And you look…fantastic."

She is wearing a beige suit, a white blouse, opaque tights, and a pair of low-heeled pumps. "You dare laugh," she says. Then, in a lower voice: "Robert helped me pick them out. He might've been a little enthusiastic. But he said I looked 'proper.'"

"I'm not laughing," Derek tells her. "I'm just really glad to see you here. I should never have let them talk me into this. Look at them! They're going to *lynch* me!"

The murmur from the crowd dies down as Bob steps out onto the stage and introduces the evening's first speaker, Derek Callahan. He begins by saying that Derek doesn't need any introduction, but then he launches into a ten-minute tribute to all of Derek's achievements and his exceptional football career. He does what he can to remind the crowd that they used to love Derek, but judging by their dogged faces, he doesn't quite manage to convince them.

Derek is frozen to the spot at one side of the stage, looking out at the sea of terrifying faces.

"Remember, you can sell anything," Stacey whispers, practically pushing him out onto the stage before taking a seat next to Joyce.

"Ahem, yes," Derek says. "Who would've thought that a quarterback could become a politician, huh? Believe me, I know it sounds crazy."

No one smiles. No one laughs. Derek glances desperately at Stacey, his anchor point. She nods encouragingly.

"So, I guess you've all heard about our idea for a more moral approach to business?" he continues. "I guess you read the article in the *Gazette*? I want you to know that no matter what you've read, we don't have a problem with *you*."

"I should hope not!" the woman from the secondhand store shouts out.

Derek forgets all about his preprepared speech, but I actually think that's a good move. He laughs and seems to remember that he knows everyone here. They transform from a frightening, anonymous mass into people he's known all his life.

"I definitely don't have a problem with you, Margaret," he says with a smile. "I'd never dare. I've got no problem admitting that."

The woman smiles appreciatively, and several others laugh.

"You business owners are the ones who built this town and who continue to take care of it," Derek continues. "I don't need to tell *you* how to run a business in a town like Pine Creek. It's not just about money—not that any of us has anything against earning a few bucks." A new disarming smile. Fewer stern faces in the crowd. "No, it's about contributing to the town. You have a responsibility. As business owners, you're role models. Our kids look up to us, and they expect us to take care of them. To show them the way and to do our best to make sure that Pine Creek is the kind of town where they can enjoy safe, Christian childhoods. Surely no one here—aside from the liberal folks at the *Gazette*, of course—could claim that our approach to business *isn't*

Christian and moral, and I can't imagine any of *you* think it should be otherwise."

His words are being met by appreciative nods now.

"But the same isn't true of the motel. It's never really been part of this town. Every other business has helped out when necessary. Just look at Ned's paint store. He's sponsoring the paint for the school. But what does the motel do? They vandalize it. *They're* the ones who don't want to be part of Pine Creek."

The woman from the secondhand store nods. "I told you they couldn't have anything against *us*. But the motel, well, that's different."

"Not part of town," the woman next to her agrees. "It's high time someone says what we're all thinking."

"And he *does* look handsome in his suit."

"I remember him in his football uniform..."

Both women smile nostalgically.

"Ask Sheriff Ed how many times he's been called out to the motel."

"That's not fair!" I protest. "Most of them were because of you!"

"Ask how many rules the motel has been allowed to break, while every other business has had to follow every last regulation Washington can come up with."

His eyes scan the eagerly nodding crowd.

"I'm not going to keep you for much longer. I'm a newbie in politics. I'm happy to admit that, but even I know that being forced to listen to politicians drone on for hours is the worst. I'm more interested in hearing what you think and feel. So, if you have any suggestions about things we could do better or just want to contribute to our campaign for a more moral approach to business, I'll be at the table all evening. Swing by. Say hi. Have a coffee."

The hall erupts into applause, and once Derek leaves the stage, people crowd around him to praise his pleasantly short speech. Women smile, men thump him on the back, and several stop to chat.

It's Stacey who spots them first.

She tenses up and unwittingly grabs Dad's arm, something that makes both of them look unbelievably guilty. Through a gap in the crowd, I catch a glimpse of MacKenzie, Michael, and Camila.

I don't know how long they've been here or how much they heard, but judging by their faces I would probably say: more than enough.

They are standing at the very back of the room, awkward and unmoving, despite the fact that they are in the way of anyone trying to get to the cloakroom or the information table by the doors.

"Excuse me," a woman says, pushing past them to get to the petition. People have formed a line to add their names to the list.

Camila gazes helplessly around the room. "Shouldn't we...do something?" she asks, and both she and I turn to MacKenzie as if we're hoping for a miracle.

"Say something!" Camila pleads.

But MacKenzie shakes her head. I don't know whether she even realizes she's doing it. She instinctively takes a step back.

Eventually, it's Michael who reacts. "I've got a thing or two I'd like to say to Derek," he mutters.

He gently but firmly pushes MacKenzie to one side and then elbows his way over to his brother.

Derek is in the middle of a conversation, but Michael doesn't care. "What the hell are you doing?" he shouts, not seeming to notice that everyone around them has stopped talking.

"This isn't the right place..." Derek begins, smiling tensely.

"I think it's the perfect place. Have you lost your damn mind? Why are you attacking the motel? You *like* MacKenzie. You were her friend. You used to work there, for God's sake."

All around them, people have paused to eavesdrop on the argument. One man has even stopped with his coat half on, one arm raised in the air.

"Since when did you care about morals?" Michael continues. "You love sin. You're an expert in it."

"He's just kidding," Derek says, grabbing Michael's arm and trying to pull him off to one side.

Michael angrily breaks free. "And you two!" he shouts at Dad and Stacey. "After everything the motel has done for you! How can you just stand there and listen to this bull? You're both staying there, for God's sake."

That spurs Derek into action. He forgets that he is a calm, reasoned politician these days. "And you're perfect, of course? First you butt into my life and tell me I need to do something with it, then once I actually do, you show up and criticize what I'm doing?"

"Don't you see how insane this is?"

"What is it that's so insane, Michael? Please, tell me. Is it that people might vote for me, or that I might be able to make a difference? Or maybe it's the fact that I could be good at something other than playing football."

"What's insane is that you're pretending to be some kind of conservative dream politician. Complete with the supportive wife by your side."

"At least *I* married my childhood sweetheart."

"And you did a good job of that, didn't you? It's not like the two of you lived happily ever after, did you?"

"Happier than you and Henny."

That's when Michael punches him.

His fist hits Derek square in the jaw, but then he seems to freeze in shock. He shakes his hand.

"That's enough," Mr. Callahan snaps furiously at Michael. "You're causing a scene. You..."

He doesn't make it any further before Derek launches himself at Michael. Both men fall to the floor. They roll around by Mr. Callahan's feet, until eventually he has to jump out of the way to avoid being knocked over.

Michael and Derek continue to brawl in front of half of town. Chairs fall over as people rush to get out of their way.

"Do something!" Camila shouts. She and MacKenzie have pushed forward to the first row around the fighters.

"I think Michael's holding his own pretty well," MacKenzie mutters, stubbornly folding her arms.

Eventually, Mr. Callahan manages to grab an arm, and someone else takes hold of another. The two men are pulled apart. Stacey helps Derek to his feet.

He tries to brush the dirt from his jacket and smiles apologetically at everyone around him. "Just a little difference of opinion," he says. "Normal brotherly love."

"Go to hell!" Michael shouts.

The windshield wipers struggle against the heavy rain as we drive back to the motel. The car's headlights only reach a foot or so in front of us. The whole world feels like it's underwater. MacKenzie is driving calmly and carefully.

Michael is sitting by the passenger-side door, and I'm not entirely sure who he is talking to when he says, "I'm an idiot. I really tried to give this place a chance. I thought if I could just see it the way Henny did, then... I don't know what I thought. I guess I thought things might be different this time."

"They still could be," Camila tells him. "Don't forget the party I'm going to throw. That's more important than ever now. We're going to prove to them that..."

But Michael continues as though he hasn't heard her. "I only spent three days with her as an adult, but somehow I thought that it meant something. Like I could learn something from her. But do you know what I should've remembered? That she always chose this town ahead of me. That's what I should have focused on."

"Of course it meant something," Camila says.

"I was crazy for coming back here. What did I think was going to happen? Everything would suddenly be fine, all of life's mysteries would reveal themselves, and our past would no longer matter? Like I'd become someone new just because I pulled up outside."

"You loved her. It isn't crazy."

"You don't understand. I couldn't, I don't know... Jesus Christ, Camila. I had to *know*." Now that he has started, he can't stop. "I left here, but I still lived half my life here. Like that film, *Sliding Doors*. Except I was aware of it the whole time, and that made it worse. No matter what I was doing, that half of me was constantly whispering about a different life. I could smell tomato and rosemary plants on a warm summer evening, picture a backyard, a barbecue, Henny and her closest friends. And sometimes, at night, if I was someplace new, at yet another motel or in a sublet apartment somewhere, I could only get to sleep if I imagined

I was in that house we could have had, in a comfortable double bed, next to Henny."

"And then you came back," Camila tells him. "You got to see her again."

"I couldn't stay away any longer. It wasn't even a conscious decision. I just woke up confused in reception one day, and there she was. Everything was right again."

"Michael, that's *beautiful*, not crazy. Right, MacKenzie?" Camila places a hand on MacKenzie's knee. "Tell him it's not crazy."

"Don't look at me," MacKenzie replies. "I agree with him. He *was* crazy for coming back. What the hell did he think would happen? They spent one weekend together. That's all. And you're just as crazy if you think you'll ever get this town to accept you."

Once MacKenzie has dropped off Michael, she lazily parks outside the motel and heads straight up to our apartment. Camila and I hurry after her.

We arrive just in time to see her on tiptoe, trying to reach her suitcase from the top of the wardrobe. Camila hesitates, then reaches up and lifts it down for her.

"I'm pretty sure I shouldn't be helping you with this," she says. "What are you doing, MacKenzie?"

"What does it look like I'm doing? I'm leaving this place." She throws a couple T-shirts into the case. "Do you know what I did while everyone else was watching Michael and Derek? I looked at the petition. They'd filled several sheets!"

"Don't go."

"I told you I'd leave you in the end."

"Me, yes. Not the motel. This is your *home*."

"You said it yourself: It's just a black hole that sucks the energy out of everything. You could work here your whole life and never achieve a thing."

"I was wrong. I forgot that I was happy here, too. We were friends. For a while, I was free here."

"I can't handle going through this again."

MacKenzie throws a few sweaters into her suitcase, a couple pairs of jeans, and the first things she can grab from the closet. Then she heads into my room and rummages through the photographs on the floor. She picks two, takes them back to her room, and puts them into her suitcase. The images facing down.

"But...you stayed after Measure Nine. And all the other votes they pushed through. You even stayed during the marriage vote, and you must have known we'd lose that."

"That was different. After Measure Nine, I never cared."

"So that...that must mean you care now?"

"No."

Camila moves in between MacKenzie and the suitcase. "Come on," she says. "Talk to me. Help me understand."

"*You* care, Camila. But you're not going to win. They're going to break your heart, and there's no way I'm going to stay here and watch."

"MacKenzie..."

"I mean it." She gently pushes Camila to one side, slams the lid of her suitcase shut, and carries it down to the car. She throws it into the passenger seat.

"MacKenzie, *stop*."

MacKenzie pauses. She studies Camila with something that looks a lot like grief.

"It doesn't matter what you tell yourself," Camila says. "You love this motel. And you like me."

MacKenzie holds a hand to Camila's cheek. Hesitates. Pushes back a lock of hair, damp from the rain. "I *told* you not to care about me. I warned you."

With that, she climbs into her car and drives off. Just like that.

Michael is still awake when I get back to the cabin. The light above the table where he is sitting is the only one turned on, and it mercilessly illuminates his weary face. There is a half-empty bottle of whiskey in front of him.

"She just drove off!" I angrily blurt out. "Threw some random clothes into a suitcase. But it must be temporary, right? She'll be back. MacKenzie could never leave the motel for good. Not really. Not forever. Right?"

Michael buries his face in his hands, and I lose my train of thought. He looks so abandoned that I don't want to force my problems onto him. Instead, I move over and place a hand on his shoulder. Outside, everything is dark. Night has settled like a damp blanket on top of our world.

"You're not going to leave, right?" I ask, but as the words leave my lips, I question whether I really believe it.

MacKenzie left.

"I can still make you all happy," I say, but I don't know whether that's really true anymore.

I wonder... Would they have been happier without me? Would it have been easier for them to move on if I had been strong enough to leave them behind?

The thought hits me so hard that I have to sit down on the bed.

They don't need to stay here. They could move on with their lives. Maybe Michael was right. Maybe there's a big, exciting world out there. Maybe it would have been kinder to them. MacKenzie and Camila could have gone off to be happy together if Camila hadn't felt my presence and thought she had to stay when MacKenzie left.

It should be easy to give up someone you can't have. I imagine it's a bit like dying. Once you've been rejected enough, you realize it's no longer worth clinging, and then...you give up. Close your eyes, stop breathing, move on, free.

Though, of course, I'm not very good at dying, either.

If only I had disappeared when I was cremated.

That probably would've been best.

And maybe...maybe my ashes could have been scattered in the wind. That way, in a small sense, I could still have come back to them.

Not in a creepy way, of course.

But I could have transformed into MacKenzie's very own sunshine, someone who followed her around and never left her side. Like when she drives all night and sees the sun come up. *Jesus,* she would think, *is it that late?* But it would just be me messing with her. Or a wind that ruffled Camila's hair. Made her slightly less perfect and got her to laugh.

Maybe I could have just dissolved in water, and that way I could have rained down on Michael. Not a cold, horrible rain. A summer rain. Nice and warm. He would smell fresh grass and realize the air had suddenly become easier to breathe, and everything would be quiet other than the sound of raindrops on puddles.

That could be me.

CHAPTER 44

Celebration

AFTER THE RESULTS CAME IN, PAT AND CAROL THREW AN impromptu party to celebrate. Their living room quickly became unbearably warm from all of the bodies crammed inside. I barely knew half of the people there, however much they claimed we had been fighting on the same side. It was the first time I ever experienced the power that victory and free food have over people.

The adults didn't seem to notice the temperature, not after all the chilled white wine they had drunk. Their faces grew redder and redder, and more flushed with victory.

"I *told you* they wouldn't manage it," said a woman I hadn't met before. She was wearing a *No to Measure 9* badge and was holding a wineglass in one hand and a miniature burger in the other. "The people of Oregon will never accept it."

"The light always wins out over the darkness," someone else chimed in.

They were right, and now they could get on with their lives. They had helped us. We had won.

I found the others in the kitchen: Pat and Carol, MacKenzie, Camila, and Michael. They weren't celebrating.

Pat and Carol had invited everyone who had been involved in some way in the No to Measure Nine campaign. It was a hastily organized affair; they hadn't been planning to celebrate at all. I think they had suspected what the rest of us didn't yet know: that election day and the result itself were things to be endured alone, rather than celebrated as a group. The fact there had even been a vote was a loss in and of itself. Not even the positive outcome could erase the memory of our neighbors, colleagues, friends, and absolute strangers fighting for the other side. We had seen it, and our eyes couldn't forget.

I wondered what visions were playing out in front of MacKenzie's eyes. All I could see was her face the day we saw Cheryl wearing her *Yes to Measure 9* T-shirt.

"Fifty-two percent!" someone shouted from the living room. The Honorable Heterosexual Housewives really were keeping spirits high.

Eventually, we were the only ones left, alone among the empty, abandoned wineglasses, the empty trays and dirty napkins. A date wrapped in bacon had been forgotten on a plate, and the last bite of a mini pizza had been dropped on the rug.

"We're moving away," Pat suddenly announced to MacKenzie.

"We didn't want you to hear it from someone else," said Carol.

"It's a nice town," Pat went on. "But we're not really from here, so we don't have any relatives or family... There's no reason why we need to live *here*."

"Come visit us if you're ever passing through Portland."

"Sure," said MacKenzie.

"It's just not the same here now."

MacKenzie nodded.

"You guys go home," said Carol. "We'll tidy up here."

I gave MacKenzie an uncertain glance. "You want to find something to do? Want to go somewhere?"

MacKenzie bent down to pick up the piece of pizza from the carpet. "I'm working at the motel tonight," she said. "See you tomorrow. At least school goes on like normal."

I nodded.

None of us said what we were all thinking. The liberal cities like Portland and Eugene were what had narrowly saved us from catastrophe. Fifty-two percent was the state average.

In MacKenzie's Pine Creek, there was no reason to celebrate. In this town, 64 percent had voted in favor of the measure.

CHAPTER 45

Thing 1...

I'M SITTING ON THE HILL BY THE MOTEL, LOOKING DOWN AT THE parking lot.

It's so quiet that I'm almost relieved to see the protesters show up and start unpacking their thermoses and placards. Their shouts about burning in hell have a mass-like calming rhythm, as does the whooshing sound of trucks driving by on the main road. The comforting routine of their presence means I can pretend everything is normal. Any minute now, MacKenzie will emerge from the restaurant and swear at them.

But there are only three cars parked in front of the motel: Camila's, Alejandro's, and Dolores's. The spot where MacKenzie's pickup is usually parked is now just empty asphalt. It's as if she took all the color with her when she left.

An icy drizzle falls on the pines and the protesters, who huddle against the wind. Their coffee quickly cools, and their raincoats are no protection against the damp chill that penetrates everything. They snuffle through their chants with frozen cheeks and red noses. There are considerably fewer of them out there today.

Camila is pushing the cleaning cart, trying to deal with the last few rooms after Mrs. Davies's visit, but it's slow work. Even from here, I can see how heavy her movements are. She emerges from the last room and dumps the dirty sheets into the laundry bag, then rests her hands on the handle and leans against it, struggling with the grayness and pointless-ness of her surroundings.

Then she abandons the cart up there.

When I step into check-in, Alejandro and Dolores are already there.

"I don't understand," Dolores says. I can tell from Camila's face that it isn't the first time she has said it. Like so many others after catastrophe strikes, Dolores seems to find comfort in going over things again and again. I should know. I spent the whole night doing it, too.

"She's never disappeared like this before. Was it something you said?"

Camila's jaw tenses, and she forces one of the new brochures into the stand. "She's a grown woman," she says. "She can go wherever she wants."

"But she's never disappeared like this before."

"Well, there's not much I can do about that, is there?"

"Come on, Mom," Alejandro mumbles. "It's time to start lunch."

"Who cares about lunch?" Dolores replies, probably for the first time in her life, but she allows herself to be led back to the restaurant all the same.

Camila closes her eyes in relief, but she barely has a moment to herself before Dad comes storming in.

"I want you to know that I wasn't at that meeting to support their proposal. But it was important to Stacey, and I've learned..." He glances around in confusion. "Where's MacKenzie?"

"She's gone."

"But she can't just leave! She's MacKenzie!"

"Well, she did."

Dad is so confused that he even goes to knock on Stacey's door before remembering that she already checked out, and then he walks lap after lap around the motel. From a distance, he's a strange little figure, a red dot against a backdrop of gray, his face bowed against the wind, taking short, quick steps.

Out behind the motel: an equally lonely figure, slowly and laboriously trying to finish a veranda that no one cares about anymore. Paul is alone now, but he tries to keep working. The veranda is barely half-finished, and in the cold drizzle, the wooden planks and the nails and the tools seem as lost and abandoned as the rest of us.

Dad pauses to watch, but he makes no attempt to help as Paul moves a long plank into place.

Suddenly, he surprises both me and himself by saying: "I was only there for Stacey's sake. It wasn't me taking a *position*. MacKenzie must have known that."

"MacKenzie was Henny's best friend," Paul replies.

"I don't have anything against the motel. I might have had a few suggestions for improvements, but I've always been open and honest about those. She can't have left because I was at that meeting, can she?"

Paul shrugs. He moves the plank an inch to the left. His hands are red with cold.

"So you're building this veranda for my Henny?"

"I still keep seeing her in front of me."

There is something so fragile and tortured about his voice that I study him more closely. He might look healthier on the outside, but on the inside, nothing has changed. The veranda is a distraction, not a cure.

"Especially when I'm sleeping. I always wake up just as the truck hits... Once it's too late."

He's still having nightmares. About *me*. It hurts to know that someone, anyone, is using me as an excuse to torture themselves, and for some reason it feels particularly bad to know that Paul is doing it. He didn't even know me while I was alive.

"Whatever I do, she's always there," Paul continues. "I try to brake, but it's too late. She just appeared in the road. The whole thing was over in a few seconds. How can that end a life? If only I'd had another cup of coffee. If I'd just picked a different job. It wouldn't have made any difference to me, would it?"

He glances eagerly at Dad, grateful to finally talk about it.

"If I'd picked a different job, she would still be alive. A car mechanic. I could've been a car mechanic. Or a cleaner. Who cares, as long as Henny was still alive."

"Paul," I say. "All those *ifs*... They'll drive you crazy. Believe me. I've already had all those thoughts."

"I thought she looked surprised, but now that I think about it, she actually seemed *happy*. That's the worst part. She was happy, and then I showed up."

But Dad has stopped listening. He turns abruptly and walks away. Paul and I are left alone.

"She'll be back," Alejandro says, passing Camila a cup of coffee as she steps into the restaurant.

Camila doesn't reply. Her eyes are on the tragic little group on the other side of the road. There are no other customers in the restaurant, and she already has a mug in her hand, but Camila goes over to the machine to brew a fresh pot of coffee.

When it's ready, she pours it into a thermos and jogs across the road.

The protesters seem skeptical as she approaches. For a while, their chanting actually increases. Camila doesn't care. When no one steps forward to take the flask from her, she just puts it down on the ground and turns and walks away.

They do actually seem tempted by the thermos. Circling around it. Looking away. Approaching it again. Waving their placards half-heartedly. When the wind really starts to pick up, one of them reaches for it and pours a hot cup of coffee with relieved, trembling hands.

Alejandro shakes his head at her. "I'm not sure they deserve that," he says.

"I'm not sure it matters anymore," Camila tells him.

The next morning, the phone starts ringing nonstop.

It's all of the businesses Camila made brochures for. After the meeting in town, they have suddenly started to wonder whether it's really such a good idea to collaborate with the motel. It's not that *they* have anything against the motel, they tell her, but you know how it is. Besides, one of them says defensively, there's no smoke without fire, and if the motel has suddenly decided that it wants to be a part of this town, we should've thought about that before, and *also*...

Camila hangs up mid-tirade.

Sheriff Ed swings by the motel just before lunch. Camila makes a valiant effort to flash him a friendly smile, but her eyes give her away.

"What can I do for you?" she wearily asks.

Sheriff Ed looks troubled. Troubled and reluctant. "I heard you were at the meeting yesterday," he says.

Camila nods.

"So you heard what they were saying. We've had quite a few complaints. People calling up to ask why we haven't investigated the motel properly. Saying that who-knows-what goes on here, and asking what we're planning to do about it. That kind of thing. Probably completely baseless, but you know how it is."

"No," Camila replies. "I don't."

"Uh. No. Maybe not. But people have been complaining to Bob, too. He asked me to come by and 'look into it.'"

"So this is a *formal* visit?" Camila sounds astounded. Sheriff Ed looks embarrassed.

"Only so we can say we took people's concerns seriously," he tells her.

Camila folds her arms. For a moment, I'm sure she is about to give him a piece of her mind. I can tell that she's desperate to take out her frustration on someone, let them know exactly what she thinks about people's concerns. I *hope* she does it! How dare Sheriff Ed come over here like this? He's been eating lunch here for years! Now I regret ever worrying about his cholesterol levels.

But then it's like Camila just gives up. She suddenly doesn't have the energy to care any longer. Her arms slump to her sides. The anger disappears from her eyes, leaving only emptiness behind. Emptiness and an indifference that's difficult to for me to see.

"Do what you want," she says.

And then she just stands there and answers his questions. He checks our reservation system, goes through our check-in procedures, asks whether we record names and license plate numbers, whether we check people's IDs, whether we've had any trouble with difficult guests, that kind of thing. Any complaints? Have we seen anything suspicious?

Camila endures his visit, and when Sheriff Ed runs out of questions, she even asks whether he wants lunch before he leaves.

Sheriff Ed looks even more pained and says, "Probably shouldn't. People might think I've picked a side."

"Sheriff Ed," Camila says, her voice flat. "Do me a favor and go to hell."

She slumps onto the couch the minute he leaves, staring at the colorful walls as though they're mocking her. MacKenzie's spirit hangs over every inch of reception.

"What am I doing here?" she asks herself.

That afternoon, we go into town together. Camila parks on Elm Street, but she doesn't get out of the car. She seems to be trying to memorize every last gray detail.

In the middle of the street: that gazebo. Cheryl looks much more enthusiastic than the protesters, probably because she isn't exposed to the elements the way they are. People are actually stopping to chat with her. Despite the weather, no one seems to be in a hurry. They just turn their collars a little higher and then nod and listen and take the leaflets they're offered.

I realize that Camila is making her way straight toward them, and I hurry after her.

"Are you sure you want to..." I shout. "There are loads of them, and only one of you!"

But Camila just walks over to Cheryl and says, "We need to talk."

See! She already has a plan. She'll be able to fix this.

"I'm listening," Cheryl replies. Her pale-pink puffer jacket is obscuring today's Christian slogan. It also clashes with her bright-pink sneakers. She has finished off her outfit with a purple scarf.

"Maybe somewhere a little warmer? I want to make you an offer."

They end up at Hank's, at a small table by the window in the back corner of the café—as far from Hank's eavesdropping as they can get. They each order coffee and ignore his inquisitive questions, and then Camila says, "If I sell the motel, will you stop the protests? I can't guarantee you'll be any happier with the new owners, but you'd get rid of me at the very least."

Cheryl takes a sip of coffee to win herself more time. "So we'd just have to hope the new owners were better?" she says after recovering from Hank's coffee.

"I can't sell the motel if there are protesters outside. So, yeah. I guess you'll have to decide whether you like the sound of those odds."

"Can't get any worse, I suppose," Cheryl mumbles.

Camila patiently waits her out. I want to shake her and say that she's crazy even to consider giving in, but I just sit mutely beside her. Her words are still ringing in my ears. *New owners. Sell the motel. She can't be serious*, I think in desperation.

"And if they don't behave, we can always raise the issue again." Cheryl sounds thoughtful.

"No. We settle this once and for all. I'm not going to sell the hotel if it just means fobbing the problem off on someone else. It isn't fair to whoever takes over."

"I'll have to think about it."

"Do me a favor and call off your protesters while you do. They're giving me a headache."

As Camila gets up to leave, Cheryl studies her intently. "And you think you'd be able to do it?" she asks. "Sell your uncle's motel, just like that? Everything he worked for, and everything you've toiled for since you came back?"

Camila sits down again. "I got the hint, even if it was nice to be back. I don't belong here. I guess your protests have already done their job. You got the message across in other ways, too, but I guess a few *You're going to burn in hell* signs never hurt, right?"

Cheryl looks uncomfortable. She even takes a sip of her coffee rather than look Camila in the eye. "That was never the intention," she mutters. Then she looks up, defiant. "It was about the motel. It's never been a part of this town, and you know it."

"No, and you've really made sure of that now. No, no, I didn't mean it as criticism. I know MacKenzie can be really irritating. She drives me crazy, too."

"It's not about MacKenzie, either!" Cheryl still can't quite meet Camila's eyes.

"Good. Because I can't guarantee she'll stay away forever. She said she was leaving for good, but she might change her mind and come back."

This time, Cheryl looks her straight in the eye. She can't help herself. "MacKenzie is *gone*?"

"Left yesterday."

"But this is *MacKenzie* we're talking about."

"Yup, guess you won in the end." Camila gets up. "So are we done here? You'll think about my offer? Give me a call once you've made up your mind."

"But about MacKenzie, I've never said that..."

"I don't care."

After her chat with Cheryl, Camila goes to see the motel's lawyer, an old man who has been helping us out since Juan Esteban's time in charge. I decide not to follow her into his office. I can't handle any more talk about the motel being sold.

When Camila and I eventually get back to the motel, she goes straight up to her room. I follow her. "You can't sell the motel," I plead with the back of her head. Then I realize she is just staring at the broken blinds, and I lose my trail of thought.

For once, she isn't looking at them with a critical eye. It's more like she is going through everything she will miss about the motel.

Thing 1: Even these blinds.

Her next port of call is check-in. This time, she finds herself smiling at the colorful walls and slowly runs a hand along the top of her pretty white desk. I wonder whether she's thinking about the time she and MacKenzie almost kissed while they were cleaning the windows.

Thing 2: The whole of check-in.

When she reaches the restaurant, she sits down for a cup of coffee with Dolores. She doesn't even protest when Dolores brings up MacKenzie. She pats Alejandro on the shoulder as she leaves.

Thing 3: The overly enthusiastic staff.

Camila visits Juan Esteban's old office next, but she doesn't seem to get much out of it. The room might be tidy now, but it's no longer the center of anything. The heart of the motel is somewhere else. She spends some time by the window, looking out at the new sign. Then her eyes are drawn to the spot where MacKenzie's car is no longer parked.

Last of all, Camila heads down to the apartment MacKenzie and I used to share. She moves slowly and carefully through my old room, picking up the hardback copy of Michael's book and putting it back on the shelf. The book looks even more lost there, alone on a dusty shelf in the middle of a trashed room. I think I hear a stifled sob, but I'm not sure.

"You know, I always thought you named your cabin the Pine Cabin to show how little you cared," I say. "Like you thought an unimaginative name would prove just how indifferent you were. The Pine Tree Cabin at the Pine Creek Motel."

Camila bends down and picks up one of the photographs. It's of the four of us, on our way to prom: me, Michael, and Camila in suits, MacKenzie in a gown. She's staring straight at the camera, trying to hide how uncomfortable she feels.

"But the most important thing about pines is that they survive. Redwoods are prima donnas in comparison, and trembling aspens pretty and fragile. But pines, they can cope with anything. And do you know something else about pines? They're really stubborn once they've put down roots. Once they've settled on a spot, it's a nightmare to get rid of them."

The photograph flutters back down to the floor, and Camila sobs. She leaves my room and tiptoes over to MacKenzie's bed. She sits with her back to the wall, hugging the pillow to her chest. I guess it must still smell like her.

Thing 4: MacKenzie.

I sit down beside Camila and rest my head on her shoulder. We were sitting the exact same way when she came out to me. It was a week after Michael had left. I didn't want to accept that she was going to leave, too. *I have to, Henny,* she said.

She made it sound like it was important to her that I understood, but I assumed that MacKenzie was the person she really wanted to convince. She said she had to leave us to be able to live her life. She couldn't give up her future, not even for the alternative community she had suddenly experienced when we organized against Measure Nine and she and

MacKenzie had worked at the motel. I could understand that, couldn't I? She would never be free here, not really.

Eventually, Camila's eyelids grow heavy, and her head slumps gently to one side. She jolts as she dozes off, but then her chin slumps down again. I pat her on the head, and before long, her breathing grows calm.

"You sleep," I say. "I'll keep you company for a while."

CHAPTER 46

Proud Home of Anti-Gay Ballot Measures Since 1992!

THE VOTE TOOK PLACE IN NOVEMBER OF OUR LAST YEAR AT HIGH school, and though nothing was the same afterward, life and school went on.

Michael and I continued to see each other, but we didn't tell anyone else. I don't think he wanted to admit there might be something to keep him here, and I didn't want to tell MacKenzie that the vote had brought us together. Still, I think she knew. I could never hide anything from her.

MacKenzie was almost always working at the motel. She attended enough classes to graduate that year, but no more than the absolute minimum, and she didn't seem to care about any of it. I found myself wondering whether she even cared about me.

She still turned up outside Dad's house from time to time. "Come on, Henny," she said like always, but there was no joy in her voice. She was no longer driving Cheryl's old car, and there were rumors in town that she had given it back by driving it into Cheryl's fence. By that point, she was driving a rusty old wreck that started on good days and refused on others.

One day in February, she came to pick me up. She was chatting away like normal, and she even laughed. But something still felt different. It was as if there was an invisible wall between us, a new limit to our friendship that had never been there before. Every conversation contained an unspoken sense of *this is as far as it goes*.

Looking back, I probably should have knocked down that wall. Smashed it to pieces. Forced her to cry and shout and break something. But I was too young to realize that sometimes, real friendship isn't about respecting your friends' wishes.

We drove toward the motel. The pines were weighed down with snow, but as we parked and the engine fell silent, I heard water dripping from the roof of the motel. Spring was coming. And there was a new addition to the motel's patchwork sign.

"What do you think?" MacKenzie asked, gesturing up toward it.

The sign read *Oregon—Proud home of anti-gay ballot measures since 1992!*

I know I should have destroyed that wall between us, but I'm grateful that MacKenzie did at least have Camila. Because Camila had also changed. When I saw them together at the motel, I couldn't put my finger on exactly what was different about her, but looking back, I think she felt freer in the spring following the vote than she ever had before. It was like she said the night before the funeral: she had discovered that there were other LGBT people in town. I often noticed her gazing at MacKenzie the same way MacKenzie looked at Pat and Carol.

Who knows? Maybe Camila was a braver friend than I was. Maybe she didn't care as much about invisible boundaries. What I do know is that they both spent most of their time at the motel, and that when the old MacKenzie came back to me, it was with a plan that involved us all.

At the time, Michael, Camila, MacKenzie, and I were together again, repainting the rooms at the motel. This was in May. Michael had received his admission letter from a college in California, but we never talked about it. For everyone else in school, there was only a month left until freedom. More importantly, prom was just three days away.

Somehow, MacKenzie managed to convince us to use prom to make a statement. Michael and Camila would attend together, and so would MacKenzie and I.

"You can go as a gay couple," she said to Michael and Camila. "And Henny and I can go as dykes. It's not exactly like any of us have anyone else to go with," she continued, waiting to see whether I would protest. I found myself glancing at Michael, but neither of us spoke. "And I'm guessing you don't care if our idiotic classmates think we're gay?"

MacKenzie made the idea sound so simple, but as we stood outside the gymnasium a few days later, I think she felt just as nervous as the rest of us. She was uncomfortable in her dress, and I stood next to her in my tux. We had drawn lots to see which of us would wear the tuxedo, and I had won. Though maybe that's not quite the right word for it. I think we both wished it had been the other way around. Michael and Camila were right behind us, both wearing tuxedos, too.

The room fell silent as we entered. An entire sports hall of shocked teenagers was left speechless by the sight of us. All we could hear was the ropy old sound system blaring out Eve 6's "Here's to the Night."

"I brought a flask," MacKenzie whispered over her shoulder. "If it all goes to hell, we can always get drunk."

CHAPTER 47

Under the River

THE PROTESTERS ARE STILL OUTSIDE. I GUESS THAT MEANS Cheryl still hasn't made up her mind about Camila's offer. I can't see their faces through the drizzle, which is making them into a murky, menacing cluster on the other side of the road. Here to remind us that we'll never belong anywhere. They've already managed to drive MacKenzie away, and now Camila is going to sell the motel.

We thought we could choose to belong here and create our own alternative community around the motel. I naively thought that it actually made us stronger, more liberated somehow. Because we didn't care about what people in town said. Because we knew how it felt to be on the outside, so we could really help people who needed it.

But I was wrong. Now that MacKenzie is gone, the motel is nothing but asphalt and concrete again. It's a building, nothing more. It can't protect us.

I go to see Michael first, then Camila. I tell them both the same thing: "Leave if you want. I won't try to stop you again. Do what you have to do to protect yourselves."

I know I won't be able to follow them. I'm as trapped here in death as I ever was in life. And I can't bear the thought of being here without them.

I walk the familiar stretch between the cabin and the motel and cross the parking lot. Before I can stop myself, I glance over at the protesters one last time, immediately regretting it. I don't want the image of them to be etched in my memory when I disappear. Paul is still working on the veranda. The calm sound of his hammer follows me all the way to the river.

I walk straight out into it. The icy water surges around me, but I don't feel a thing. I sink beneath the surface. Anything to get away. The world above is distorted. From here, everything seems to glitter, but it also looks so fragile. The drizzle forms rings on the surface above.

Become one with the water.

If I could just dissolve right here, I could rain down on them later. I wouldn't have to stay and watch them go their separate ways. They would be freer without me.

Time passes.

All that happens is that the branches of the silver birches become darker and more depressing as afternoon edges toward evening. I'm bored long before I disappear.

And then I feel angry.

How *dare* they? They made MacKenzie leave us! Camila is going to sell the motel! How can they stand over there, so self-righteous and evil and... Jesus Christ, is that a *fish*?

I jump out of the river, still full of anger. Camila was right. We *were* happy here, and even if MacKenzie and Camila and Michael give up, I'm not going to.

Not yet, anyway. Not until I know that I've done all I could.

And they're definitely not going to make me spend my time surrounded by disgusting fish.

I have an idea, but I'm not sure it's going to work. It's worth a try, in any case. I wait all evening, and as the clock approaches two in the morning, I stride toward town.

The distant glow of the streetlamps on Elm Street guides me, and once I'm there, I have no trouble finding Cheryl's house. It's two in the morning, and the place is dark and quiet.

Good.

But it's actually pretty hard to move through a strange house without any lights on. The darkness is so compact in here. The clouds break and a faint pool of moonlight finds its way in through the window, but that doesn't really help.

I have no idea how burglars do it. I manage to walk into an umbrella stand and am halfway through a huge chest of drawers when I realize that I can only see the top half of my body. The way my lower half vanishes into what must be polished wood would be alarming if I wasn't so focused on my task.

I step away from the wall and see the faint outlines of my legs beneath me. That's better.

The bedroom is on the first floor. No surprises there. It's actually quite easy to find by following the sound of Cheryl's husband's snores.

The electronic digits on the alarm clock glow eerily in the darkness: 2:07. I bend over her and whisper, "You don't care about the motel anymore. You want to take up a new cause. There are so many other unchristian issues to deal with. But not LGBT people," I quickly add. "Something else. I don't quite know what. But you feel like it's time to move on from the motel."

I repeat the same words several times, hoping that they have somehow managed to penetrate her subconscious. "You're bored with the motel. The issue is overplayed. You don't care about the motel. There are other things you want to do. The motel isn't interesting."

But then I pause. She looks so...vulnerable in her sleep. She is wearing baby-pink flannel pajamas, and her pillow has left a crease on her cheek. Her hair is sticking up in all directions. Right here and now, she seems younger than when I first met her. I think back to hot chocolate and peanut butter and jelly sandwiches.

"The real Cheryl is in there somewhere," I say to her. "The one who took care of a couple of lost teenagers and taught MacKenzie to drive and bought a new car just so she could give the old one to her."

A frown appears on Cheryl's forehead.

"You're in there somewhere. You just need to rediscover yourself, I guess."

She must be in there, I think. Otherwise I don't know whether I can still love this town.

I'm more confident when it comes to my next break-in. I've learned just to stand by the front door and listen for snoring. Haunting a house with a sleeping man in it is practical like that.

Derek's snores immediately show me the way.

The moonlight illuminates his shirts and Stacey's new "proper" clothes. They are in a messy heap on the armchair in one corner and scattered across the floor. Derek is asleep with his mouth open, one arm beneath Stacey's shoulders.

"You're an expert at fixing things," I say to him. "So fix *this*."

I say the same thing three times, and then I move on to Stacey. "And you're too tough and funny to be wasting your personality on pretending to be respectable! You got Dad to throw flour at you, and now he walks around wearing that red coat. He still needs you, and you need the motel."

I sit down on top of the clothes on the armchair and talk about the motel and Derek's football career and how much Michael admired him; I talk about Stacey's toughness, how pretty she was when she was younger, how pretty she still is. When the sun finally comes up, I head home.

Some *of that must have sunk in*, I think.

CHAPTER 48

Moats and Drawbridges

I WOULD RECOGNIZE MACKENZIE'S PICKUP ANYWHERE, SO I spot her approaching from a way off.

I'm so relieved that I almost feel like crying. And laughing. And shaking her and asking what the hell she was thinking, disappearing like that. And hugging her. Mostly the last one.

She slows down, indicates a left turn, waves to the protesters, parks in her usual spot, and practically runs over to reception. She enthusiastically waves a magazine in the air.

"Check this out!" she says to Camila as though she had never left.

As she looks at MacKenzie, all the tension and hardness within her seem to disappear. But only for a brief moment, before she composes herself and continues to pull all of her pretty new brochures from the stand.

"Did you know that Mrs. Davies writes a column for the *New Yorker*?" MacKenzie asks. Her face is deliberately nonchalant. I think she is trying to convince both Camila and herself that she didn't just leave. "She's the one who writes In My Humble Opinion."

Camila looks up from the brochure stand. "The column that always eviscerates everything? Films, restaurants...hotels."

"Yup!" MacKenzie sounds cheerful. I take a closer look at the magazine she is holding. It's the latest edition of *The New Yorker*.

"What has she written?"

"The headline of her column is: "Would Jesus check in here?" She writes that she's always thought Jesus had some morally sound principles, but that it doesn't seem like he had much of a sense of humor. He'd be a nightmare guest unless there was a fish, bread, or wine shortage."

"Great. They're going to crucify us."

"I doubt anyone here reads *The New Yorker*. Anyway, she's written such nice things about the motel. She says she can't think of a better place to pine away. The idea of a home might be a modern illusion in these restless times, but she admits that we can all benefit from duping ourselves from time to time. And if any of her readers happens to be Jesus, they'll also get a 10 percent discount."

She shows Camila the article, and I read it over their shoulders. It *is* an incredibly nice piece. It starts out mocking and superior, a big-city perspective on a conservative small town, but then she becomes serious, almost despite herself. The ending is warm and honest. She might joke about Jesus being an awkward dinner guest at the outset, but by the closing paragraph, she describes our motel and its collection of damaged individuals as "truly Christian" and "more like the biblical Jesus than anyone she has ever met before."

Camila smiles weakly as she hands the magazine back. MacKenzie must have seen something in her eyes, because she involuntarily mumbles: "Camila..."

Camila quickly shakes her head. "Don't worry. You said you'd leave, and you did. No expectations, right?"

"I came back," MacKenzie tells her. "I couldn't leave before your party."

"It's canceled."

"And Mrs. Davies's column reminded me that I couldn't give up without a fight. I love this motel."

"The shop owners have been calling all day," Camila explains. "They aren't interested in having their leaflets here anymore. But they say that they wish us good luck. That they're sure I understand."

"I'm sorry for leaving like that. One of these days, I'll leave, but I shouldn't have abandoned you with all this to deal with."

"You were right. It's pointless even trying," she says. "This is what happens when you start caring about things. I should've given in right away. Like you. Just left."

MacKenzie steps forward and takes Camila's face in her hands. She kisses her. For a moment, Camila tenses up, but as MacKenzie pulls her close, she shuts her eyes and clutches MacKenzie's jacket. MacKenzie holds Camila's body against hers and sighs involuntarily.

I'm just about to leave them alone, but as I turn around, I see Camila pushing MacKenzie away. "MacKenzie…" she begins.

MacKenzie glances around. "We can't talk here," she says, dragging Camila into the office. She lies down on the sofa and pulls Camila on top of her. "Better," she says once she has both arms wrapped around her.

I pause in the doorway.

"Tell me about Henny," Camila says.

MacKenzie stiffens up. "Why? She doesn't have anything to do with us."

"You never talk about her."

"There's nothing to talk about."

Camila struggles into a sitting position on the edge of the couch. "Until you left, I'd always thought we were friends at the very least."

MacKenzie seems touchingly unsure. "We are friends, aren't we?"

"Friends *talk* to each other. They don't just clear off like that."

MacKenzie looks like she wants to say something, but she has no idea what. Her heart is beating so hard in her chest that I feel as if I can see it through her top. Her face is naked and vulnerable. The slightest shift in her thoughts is visible on it, waves of fear and panic and uncertainty washing over her eyes, her skin, the fine lines on her forehead.

"Start with Henny," Camila tells her. Then she waits. She lets MacKenzie pull her close again.

"I was never in love with her," MacKenzie explains. "We were just friends."

Camila's fingertips push back the stubborn lock of hair that is always falling into MacKenzie's eyes. "Hardly just," she says.

MacKenzie takes a deep breath.

"You're right. There was no 'just' about being friends with Henny. She was my best friend. She was always there. Nothing feels right anymore. I don't know how the world works now that I can't talk to her. She was like a…compass. I could always find the right direction by talking to her."

Camila's fingertips continue to explore MacKenzie's face. Unconscious, featherlight movements across her forehead, down onto her cheeks and neck.

"She never said much," MacKenzie continues. "But she had a special way of listening. Focused, natural, like everything you said was exciting and interesting."

This feels like far too a private moment to be eavesdropping on, but I can't tear my eyes away from MacKenzie. Years of toughness and self-sufficiency have been peeled away, and I can see the old MacKenzie again, the way she was the summer we built the cabins. The MacKenzie I've been looking for all this time.

"She could see right through me and liked...no, loved me no matter how I behaved. Henny was unconditional love and I took her for granted, and now she's gone." She closes her eyes. "I loved her, even though I wasn't as good at listening. I was never as good a friend as she was. I just wasn't as good a person as her."

Oh, MacKenzie. That's only because you *did* things rather than sitting around, listening to people talk.

"You made my life more exciting, in any case," Camila says. Her tone of voice is deliberately easygoing. "Everything was an adventure with you. I never knew what was going to happen."

MacKenzie's eyes are focused on anything but Camila. Then she says, "Why did you never come out to me? Before you left, I mean."

It's Camila's turn to look away. "I just couldn't."

Then she smiles. It isn't an entirely happy smile. "Did you know I wanted to take you to prom? In a dress. But I was never as brave as you."

"I'm sorry," MacKenzie eventually replies. "I didn't know."

"MacKenzie, it's all right. I never told you."

"I should've been a better friend."

And then MacKenzie kisses Camila, hard, and I throw myself out of the room as the first piece of clothing flies through the air. The last thing I hear is MacKenzie insisting that Camila will have her party, whether she wants it or not, accompanied by the fantastic sound of Camila laughing again. But then she says, "MacKenzie, we don't have to throw a party unless you want to."

"We're having a party," MacKenzie says, and I hum to myself as I walk away.

I walk around the edge of the motel and find Michael and Paul by my veranda. The two men are working silently and efficiently, but Michael keeps pausing and staring straight ahead.

He got a call from his agent an hour ago and said yes to a lecture tour in Canada, given that he would be in British Columbia anyway.

"You know," I say, "I barely even remember my mom. I was five when she died, and I have no idea which memories are real and which are imagined, planted through photos and Dad's and Grandma's even more unreliable memories. There was a period when I used to ask Dad about her all the time. I was six or seven, and every day was full of questions like: Did Mom like ice cream? What was her favorite color? Did she have a favorite TV show? What color hair did she have? What about her eyes? The pictures didn't give me anywhere near enough information. Yes, her hair was blond, but what *kind* of blond? Honey blond? Strawberry blond? Dark blond? I thought honey blond sounded nicest."

I move over to him, standing as close as I can get. He smells like motel soap, wood, and cold air.

"There were a couple of girls at school who had those My Friends books, and I used to memorize the questions from them so I could ask Dad and fill in my own version in my head. 'What about her favorite animal, Dad. What was Mom's favorite animal?' Dad said it was dogs, but he didn't know what *kind* of dog, so now I wonder if he just made up an answer. Maybe he didn't really know her, either. 'Ask your grandmother.' That's what he often said, but I knew that the image of Mom that lived on in her mind had very few similarities with any living person. Am I going to disappear like that? Will anyone remember my exact hair color? Will you remember the exact shade of my eyes? Does MacKenzie know what my favorite color is, so she can pass it on? I think it's yellow."

I glance at him. "You'll remember me, won't you? Anyway, I'm still here. I'll remember everything you've said and done and thought, and you'll remember me. Teamwork."

My mountains are dark against the bare trees. The damp, brown grass of the meadow in front is wrapped in a faint haze, wild and lonely and beautiful.

"I never picked the town ahead of you," I say.

It's just that I had never known anything but Pine Creek. Whenever

Michael told me about the rest of the world, it was like trying to imagine what existed beyond the universe. Thinking about that too much would drive anyone crazy. Or so I thought. And how was I supposed to know whether I would be able to breathe anywhere else?

"It was *you* who left me," I say. "I was always here. You knew where to find me."

For a moment, I'm convinced I can actually feel the warmth of his body.

"I would have made you happy if I'd had the chance," I say.

MacKenzie is nowhere to be seen the whole next day, out on errands I should probably be worried about. That dangerous glimmer in her eye is back with a vengeance. When she returns, she takes over the practical side of running the motel so that Camila can focus on the preparations for her party.

Camila tries reorganizing the furniture in the restaurant, while MacKenzie cleans the last few rooms that Camila didn't get around to. Camila makes posters; MacKenzie deals with the accounts in the office.

I hop up onto the desk beside her. "I'm sorry I said you should be strong and do things," I say. "I was wrong. You don't need to be strong at all."

The door into reception is open, and we can both see Camila hunched over the computer, working away on her posters.

"I've been thinking about love a lot lately," I continue. "Do you remember how it felt just after I died? How everything seemed to really affect you? Every sound cut into your soul, every irritating moment or idiotic person made your bones ache; your temper flared up without warning, and the smallest task felt like a visit to the dentist. Like you were skinless. I think that's how life should be lived. We *should* be skinless.

"We should cry when we watch sad films and laugh when we see a clip of dogs doing stupid things; we should feel love without warning, sudden bouts of joy. And anger and irritation, too, of course. It's not all positive. But we're *supposed* to feel life. You can try to shield yourself from it, but that won't make you any safer. It's a false comfort, thinking you can build moats and drawbridges and defensive walls around you. The first catastrophe that comes along will flatten them all. The only thing you'll actually manage to do is shut out love."

I think MacKenzie might have learned that lesson now. She *was* vulnerable with Camila. I saw it in her face. It's just so difficult to know whether it's going to last. From time to time, she glances over at Camila. Sometimes she smiles as she does it, but then her face becomes closed off as she goes through the figures, our expenses and the meager income we've had lately.

I jump down from the desk.

"Love is giving in. Unconditionally. Lowering the drawbridge. You'll be surprised by everything that comes flooding in. You can find help and support from people you don't even know, see love marching in and friendship making itself at home. The only way to protect ourselves from loss is never to have anything to lose, but that's such an empty way to live. Our hearts can handle more than we think. They keep beating long after we've been cremated."

When I come out into the reception area, I realize that the protesters have gone. It's the middle of the day, the sun is even shining, and there is nothing but pines and emptiness on the other side of the road.

This worries me.

Camila prints out her posters on the old printer in the office, and then she puts them up all over town. It's a glorious day and there are people all around, taking time with their errands and watching with fascination as she makes her way down Elm Street. They pause by her posters, hesitate, and then move on.

All but Cheryl, who quickly skim-reads one of them and then runs to catch up with her. "I thought you were going to sell the motel," she says, out of breath. Camila still has a stack of posters in her arms.

"That's the plan."

"So what's the point of this party?"

"Think of it as a leaving party. You're invited, of course." She pauses. "I don't know whether it matters to you, but MacKenzie is back. I have no idea how long she'll stay this time."

I can't be sure, but Cheryl almost looks...relieved?

Derek is standing in the middle of a group of men, nodding and laughing and shaking hands. Beneath his black sports jacket, I catch a glimpse of an impressively crisp white shirt collar.

"Excuse me, boys," he says when he spots Cheryl. He jogs over to her. They are standing just outside a shop, and the owner waves cheerily to Derek, who waves back before he leans in to Cheryl.

"What's this I hear about taking a break with the campaign?" he asks quietly.

"We haven't given in. It's more like a...cease-fire."

"Sounds a lot like giving in to me. What's going on?"

"Camila has agreed to sell the motel," Cheryl explains. "The new owners might be better. We can influence them to..."

"So what? We'll have some cheap motel chain instead? And that's meant to solve everything?"

"We're not against motels per se, just the way this particular motel has been run. And with another owner, well..."

Eventually, Derek tells her what's really on his mind: "But what about MacKenzie?"

You should have thought about that before you began all this, I think.

Cheryl looks away. "She isn't our responsibility. We're here to make this town into a better place for our kids, and..."

"Yeah, yeah, I know. No need for the speech." He shakes his head. "I just didn't think she'd give in like that."

"Who?"

"MacKenzie. She's always been at that motel. She's crazy and a pain in the ass, but, you know, this is *MacKenzie* we're talking about."

"Camila is more reasonable; it's as simple as that. Or smarter, perhaps."

"And that's it? All this work for...well, this?"

"This *is* what we've been fighting for. The new owners will change things. I'm sure Robert will be able to move home now."

"I just thought we wanted more than this."

"It's just one battle in the wider war. There'll be more. The world can't be saved in a day. It's about endurance, and..."

"All right, all right," Derek looks weary. He gives her a disillusioned glance. I wonder whether he is thinking that Bob was right.

CHAPTER 49

Tougher than Others

DAD ANXIOUSLY FOLLOWS ALL OF THE PREPARATIONS FOR THE party. He even goes into town to gauge the general mood. Once he returns to the motel, he inspects the veranda, sees Camila working in the restaurant, eavesdrops on a conversation she is having with Dolores, and shakes his head.

He is so worried that he even talks to Clarence about it—though, in truth, he might be talking more to himself than anything. He is sitting on the bench outside the restaurant when Clarence joins him, and Dad suddenly says, "It's not going to work."

"What's not?"

"The party. People won't come. They'll stay away. People try to avoid controversy, and the motel is still too controversial." Dad nods to himself. "They're going to be upset here. I don't like the thought of them being upset. What if MacKenzie disappears again?"

"Well, you'll have to do something about it," Clarence says with the calmness of someone who has no intention of leaving his seat in the sun. He is enjoying the warmth from its weak rays, a blanket on his knees, and a mug full of liquor in his hand.

"Do something?" Dad sounds shocked.

"Yeah. Sort it out."

"But what can *I* do?"

"Well, I don't know. I'm not the one sitting here talking about catastrophes. I just want to enjoy the first nice day in forever. You know, people worry too much. I've always said that. I think it's because they don't drink enough..."

Fortunately, Dad is no longer listening. Instead, he is staring at the man who has just parked outside the motel.

It's our lawyer, a kind, old man who has spent the past ten years trying to retire. He is wearing boots, jeans, and a warm, padded jacket. I'm pretty sure I can see a fishing rod waiting for him in the back of his car.

He also looks more nervous than I've ever seen him before.

Dad gets up from the bench and cautiously follows him. When the lawyer finds MacKenzie, Dad hides around the corner to eavesdrop on their conversation. I don't need to hide, of course, I can eavesdrop in the open, but the sight of Dad's mop of gray hair peeping around the corner distracts me.

"Camila stopped by the office the other day," the lawyer says. "I shouldn't be telling you this. I *really* shouldn't. The bar association would have a fit."

"In that case, maybe you shouldn't tell me."

"But I've known you since you were a kid, when you turned up at my office to ask how an eight-year-old could leave home."

"You weren't much help, if I remember correctly."

"And if *I* remember correctly, you suggested pitching a tent in the schoolyard."

MacKenzie shrugs.

He glances around. Dad's head disappears around the corner. "You didn't hear it from me, all right?"

Dad's head pops out again.

"Camila wanted to talk to me about selling a motel. Asked for the necessary forms. Wanted me to take her through how to fill them out. I asked if you knew about it, and she said, 'It's still my motel. For now, anyway.' I thought you should know what she's planning. I can't do anything about it, I hope you understand that. You might've been running this place for years, but from a legal perspective, she's the owner. Still, this way you'll have time to prepare. Maybe look for another job."

MacKenzie pats him on the shoulder. "I appreciate the warning," she says.

"It's not right," he mutters. "The bar association can go to hell."

MacKenzie shoves her hands into her pockets. "A commendable attitude."

"Okay, Robert, you need to do something," Dad mutters to himself. "Think. An idea. That's all you need."

He sits down on the bed in his room—everything is manically tidy—and stares at my urn. I see his lips move, followed by a slight shake of the head, a nod, a new shake. Maybe he is weighing up different options, or going through the pros and cons.

He continues this for roughly an hour before suddenly standing up. "Yes, the situation demands it," he says. "It might be presumptuous, but it has to be done."

He puts on a fresh, ironed shirt.

"I don't want to get involved, but someone has to."

His hands are trembling slightly as he knots his tie. Then he smooths it out, checks everything is hanging properly, and pulls on his red coat.

"I guess she can always say no."

"I know you don't really want to sell the motel," Dad says.

Camila looks up from the reception desk in surprise. "Sell the motel?"

"You can't be serious about it."

She gets up and walks around to him. "How on earth do you know about that?" she asks.

Dad's face turns red. "I...happened to hear your lawyer warning MacKenzie about it. He had to," he quickly adds. "He's known MacKenzie all her life. And she *has* worked here all this time. I hope he's not going to get into trouble..." He mutters to himself. "I never thought about *that*."

Camila seems taken aback: "*MacKenzie* knows?"

"Um, yes. I'm afraid so."

Her voice is nothing but a whisper: "What did she say?"

"Nothing. She didn't say anything."

"Where is she?"

"Gone. But not forever," he says as Camila's face turns pale. "I think.

I think she's just out running some errands. She drove off an hour or so ago, though she didn't have any bags with her. But that's not what I wanted to say. The point is that, well, I hope this isn't presumptuous of me, but I think I have a plan."

"Funny," Camila replies. "Because I thought I did, too."

Camila spends the rest of the day watching out for MacKenzie's pickup. No matter what she's doing, she keeps half an eye on the parking lot and the road beyond. But when MacKenzie eventually returns just after five, it's Dad who spots her first.

"MacKenzie!" he says as she calmly climbs out of the car. She is holding a slim cardboard box in one hand and has the motel's master key in the other.

I nervously scan her eyes for any sign of madness, some kind of crazy new plan, but all I see is calm satisfaction. She's *pleased*. With herself, I think, but it's hard to know for sure.

That doesn't exactly reassure me.

"I want to organize a memorial for Henny," Dad tells her.

"Wasn't the funeral enough?" she asks.

"No, I want it to be more...fun. I want people to talk about Henny. I want to hear their stories."

"Sure, sure. I'll stay away. You don't need to send Cheryl this time."

"No, I mean, I want to hold it here."

"Here?"

"Yes. I was wondering... Do you think Camila would mind if we combined her party with Henny's memorial?"

"You'll have to ask her."

"But is it all right with you?"

"They're not going to come. People from town, I mean. Not even for Henny's sake."

"We'll see," Dad says, and MacKenzie shrugs and continues up the stairs. She uses the master key to let herself into Camila's room. She only spends a few minutes inside, but by the time she reemerges, she is no longer holding the box.

Camila intercepts MacKenzie in the parking lot, but she seems too nervous even to look at her. She swallows and says, "I can explain."

MacKenzie raises an eyebrow. I don't think she seems angry, but Camila's nerves are rubbing off on me.

"About the motel. I know you know I'm going to sell it."

"Harry has known me since I was eight. If you wanted to keep it a secret, you should've asked a different lawyer for advice."

"I was planning to tell you later. Maybe I should've done it right away, but..."

MacKenzie interrupts her. "You don't need to explain anything," she says. "I know you wouldn't do it unless you had to. I know the state our finances are in. And you'd never sell it unless you were sure the new owners would keep Dolores on."

"They'll definitely keep her."

"Yeah, they'd be crazy not to." MacKenzie shrugs. "And I'll always be fine."

"But that's what I'm trying to say..."

"Come with me, Camila. I want to show you something."

She takes hold of Camila's arm and leads her up to her room. Camila still seems tense, but she follows MacKenzie blindly, as if she can no longer think for herself.

The box that MacKenzie left in Camila's room contains a gown.

A ball gown.

An utterly fantastic gown, but I think the word Camila might be looking for is *senseless*. Or *incomprehensible*. The kind of gown you would wear once at prom and then never again. It looks like something from a Disney film: shimmering pink, with tiny embroidered pearls on the bodice and a sea of tulle and satin beneath. On a teenager, it would look enchanting; paired with Camila's dogged face, it seems more like the mice smoked something before they were let loose on the fabric.

Camila is staring at it with a skeptical expression.

"What's going on, MacKenzie?"

"What do you think's going on? I'm giving you a dress."

"I've worn dresses before."

"But never one like this."

There's no arguing with that.

"Meet me in the parking lot at seven."

The parking lot is dark and empty when Camila steps outside at seven on the dot. She strides down the metal steps with as much dignity as she can muster in her pink tulle gown. The skirt sweeps over the steps, and in the glow of the streetlights, the pearls glitter against the dark asphalt. Her hair is tied up in a deceptively simple bun, with two soft curls framing her face.

She looks heartbreakingly beautiful. MacKenzie follows her every movement. For once, she can't think of anything to say.

Camila tugs nervously at the dress. "I look like an idiot," she says.

"You look incredible," MacKenzie tells her. She is still just staring at Camila, and only springs to life to open the car door when she notices Camila raise an eyebrow.

"And I look like an uncomfortable teenage boy who's been forced into a tux against his will," she says.

But if you ask me, they both look fantastic, and they can't help but steal glances at each other as MacKenzie drives toward the school. I'm in the bed of the truck and can't tear my eyes away from them.

MacKenzie pulls up outside the gymnasium.

"Should we really be here?" Camila asks.

"Relax," MacKenzie tells her, which only makes Camila more nervous. MacKenzie leads her across the yard and around the freshly painted building.

"The dress is great, but can we go home now?"

"You worry too much. You'll get premature wrinkles."

"MacKenzie! You can't break into the sports hall, and I can't run from the cops in these heels. You *promised* you wouldn't do anything to piss them off."

But the doors swing open as MacKenzie turns the handle. "After you," she says.

"If the alarm goes off, I'm…"

Camila's voice trails off.

The sports hall has been transformed for the evening, decorated with the same confident taste as all school dances. Delicate pink drapes hang from the ceiling in an attempt to soften the lighting. There are fabric runners on the walls, all dramatically lit by spotlights. The hall smells like rubber flooring and teenage angst, but there is also a disco ball. It spins lazily on the ceiling, scattering beams of light across the empty floor to the tones of…

Bruce Springsteen.

"Michael convinced Coach Stevenson to let us hire the gym for the night. We even got to use the decorations they save for prom. Clarence and Buddy helped out."

I take a deep breath.

Camila does the same. She steps forward onto the empty dance floor and gazes around in wonder. The light dances over her and her dress as she slowly spins around.

I wonder whether she has also been transported back in time, whether she can see our old classmates just as clearly as I can. I take a step forward, just like I did back then.

I'm a firm believer in decisive moments in life. Instants in which we change radically and irrevocably. I experienced one of those moments on the dance floor fifteen years ago, as I stood next to MacKenzie in the compact silence that greeted us.

I should have been terrified. I *was* afraid, but it was as if I had decided I was brave enough to ignore their glances, to raise my chin and refuse to care.

It was the biggest step I had ever taken, and it might not sound like much now, but it tore me away from everyone else in town and put me firmly on the side of the motel. I never looked back.

I don't think I was aware of it at the time. Not really. I knew something had happened, but I wasn't quite sure what. I think maybe that's what happens in these decisive moments. They can be so brief that we don't even realize we've changed course. It might only be by a few degrees, but it's enough to shift us onto a completely different course, and as the years pass, those few degrees take us further and further away on our new trajectory. For better or worse, I'm not entirely sure, but I'd like to believe that our lives choose us for a reason. Think of it as a new course, rather than being knocked *off* course.

I wonder whether Michael experienced the exact opposite back then. His face was haughty, his gaze ice-cold. He looked at everyone around us as though nothing they said or thought would affect him in the slightest. Camila was half a step behind him.

But it was our evening all the same. I felt remarkably free. Everyone's opinions of me, their views and remarks; all those things got pushed back. Just like the other students as we walked across the dance floor.

After a while, the conversations started up again. The people on the dance floor started dancing. MacKenzie and I danced together, and argued about who would lead. I danced with Michael after that. He led. I was amazed that everything seemed so normal. I guess I had imagined the roof of the sports hall crashing down on us.

Michael's back was tense beneath my hand. I could feel his knotted muscles, but I also couldn't stop smiling. I was wearing a tuxedo and was drunk on the freedom of having escaped people's expectations without making the world go under. The dark arm of my jacket looked absurd against the matching fabric on his shoulder.

Michael's gaze softened as he looked at me, and that made me feel even stronger.

He can't leave, I thought. There's no way he can want to leave, not if he can look at me like that. Green Day's "Good Riddance" was playing through the speakers, and I decided it would be our song from that point on.

I think I thought of Michael as a tense knot of contradictory impulses. Wants to, doesn't want to. I thought that with time, the knot would loosen, whether because of me or because of life, but what I didn't realize was that knots don't loosen when they're pulled in opposite directions. They just get tighter and tighter.

Still, then and there, he laughed and shook his head and spun me around, and I remember thinking: *See, he loves me.*

The memory dissolves before my eyes. I'm still spinning around on the dance floor beneath the disco ball, but I'm alone again.

Camila is standing perfectly still, staring helplessly at MacKenzie. She has tears in her eyes.

"Camila!" MacKenzie sounds dismayed and instinctively moves toward her.

"I know you said you'd break my heart," Camila says quietly. "And I know I told you I could look after myself, but Jesus Christ, MacKenzie, I didn't realize how completely you'd do it."

She blinks several times.

"I'm sorry, I thought I could manage to keep things easygoing and no strings, but..."

"Shh," MacKenzie tells her, holding out a hand. "May I?"

She takes Camila's hand and wraps an arm around her waist, leading her out onto the dance floor. Bruce Springsteen is singing that he's tougher than the rest, and Camila finally relaxes in MacKenzie's arms. She closes her eyes and lets herself be taken along on yet another of MacKenzie's adventures.

I stick to the shadows along one wall, watching them dance. Here and now, I think Camila would follow MacKenzie anywhere, and MacKenzie will never be able to leave her after this. But I wonder whether that's what this is really about. Regardless of which path they take in the future, no one can take this moment away from them.

The memory will always be there inside them, in a place where time doesn't work the way it does here. A small part of them will always be able to dance around this empty sports hall, not caring about the fabric starting to come loose from the wall, or Clarence and Buddy having forgotten to fold up the basketball hoop.

MacKenzie pulls Camila closer. "You know when I said I would never fall for you?" she says quietly.

Camila nods.

"I was lying."

CHAPTER 50

One Day, I'll Leave All This Behind

THE NEXT DAY, I JOIN MICHAEL IN HIS CAR AS HE SETS OFF somewhere. My mind keeps returning to the image of MacKenzie and Camila dancing together, but no matter how hard I try, I don't seem to be able to hold on to the feeling I had yesterday. I'm tired, hungover on feelings, and oddly anxious.

Something is refusing to leave me in peace. It isn't quite a memory. More a shadow of one. Something itching and rubbing and irritating me, like a splinter I can't quite see to extract or even ignore.

I stiffen up next to Michael.

It can't have been, I think.

If those decisive moments change the course of our lives, that must mean we were already moving away from each other on prom night. I was free and happy, and "Good Riddance" was our song. How can a happy moment go on to make us unhappy? That's not how life is meant to work.

"If only you'd asked me *then,*" I say to Michael. "I was invincible that evening. I would have followed you anywhere. You could've dragged me out to the car and driven me off into the world."

But as the words leave my mouth, I wonder if it's true. Would I have done that? Maybe I was already moving away from him, however incomprehensible that sounds.

I stare out through the windshield. I know where we're going. He's driving to our place. The place he first kissed me, and where we always went when we wanted to be alone.

The whole of northeast Oregon is so beautiful that it was pure chance we picked this place, but ever since that spring, it's how I've always pictured paradise.

I never went there during all the years Michael was away. To me, it became somewhere half-mythical and half-real.

I cover my face with my hands to make the memories disappear.

"Why are we going there?" I ask wearily. "Why are we torturing ourselves with memories? It happened. It's over. Dwelling on it won't change a thing."

But when he parks the car, I follow him. Of course I do.

You get to our place by walking for an hour along a narrow, winding path through the pine forest. It's uphill all the way, until your thighs burn and all conversation stops because you need every last bit of air in your lungs.

It's an odd sensation to walk up there without getting the least bit out of breath.

I wish I *did* feel exhausted. It would give me something else to think about, at the very least. Michael is going to move on with his life without me, just as he did fifteen years ago, and I don't want to think about it anymore.

"I've thought about everything I want to think about," I announce to Michael's back. "Why couldn't it all just end at prom, while we were dancing and laughing and you spun me around? Surely that was as good a point as any to leave us."

What do the last few weeks matter? They're *my* memories. I'll do what I want with them.

The trees become increasingly sparse, and we reach a small ledge, just big enough for a camping stove and two people. Beneath us, Pine River flows sluggishly, as it always has.

But Michael's eyes are fixed on the ground, on a piece of rock. He takes out his hammer and carefully hits one edge of it until the section he has chosen breaks loose. The sound of his hammer on the rock echoes around us.

He is re-creating his photo album of rock.

"You came back here before you left, didn't you?" I ask quietly.

Michael sits down on the rock. I gently lower my head to his lap.

This was how we used to sit. He would run his fingers through my hair, slowly and gently, as if unaware he was doing it.

Then he always said, "One day, I'll leave all this behind, Henny."
As though he needed to remind himself.

Prom definitely gave our classmates something to talk about, but more than anything, it changed us. MacKenzie had made up her mind. She was going to work at the motel and ignore what anyone in town thought. Camila was quiet and withdrawn, the way she had been before getting involved with the Measure Nine campaign. When she came out to me, I thought that was the reason, but looking back now, I think it was more to do with the fact she had realized she would need to leave Pine Creek in order to be herself. Prom had simply confirmed that for her. I noticed she had started looking at MacKenzie with some kind of fond distance, as though she was already thinking of her as a memory. And then she forced herself to leave MacKenzie and the motel without ever looking back. Until I died.

Michael became increasingly tense during the last few weeks of school. I knew he was fighting constantly with his dad. It had started during the campaign, but things escalated after prom. Mr. Callahan didn't like Michael's political views, and he really wasn't happy when people started talking about how he had gone to the dance with another man.

Before that, their arguments had mostly centered around Derek and Stacey's wedding. They were getting married right after school ended, and everyone was expecting great things from them. Derek may have lost his scholarship due to an injury, but he was still destined for something big. Someone with that much talent forged their own path, they said; normal rules didn't apply.

One week after prom, Michael showed up in town with a black eye. He wore it with a kind of strange pride. Everyone knew it was his dad's handiwork. That evening, he moved into the Redwood Cabin.

I didn't know how he could afford it, but maybe the black eye had convinced Juan Esteban. Back then, he was still incredibly generous. MacKenzie was already living at the motel by that point, so I guess it made no real difference whether he was helping out one teenager or two.

I went to see Michael as soon as I heard about the bruise. He didn't tell me about it himself. I had to hear it from someone else in town, and though I had been forewarned, I still got a shock when I finally saw it for myself. The purplish-blue parts were surrounded by yellowish-green.

I swallowed nervously as I glanced around the cabin. The walls had been given a fresh coat of pale-gray paint. I knew that—we were the ones who had done it, after all. But somehow it felt wrong, immoral almost, to be there as a guest. As if we were stealing an experience that didn't belong to us. Everything still smelled new.

Michael's backpack was on the couch, and his geology books were spread out across the table.

"By the time you get to UC Berkeley, you won't have anything left to read," I said.

"I like to be prepared."

"Your eye looks much better today," I lied.

Michael turned to me and gave me an intense look. "Come with me," he said.

"To college?"

"Anywhere. First college, then the world. We could live anywhere. Go wherever we want. Travel together."

"How would we ever have a home, then?"

"We'd find somewhere we loved, somewhere we'd chosen ourselves. We'd still travel from time to time, but we would have a home to come back to. A real home. With a barbecue in the backyard. A full set of plates and glasses. A white picket fence out front. We'd even have one of those doormats that say *Welcome*."

"We already have a home *here*. We know what it's like. We know everyone, and..."

"I know! That's exactly my point. We know what people are like here. There are so many other people to meet."

I shuddered. "So we would travel the world until we found the perfect place?"

"Not every day. We could stay longer from time to time. But you know what I mean. I'd be happy to stay in boring motel rooms so long as I was with you."

"But we have a whole motel here!"

"*You're* my home. You're the only thing I need. If you want me to, I'll pack a doormat for you. Spread it out in front of the door wherever we stay."

He took hold of my arms as if trying to convince me by using some kind of inner strength. It worked. I felt it. I was standing in front of a precipice and could hear some ancient, primordial power calling to me. Whatever he was radiating said *Jump*. As if it was a simple matter of taking a small step forward and letting myself fall. *This whole fantastic view could be yours. Don't worry about hurtling downward. It's only temporary.*

It was terrifying and it was perilous; that's how it felt.

"Michael," I said hopelessly.

"And then, once we've seen a few places, we'll find our home. I could make you happy. I swear. I'd give you the world, millions of years of it, and no matter where we are, we'll wake up together. That's all I need. That's home to me. Falling asleep and waking up next to you."

"Michael!"

He finally fell silent.

"I can't," I said, sounding desperate. "I can't just leave everything like that. My whole past and my life and...Dad! What would he do all on his own?"

"He'll be fine. You can't shape your whole life around him."

"Why not? He's my *family*. And MacKenzie? Am I just supposed to leave her, too? I love you, Michael. You know I do. You're fantastic and incredible, and you're going to do everything you want in life, but Pine Creek...everyone here... That's my home."

"Not me, then."

"You too. Here. Where we are now. We can wake up and fall asleep together here, too."

"Where your home is."

"Now you're being unfair," I said quietly.

Michael moved back and forth as though the walls were closing in on him. "We choose our family, Henny," he said. "And you're choosing *them*. That's just how it is."

"I can't think," I said. "Not now. Not suddenly, like this. You always make decisions so quickly. You know what you want. You're so sure of everything in life. But I'm not like that. I..."

"It's not exactly a difficult question. Either you love me or you don't."

"That's not true! I love you. You know that."

"Just not enough."

Every time I looked into his eyes, I had to fight to remember who I was. I knew my life was on the line, but I couldn't defend myself, not against him. I was powerless to resist him. The freshly painted walls aged before my eyes. I found myself missing the scent of wood, missing that summer when everything was still new between us. Everything had become stifling and suffocating. My cheeks flushed in the heat.

He ran a hand over the half of his face that wasn't bruised. "Do you want something to drink?" he asked.

I nodded. Swallowed. There was an empty bottle of Coca-Cola on the counter, but he had another in the refrigerator. Eggs, milk, ketchup, and hot dogs, too. The surreal sense that we were playing adults in the cabin grew, but I knew I was the only one who felt it. Michael *was* an adult. He had his own refrigerator now. He had filled it himself with things he wanted, and if he got hungry, he just could just make himself something to eat.

The black eye was his decisive moment. I knew that. Everything was suddenly crystal clear to him. I could see it in the new sense of confidence he had. There was no longer any hesitation in his movements, not the slightest hint of doubt in his eyes. He was free. Nothing could hold him back.

Except for one thing. My hand trembled as I took the glass of cola.

He noticed, and his eyes softened. "We don't need to decide right now," he said.

I nodded again. Retreated slightly. Realized, in desperation, that I couldn't think of anything else to say.

We had sex that evening, with an oddly calm intensity that I had never experienced before—and haven't since. All of our energy was focused on the parts of our bodies that were touching; time came to a standstill, our thoughts stopped, and nothing else existed. Our brains might have been refusing to think about the future, but our bodies knew that they needed to concentrate two entire lives into one single night. All we wanted and desired was caught up in that moment.

Afterward, I lay naked against his body, completely open. I didn't need any covers. I felt no shyness, no cold. I looked him straight in the eye, those absurdly long lashes of his, the greenish-yellow tinge of his skin, and I stroked his face with my fingers. My eyes said, *You're mine*. I tried to convince us both. Whatever happened going forward, all of his future adventures, all of his future *women*, would pale in comparison with that moment. It would last forever, and he would never really leave me. The intensity in my gaze made his heart beat quicker. I felt it against my skin, much clearer than my own pulse.

Then I lay my head in the space between his shoulder and his neck, my space, and felt his arms loosen around me. When I glanced up at him, one eye was half closed with sleep, the other because of the bruise.

Then he said, possibly in his sleep, "I'll stay if you ask me to."

CHAPTER 51

What Henny Would Have Wanted

DAD SEEMS TO HAVE GATHERED HIS...TROOPS IN THE RESTAU-rant. He, Clarence, and Buddy are sitting at a table in the corner, their heads together, whispering away as the preparations for the party go on around them.

"No one from town is going to come," Dad says. "Not as things stand. Camila's posters won't make a difference. People might be curious, but they also want to avoid any conflict."

Clarence shrugs. Buddy looks anxious.

"So we need to do something about it," Dad tells them.

"But the party's tonight," Buddy replies. "What can we really do in one day?"

"If this madness could flare up that quickly, we can put a stop to it just as quickly. We just need to talk to the right people. You two can take care of Stacey."

Buddy grimaces nervously. "She's, uh, a little scary."

Dad finds a scrap of paper in his coat pocket and scrawls something down. "Here," he says. "Just say this. And tell her I say hello. Tell her it's a memorial for Henny. Get her to talk to her husband. Derek should definitely be able to get people over here. And I have something else for you to take, too."

Buddy and Clarence find Stacey at Raymond's Steak and Grill, the best restaurant in town. It's right by the river, with huge windows looking out onto the water. Stacey and Derek are sitting by one of them, at a table with maybe ten others. The majority are middle-aged or older and radiate success and comfortable lives. All the usual signs of a long Sunday lunch are dotted around the table in front of them: wineglasses, empty plates, coffee cups, cognac glasses. The decor in the restaurant is dominated by dark brickwork, gleaming mirrors, and dazzling windows. A large fire is burning in the oversize fireplace, keeping the damp autumn weather at bay. The cream of Pine Creek's citizens are scattered around the room.

Buddy and Clarence are lingering in the doorway, waving frantically at Stacey.

"Can I help you, gentlemen?" the maître d' asks. His voice is cooler than the ice bucket on the nearest table.

"No, no, don't mind us," Clarence cheerily replies. "Stacey!" he mimes, waving even more wildly.

"Do you have a reservation?" the maître d' asks. "I'm afraid we're fully booked today."

"We're just looking for a friend." Clarence abandons his waving and pushes past the maître d'. "Excuse us," he says, patting the man on the shoulder.

The maître d' casts a single glance at Buddy, who looms up behind Clarence, and abandons any attempt to stop them.

Stacey sees them coming and quickly gets up. She smiles apologetically and practically drags Buddy and Clarence outside.

"What the hell are you doing here?" she snaps once they are out of earshot.

"See what I mean? She's scary," Buddy mutters to Clarence. He turns to Stacey: "Robert wanted us to give you this."

He holds out a plastic bag that he has taken great care to keep level.

Stacey peers inside. "An...apple pie," she says.

"Don't ask us what you're meant to do with it," Clarence tells her. "He just said it would mean something to you. But we were also supposed to say... Buddy, do you have that piece of paper? He wrote it down just to be on the safe side. I'm normally pretty reliable until my third cup, but..."

"Clarence," Stacey interrupts. "What were you supposed to say?"

"Okay, okay." He squints down at the paper. "He said that it's boring living by other people's rules and that you should have fun and swear more—no problem with that, huh? And...wear a bright-red coat? This makes no sense at all. He must've been even more wasted than me." Clarence throws the piece of paper over his shoulder. "Look, here's the deal. The motel needs help. They're throwing a big party tonight, and Robert is worried no one will show up."

"But what can I do?"

"Talk to Derek. Get him to help. Tell him to focus on the shop owners and the football fans. Buddy and I are going to the bar. If no one shows up, we can always take a few of the regulars along."

With those words of wisdom, they turn and leave Stacey alone outside the restaurant.

She is shivering in her black dress, but she doesn't turn to head back inside. She is still clutching the bag containing the apple pie when Derek comes out to check on her.

"What are you doing?" he asks. "And what the hell's that?"

"Apple pie."

Derek mutters something to himself and drapes his jacket over her shoulders. She turns to him. "You know that I'll support you in this whole becoming-a-politician thing," she says. "But do you have to be a *boring* politician?"

"Is there any other kind?"

"*You* could be. These...shirts and jackets and a dress that goes down to my knees. It's not us."

"You're right about the dress," he says. "It's definitely too long."

"There's a party at the motel tonight."

"And you want to go?"

"That's not all. I need your help before then."

Derek's eyes dart back and forth between Stacey and the restaurant. "Jack's in there. Won't it be a little weird if we just take off? What are we meant to say to them?"

"Forget Jack. I want to help out with the party. We have a couple of hours to get people over there. It's going to take a miracle, and you're the only one who can do it."

That decides it. Derek tosses his car keys to her. "You bring the car around. I'll get our coats."

"Derek?"

He pauses. I'm sure she is about to thank him, but instead she says, "Get rid of that tie. And you should probably think about what you're going to say to Michael."

Derek shakes his head. "You're lucky I like strong-minded women."

"Lucky for you, too." Stacey looks happier than she has in years.

Dad's house feels even more depressing now that it has been empty for so long. It smells stuffy and abandoned, the rooms are dark and gloomy, and there is a fine layer of dust on everything. The whole house just seems so sad.

Dad seems to feel the same way. He shivers as he walks down the hallway, and when he sees the armchair in the living room, with Jesus and his bird's nest dejectedly looking down at it, I think he starts to wonder how he could have lived alone here all these years.

I'm glad he's at the motel now. I should have taken him over there a long time ago. It's the right place for him, simple as that; he needs chaos and people and things to get annoyed about.

Dad turns on all the lights, opens the windows in every room, and then heads into the kitchen to unpack the bags he brought with him. Before long, the counter is full of flour, apples, nuts, chocolate, baking powder, sugar, and mountains of other ingredients. He pauses to throw away all of the withered flowers from the kitchen table.

After that, he really gets to work. Flour swirls through the air, pieces of nut fly in every direction as he starts chopping, and the stuffy smell is soon replaced by heat of the oven and the scent of freshly baked pies.

There are pie dishes covering every free surface in the kitchen, all different shapes and sizes. Pecan pie, toffee pie, several apple pies, two chocolate tarts, what I think looks like a lemon meringue pie, and a key lime pie. The sink is full of sticky spoons and ladles, messy stacks of pans and bowls.

Dad doesn't even need to call Cheryl. She is drawn to the light behind the steamy kitchen window like a moth to a flame.

"You're back!" she shouts.

"Come in, Cheryl, come in," Dad sounds exuberant. He is still wearing his apron, and he holds out an oven-glove-clad hand and leads her into the kitchen. "You got here just in time," he says.

"In time for what?"

"For pie!"

He sits her down at the kitchen table, quickly moving some of the pie dishes out of the way. He then cuts her a piece big enough to feed at least five hungry children and smothers it in whipped cream.

"Have a taste," he says, giving her an expectant look.

"I don't understand," Cheryl says. "Are you back for good? Have you finally left the motel?"

But she obediently takes a bite of pie.

If Dad had been planning to convert her with the power of his apple pie alone, he'll have to reconsider. He seems to realize this, because he sits down opposite her and says in a serious tone, "I know that you care about me."

"Of course I do!"

"You've got a good heart, Cheryl. You were there for me when Henny died. I know you think the motel contributed to my problems, but..."

"Your *drinking* problem, Robert. There's no shame in admitting it. In fact, admitting it is the first step to recovery. Everyone knows that."

Dad looks her straight in the eye and does what he has to do: "When I had my *drinking* problem," he lies, almost without making a face, "it was MacKenzie who helped me sober up."

"Robert, is this one of your *steps*?"

"Uh, sure. Of course. I admit my faults and shortcomings and am trying to fix them and, uh, help others." He's improvising wildly, but I think he has done a good job.

Cheryl blinks away tears. "I'm so proud of you."

"Thanks. But what I'm trying to say is that it was the motel that helped me. MacKenzie has an incredibly motherly side."

"Careful, Dad," I warn him. "There are some things she won't believe."

Cheryl raises an eyebrow.

"Maybe not motherly," Dad says with a faint smile. "But she's a good friend. Have a little more pie."

Cheryl struggles valiantly with her apple pie.

"This party they're throwing at the motel," Dad continues. "It's also a memorial for Henny."

"A memorial?"

"Yes. The more I've heard people talking about her, the more I've realized I want to get to know her as an adult."

"I would have organized it for you if you'd asked."

"I know, I know. But this is a way for me to try to right what went wrong. With the funeral. My steps, remember."

"Maybe. Camila said it was a leaving party."

"More pie?"

Cheryl forces down another enormous slice. She looks slightly ill during the last few mouthfuls, but I don't think it has anything to do with the motel. I think it's more that the thought of another spoonful of cream is making her feel queasy. Once she finishes, she breathes a sigh of relief and pushes her plate as far away as the other pies will allow. She gets up before Dad has time to suggest that she try the cherry pie.

"Why don't you swing by tonight and talk to her?" Dad says. "At six."

Cheryl doesn't ask who he means. I have no idea whether he has managed to convince her.

Over in town, Clarence and Buddy aren't having much more luck. They are standing on Elm Street, handing out flyers for the party, and every time Clarence manages to push one into someone's hands, he says, "And a memorial for Henny Broek, the girl who died."

Another passerby, another: "Here you go. Memorial for the girl who died."

Oddly enough, I don't think it makes people any more eager to go to Camila's party. They stare at him in shock and then hurry away as though they think death might be infectious.

Buddy looks deeply uncomfortable, but Clarence refuses to give in.

The next time someone passes, he tries a different sales pitch: "Free punch! Guaranteed to be spiked!"

The mother of the seven-year-old child glares at him.

I really hope Derek is having more success, but the more I think about it, the more I wonder how much he can really be expected to achieve.

He only has half a day, after all.

I don't know who looks more nervous, Camila or MacKenzie.

It's five to six, and Camila is pacing around the restaurant, straightening paper tablecloths that are already straight, moving the piles of plates a fraction of an inch to the right and then back again, and inspecting the buffet and Dad's dessert table.

MacKenzie follows her every movement.

"Stop worrying," she says. "It looks fantastic."

Camila has transformed the restaurant with the paper tablecloths. Pink, purple, baby blue, and bright yellow: the room is now bathed in color.

Buddy has strapped eight plastic boxes together in the corner by the windows, forming a stage of sorts. He has even added a microphone and a simple sound system. Dad has spent the last few hours working on a secret project with Alejandro: one wall of the restaurant is currently hidden behind MacKenzie's banner. The words *Welcome, Mrs. Davies* are still visible.

I can barely see the counter beneath all the food. Huge bowls of potato salad, trays of cold cuts, chicken wings, and spare ribs, two baskets of corn bread, cobb salad, bean salad, and a simple tomato salad, plus a huge dish of mac and cheese and a pot of Dolores's special chili. If Dolores had been around at the same time as Jesus, the world would have been one miracle poorer; she wouldn't have had a problem feeding thousands of unexpected guests.

Dad's pies are lined up at one end of the counter, and on the small side table where we usually keep plates, silverware, and menus, MacKenzie has set two enormous bowls of punch.

"Do you think we have enough chairs? Do you think we should've brought more down from the empty rooms?"

"We can always go get more if we need them," MacKenzie replies. She keeps her voice light and friendly, but I can see the absolute conviction that we won't need any more chairs in her eyes. She still doesn't think anyone is going to come, and the more eager Camila seems, the more she fixes things and tries to make them perfect for the guests she thinks are coming, the more tense MacKenzie becomes.

I pray that Camila isn't going to be disappointed.

"Do you think I'm too dressed up?" she asks. "I knew the skirt was a bit much."

"You look perfect. Here, have a glass of punch."

"You've already spiked it, haven't you?"

"Only one of them. People expect it." MacKenzie turns to Michael and quietly adds: "Besides, if no one turns up, I'll need to get drunk."

Dad glances at Alejandro. "I think this could be a good time to show you what we've been working on this afternoon."

Alejandro looks almost embarrassed. "It's nothing special," he mumbles. "Just a little project. I thought it could be nice. But you don't have to say anything about it if you don't want to; we can always put the banner back up again."

"Come on, don't leave us hanging!" MacKenzie shouts. Alejandro lowers the banner.

The whole wall behind it is covered in photographs. There must be hundreds of them. Of the motel, the new sign, Dad in his bright-red coat. Michael and Paul building the veranda, Camila in front of her new reception desk, MacKenzie painting the walls, and then...me.

I move toward the wall and squint up at the pictures. I'm everywhere. Alejandro has somehow managed to reprint my old pictures on glossy photo paper. Michael, MacKenzie, Camila, and me at prom. The picture from the summer the cabins were built. MacKenzie and me in front of the world's biggest beagle, grinning the way only MacKenzie could make me. Embarrassing pictures of me as a kid. Those must have come from Dad.

No one seems to know what to say. They just stand there, staring at the photographs on the wall. My entire life, gathered in one place.

"Are you okay?" Camila asks, reaching out for MacKenzie. MacKenzie nods slowly. She finds Camila's hand and then moves closer to the pictures. An odd little smile spreads across her lips. "Jesus, look how young we were," she says, pointing to a picture of all of us from our first year in school. My hair is tied in ponytails; hers is as wild as ever.

The sound of a car makes everyone turn toward the road, but it drives right on by. MacKenzie smiles tensely.

"It's fantastic," Michael blurts out. "It's worth throwing a party just for these pictures."

"And we're all here together," Alejandro points out. The three of them keep glancing at Camila.

Dad's shoulders slump. "I was sure she would come," he mutters quietly to himself.

Then we hear the sound of cars again. This time, no one dares turn to look. They don't want to tempt fate.

But the cars are slowing down! I run over to the window just in time to see car after car pull up outside.

Derek and Stacey's car is the first to arrive. Stacey hugs Dad, to his delight and horror, and Derek glances at Michael and flashes his most charming smile, ready to meet his public. Everyone gathers around him as they climb out of their cars.

"Welcome!" he shouts. "They've got good food and good drink, and you can check out the famous motel as you eat, have a chat with the current owners. Most of you know MacKenzie, but Camila here might be a new...face. Juan Esteban Alvarez's niece. I know we've had our differences, but after careful consideration, I decided it was time to settle things peacefully. Our town has always prided itself on cooperation and friendship, and when it comes down to it, Jesus tells us all to turn the other cheek."

Derek is actually pretty convincing. He has so much charming nerve that, for a moment, I forget that just a week earlier, he was preaching the very opposite. He even winks at Michael when he spots Michael's skeptically raised eyebrow.

Derek's going to be a great politician, I think.

But he is also honest enough to linger outside as everyone else heads indoors. Michael shoves his hands into his pockets. Neither of them seems to know what to say.

Derek eventually speaks up. "You were right. Bob, too, for what it's worth. It was idiotic to take on the motel."

"Friendship and cooperation?" Michael asks.

Derek shrugs. "Well, I guess it's true." He smiles. "Plus, I had to say something."

Michael shakes his head. He seems reluctantly amused.

"I heard you built a veranda for Henny," Derek says.

"How?"

"Stacey told me." He walks around to the back of the truck and removes the tarp that's been covering whatever is there. "And since I know a guy who gave me a damn good price, I thought I'd contribute a little something to your project."

I blink. Inside are four incredible oak armchairs.

Derek pats Michael on the shoulder. "Think of it as a peace offering."

Before long, there are people everywhere. Someone props open the door to let some fresh air inside, but everyone is still sweating as they crowd into the restaurant, juggling plates and glasses and helping themselves to food.

The majority are peering around the room in surprise. *Is this it?* they seem to be thinking. The woman from the secondhand store actually looks disappointed. I think she must have been hoping for a bit of good old sin and immorality now that she has finally come to visit.

Then, suddenly, Cheryl is in the doorway, looking stiff and lost. I don't know how long she has been there, but she doesn't seem to be able to bring herself to either leave or come in. When Dad spots her, he immediately goes over to her.

"Robert!" She sounds relieved and allows him to lead her inside.

She spots MacKenzie and pauses. The two women face each other in silence. Neither of them wants to make the first move. They are both trapped by their past, but the same shared memories also bring them together.

"I'm not going to apologize," Cheryl says, stubbornly raising her chin.

MacKenzie folds her arms. "Me neither."

Cheryl spots the pictures on the wall, and when she moves over to take a closer look, MacKenzie follows her.

"My goodness, you were so young," Cheryl murmurs. She doesn't turn to look at MacKenzie as she says, "I'm sorry for hurting you. I'm not going to apologize for my views. I hope you know that. I did what I thought was right, but I never wanted to upset you."

"I'm sorry I crashed your car into the fence. And for the rainbow flag on the school."

Cheryl laughs and shakes her head. "You aren't the least bit sorry, MacKenzie Jones. You'd do it all over again if you had the chance."

MacKenzie smiles. "I was just trying to be polite."

"So who's the new owner?"

Dad and Camila glance at one another. "I guess now is as good a time as any?" Camila says. Together, they go over to the little improvised stage. Camila hops up onto it, and Dad hesitantly climbs up beside her.

"I'd like to thank you all so much for coming here tonight," Camila says once the murmur has died down. "I know you've probably already heard quite a lot about the motel. And I'm sure most of you know that we recently lost a dear friend here."

The last of the talking has definitely stopped now.

"I didn't get a chance to spend any time with her as an adult, but I knew her when we were younger, and I know Henny always loved this motel. I came back just in time to try to save it for her. Whether I managed that is up for debate, but I've done my best, and I've always tried to keep in mind what Henny would have wanted. That's all she ever asked of anyone. So, I'd like to take this opportunity to introduce you to the new owners."

"Owners?" Cheryl pipes up.

"I'm going to transfer 30 percent of the motel to Robert here, who already has many ideas for...improvements."

"*Robert*," Cheryl gasps. I have no idea what she's thinking. She actually looks about as shocked as MacKenzie.

"Twenty percent to MacKenzie"—MacKenzie's face is now completely expressionless—"10 percent to Stacey Callahan, and 10 percent each to Dolores and Alejandro."

A surprised shout can be heard from the kitchen.

"Twenty percent also goes to Michael, in the form of the Redwood Cabin. That's all. Thanks. Enjoy yourselves."

In the brief silence that follows as Camila passes the microphone to Dad and steps down from the stage, people begin chatting eagerly. MacKenzie grabs her arm as she passes.

"You forgot yourself," she says.

"I promised Cheryl completely new owners. Besides, I always planned to marry a rich motel owner. But first, I thought we should go on that road trip together. Visit all your motels, or the ones that are still open, anyway."

MacKenzie relaxes. "Great idea," she says. "We can let Robert hold the fort while we're gone."

"Well, he *is* the only one paying anything for it. He's going to sell his house and move over here for good. I thought we could give him one of the cabins."

"Is this on?" Dad asks, tapping the microphone—which is definitely working properly. He clears his throat. Loudly. Into the microphone. "During my time here at the motel, I've learned many things about myself, but also about Henny. I've realized that maybe I never really knew her as an adult. I suppose I always thought there would be more time. But, well, that didn't turn out to be the case. So, this memorial party is my way of getting to know her. I'd like to thank all of you for coming, and I'd encourage you to share your memories of her."

Dad steps down from the stage. The music starts up again, but Buddy is poised and ready to hit Pause the minute anyone decides they want to say a spontaneous few words in my memory.

And they do!

Several people get up and tell their favorite anecdotes about me. I smile and shake my head and laugh, but mostly I just look at Michael. He is standing at the very back, by the wall, alone. It might look like he's only half listening, but I can see something moving inside him. His body is pulsing with repressed energy, and his gaze is focused inward on something no one else can see.

"Henny loved Bruce Springsteen," Buddy announces through the microphone. "So I'd like to play a little song for her." He nods to Clarence, who has taken temporary control over the sound system.

"Brilliant Disguise" starts playing across the room.

"Wrong track!" Buddy shouts, pushing Clarence out of the way. He puts on "My Lucky Day" instead. Everyone makes a valiant effort to bob their head in time with the music, to listen respectfully, as though they're in church, but I dance away next to Michael. I've never been able to keep still while this song was on.

"I'm not really one for making speeches," Derek begins as he takes over the microphone. He winks exaggeratedly. "See, I've already learned how to start a speech. As some of you might know, I've had the misfortune of becoming a politician lately. But don't you worry, I'm not going to talk your ears off. I'm still pretty green around the gills. I haven't learned how to talk and talk yet."

Appreciative laughter.

"Speaking of misfortune, a few of you might also remember that I played football as a youngster."

More appreciative laughter.

"Then, unfortunately, I got injured. No, no, that's just life. But it was a bit of an adjustment to come back. I don't want to be too serious now. I just wanted to say that Henny was the only person who looked at me the same way when I came back injured." He raises his coffee cup full of spiked punch and nods to Michael, who is standing next to Camila and MacKenzie at the back of the room. "Maybe because, in her eyes, I was always overshadowed by my little brother."

"Smart woman, that Henny!" Stacey shouts, winking even more exaggeratedly at Michael.

But Michael shakes his head and leans back against the wall. Something within him has relaxed. No, that's the wrong word. It's more like something inside him has fallen into place, like he has found a new purpose or meaning.

"And now *I* want to play a Bruce song in Henny's memory," Derek says. Buddy hits Play on "Glory Days." Everyone laughs and applauds. Derek walks over to Stacey and bows. "May I?" he asks, and they start dancing in the small area of free space in front of the stage.

This time, everyone else starts dancing, too. There's barely room to move, but they improvise around the tables, the buffet, and the punch.

Everyone but Paul. He is standing by the wall of pictures, staring at... well, me. Me when the cabins were being built, in the schoolyard, in reception. Me, living. Me, not in his nightmares.

Dad isn't dancing either, of course. He moves over to Paul and mutters "I forgive you," walking away before Paul even has time to speak. Both he and I are left behind, watching as Dad disappears into the crowd.

MacKenzie looks amused. "Henny would've forgiven you a long time ago," she says.

Maybe that's when it finally sinks in. Paul is still staring at the pictures, but his eyes seem calmer. They are no longer trying desperately not to see what his brain remembers.

MacKenzie pats him on the shoulder. "My Henny would have been the friendliest ghost ever," she says.

I smile and shake my head, and then turn to Michael to share the moment with him. Michael smiles at the memory of me the way he used to smile every time he saw me. It's a smile that begins in his eyes—a subtle softening, invisible to everyone but me. Then, much later, it reaches his lips, slow and lingering, like an afterthought.

Jesus, I've missed that smile.

The noise from the restaurant carries through the darkness, down the slope, and all the way to the Redwood cabin: a heady mix of voices, Bruce Springsteen's bass, and the occasional snippet of conversation from people who have stepped outside for a cigarette or some air.

The door at the back is open, but I'm sure that Michael still hasn't noticed the noise.

He quickly clears the table. Moves dirty dishes to whatever free surface he can find. A couple of old plates end up on the chest of drawers in the hallway. He dumps the papers that were on the table on the floor. He impatiently pushes the notepad he started earlier to one side and rummages through his backpack for a new one, which he ritually places in front of him on the empty table.

Michael has had an idea.

He moves over to the window and waits for it to take shape.

"It wasn't just you who left me," I say. "I let you go."

One last memory for me: the way I gathered my clothes together in the darkness. I crept out of the cabin as quietly as I could to avoid waking him. It was all I could do. I swore to myself I would never give in to the temptation to ask him to stay.

"I wasn't some passive bystander who stood still as you moved on with your life," I say. "I carried on down my own path."

I guess we both did. And in the end, that's what brought us back together again. Two roads we traveled down for fifteen years, heading to this exact point, this exact moment, even though we had no idea we were doing it. We became who we are now either thanks to or because of the different routes we took, and I wouldn't change a single thing about him.

Without thinking, Michael takes a sip from his mug. He makes a face. He hadn't realized his coffee had gone cold.

Then he gets to work.

On the front cover of the new notepad, he slowly and methodically writes his preliminary working title. Then he releases all his repressed energy, flicks forward to a new page, writing quickly and without pausing to think. It's a draft table of contents. He writes the titles of the first chapters carefully, but his handwriting gradually becomes more ornate and cursive as he struggles to jot down all of the ideas rushing out of him. New page, more writing. Side after side fills up with outlines, first sentences, notes for himself, quotations, ideas for possible sources.

Eventually, he leans back in his chair. He pauses for a moment, almost as if he's trying to see whether any last few ideas might come to him, but then he nods to himself and closes the pad.

I place a hand on his shoulder. "You know when you asked what I wanted from you?" I say. "I want you to be happy. I want you to have everything you've always wanted in life. I know no one can have everything, but I don't care. I never said that what I wanted from you was realistic."

We'll make it, I think. Camila and MacKenzie's roads led them to the gym, and who knows what's going to happen between them going forward? Dad will have his hands full with the motel. He and Stacey can spend their days baking apple pies. And Michael? He'll be happy again one day. He just needs to find his way back to his rocks.

"Do what you need to do to live the life you want," I say. "Leave. Find more fantastic rocks. Be happy somewhere else. But then come back. You belong here, whether you like it or not."

I'm not worried. I know he realizes that now. On the front of the notepad, the name of his new book is written in huge letters: *Conversations with Henny, or Once upon a time hundreds of millions of years ago, Boise was a coastal city.*

CHAPTER 52

Loved by Henny

"ARE YOU SURE WE SHOULD BE DOING THIS?" CLARENCE ASKS.

"Just stay there and keep a look out," Buddy tells him. "Paul? You ready? Lift me up."

"And they're not going to be angry?" Paul sounds worried.

"MacKenzie will like it."

"So long as it doesn't upset them."

"The only person who'll be upset is you, if you don't lift me up right now. We need to do this now, while they're still celebrating their new veranda. Keep an eye out around the corner in case they come."

But Buddy isn't worried. I know that, because he has Bruce on in the background. In the darkness of the near-empty parking lot, Bruce is singing "None but the Brave."

Two hours later, the motel has a new addition to its sign.

"This one's going to end up as chaotic as the old one!" I say with delight.

Derek's four armchairs are lined up on the veranda. I'm sitting in one of them, and I'm the only one who doesn't need to wrap up in blankets and coats and scarves to protect myself from the cold. There are two six-packs of beer by MacKenzie's and Camila's feet, and Oregon's night sky spreads out above us.

"These are good chairs," MacKenzie says. "Armrests wide enough for a can of beer."

"I don't want to be the kind of person who says *I told you so*," I say. "But have you noticed that we're lined up in four armchairs on a veranda? Getting old together." I nod appreciatively. "Just thought I'd mention that."

"Do you know what I thought at the party yesterday," Camila says. "I thought: what a fantastic thing to have been loved by Henny. I'm going to take that love with me. Whatever happens, we were loved by Henny."

"That's not something everyone can say," MacKenzie agrees.

Michael swigs his beer. "Do you think we would've been happy together?"

It isn't a tortured question. He has spent the entire day writing, and is almost done with the first couple of chapters: "A Story about a Fish (I'll get to the rocks, I promise)" and "A Photo Album of Rocks."

"I think it would've been impossible not to be happy with Henny," MacKenzie tells him.

"Do you think Henny is happy wherever she is now?" Camila asks.

"God and I have had our disagreements," MacKenzie says, "but not even I can imagine he'd let her be unhappy."

"She wouldn't like it if *we* were unhappy," Michael says.

"Then we'll have to make sure to be happy."

Camila smiles. "You know, I think Henny might be working on that. She would hardly let God make us unhappy."

"True, but she wouldn't give him a talking-to," MacKenzie agrees.

"Uh," I say.

"Or complain," Michael adds.

"No, no," I say.

"She would just give him a wounded look, like she didn't understand how he could do that to us. She would tell God she knew he was kind deep down, and surely he couldn't want us to be unhappy? It must be some kind of misunderstanding, right, God?"

"I don't know," Michael continues. "If she was upset enough, she might yell at him. Like she did with the man who ran the candy store. So if it suddenly starts raining candy, we know she's involved."

"Amen," MacKenzie agrees.

"Do you think..." Camila begins. "Do you think she was always supposed to be the one who left us first? Because none of us would've been strong enough to manage it? This way, we know Henny is waiting for us somewhere."

I lean back in my armchair and look out at the mountain and the stars. "Yup," I say. "I'm much closer than you think."

Right then, Buddy, Clarence, and Paul come over to join us. Buddy and Clarence each take a beer, but Paul sticks to coffee. Before long, their cheery voices even bring out Dad and Stacey. They are wearing matching aprons, and their cheeks are flushed from the heat of the kitchen. Suddenly, the veranda is full of people. But they leave my armchair free.

I glance around at them.

"I think we're going to need more armchairs," I say.

The Very First Time

THEIR BREATH FORMS CLOUDS AS THEY DRAG THEIR SUITCASES over to Camila's Honda. It's more reliable than MacKenzie's pickup; that's what they have agreed.

I walk alongside MacKenzie and Camila, breathing out as hard as I can and laughing at the novelty of not being able to see my own breath in the cold air. All around us, the frost makes it look like everything is brittle and glistening.

"You're the one who wanted to set off early!" Camila suddenly snaps.

MacKenzie gives her a questioning look, but then she grins. In an excessively whiny voice, like one of the many couples checking out of the motel, she says, "If *you* hadn't insisted on unpacking everything for a one-night stay, we would at least have had time for breakfast. How much luggage does a woman need?"

Camila throws the first case into the trunk and starts scraping the windows. She tries to keep a straight face, but a smile keeps threatening to break through. She has heard enough arguments to know how they go. "And if *you'd* just asked for directions, we would never have even ended up here!"

"You were the one reading the map. 'Turn left,' you said. Sure, sure." MacKenzie throws two more bags into the car. "All this just to visit your mom!"

"Why don't you say what you *really* think of her."

"Because you're always pissed off for days when I say that your mom is a hysterical, passive-aggressive sociopath whose only joy in her dead, empty life is to drive me crazy."

"That's just because she doesn't laugh at your jokes," Camila tells her, laughing when MacKenzie suddenly wraps her arms around her and pulls her close. She takes off her scarf and loops it around Camila's neck, kissing her on the tip of her nose—the only thing not covered up.

I'm sure everyone is going to come out and wave them off. It's just that we're pretty busy right now. A busload of Christian senior citizens has just arrived and are currently swarming across the parking lot.

They're here to experience God in the American wilderness, on a singles trip organized by a congregation in Colorado. They're heading for the Canadian border, but when they read Mrs. Davies's column, they couldn't resist stopping off here. They have clearly been enjoying some songs on the road, because several have lyric books in their hands, open to "'Tis So Sweet to Trust in Jesus." It's one of my favorite psalms.

Dad and Stacey are ready to welcome them. Clarence has been given strict orders to stay away, and Paul has left brand-new Bibles in every room.

Paul seems to be doing much better now. I think he might even have put on a little weight. Dolores has never been able to resist a skinny man. He is still refusing a proper room at the motel, but he has put up curtains in the office and hung a picture of me on the wall. Alejandro enlarged it for him and put it into one of the frames Camila bought from the secondhand store.

Alejandro's collection is still on the wall in the restaurant, though pictures keep disappearing. Just the other day, I spotted Cheryl taking one of me and MacKenzie. Alejandro keeps it refreshed with copies and new photos when he finds time between Instagram updates and his own projects. He has an exhibition in Portland next spring.

MacKenzie and Camila wait patiently for the chaos to be dealt with.

"Off with the two of you!" Dolores eventually announces, holding out her arms so that MacKenzie and Camila can hug her from both sides.

Dad's bright-red scarf is left slightly lopsided as they hug him, too.

Stacey gives them a warning glance, and they do actually hesitate for a few moments before hugging her. "God knows whether 10 percent of the motel is worth it if we're going to carry on like this," she mutters, but then she disappears inside to fetch two enormous paper cups of coffee for them.

Dolores has already given them enough food to reach Arizona, of course. At least. Their first stop is Idaho, and she clearly doesn't trust that they also have food there. This is MacKenzie's first long holiday in... well, ever. But they'll be back in time for Christmas.

Michael too. He leaves a few hours after them, and I'm back in the parking lot to see him off.

I thought it would be sad, but it's not at all. He'll be back. Maybe I'll still be here then, maybe not. That thought doesn't scare me anymore. I don't think time is as linear as we assume it is. I think everything exists simultaneously, all of the time.

Somewhere, right now, we're meeting for the very first time. Somewhere, he is stepping into check-in fifteen years later, and I don't know which of us is most nervous. Somewhere, my body is pressed against his, and time and space have ceased to exist. All that matters is the heat of his skin. Somewhere, we're parting ways for the very last time. I laugh. *Michael's body*, I think as though I'm repeating a miracle that will never cease to amaze me.

Somewhere, I'm waiting for them.

As Michael drives away, the manuscript of his new book is in the seat next to him. I read the dedication over his shoulder. *To Henny, who left all this behind.*

It's a beautiful thing, to be loved, I think as I wave until I can no longer see his car. I stay in the parking lot for quite some time after he is gone.

And then the first snow starts to fall. Huge, wet flakes sail down through the air, slow and almost confused. They don't seem to have quite mastered this whole falling thing yet.

"It's snowing!" I cry. I turn to Dolores and whisper in her ear: "You want to make hot chocolate. Hooot chooocolate. With plenty of marsh-mallows!" I shout the last part over my shoulder as I run across the parking lot.

The snowflakes land softly on trees and road and parked cars, tumbling through the air as if they don't have a single concern in the world.

One day, I'll leave all this behind. I know that. But right now, I look up at the sky and see the white flakes slowly fall, only to swirl away right when they should have landed on my nose. I stretch out my arms and take a couple of hesitant dance steps. I pick up speed and spin around and around, out on the road, surrounded by snow and winter and cool, crisp air.

Through the swirling snow, the latest addition to our sign shines bright and clear. In brilliant neon, it reads:

Henny was here!

Read on for a look at

The Readers of Broken Wheel Recommend

by Katarina Bivald

Available now from Sourcebooks Landmark

Books 1–Life 0

THE STRANGE WOMAN STANDING ON HOPE'S MAIN STREET WAS SO ordinary it was almost scandalous. A thin, plain figure dressed in an autumn coat much too gray and warm for the time of year, a backpack lying on the ground by her feet, an enormous suitcase resting against one of her legs. Those who happened to witness her arrival couldn't help feeling it was inconsiderate for someone to care so little about their appearance. It seemed as though this woman was not the slightest bit interested in making a good impression on them.

Her hair was a nondescript shade of brown, held back with a carelessly placed hair clip that didn't stop it from flowing down over her shoulders in a tangle of curls. Where her face should have been, there was a copy of Louisa May Alcott's *An Old-Fashioned Girl*.

She didn't seem to care at all that she was in Hope. It was as if she had just landed there, with book and luggage and uncombed hair, and might just as well have been in any other town in the world. She was standing on one of the most beautiful streets in Cedar County, maybe even the prettiest in east central Iowa, but the only thing she had eyes for was her book.

But then again, she couldn't be entirely uninterested. Every now and again a pair of big gray eyes peeped up over the edge of the book, like a prairie dog sticking its head up to check whether the coast was clear. She would lower the book further and look sharply to the left, then swing her gaze as far to the right as she could without moving her head. Then she would raise the book and sink back into the story again.

In actual fact, Sara had taken in almost every detail of the street. She would have been able to describe how the last of the afternoon sun was gleaming on the polished SUVs, how even the treetops seemed neat and well organized, and how the hair salon 150 feet away had a sign made from laminated plastic in patriotic red, white, and blue stripes. The scent of freshly baked apple pie filled the air. It was coming from the café behind her, where a couple of middle-aged women were sitting outside and watching her with clear distaste. That was how it looked to Sara, at least. Every time she glanced up from her book, they frowned and shook their heads slightly, as though she was breaking some unwritten rule of etiquette by reading on the street.

She took out her phone and redialed. It rang nine times before she hung up.

So Amy Harris was a bit late. Surely there would be a perfectly reasonable explanation. A flat tire maybe. Out of gas. It was easy to be—she checked her phone again—two hours and thirty-seven minutes late.

She wasn't worried, not yet. Amy Harris wrote proper letters, on real, old-fashioned writing paper, thick and creamy. There wasn't a chance in the world that someone who wrote on proper, cream-colored writing paper would abandon a friend in a strange town or turn out to be a psychopathic serial killer with sadomasochistic tendencies, regardless of what Sara's mother said.

"Excuse me, honey."

A woman had stopped beside her. She gave Sara an artificially patient look.

"Can I help you with anything?" the woman asked. A brown paper bag full of food was resting on her hip, a can of Campbell's tomato soup teetering perilously close to the edge.

"No, thank you," said Sara. "I'm waiting for someone."

"Sure." The woman's tone was amused and indulgent. The women sitting outside the café were following the whole conversation with interest. "First time in Hope?"

"I'm on my way to Broken Wheel."

Maybe it was just Sara's imagination, but the woman didn't seem at all satisfied with that answer.

The can of soup wobbled dangerously. After a moment, the woman said, "It's not much of a town, I'm afraid, Broken Wheel. Do you know someone there?"

"I'm going to stay with Amy Harris."

Silence.

"I'm sure she's on her way," said Sara.

"Seems like you've been abandoned here, honey." The woman looked expectantly at Sara. "Go on, call her."

Sara reluctantly pulled her phone out again. When the strange woman pressed up against Sara's ear to listen to the ringing tone, she had to stop herself from shrinking back.

"Doesn't seem to me like she's going to answer."

Sara put the phone back in her pocket, and the woman moved away a little.

"What're you planning on doing there?"

"Have a holiday. I'm going to rent a room."

"And now you've been abandoned here. That's a good start. I hope you didn't pay in advance." The woman shifted the paper bag over to her other arm and snapped her fingers in the direction of the seats outside the café. "Hank," she said loudly to the only man sitting there. "Give this girl here a ride to Broken Wheel, OK?"

"I haven't finished my coffee."

"So take it with you then."

The man grunted but got obediently to his feet and disappeared into the café.

"If I were you," the woman continued, "I wouldn't hand over any money right away. I'd pay just before I went home. And I'd keep it well hidden until then." She nodded so violently that the can of tomato soup teetered worryingly again. "I'm not saying everyone in Broken Wheel is a thief," she added for safety's sake, "but they're *not* like us."

Hank came back with his coffee in a paper cup, and Sara's suitcase and backpack were thrown onto the backseat of his car. Sara was guided carefully but firmly to the front seat.

"Go on, give her a ride over, Hank," said the woman, hitting the roof of the car twice with her free hand. She leaned toward the open window. "You can always come back here if you change your mind."

$\backsim$

"So, Broken Wheel," Hank said disinterestedly.

Sara clasped her hands on top of her book and tried to look relaxed. The car smelled of cheap aftershave and coffee.

"What're you going to do there?"

"Read."

He shook his head.

"As a holiday," she explained.

"We'll see, I guess," Hank said ominously.

She watched the scenery outside the car window change. Lawns became fields, the glittering cars disappeared, and the neat little houses were replaced by an enormous wall of corn looming up on either side of the road, which stretched straight out ahead for miles. Every now and then it was intersected by other roads, also perfectly straight, as though someone had, at some point, looked out over the enormous fields and drawn the roads in with a ruler. *As good a method as any*, Sara thought. But as they drove on, the other roads became fewer and fewer until it felt as though the only thing around them was mile after mile of corn.

"Can't be much of a town left," said Hank. "A friend of mine grew up there. Sells insurance in Des Moines now."

She didn't know what she was meant to say to that. "That's nice," she tried.

"He likes it," the man agreed. "Much better than trying to run the family farm in Broken Wheel, that's for sure."

And that was that.

Sara looked out of the car window, searching for the town of Amy's letters. She had heard so much about Broken Wheel that she was almost expecting Miss Annie to come speeding past on her delivery bicycle at any moment or Robert to be standing at the side of the road, waving the latest edition of his magazine in the air. For a moment, she could practically see them before her, but then they grew faint and whirled away into the dust behind the car. Instead, a battered-looking barn appeared, only to be immediately hidden from view once more by the corn, as though it had never been there in the first place. It was the only building she had seen in the last fifteen minutes.

Would the town look the way she had imagined it? Now that she was finally about to see it with her own eyes, Sara had even forgotten her anxiety about Amy not answering the phone.

But when they eventually arrived, she might have missed it entirely if Hank hadn't pulled over. The main street was nothing more than a few buildings on either side of the road. Most of them seemed to be empty, gray, and depressing. A few of the shops had boarded-up windows, but a diner still appeared to be open.

"So what d'you want to do?" Hank asked. "You want a ride back?"

She glanced around. The diner was definitely open. The word *Diner* was glowing faintly in red neon letters, and a lone man was sitting at the table closest to the window. She shook her head.

"Whatever you want," Hank said in a tone that implied "You'll only have yourself to blame."

She climbed out of the car and pulled her luggage out from the backseat, her paperback shoved under her arm. Hank drove off the moment she closed the door. He made a sharp U-turn at the only traffic light in town.

It was hanging from a cable in the middle of the street, and it was shining red.

e⁓

Sara stood in front of the diner with the suitcase at her feet, her backpack slung over one shoulder, and one hand firmly clutching her book.

It's all going to be fine, she said to herself. *Everything will work out. This is not a catastrophe...* She backtracked. As long as she had books and money, nothing could be a catastrophe. She had enough money to check in to a hostel if she needed to. Though she was fairly sure there wouldn't be a hostel in Broken Wheel.

She pushed open the doors—only to be confronted by a set of real saloon doors, how ridiculous—and went in. Other than the man by the window and a woman behind the counter, the diner was empty. The man was thin and wiry, his body practically begging forgiveness for his very existence. He didn't even look up when she came in, just continued turning his coffee cup in his hands, slowly around and around.

The woman, on the other hand, immediately directed all her attention toward the door. She weighed at least three hundred pounds and her huge arms were resting on the high counter in front of her. It was made from dark wood and wouldn't have looked out of place in a bar, but instead of beer coasters, there were stainless-steel napkin holders and laminated menus with pictures of the various rubbery-looking types of food the diner served.

The woman lit a cigarette in one fluid movement.

"You must be the tourist," she said. The smoke from her cigarette hit Sara in the face. It had been years since Sara had seen anyone in Sweden smoking in a restaurant. Clearly they did things differently here.

"I'm Sara. Do you know where Amy Harris lives?"

The woman nodded. "One hell of a day." A lump of ash dropped from her cigarette and landed on the counter. "I'm Grace," she said. "Or truth be told, my name's Madeleine. But there's no point calling me that."

Sara hadn't been planning on calling her anything at all.

"And now you're here."

Sara had a definite feeling that Grace-who-wasn't-really-called-Grace was enjoying the moment, drawing it out. Grace nodded three times to herself, took a deep drag of her cigarette, and let the smoke curl slowly upward from one corner of her mouth. She leaned over the counter.

"Amy's dead," she said.

⁓

In Sara's mind, Amy's death would forever be associated with the glow of fluorescent strip lighting, cigarette smoke, and the smell of fried food. It was surreal. Here she was, standing in a diner in a small American town, being told that a woman she had never met had died. The whole situation was much too dreamlike to be scary, much too odd to be a nightmare.

"Dead?" Sara repeated. An extraordinarily stupid question, even for her. She slumped onto a bar stool. She had no idea what to do now. Her thoughts drifted back to the woman in Hope, and she wondered whether she should have gone back with Hank after all.

Amy can't be dead, Sara thought. *She was my friend. She liked* books, *for God's sake.*

It wasn't quite grief that Sara was feeling, but she was struck by how fleeting life was, and the odd feeling grew. She had come to Iowa from Sweden to take a break from life—to get away from it, even—but not to meet death.

How had Amy died? One part of her wanted to ask; another didn't want to know.

Grace continued before Sara had time to make up her mind. "The funeral's probably in full swing. Not particularly festive things nowadays, funerals. Too much religious crap if you ask me. It was different when my grandma died." She glanced at the clock. "You should probably head over there now, though. I'm sure someone who knew her better'll know what to do with you. I try to avoid getting drawn into this town's problems, and you're definitely one of them."

She stubbed out her cigarette. "George, will you give Sara here a ride to Amy's house?"

The man by the window looked up. For a moment, he looked as paralyzed as Sara felt. Then he got to his feet and half carried, half dragged her bags to the car.

Grace grabbed Sara's elbow as she started off after him. "That's Poor George," she said, nodding toward his back.

Amy Harris's house was a little way out of town. It was big enough that the kitchen and living room seemed fairly spacious, but small enough that the little group that had congregated there after the funeral made it seem full. The table and kitchen counters were covered with baking dishes full of food, and someone had prepared bowls of salad and bread, laid out cutlery, and arranged napkins in drinking glasses.

Sara was given a paper plate of food and then left more or less to herself. George was still by her side, and she was touched by that unexpected display of loyalty. He didn't seem to be a particularly brave person at all, not even compared to her, but he had followed her in, and now he was walking around just as hesitantly as she was.

In the dim hallway there was a dark chest of drawers on which someone had arranged a framed photograph of a woman she assumed must be Amy and two worn-looking flags, the one of the United States and the other of Iowa. *Our liberties we prize and our rights we will maintain*, the state flag proclaimed in embroidered white letters, but the flag was faded and one of the edges was frayed.

The woman in the photograph was perhaps twenty years old, with her hair pulled into two thin braids and a standard issue, stiff camera smile. She was a complete stranger. There might have been something in her eyes, a glimmer of laughter that showed she knew it was all a joke, that Sara could recognize from her letters. But that was all.

She wanted to reach out and touch the photograph, but doing that felt much too forward. Instead, she stayed where she was in the dark hallway, carefully balancing her paper plate, her book still under her arm. Her bags had disappeared somewhere, but she didn't have the energy to worry about them.

Three weeks earlier, she had felt so close to Amy that she had been prepared to stay with her for two months, but now it was as though every trace of their friendship had died along with her. Sara had never believed that you had to meet someone in person to be friends—many of her most rewarding relationships had been with people who didn't even exist—but suddenly it all felt so false, disrespectful even, to cling to the idea that she and Amy had, in some way, meant something to each other.

All around her, people were moving slowly and cautiously through the rooms, as though they were wondering what on earth they were doing there, which was almost exactly what Sara was thinking too. Still, they didn't seem shocked. They didn't seem surprised. No one was crying.

Most of them were looking at Sara with curiosity, but something, perhaps respect for the significance of the event, was stopping them from approaching her. They circled around her instead, smiling whenever she accidentally caught their eye.

Suddenly, a woman materialized out of the crowd and cornered Sara halfway between the living room and the kitchen.

"Caroline Rohde."

Her posture and handshake were military, but she was much more beautiful than Sara had imagined. She had deep, almond-shaped eyes and features as pronounced as a statue's. In the glow of the ceiling lamp, her skin was an almost shimmering white across her high cheekbones. Her hair was thick and streaked with gray. Around her neck, she wore a black scarf made from thin, cool silk that would have looked out of place on anyone else, even at a funeral, but on her it looked timeless—almost glamorous.

Her age was hard to guess, but she had the air of someone who had never really been young. Sara had a strong sense that Caroline Rohde didn't have much time for youth.

When Caroline started talking, everyone around her fell silent. Her voice matched her presence: determined, resolute, straight to the point. There was, perhaps, a hint of a welcoming smile in her voice, but it never reached as far as her mouth.

"Amy said you'd be coming," she said. "I won't claim I thought it was a good idea, but it wasn't my place to say anything." Then she added, almost as an afterthought, "You've got to agree that this isn't the most... practical situation."

"Practical," Sara echoed. Though how Amy was meant to know she was going to die, she wasn't sure.

Others gathered around Caroline in a loose half circle, facing Sara as if she were a traveling circus making a brief stop in town.

"We didn't know how to contact you when Amy...passed away. And now you're here," Caroline concluded. "Oh well, we'll just have to see what we can do with you."

"I'm going to need somewhere to stay," said Sara. Everyone leaned forward to hear.

"Stay?" asked Caroline. "You'll stay here, of course! I mean, the house is empty, isn't it?"

"But..."

A man in a minister's collar smiled warmly at Sara, adding, "Amy specifically told us to let you know that nothing would change in that regard."

Nothing would change? She didn't know who was madder—the minister or Amy or the whole of Broken Wheel.

"There's a guest room, of course," said Caroline. "Sleep there tonight, and then we'll work out what we're going to do with you."

The minister nodded, and somehow it was decided. She would stay, alone, in dead Amy Harris's empty house.

She was bustled upstairs. Caroline went first, like a commander at war, followed closely by Sara and then George, a supportive, silent shadow. Behind them, most of the other guests followed. Someone was carrying her bags, she didn't know who, but when she reached the little guest room, her backpack and suitcase miraculously appeared.

"We'll make sure you've got everything you need," Caroline said from the doorway, not at all unkindly. Then she shooed the others away, giving Sara a brief wave before pulling the door closed behind her.

Sara sank onto the bed, suddenly alone again, the paper plate still in her hand and a lonely book lying abandoned on the bedspread next to her.

Oh hell, she thought.

Reading Group Guide

1. Describe the relationship between Henny, Camila, MacKenzie, and Michael. Would you want to be friends with them? Who was your favorite?

2. Talk about the influence of social media in this book. How did it help the motel? In what ways did social media harm it?

3. Many people in the town claim that they don't hate gay people, but they never speak up in defense of MacKenzie, Camila, or the motel. Does their silence inflict damage? In what way?

4. Discuss Robert, Henny's dad. What is he like? How does he change by the end of the book?

5. Pine Creek is a small town where everyone knows everyone else. Would you, like Henny, want to stay in a place like that? Or would you, like Michael, want to leave?

6. Pine Creek is host to a quirky cast of characters. Did you have a favorite townsperson? Why?

7. You can learn a lot about a person by looking at the people who love them. After reading about MacKenzie, Dolores, Buddy, Alejandro, Camila, and Michael, just to name a few, what did you learn about Henny?

8. As a ghost, Henny tries to influence the people around her by whispering to them. Do you think her efforts work, or do her friends save the day on their own?

9. Talk a little about Stacey and Robert's friendship. How do they help each other?

10. MacKenzie spends her life in a town that unfairly condemns her identity. Why do you think she stays? What would you do?

11. Describe why it was so difficult for Camila to return to Pine Creek. What obstacles did she face? How did she overcome them?

12. How did you feel about Henny staying behind at the Pine Away Motel at the end of the story? Did it strike you as sad?

13. Do you think the town will be able to put aside its differences after Henny's memorial? Why or why not?

14. What do you think happens to Henny after the story ends? Does she stay in Pine Creek? Does she move on?

A Conversation with the Author

Tell us a little bit about your writing process.

The first thing to mark a new project is when I get a sense of at least one of the characters, often the main one. This usually comes to me in a series of scenes or situations, even though they don't always end up in the book. In *Welcome to the Pine Away Motel and Cabins*, it was Henny standing alone by the road, looking down at her own body and realizing that something was wrong here. From that moment, Henny walked by my side as a very friendly ghost. I've doubted a lot of things with this book—at times it was a difficult and challenging book to write—but I've never doubted Henny.

Your first book, *The Readers of Broken Wheel Recommend*, also takes place in a small town. What is it about these communities that makes you want to use them as settings for your stories?

I think small towns are like a microcosm of human life. People are closer here—literally, geographically—so they offer a great way to show how different and quirky or downright crazy we all often are. I think small town also forces you to meet people who are different from you, which is always a great thing in a novel—and in real life.

This book takes on some serious political issues—namely, the right-wing media and the widespread prejudice against the LGBTQ community. Why did you decide to write a story about these conflicts?

I am bisexual myself, and I have LGBTQ friends from Oregon. When I began writing this book, I was worried about the increasingly vocal and violent racist movement and the rise of homophobia and transphobia.

And at its core, racism, xenophobia, homophobia, and transphobia all lead to people having to justify their right to live and love and exist. And never is this clearer than in elections, when you basically have to campaign for your right to exist—especially if the topic is literally you. It does something to you, having to convince your neighbor or coworker or family member that you are a human being.

What inspired you to write a protagonist who, as a ghost, is present but unseen by the rest of the primary characters? Was it difficult writing a character like this?

I think there are two kinds of people in this world: those who like the idea of being a ghost, and those who are terrified of it. I'm very much in the first category. The idea of not existing is much more frightening than any of the, well, practical difficulties that being a ghost entail. So this book began as the simple question about what it would be like if I did die and remained as a ghost. When Henny and MacKenzie arrived, it turned into a much deeper story about love, friendship, and community. Henny is simply a better, braver person than I am.

Do you feel that not having been raised in the U.S. offers you a clearer perspective on American issues?

No, not really. You have a deeper understanding of a place if you've lived there all your life. But maybe it offers me a different approach to them at least: if I don't understand something, I have to look deeper into it.

Out of all the quirky characters who inhabit this story, which was your favorite to write?

I love them all. Cheryl was perhaps the one I struggled most with to understand and accept, and therefore, she's come to mean a lot to me, even though her approach to God is very different from my own. And I have a special soft spot for Clarence and Buddy.

What kind of books are you reading these days?

I've read a lot of books about death and dying lately. They can teach you a lot about life. I recommend everyone read Elisabeth Kübler-Ross and David Kessler's *Life Lessons*.

What made you choose to have this narrative revolve around a motel?

It's an irresistible setting for a novel. Anything can happen at a motel. I think we all know this.

Through their friendships with Henny, the characters in this book learn how to be better, happier people. Did you learn anything from her?

For years, Henny has walked by my side as a very friendly ghost. She has represented everything that is most brave and loving. She might not have led a very exciting life, but she's a better person than I'll ever be. So yes, I have learned a lot from her and continue to do so. I think we all need someone to remind us about what's important in life. It's a lesson that's so tragically easy to forget in the general humdrum of existence.

Were there parts of the story that were difficult to write? Which ones?

As a Christian, I still struggle to understand how someone could take the love of Jesus and use it as a weapon against people, especially vulnerable people who should instead inspire our help and compassion. What's most difficult for me to accept is that these are often also people who *are* loving and compassionate and helpful, in a far greater way than I am, for example. They just seem to be able to draw, in their mind, a sharp line between those who deserve help and those who don't—and to combine this limit to their compassion with being a Christian, which is incomprehensible to me.

At the end of the book, the town overcomes its differences by celebrating Henny's life. Do you think this same principle can be applied to conflict in real life?

I sincerely hope so, or else I see little hope for us. But yes, I do think so. I think each generation has the potential to create the world anew. Even if many of the old battles need to be fought again and again and again, I have to remind myself that we've done it before, we can do it again, and we're better prepared for it now. And that I think all human beings have the capacity to learn, love, and grow.

What do you hope readers will ultimately take away from Henny's story?

That to set limits to our communities belittles us all. It's not enough to love only our closest friends and family or congregation; we're bigger and braver than that. If there's one thing I want readers to take with them from Henny is how great our ability to love is.

Acknowledgments

It is a difficult, frustrating, very lonely, and often incredibly ungrateful job, being the friend of a writer. And never is this more true than when the writer has spent three years thinking about death. To my long-suffering friends, family, colleagues, and publishers: thank you.

To rocks, of course, none of this matters. They were here long before humans arrived, long before we started telling stories by the campfire, or invented printing techniques, or felled trees to turn into paper. They will be here long after we're gone. When I wrote this book, Marli Miller and Sam Castonguay generously gave of their time, knowledge, and passion for rocks. If I've made mistakes or taken liberties with the immense history of the earth, please note that it's not their fault. They did their best.

And finally, a special thank-you to Basic Rights Oregon. Anti-gay ballot measures are a part of Oregon's history, but so are organization and resistance. Basic Rights Oregon made the happy ending of this story possible, and their important work continues today. You can read more about it and support the organization at basicrights.org.

About the Author

Katarina Bivald is the *New York Times* bestselling author of *The Readers of Broken Wheel Recommend*. She lives in Stockholm, Sweden, with a great many bookshelves and an impressive collection of rocks.